CURSED
BLACK SWAN
A FIXER NOVEL

CURSED
BLACK SWAN
A FIXER NOVEL

RYAN T. MCFADDEN

CURSED
Copyright © 2015 Ryan T. McFadden

Cover Art by Happi Anarky

ISBN 13 978-1-897492-90-1

Printed on acid free paper

www.dragonmoonpress.com

DEDICATION
To Paige and Cordelia

ACKNOWLEDGEMENTS
I cannot express enough thanks to my own Fixers and Scoundrels: my publisher, Gwen Gades and Dragon Moon Press; my editor Gabrielle Harbowy, who surely needed a whip and a firm voice to tame this manuscript; Eileen Bell who kept me focused even when I wanted to wander into the wilderness alone; Robert J. Sawyer who spilled some of my blood when it was necessary; Sherri McPhee who kept me going when the clouds were dark; to my ever-honest readers for their unflagging support over the years (years!): Brian Garside, Kari McFadden, Bev Geddes, my Mom, and my sister Kim Ziebell; and all the others too numerous to mention who helped support me in the immeasurable ways throughout the years.

CHAPTER ONE

CROSSBOWS AND BUREAUCRACY

We lay naked in the candlelight of her apartment. Rain thrummed on the baked clay roof, muting the night sounds of Havencastle. Amber ran her finger along the straight pink-and-white scar under my left nipple. "How'd you get this one?" she asked.

"Hugo the Hellion stuck his knife in me."

"I heard Hugo was dead."

"He was after he stuck his knife in me."

She looked at me with a tightened expression. "I was there when Hugo and his attack dogs plundered the Fjords near Oldbank. His sword was so great it took two slaves to carry. You're telling me that *you* brought down the Scourge of the Succession?"

"A man has to defend his honour."

"I didn't...well, I didn't think you had honour."

"It wasn't *my* honour. He caught me cheating at dice and stabbed me. You remember O'Meara? With me bleeding on the floor, he went into a rage and brutally beat Hugo. The sawbones sewed me up but there wasn't much they could do for Hugo."

"That's quite a friend you have."

"O'Meara? He didn't do it out of friendship. He did it because I owed him money. He owes *me*. Instead of jailing him for murder, the Bronze appointed him the Sherriff of Havencastle."

She tucked a loose strand of auburn hair behind her ear. She was attractive, her skin soft, her earlobes delicate and flowing into a perfect line of her pronounced neck. She regarded me thoughtfully, her grey eyes dark in the meagre candlelight.

"And this one?" Her fingers played at the edges of a messy puckering of tissue along my side.

"A rhino."

She slapped my stomach, a little too hard. "Now you're mocking me."

"I'm not," I protested. "You've heard of the Grand Violence?"

"*The* Grand Violence?"

They were the most famous, and most dangerous, performance troupe in the Succession. "I joined them in DunGhūl. They were the perfect cover when I needed to blackmail the Merchant of Maul."

"You're an acrobat?"

"No, and that was the problem. The whole debacle ended with a rhino loose during the performance. The rhino gored me and trampled the Merchant." I smiled fondly at the memory. "The rhino rampaged across DunGhūl for three days before the City Watch were finally able to chase it over a cliff. After my performance, the Grand Violence was able to double their admission price."

She asked about my scars and I explained each of them: shark, molten gold, cedar tree, razor-tipped sawfish. Finally, exhausted of stories, we fell into a relaxed silence. As I was drifting to sleep she asked, "Who were you running from tonight?" When I didn't answer, she added, "They would've done far more than give you scars if I hadn't hidden you, I suspect."

It was her way of saying that I owed her. I guess I did.

"The Crucifers. They want me for questioning." Being questioned by the Crucifers involved being strapped to one of their stone tables and dissected slowly. From what I'd heard, sometimes they didn't ask questions at all.

"There must be a sizable bounty to bring you in." Her voice had taken on a darker and more ominous tone. Dammit. No longer were we talking about past adventures—this sounded more like business. I was a wanted man in nearly every city in the Succession. You don't get an inventory of scars from molten gold, rhinos, and razor-tipped sawfish from living a quiet life.

"Perils of the trade," I replied. I had tucked my hand crossbow safely under my pillow and I estimated the time to throw her from the bed, grab my weapon, and shoot. Realistically I doubted shooting her would do any good at this point. Whatever Amber had planned was already in motion. Maybe she intended to drug or poison me. She could've slipped something into my drink earlier, or loaded her lips with a two-part poison. Or maybe it was even contact venom smeared on her breasts.

Amber and I went way back. Maybe that was what worried me so much. I didn't have friends—life was less complicated that way. I just had people like Amber who I could count on occasionally to not screw me over. I wasn't sure this was one of those times. And yet, I was here cuddled with her naked in the dark because she was hiding me from my pursuers.

"I heard about the *DragonRoot* job." She gazed up at me, resting her head on the backs of her hands folded on my chest.

The *DragonRoot* job had been my most recent heist, though heist made it sound like I had succeeded. The job had been a resounding failure, complete with shattered wagons and burning buildings.

"Next time don't drug your camels," she said.

My gaze flickered to the exit points of her darkened apartment. There was the wooden door fastened with four sets of locks, and a shuttered window. I had come in through the door but I suspected I'd be leaving through the window.

She must've noticed me stiffening because she slapped me playfully. "Relax, we go back too far for me to screw you over for a few brine."

I was worth a whole lot more than a few brine. I knew how much I was worth in every city in the Succession. Such knowledge kept me alive because once I knew my worth, it was a simple equation to determine how desperate people would be to capture me. Would they risk their lives? Would they risk the lives of others?

I came here to this hellhole of a city thinking I was staying ahead of the bounties on my head. Then, a day ago, I spotted the Crucifiers, which wasn't usually too difficult considering all their armour and shields and squires. Regardless, they almost got the drop on me at the Dog and Mustard Pot. I hadn't expected them to make a move this far from home and that carelessness was how a man could find himself strapped to one of their interrogation tables.

Once outside the Mustard Pot, they pursued me in numbers. They had hunting dogs too—big slavering beasts with muscles like heavy ropes and jaws that could crush a man's skull. I was forced to the rooftops so they'd lose my scent. Still, the net was tightening.

That was when I remembered Amber. I had gotten her out of a jam a year earlier. She had been on a pleasure barge on the White Gravel River attempting to swindle Lord Hayminch out of a small portion of his fortune when her cover was blown. If it hadn't been for me, Hayminch would've cut out her tongue. She had a talented tongue, both in spinning lies and in the bedroom. I wasn't sure which skill he wanted to punish—maybe both.

She owed me.

"What happened to the five crates of *DragonRoot*?" Her hand wandered down my stomach and between my legs. Despite myself, I hardened under her touch. I resisted giving in fully, as I had to be careful lest she trap me in one of her games.

"I attempted to steal five crates of *DragonRoot*. Like you heard—it went bad."

"I thought you weren't a thief," she said, stroking me softly.

"If I were a thief, I would've stolen five crates of *DragonRoot*. I'm a fixer. Big difference." I tried to stay focused but she was manipulating me with a professional touch.

"So they're not stashed somewhere?"

"Is that your angle? You want some of the action?" I moved her hand off me. She made a soft mew of protest.

"I'm just curious," she pouted. "I just don't know how you ended up in bed...with the Crucifiers."

"I didn't end up in bed with them," I replied tersely. "It was a job."

She moved from the bed gracefully, her body curving in all the right ways. Despite my arousal, I reached under my pillow to retrieve my hand crossbow. Except it wasn't there. Had I forgotten to put it under the pillow in our rush to strip ourselves of clothing last night? Never. I'd never forget to put it in its proper place. Carelessness like that could get a man killed. Of course, falling into bed with a woman selling you out could also get you killed.

She opened the shutters. It was still dark outside, a heavy rain falling. Before I protested and told her to shut them, a man plunged through the opening. He landed gracefully, rolled, and was on his feet. I should've been doing something: lunging from bed, trying to get dressed, running for my life. Something. His face was hidden behind a great tuft of hair that I took to be a mask. I didn't react, however, because I was still trying to figure out why someone had just tumbled into the room. We were on the top floor of the inn, thirty feet above the street, high enough that people don't jump through your window. I hated to admit it but he caught me, literally, with my pants down.

For a brief, irrational second, I thought that maybe she was reuniting me with the Grand Violence troupe. That ridiculous idea was dispelled when someone pounded on our door, followed by muffled yelling. Another man, this one wearing a white mask, tumbled through the window. Amber was backed up against the wall watching the scene unfold. When I caught her gaze she shrugged guiltily.

I jumped from bed naked, not sure how the hell I was going to get out of this mess. Two were already in the room and another plunged through the window. Odds were getting worse, and the longer I stuck around, the worse it was getting.

"You owed me!" I yelled at Amber, though it didn't matter now. The situation was out of her control once she'd opened the shutters. "I saved you from Lord Hayminch cutting out your tongue!"

"You're the one who blew my cover," she snapped.

Details, details.

Something big and heavy hammered on the other side of the door. Once, twice, and the third time the wood gave way and splinters flew. I turned to Amber to implore her to give me something to defend myself. The first man's fist cracked across my jaw, turning my world grey before reality snapped back. At least he hadn't shot me—which meant they were planning on taking me alive.

The door failed, a ruin of splinters and snapped wood. The killers flooded the room. Too many. They swarmed me. A bad scene. Someone kicked me in the gut. Of all the places to die, I hadn't wanted it to be in this craphole called Havencastle.

"You shouldn't have crossed us, Nathaniel."

He punched me in the gut and I couldn't breathe.

"You think it's funny now?"

"You know those five crates of *DragonRoot* you stole are worth more than you'll see in a lifetime?" a jester bellowed. Another punch, this one aimed at my lower back, and my legs went numb and I collapsed.

"Bring him," a calm, soft voice said. They hefted me by my armpits, my head lolling.

They carried me through the broken door, down the stairs, and into the tavern. These weren't the Crucifiers. They wouldn't have bothered coming in through the window. I realized that they weren't wearing masks at all—those were their real faces. Which made these the Pariahs—the guild I had tried to steal the *DragonRoot* from.

Amber had hidden me from the Crucifiers because she was selling me to the Pariahs. Better than the other way around. The Pariahs used crude interrogation methods like whips and chains, but they wouldn't get too barbaric. The Crucifiers, now they would've cut me up right good.

My smile dripped blood. I could get out of this. The odds would be high, but the challenge didn't scare me. Then the bag went over my head. Not good. My vision exploded in bursts of white, followed by nothing.

∽

The Dark scratched at the worn, dusty boards with long, chipped nails. It wanted out from the recesses of my soul where it lie trapped. I tried keeping it in shackles with chains and locks inside of me but sometimes I worried it would break free. Like now. The Dark navigated every labyrinth I threw at it, every obstacle that I could to keep it away. No matter how far I ran, it was always there. I had finally come to accept that the only thing stopping it were those meagre locks and that old warped door.

Now, with my head lolling on my shoulders, I smelled its foul breath. I could say that it smelled like death, but death had so many smells. There was the smell when a body swelled in the sun like an oversized sausage, waiting to split along a seam, entrails bursting in a cascade of offal. Or the death crap, when at expiration the bowels released a spew of brown slop.

The Dark smelled more like the shed. When I was four, just around the time when memories ripened and became permanent, the scholars locked me in the shed with the corpses. A lesson, they had told me. Some lesson. That smell—it soaked into my pores and my mind. Took weeks to scrub it out of my skin. I could never remove it from my memories. Kind of like the Dark. I actually wondered if maybe the Dark took that smell because of the power it had over me. The wash of emotions, the reoccurring images of the slaughter.

The twisted nails clicked at the locks. On bad days, I sometimes forgot to fasten all of them. The Dark liked those times, playing around the edges, touching, caressing, teasing. Today, despite my beating, the locks were fastened. I knew all I had to do was unlock the door. Let the Dark roam free. Let it into the world and the Pariahs would be gone. Wiped away. The problem was that one of these days, I knew the Dark would control me completely and I wouldn't be able to throw it back into my internal prison.

"*Open the door,*" it said. The Dark didn't have a mouth. Didn't have eyes either, but that didn't prevent it from staring directly through me. It was just there, pulsing with its malevolence like a spider's egg sac ready to burst.

The Pariahs didn't understand. How could they? All they knew was that someone had tried to steal five crates of *DragonRoot* from them.

"Get away," I slurred. There was a bag over my head. I saw silhouettes floating around me and I worried that they might crack me across the back of the head again. Then the Dark would come. The last time that had happened—well, I didn't want to dwell on that.

"*Open the door,*" it said again.

"Leave me alone." I wasn't sure if I spoke aloud.

"He's coming to." A real voice.

Scratch, scratch, scratch.

I focused on the physical sensations like my legs that I couldn't seem to control, my feet dragging behind me. I tried pulling them under me but they slid away as if I were a newborn calf. Hands under my arm pits. The clack of footfalls on stone.

Scratch, scratch, scratch.

I pulled against my captors but their grip was too strong. My weakness, however, must've been brought on by more than just a sap to the back of the head. Drugged.

"*Let me out!*" the Dark yelled.

"Hit him again," the voice said. Calm. Efficient. No emotion. Had to be wary of that one.

A crunch. I realized it was the back of my skull that made that terrible sound. They'd crushed it. Broken my head. Worse, it was the sound of the door breaking. The Dark was there. Slavering. Roaring at me.

No! A silent scream. I met the Dark in the recesses of my mind. Couldn't let it out. This wasn't Cresek-Tawn and I wasn't about to let that happen again. But the Pariahs were weakening me. If the Dark did escape, terrible things would happen.

"He's still awake," one of the Pariahs said.

"Of course he is. You hit him too high. Down here. Lower."

I felt my brains leak along my shoulders.

The second time, my assailant got it right, hitting me along the base of the neck. There was no crunch or explosion of lights. Only black.

⤚⤙

Havencastle wasn't my first choice of cities to call home. It wasn't even my third or fourth. I had tried other places first. In DunGhūl it was the whole Machine of Doom fiasco. In Sintium, it had been smuggling contraband to the royal family. In Moregeth—well, Moregeth was where the *DragonRoot* caper had gone terribly wrong. Luckily, no one had been killed in Moregeth (most thankfully me) but the Pariahs and Crucifiers were both mighty annoyed. I was hoping I had outrun them, but considering the bag over my head, I was guessing that I'd worn out my welcome in Havencastle, too.

A sliver of hope remained. If the Pariahs had wanted me dead, I'd already be gone and buried. They had something else in mind. Perhaps torture or mutilation but something less than death. Anything that delayed the inevitable gave me a bit longer to keep running. Except I hoped it wasn't too much torture. I had somehow managed to keep all my digits over the years and

I preferred to keep it that way. Losing my eyelids, teeth, fingers, toes or something in my lower regions would be a handicap I wouldn't want to deal with.

Through the canvas bag I heard muffled talking from another room. Sweat dripped down my nose.

Unfortunately, I didn't know a lot about the Pariahs. Maybe I should've done some research before trying to rob them but it didn't seem important at the time. What I did know amounted to rumours and drunken gossip. They ruled Moregeth after winning a bloody war of the underworld. Crazed freaks, mutants, rejects, and Rapespawn— outsiders. There were crazy origin theories, but they were just that—crazy. As if they had actually come from the Desecration—that was a story designed to scare kids at night; everyone knew the Desecration was a fairy tale.

What wasn't a fairy tale was that they had captured me, too easily, and now I was tied naked to a chair.

The door opened and a refreshing breeze washed over me. Footsteps. Then the bag was yanked from my head, and I winced from sudden brilliance which increased the agony in my cracked skull.

The first thug was two-hundred-fifty pounds of corded muscle and smelled like a barnyard. His flesh was black, his skin gleaming like polished obsidian, his sharpened tusks dripping a trail of mucous. A black goblin. I tried to hide my surprise— black goblins didn't come this far north and didn't associate with humans.

Except I guess the Pariahs really weren't human.

The second thug might've had some human in him—but all rearranged as if his face had been made out of clay and someone had reached in and twisted everything. His left eye was higher than the other and his mouth was crooked.

I knew the third was the leader because I recognized him. *Shyst*, I cursed to myself. If their leader was here, I was in a whole load of trouble. You never send the leader unless something serious was going down. He had a slight build, almost feminine, with long blond hair. The perfect type of body for thieving— light, agile, able to slip between crowds or dash along rooftops. His ears were pointed, the only indication he was Rapespawn. If I had to face him in an alleyway, I wouldn't have been worried until we made eye contact.

His name was Airlik.

He leaned close.

"You're a fixer."

"At your service," I slurred. I had hoped to deliver that line with more grace, but it was hard to sound dignified when your lips were swollen. My tongue did a cursory check but found no broken teeth.

"What do you think we should do with you?"

"I don't know if you're allowed to do anything to me." The goblin stepped forward, fist drawn back. I didn't want him doing that. My head hurt enough. "I'm just saying, that whole five crates thing," I continued quickly. "That was back in Moregeth. We're in Havencastle now. This is Syndicate territory, and they don't take kindly to outsiders on their turf." I didn't have many cards to play. Actually, I think that was my only card.

"So you're hoping...bureaucracy will save you?"

"It's pretty much all I've got."

Airlik lowered himself to my level. "You don't need to worry about us. We have their permission." He motioned to the twisted-face guy who flapped papers before my blurred vision. Could've been anything on those sheets but I knew that his look of triumph meant that he held an official license from the Syndicate. Probably to torture me or other such mayhem. So much for bureaucracy.

Perhaps these Pariahs weren't such amateurs after all.

"Or maybe I should hand you over to the Crucifiers."

"Shyst." I wasn't sure if I said that out loud, though the laughing goblin made me think I did.

"Because they might be interested in having a chat with you."

The crates of *DragonRoot* had originally belonged to the Crucifiers. How they ended up in the Pariah's warehouse hadn't mattered to me. What had mattered was that the Crucifiers had wanted it back. But let me explain. I never worked for free, and this was no different. They paid me a small amount, so we signed a binding contract between an illegal association and a fugitive, with the objective of stealing *DragonRoot* from an outlawed guild. My rate should've been much higher.

Airlik continued. "You stole five crates of *DragonRoot* from us."

"I didn't steal them. I tried. Remember that whole ambush thing?"

"I remember." Airlik straightened. "Are you uncomfortable?"

"I'd love some water."

"Water?"

"Just a sip." This was usually when the torturer would attack with merciless glee, dunking the victim (me) into a vat of water, or water torture, or water boarding...really, anything to make my request overly ironic.

"Bratic, get our guest a cup of water."

Here it comes. My head was about to be shoved into a bucket. Wait, the goblin was using a ladle to pour water into a wooden cup. What form of trickery was this?

The goblin held the cup to me. Of course, I couldn't reach for it since my hands were tied behind my back. Damn. So that was how they were going to antagonize me.

"His hands aren't free. Untie him."

The twisted-face guy loosened my bonds. I still waited for the ironic punishment. The three did nothing, the water cup held before me. I briefly rubbed my wrists, then took the cup. Paused. Finally shrugged and chugged it down. The water tasted like nectar.

When I finished, I sighed. I didn't presume to stand, however. The last thing I wanted was another sap to the skull. I appreciated that some of these guys were apprentices, but I didn't need them practicing their shots on my head. I touched the back of my skull and winced. A sticky, congealed mess back there. Felt a stab of panic.

"I think you broke my skull."

"It's a bit of blood and some tangled hair. You'll be fine."

Of course, he could say that. His brains weren't splattered everywhere.

The goblin named Bratic handed me a sack. I took it tentatively, waiting for permission from Airlik. He gave a brief nod and I glanced inside and gave him a questioning look in return.

"Your possessions."

I pulled out my loaded hand crossbow. No one moved. I shrugged and began to dress.

"You're not our prisoner."

"Really? Then did you really need to beat me, bag me, and tie me to a chair?"

"After the heist in Moregeth, we looked into your history. Seems that you've been known for your... unpredictability. I consider myself a risk assessment expert. And your history has too many gaps."

"So I hear."

"That's your business. But those five crates were ours. Made us look bad to the city. How many more will make an attempt to hit us because of that? Every two-brine thief will take a run at us. You know how this works."

"Usually, you'd need to make an example of me."

"Like getting Bratic here to pop your head off like a nut? Hang your head, feet and hands at the four points of the city?"

"That sounds about right, if a little barbaric."

"How are you going to repay us, if you don't want us chopping you into pieces?"

I pulled on my breeches. "I'm between jobs right now, so cash is tight. But maybe some type of payment schedule..."

"Payment schedule?" He wasn't smiling, but I saw the amusement in his eyes. Almost a twinkle. I couldn't be sure if it was from my statement, or because he was going to order his brutes to rip me down.

"We may look savage, Nathaniel, but we're not. That's why you managed to get as far as you did with the five crates. We're not murderers, we're thieves like you."

"I'm a fixer," I scowled. Too many people confused me with a thief. I fixed trouble. Damn it, why couldn't anyone get it right?

"Even better. Because you're going to do a job for us."

I fastened my belt and checked my tiny metal vials of venom and toxins. They were all intact. "I see. A job. What type of job?" A suicide mission probably. Something so diabolical my chances of success would be non-existent. Airlik had already tried to show me that he was the boss. Apprehending me with little trouble, then letting me sweat it out under that stupid bag.

"You heard of the Vera Velat Temple in Shambri-Gal?"

"Here in Havencastle?" I clipped my crossbow to my belt.

"That's right,"

"What about it?"

"There's something in the temple I need."

"Need?"

"Want."

"Like I wanted five crates of *DragonRoot*?"

"Exactly."

"Aren't you guys thieves?"

"It's complicated."

"The job?"

"The politics."

Politics. I never did well with politics. Whenever I dabbled in politics it always seemed to end in bloodshed or revolution.

"You a religious man, Nathaniel?"

"Can't say I am."

"Good."

"Would that have made a difference?"

"Of course not. Bratic." The black goblin swept a table top

clear with a crash of cutlery, junk, and plates. He unrolled a sheet of blue vellum in its place.

"The Vera Velat temple: the Holy House of He Who Rains Fire in the heart of the Shambri-Gal district here in Havencastle. An easy job. Get in, steal something, get out."

I studied the blue vellum and found drawings of the temple though I didn't know how recent they were. Couldn't fully focus, as my vision was still hazy from the practice sessions earlier.

"Do I have a choice?" I asked.

"Of course. There is always a choice."

"What if I decline?"

He smiled but said nothing.

"Right. What am I stealing then?"

Airlik leaned forward, hands on the table. "A sword."

"A sword?"

"An exceptional sword. One that wasn't crafted by mortal hands."

I suppressed the desire to roll my eyes. Did he really think I was going to believe in fairy tales? He already told him I wasn't into all that religious nonsense.

"What else can you tell me?"

"It's called Black Swan, and it was a gift from the King of the Light of Righteousness to the first emperor in the Times Before. It was handed down through the generations and now is protected by the Monks of Titus."

"Monks?" Didn't sound too tough.

"Fighting monks."

"Are there any other kinds? This Black Swan...it's here?" I jabbed at the vellum.

"Yes. It'll be well guarded."

"By fighting monks. Got it."

"In a vault."

"So I need to pick a lock."

"And no one knows the combination."

"They never do. How long do I have?"

"Time is a factor."

"If this sword is so old, what's the rush?"

Airlik smiled. "Politics."

"Okay. I'm in. I get you this sword, we're even. Right?"

"All debts will be paid. Then you can return to your life."

Now I paused. Little did he know that this was my life.

CHAPTER TWO

TOWERS, GIANTS, AND RED EMERALDS

Shambri-Gal—a cultural bastion for the islanders, fully insulated in their own world. A country within a city. If you couldn't go to Moragorat, why not bring Moragorat to you? Instead of taking a five-day journey on the dead-rails to the port of Eval King and an arcane steamer through the Hollow Straights to Cowra Bay, then simply take a five-minute carriage ride through the Ridges and you'd be at Shambri-Gal.

After the Genocide Wars, refugees from the ruined island of Moragorat had settled the outskirts of Havencastle and what had begun as a refugee camp became permanent. Temples were erected, houses built, and over the years Havencastle swallowed the enclave but couldn't digest it. The former islanders resisted the pull to amalgamate and continued with their own culture. They paid their taxes and lent their resources to the benefit of Havencastle, so the ruling class kept their distance.

But it had been eighty years since the Genocide Wars, and the original culture had mutated into something not quite from Moragorat and something not quite from Havencastle. Shambri-Gal was the cross-gender offspring of two distinct cultures.

The bustling bazaar was known across the Succession as the place to buy and sell the exotic. From pottery, jewellery, carpets, and spices, all openly available, to the slightly less legal like drugs, prostitution, and gambling dens—all kept in the hidden basements.

The alleys were narrow, almost claustrophobic. Frayed burlap awnings stretched over the continuous store fronts, keeping the scents of *DragonRoot*, exotic spices, and the pungent smell of unwashed human flesh from being blown away by the wind.

I was a foreigner here. Always would be a foreigner. I stood six inches taller than the average Moranian, with skin two shades lighter. They spoke Metashe in a dialect I barely understood, cursed in Conragess that made even the harshest words seem sweet—and they talked in a rushed patter that combined into an aural stew as repulsive as the strange offerings from the vendors: eels, fried scorpions on a stick, blood fish, chocolate dipped razor-tipped sawfish.

And noodles everywhere. I hated noodles. Fried, boiled, steamed, baked, rolled, smothered. It was an obsession I didn't understand. Everything was damned noodles.

Bodies jostled, twisted, bumped. Made it difficult to eat my fried scorpion (on a stick) and I worried that I might jab myself with the black pincer.

I didn't bother trying to blend into Shambri-Gal. It would've been a losing proposition. So I wandered the alleys like a lost tourist, which I pretty much was. My Metashe was awful. So awful that the locals would curse at me for butchering their language.

I broke free from the bazaar near the Vera Velat pagoda. It had been easy to find the compound in the claustrophobic layout of Shambri-Gal. At two-hundred feet tall, the pagoda was the tallest structure in Havencastle. An impressive building.

It had an octagonal base of solid brick with thirteen tiers of wooden eaves. Taut chains stretched from the top of the copper finial to four statues at the corners of the uppermost eaves as if holding the steeple in place. Inspiring architecture indeed, but really the world's most overwrought lightning rod. Only the five upper floors sported balconies. Set into the brick on the lower floors were fake doorways and small notches in the stonework, either to allow air flow or to shoot crossbows at attackers. I couldn't help but think that the Vera Velat appeared more like a military installation than a religious temple.

Unless you could fly, there was only one real way in or out—an iron gate at an oversized vaulted door.

Surrounding the Vera Velat were five scaled-down pagodas. On each, the three lower levels were constructed of green, blue, and red bricks while the upper four levels were ornamental wood.

Each of the five buildings was equidistant from the Vera Velat, their finials connected to the larger pagoda by cords adorned with paper lanterns. An eight-foot stone wall surrounded the towers with a solid iron gate as the only entrance into the compound. The place seemed pretty secure for a religious temple. More like the hiding place of something very valuable.

I surveyed the Vera Velat temple using my eye glass.

Spotted a monk on the wall. I wondered what type of monk he was. In Shadowdark, the monks used their fists and feet as weapons. In IronDale, the monks preferred blessed steel and heavy plate to help resolve their spiritual differences. This monk wore the red religious robes of *He Who Rains Fire*, but he was hardly Moranian. He looked like he could've been my brother. So if he wasn't a monk, did that make him military?

My gaze shifted to the gate. Iron. There were several peer slits but otherwise solid. Probably reinforced from the other side.

According to Airlik, somewhere in there was Black Swan. All I had to do was get it out. Could be difficult. It would take some planning. Definitely more planning than my last job—which had somehow turned into this job. If I had learned anything over the years, it was to never make the same mistake twice.

I needed to visit an old friend. Well, he might not have known we were friends, but he was somewhat trustworthy and that was enough for me.

He had a small shop dealing in antiquities and rare artefacts. A quaint little place with a front window with his name stencilled across it: LaFage the Friendly. The tiny bell above the door tinkled when I opened it. Real cute. No matter where LaFage set up shop, it always had a familiar smell: mold and cinnamon.

He sat behind his old wooden desk, his face buried in a leather-bound book. He glanced up, intent on returning to his reading. When he recognized me, his face paled and he fumbled his book.

"Good to see you, LaFage."

"Nathaniel? I didn't know, I mean...what are you doing in Havencastle?"

"The usual. They ran me out of DunGhūl and New Eval King. I left Moregeth last month." I checked the price tag on a stuffed owl and blanched at the cost.

"That's a genuine Snow Owl from the reaches of Hammerthrone— worth every brine." LaFage was diminutive with fox-like features: small and sharp, eyes always darting as if he was either looking for danger or a way to make off with someone's money. He was the best fence I'd ever known, able to move anything with little or no attention from the authorities. We knew each other from Cresek-Tawn. Things went bad for him shortly before everything went wrong for me. We had met in other cities. Maul, Sintium, New Eval King. And now Havencastle.

"You're not here to shop," LaFage stated.

"Nope."

"You owe me from your last visit," he said.

"Owe you? You should pay me for damages. I was nearly killed because of the shoddy workmanship."

LaFage slammed his book shut, his wiry frame shaking with sudden anger. "It wasn't flame resistant! I never promised flame resistance! It was supposed —"

"All right, LaFage. Let's calm things down a bit. I'm not here to talk about old times."

He took deep breaths, then sat himself on his stool and composed himself like a true professional. "That was good merchandise," he mumbled to himself.

"I'm a wanted man, LaFage. A small incident with a few crates of *DragonRoot*. Now I owe the Pariahs big time."

"Next time, don't drug the camels."

"You heard about that?"

"Yes, I heard about that," he replied tersely. "Your mistakes always have a way of filtering back to me. It's bad for business, you know. People sometimes think it's the merchandise."

"Well, I didn't want to say it, but if I could depend more on my equipment, I wouldn't keep getting in harm's way."

"Your equipment?" He was coming from around his counter. "Was it your equipment that caused you to bury nearly all of Maul under an avalanche? Or was it the equipment that caused you to inadvertently destroy the monarchy of Rangkat?"

Maul and Rangkat weren't failures—merely temporary setbacks. Someday, I would right those wrongs and complete the missions. Well, once they took the bounty off my head.

"You're getting yourself worked up. I'm here for some information."

He huffed his annoyance but he knew that information usually led to a job. And a job meant I'd have to equip myself, which resulted in some hefty purchases from his shop. Sometimes I even had money to pay him.

"What type of information?"

"What do you know about the Vera Velat temple in the Shambri-Gal district?"

"Didn't know you were the religious type."

"I need to break in." I stared into a glass cabinet full of silver rings stolen from some graveyard. I knew they were from a graveyard because they were still attached to the skeletal fingers.

"I can tell you that nothing good ever comes from Shambri-Gal."

"So I've heard. This'll be different."

"Isn't that what you always say?"

"Consider me an optimist." I tried on one of the wide rim hats. Didn't like it, so I stuck with my own.

"Why do you need in?"

"To steal something."

"I thought you weren't a thief?"

"I'm not. But sometimes, I have to improvise."

"What are you stealing?"

"A sword."

"Are we going to play this game all day? Because I'm busy."

"All right, all right." I lowered my voice as if someone might overhear the conversation in the empty shop. "I have to steal Black Swan."

"*The* Black Swan?"

"You've heard of it?"

"Of course I've heard of it. And it's here, right in our city?"

"Shouldn't a fence know that?" He scowled and I continued. "In that temple. The temple I've got to get into."

LaFage whistled. "This is big news. Do you know what that sword is?"

"Handed down by so-and-so to a bunch of spitting monks. Right. Got it."

"That sword is supposed to herald the End of Days."

"That true?" Tried on a set of riding gloves. I liked them and slipped them into my pocket.

"Hope so. The Apocalypse would be good for business. But I think it might be a vestige from the Times Before. They're trusting this thing with you?"

"I think they liked the way I do business."

"Poorly?"

"With flair. But I need to know if I can get in."

LaFage shrugged. "Shouldn't be a problem getting in."

"And getting out?"

"Alive?"

"Preferably."

"Could be a little more difficult. But that's not really my line of work. That's more yours."

"I need you to put me in contact with some people."

"What kind of people?"

"The place is only a few decades old. People have long memories. I need to talk to the designers, the architects, even the workers if you can arrange it."

"How long do we have?"

"I've got timelines. I think someone else is going to make a move on this thing."

LaFage stared at me a moment. "You surprise me. Never thought Nathaniel would be afraid of a bunch of thieves."

"Hey, if the Pariahs put a number on my head, soon every amateur bounty hunter will be looking for me. Someone could get hurt, and it wouldn't be me."

He began scribbling. "How can I contact you?"

"I'll return in a few days. Time to poke around Shambri-Gal and see what I can find out about the place. Somehow, I think it's more than it appears to be." I stared at a display of hand crossbows mounted on the wall. "Hey, is that the new model?"

LaFage shoulder's sagged. "Put it on your tab?"

"Yeah, put it on my tab."

CHAPTER THREE

FESTIVAL OF PAPER LANTERNS

The Festival of Paper Lanterns—the perfect backdrop for crime. Festivals had a way of creating noise, rowdiness, and a whole load of strangers. The Bronze would be stretched to their limit handling the usual pains that accompanied the happiest day of the year—pickpockets, drunks, thugs, stabbings. Plus witnesses tended to be a little less observant when they were stinking, filthy drunk.

So not only did the festival give me the best scenario, it was also the one night of the year when the doors of the Vera Velat temple were opened to visitors. As I discovered earlier in the week, the place was fortified and heavily protected.

I had used a six-pack of camels to test the front gates of the pagoda. The monks' response was impressive. Not only were the gates reinforced, the monks were quick to respond by putting my poor camels out of their misery with some well-placed arrows. I had hoped to have tempted them out of the compound, but instead they waited for the Bronze, who cleaned up the mess several hours later.

I had tried other methods. Scaling the ten-foot stone wall seemed easy enough, but there were dogs on the other side snap-snapping at me. Rottweilers. These were particularly nasty dogs bred for war with impressive looking cords of muscle. I surmised that the monks kept them just hungry enough to view any type of intruder as potential food. I didn't want to be food.

Unexpected deliveries were ignored. A wagon full of supplies sat outside the front gates for three hours while the merchant yelled up the wall at a stone-faced monk. Three hours of pleading. The monk never even acknowledged him. That unexpected delivery had cost me a lot of money to buy.

Still, I hadn't expected to get inside so easily. Those were fact-gathering missions, and I considered them a resounding success (though the camels would've disagreed). I discovered the defensive response of the monks—if they were even monks. For while I saw them practice endlessly their hand-to-hand skills and weapon arts, I never once saw them engage in anything deemed spiritual. No prayers, no worshipping at altars, no meditating or reflection. I began to surmise that this was a military outfit, which wasn't a bad thing. I never understood divine worshippers. Especially monks. Why would they hole up for their entire lives to pray to an imaginary friend, even if they *believed* that imaginary friend was real? I just couldn't understand their motivations and that meant I couldn't fully predict their responses. Military men—I understood them. Predictable. Dependable. They followed orders. They'd want to repel invaders, probably by skewering them with weapons before asking questions. That I understood.

I would've liked more preparation time but the Pariahs were impatient. While I never actually saw them, I sensed they were there: a stranger's weird look, a sudden silence in a restaurant, footsteps in a darkened alley. I could've made a break for it, but I had run out of safe havens in the Succession. I had to take this job. Besides, this one interested me.

Still, I'd put the week to good use. Interviews (some friendly, some not so friendly), recovery time (because my head still hurt from the sap training), and research. The research left me bruised but a little more knowledgeable.

A canopy of lanterns hung above the streets. An hour after sunset and the festivities were in full swing. The alleys were flooded with locals and foreigners—the one day a year when they danced arm-in-arm. Tomorrow, the two groups would look at each other with disdain again. For now, they were compatriots, singing, dancing, drinking.

I didn't know the origins of the Festival of Paper Lanterns. Probably some long forgotten tradition handed down through the generations, the original meaning and purpose perverted, forgotten, twisted, and now celebrated by hanging coloured candle houses above the streets while getting rip-roaring drunk. I knew there sure were a lot of lanterns, glowing warmly in the cool night air, swaying with the wind. I drank in the atmosphere.

I felt a twinge of something. Nostalgia? Impossible. I frowned, tried to wipe it away but there it was again. I tried to keep it down, but the memory bubbled to the surface. Jane holding my hand. We were at a festival, in Cresek-Tawn. Different place, different life, but the memory was so strong that I nearly felt her beside me. Smelt her intoxicating scent, heard her laugh, or the way in conversations she closed her eyes momentarily as she formulated her thoughts.

Firecrackers exploded in staccato bursts, followed by applause. The memory popped and I couldn't say I was displeased. Some things were best left in the past. Besides, tonight wasn't a good night to get distracted and careless. Tonight I had to focus.

Kids ran through the crowd, tossing lit crackers at the feet of merchants, laughing as people shrieked and danced away from the pyrotechnics. To be a kid again.

A stout was pushed in front of me; a strange cane-shaped glass bottle. The guy was speaking in Conragess and from what I gathered, he was offering me a drink, no doubt elderberry liquor. And while I wanted nothing better than to take a healthy swallow, I knew that one drink would lead to twenty and I'd be rolling in the gutter piss drunk within a few hours. No, I'd wait until the job was over. I only had one night to get this job done. A couple hours. I could wait a couple of hours, couldn't I?

The women wore knee-length gowns with slit sides and white trousers underneath. The gowns traced the women's family histories with embroidered motifs of trees, stars, and sugarcane leaves.

The men wore similar gowns except they had stiff, standing collars in a contrasting colour. Mine was a deep crimson with flashes of blue dragons across the back. I wasn't sure what it meant but everyone was keeping their distance so I must've been someone important. Hopefully not too important—I didn't want to be remembered. LaFage had gotten me the outfit. For all I knew, he could've labelled me as a bastard child raised by donkeys. His humour usually worked in strange ways.

The locals called these garments aki-dos but I called them ugly. The conical palm hat was the ridiculous finishing touch and was just plain uncomfortable. Considering that there wasn't a rice paddy within three hundred miles of Shambri-Gal, there was no use for them. Havencastle wasn't known for its torrential downpours, nor its blazing hot sun. I missed my own hat.

The multitude of temples in Shambri-Gal were busy. People lined up to pay their respects to the deities in a strange water-dousing ritual. The worshippers would remove their palm hats, get their hair dunked in a vat of perfumed water, then head back to the festival.

And the real benefit of the Festival of Paper Lanterns—the gates of the Vera Velat compound were opened and practically unguarded. The very doors that had broken six hard-charging camels had been defeated by some paper lanterns. The holy house of He Who Rains Fire was a hub of activity. Other people were as curious as I was to discover what was past those iron gates.

I walked in through the front gates, noticing the monks on sentry duty and three more patrolling the walls. These men had hard faces, though being locked up in a compound for weeks on end might do that to someone, no matter how devoted.

I glanced over at the central pagoda. I had considered that the main tower might be merely a diversion though the Pariahs' sources were certain that Black Swan was locked inside an impenetrable vault inside that tower. Of course, they wouldn't reveal their sources, which was a bit disconcerting. I was basing this entire job on hearsay from someone whose identity I didn't know, proclaiming something I couldn't confirm. Blind faith usually got a man in trouble. But considering I was accustomed to being in some form of trouble, this was a gamble worth taking.

The other six towers were the barracks, storage, and prayer rooms.

I joined the queue of revellers moving toward the oversized tub of perfumed water in the central courtyard. Three monks performed the ritual. Ironic that they were using water to baptize worshippers of He Who Rains Fire, but religion never made much sense anyways. Shouldn't they be branding people with flaming irons? Or setting them afire? Perhaps it wouldn't have been as popular, but it would've been more consistent.

Still avoiding the booze that was flowing freely around me, I palmed a vial of Ramzikil, twisted off the lid.

When it came time for my baptizing, I removed my hat and bent over the oversized bucket. I shivered as the cold water splashed across my neck and dripped down my face. I grabbed the edges of the tank, breathed deeply of the perfumed vapours, and began incanting an ancient prayer. Or what they thought was a prayer. I didn't know a lot of prayers. Actually, I knew none. But I was betting that these monks weren't really monks and that their knowledge was as limited as mine. So I recited *The Rime of the Lost Sailor* in a backwards dialect of Ragese.

They grew impatient after four lines of the delightful poem and a hand was on my shoulder, indicating that I had overstayed my welcome at the font. I continued the poem.

I wasn't certain whether or not they recognized my prayer as a kid's poem, but I was certain that they wanted me to move. I had incited the monks into action. A set of hands on each of my arms, trying to draw me away from the bucket. In the brief moment of activity, I dropped the open vial of Ramzikil into the water. The whole mission rested on the proper application. If they noticed the vial, then surely they would empty the contaminated font and begin again. That wouldn't have been good for me.

They dragged me away, then gave me an unceremonious shove out of the parade line. I bowed several times, then replaced my hat.

Several areas of the compound were cordoned off with twisted ropes, stoic monks trying their best to keep the area clear. But with the monks outnumbered by the visitors nearly twenty to one, it was simple to sneak away from observing eyes. After all, the small, squat building off to the side didn't need safeguards—no one in their right mind would want to break in there.

It was away from the lanterns and the festivities. The door was bolted shut with a heavy iron padlock. Bolt cutters, previously strapped to my leg, made quick work of it. The time for a delicate hand had passed.

I slipped inside the kennel, greeted by the pungent smell of dog. The room was dark except for a small, square window which permitted the lights of the festival to cast a orange glow across the cages. Twelve sets of glittering eyes glared at me from within those cages. I saw the winking of the upper teeth, felt the aggression suddenly build in the air like an electrical storm.

The dogs were in a foul mood tonight. Their entire lives they had been trained to keep people out of the Vera Velat. Yet tonight, they smelled the scent of invaders, laughing, taunting, and defiling their territory, the very territory they would die defending.

These were hounds bred for battle. Massive dogs with thick torsos rippling with strength and knots of muscles, necks protected with studded collars. They paced their cages, their nails click-clicking on the stone floor. When they growled they revealed enviable sets of teeth.

These dogs were trained to tear down armoured invaders, their jaws powerful enough to shatter bone. Their short black fur glistened in the paper-lantern light.

Their growling was a deep rumble, escalating as I marvelled at them. Their intensity was unnerving—each dog wanted nothing more than to rip out my throat.

"Good dog," I whispered, more to steady myself than to calm them.

All I had to do was convince these dogs that I wasn't one of the outsiders. In fact, if I could somehow convince them that I was one of the pack, then they'd become enviable allies.

There was only one way to find out if I was an enemy or a friend.

There were no locks on the cages. After all, who would be crazy enough to free the dogs? The hound's body tensed as I unlatched the cage. I had fought a dog once. It was half the size of this one. The fight hadn't gone well for me.

"Good, doggie. Nice boy."

Its growl was low pitched, as if gathering aggression in its belly before unleashing hell upon me.

So I threw the gate wide. The rumble subsided and it cocked its head at me. Questioning. Questioning was good because that meant it wasn't ripping chunks of meat from my carcass.

I walked into the pen.

It sat back on its haunches and let me scratch behind its ears. The hound really liked that, the rumble more of a pitiful mutter.

It nuzzled my hand in return.

A friend. One of the pack. Just another dog. It followed me from pen to pen as I inspected each dog, let some out, and passed others by. Those I released gave me a wag and a lick. I released eight dogs.

So far, so good. The fact that they hadn't ripped out my throat was definitely appreciated. The thing was, I smelled like one of them. LaFage had acquired a batch of Bombyx, a very powerful chemical emitted by dogs through their urine. I had tried to ask LaFage how exactly Bombyx was distilled from its natural form, but I had a feeling that there was no distillation process. I accepted that I was just dousing myself in concentrated dog piss. The theory was that the stronger the scent, the more powerful the signal it would send to the pack that I was the biggest and baddest of them. Of course, this was the first field test. LaFage was particularly interested in whether they would tear me apart.

They lowered themselves onto their bellies, eyes down. I opened the front door for them, ushering them outside into the cacophony of the festival. The firecrackers, the laughing, the strange smells. The very strange smells.

Their noses lifted, sniffing the air. Throaty growls met the strange scents and I stood off to the side. The transformation was quick. They became agitated, confused. The more they sniffed, the more agitated they became. Their yellow eyes shifted across the churning crowd, their tongues lolling from their mouths, saliva dripping.

The first hound tore off after the scent. The pack broke, each immediately out for itself. They became beasts from Hell, like a spear into a crowd. They dove into their victims, eighty pounds of muscle tearing people to ground. The crowd rippled with shock, then confusion, then panic.

Yet, the canines didn't tear down their victims to rip throats in an orgy of blood. No, they were concerned with quite another orgy. One that I didn't really wish to witness. The dogs were merciless, pinning their victims, mounting them.

I loved working with animals. So predictable.

I had spiked the baptismal font with concentrated Ramzikil; concentrated enough to send scent signals to the Rottweilers' brains. While these people looked like humans, talked like humans, they scented like bitches in heat. And I had only released the males.

My intention was never to hurt anyone. Not for a sword, no matter how superstitious people got about it. My intent was only to create widespread confusion. And these eight horny dogs were just what I needed.

Mayhem.

People fled across the compound like a wave over a broken dike. To my left, the ropes were trampled. A single monk, trying to stay the flood, grabbed one person, only to be pushed back by ten more. Everywhere, the simple barricades fell as horny dogs violated the recently baptized.

Order amongst the monks had broken down. They were overwhelmed, making my job that much easier. With a backdrop of fornicating and screaming, I swam through the crowd to the Vera Velat pagoda. Two ornately carved ivory doors were guarded by a single monk. His grim expression had cracked and now he had retreated to the doors, unable to hide his confusion and a trace of fear. After all, he had probably realized what was happening—that the chaos was a deliberate attack. That someone had come here to take the sword. Reinforcements would be arriving soon, probably with the same conclusion. I had to move fast.

While I still didn't like my odds, my only obstacle was a single monk. This was as good as it was going to get.

I pulled myself from the crowd.

He must've realized my intentions because he was reaching for a weapon in his robe. He fumbled the flaps and I got the drop on him. I shot him. He gasped, his eyes rolled back into his head, and he collapsed. He hadn't even had a chance to raise an alarm—not that it would've done much good in the chaos.

I tried opening the door. Damn, just as I had suspected. Bolted. They wouldn't have left the tower unsecured. After all, what would happen if someone attacked their compound with lust-struck dogs?

However, my unconscious companion had the key on him. I used it quickly and opened the door just enough to drag him inside. The door closed behind us, the shouts of terror and the growling of the hounds suddenly muted. Inside, I remained crouched over my unconscious friend, waiting for my eyes to adjust, scanning the interior. The place appeared quiet. Numerous lanterns were set into alcoves, though only two were lit, inadequate after the festival lights.

A spiral metal staircase twisted into the darkness of the upper reaches of the pagoda. Then I saw the mural. Awe inspiring, it circled the expanse of the inner column. It was so perfectly textured and shadowed that I felt like I was standing on an open plain in the dead of night. All alone. So realistic that I had to blink to clear the sensation. I turned to view the rest of the mural. In a small section behind me, a group of warriors held back the night.

The focus was a king riding on a black charger, hands gripping the reins while his mount reared up, nostrils flaring. The king, for his part, appeared determined, a glorious sword held overhead, the blade shining as if it held the power of the morning sun. I blinked several times. The blade was so expertly rendered that it appeared real, as if those gleaming rays were lighting this hall. Foot soldiers surged around him, the combatants seemingly rallying to the flag of a black swan.

I realized I was looking at the Crusader, the holy leader of Havencastle. He wore gleaming white armour though no helm, his white beard splattered with blood.

A chill ran down my spine. Who was the unseen enemy in the mural?

Though he was named the Crusader, he hadn't actually launched any crusades, nor had his father before him. I wondered if this mural was some narcissistic fantasy commissioned to satisfy his own ego.

I shook myself from my sudden stupor to continue my investigation. The floor was a mosaic of glass tiles, however, the area was too expansive for me to make out details. I padded to the spiral staircase, taking it up several spins until I was far enough off the floor to get proper perspective.

The mosaic was a black swan with red eyes and tongue, mouth open in a hiss, wings spread in an attack dance. If I needed more proof, this was it. Black Swan was here in this pagoda. If you wanted to hide something, hide it right where no one would bother to look. In the middle of Shambri-Gal.

I spotted something else on the floor.

I returned to the bottom of the stairway to investigate.

Two knives, ten paces from each other. The first had a shattered blade but the other was intact. How had they gotten here? Discarded? Dropped? This was a complication I didn't understand and didn't need. I'd need to move fast.

The vault was off this inner chamber. The doors were blended so perfectly with the wall that I wouldn't have found them if I hadn't spoken to the vault engineer earlier in the week. It had been easy to ply information from him, threatening to reveal incriminating evidence about his infidelity. He swore that he hadn't cheated, and I believed him, but I never let a thing like the truth slow me down. Once I had explained that if I told his wife about the fake infidelity, she'd probably believe me over him, he gave me all he knew about the vault. He didn't know what it stored, only that he had designed it to be impregnable. The walls were reinforced, strong enough to withstand siege weapons, or the temple collapsing, or even the hand of god from the way this guy talked. So all thoughts of getting into the vault with explosions, drilling, or earthquakes were out of the picture. I had to do this the old fashioned way—safe cracking.

The monks of Vera Velat should've been more careful with their contractors. They should've hired a true outsider—one further away than a fifteen-minute walk. Or they should've killed their engineer.

The vault doors were secured with a hidden combination lock. He knew the location of the lock, but not the code. No matter. At least he had given me a start.

I found the eye of the swan in the mosaic pattern. Used

my jack knife to pry at the edges. A glass tile shifted and popped loose. I pushed it aside to reveal a series of seven black combination dials set into a recessed space.

Luckily, the woman who had constructed the locking mechanism happened to be the wife of the vault engineer. I liked nice coincidences like that. I bribed her. I told her that I would kill her husband if she told me the combination. Seemed that they weren't happily married after all. She joyfully jotted down instructions for me, along with diagrams.

Of course, I didn't intend to kill her husband. But, as I said, I never let a thing like the truth slow me down.

I manipulated the combination locks with an artist's touch, moving from one to another, in the sequence she had given me. I had practiced for three days on a set of dummy knobs I'd constructed. This all hinged on her having given me the correct combination, but I had told her that I wouldn't kill her husband until I verified that the sequence worked. I trusted that her hatred of her husband was enough to keep her honest.

The seventh dial spun freely and I stopped it with a sudden push.

Oversized tumblers in the door disengaged with the heavy boom of stone on stone. I winced, glancing about me, making sure that no monks had decided to join me. With a low rumble, the doors began to open on an unseen mechanical pulley. As the sliver of an opening widened, white light washed from the chamber—too pure to be created by torch or lantern. I shielded my eyes from the brilliance, half expecting fighting monks to rush me.

When no one tried to kill me (a good thing), I proceeded inside. An oversized statue of a swan, positioned like the mosaic on the floor, stood at the doors, sculpted from the darkest obsidian. I walked between its massive legs and took a step down into the main chamber. At each corner of the room was a statue of a swan taking flight, each facing the center of the room. There was a sword set atop a pedestal. The black hilt was shaped to resemble the mouth of a swan, as if swallowing the blade whole. That pure, white light came from the sword and my eyes were drawn to it. The silver blade, so bright that it stung my eyes. Awash in the glow from this artefact, the hair on the back of my neck standing up and gooseflesh rippled along my arms. What form of sorcery was this? I had always firmly disbelieved in magic and the arcane. But this, this made me doubt my doubt.

I understood. Whether or not that blade housed anything more than some overactive crystals, its very presence made me feel like it I had to have it. If it affected everyone the same way... throw in a bit of religious fervour and irrationality, and you'd suddenly have a pagoda protected by fighting monks.

I shook my head. Just a sword. I had to stay focused on the mission.

I paused, suddenly wary. As a fixer, my instincts were often two steps ahead of my senses. Something was wrong but I didn't know what.

I retreated to an alcove, hiding behind the statue of a black swan, its wingspan giving me adequate cover. My senses searched for the disturbance. There. A small sound like a hard sole striking a marble floor. A monk? I wasn't sure how I would get out of this place if those doors closed. Could the doors be opened from the inside? I cursed myself for not asking that question from the vault engineer.

I heard that leather slap again and chanced a look.

The situation had suddenly gotten complicated.

He wasn't a guard, soldier, or worker. I didn't even think he was a thief. At least not like any thief I'd ever seen.

He was a juggernaut.

He was not an attractive man and as he laid eyes upon the sword and his concentration heightened, so did his ugliness. His body was a slab of meat with large, oversized hands even too large for his monstrous body. While his left eye was blue, his right was white, perhaps useless. He had no hair, but his scalp was so laden with scar tissue, I wasn't sure he could grow any.

His face was almost as equally scarred. His exposed hands and arms were covered in a matte of dark, course hair.

I cursed myself. I had opened the vault so that riff-raff like him could walk right in and steal Black Swan. Damn it!

I loaded my crossbow with a poisoned dart. Coral snake venom. The poison wouldn't kill someone of his size; only send him into a coma for a few days. After the monks caught and interrogated him, perhaps he would wish for death, but that wasn't my concern. From the safety of my vantage point, I aimed my hand crossbow. But I didn't shoot. Maybe instead of incapacitating him, I'd use this to my advantage. Let him face the dangers of getting out of the Vera Velat. If he succeeded, then I'd shoot him in the streets and take the sword. If he failed, well, I'd simply wait for the excitement to die down, then steal Black Swan. Simple.

His hand fastened on the hilt. So many emotions raced through me: jealousy, rage, disbelief. Like walking into a bedroom to see a wife with another lover. Again, I had to resist shooting him.

The juggernaut closed his eyes and shuddered, as if revelling in the feel of the hilt. He stood motionless until I wondered if he had fallen into a strange stupor or sleep. Then the intruder opened his eyes and drew the sword from the pedestal.

He held Black Swan aloft and smiled, revealing a set of yellowed teeth encrusted with grime. He inspected the blade, marvelling at its design. He swung the sword experimentally, and each time, light appeared to spill from it, sending strange shadows dancing through the chamber.

With Black Swan in hand, he left the chamber and I shook my head in disgust. This guy had left the doors to the vault open. His carelessness could get himself, and maybe me, killed.

I expected him to walk out the front doors. Seemed like his kind of style. Direct, confrontational. But he surprised me by heading up the rod iron spiral staircase.

The giant never glanced behind, as if he didn't care if anyone followed him. Why up? Why not just walk out the front doors? The metal stairs thrummed with his powerful steps. I had expected him to slow from the exertion but he kept a consistent pace. I waited until he was a good ways above me before starting after him.

The metal staircase kept a tight diameter and my steps kept pace with his. Every full turn, we'd pass a notch in the brick, allowing me a quick view of Shambri-Gal. The festival was in full swing though from my vantage point, I couldn't see what was happening in the Vera Velat compound. Had the dogs been recaptured?

I knew from studying the plans that these stairs didn't lead anywhere. The pagoda was a hollow core. The upper four floors had balconies, but there were no rooms or chambers.

While his pace wasn't slowing, my breathing had quickened. It was a lot of stairs. Through one of the undersized windows, I saw that we were at least a hundred feet above street level and still climbing.

We reached the beginning of the upper stories. Not that he slowed. He kept going right to the top. Then his footsteps disappeared. Was he waiting at the top to see if anyone followed, or had he exited onto the upper balcony? Did he perhaps plan to hide at the top of the tower until he made an escape later? I had incapacitated the dogs and half the compound, so making a quiet exit wouldn't get any easier than it was right now.

I didn't wait long, chancing that he had gone onto the upper balcony, and I rushed upward. As I reached the third highest floor, I saw a body, broken, on the floor. A fighting monk who should've spent more time learning to fight. His body was twisted on itself, blood smearing his face, his jaw smashed out of alignment. My oversized companion had beaten this guy to death.

I felt his exposed flesh. The skin was cold. He had been killed earlier this evening.

I parted the top of his robes to reveal rows of metal links. I yanked the robes open fully. He wore a sleeveless tabard over chainmail. Some monk.

"Oh, shyst."

The tabard was a heavy golden cloth, two rearing red lions facing each other above a moon. The markings of the Legion, the Crusader's personal guard. Here, in the pagoda. I recalled what Airlik had said: the situation was complicated. Complicated indeed, if the Crusader was involved. Even more complicated if one of the Legion was here, dead.

The game had changed. First, once this corpse was discovered, the other monks would want me dead. As I realized this, my hands worked unconsciously, replacing the coral snake venom dart with another dart—cyanide.

The Legion weren't to be trifled with. They were formidable warriors. The legends had it that they weren't born as babies, they were born men with swords in their hands. The only thing that matched their martial skill was their zeal for the throne.

And this giant had seemingly dispatched one of the Legion without missing a step. My confidence wavered.

No matter. I had been in difficult scrapes before. This was no different. My objective was the same—Black Swan. Only the stakes had been raised. I thought briefly of trying to hide the corpse, but I had no place to put it, nor the time for such frivolities.

Now, however, I knew that my only choice was to kill this guy and take the sword. There was no bartering with him. The broken body was testament to that.

I loped up the stairs after my quarry and found another body, this one bent backwards over the railing, his spine snapped, mouth agape. His robes were torn, revealing his chainmail and a set of smaller blades around his waist. Two sheaths were empty. The source of the blades at the bottom of the tower, dropped upon his death. An unarmed intruder had taken out two trained warriors. Impressive.

Five years ago, right after fleeing from Cresek-Tawn, I had encountered a traveling sideshow who worshipped the Way of the Open Fist. With their bare hands, they could catch blades, smash armour, rend shields. Luckily for most, the abbots were peaceful, using their abilities only in self defence. I had seen them fight (not against me). It was an art form. A blur of arms, legs, and spinning torsos.

The intruder, however, was different; he had killed these men with brute strength, pounding the soldiers to their death.

I reached the top of the tower and stepped out onto the platform, the gusting winds threatening to lift me from my feet. There were no rails or banisters which made me wary to get too close to the edge with the ferocity of the winds.

The top of the pagoda was nearly two-hundred feet above street level. Shambri-Gal appeared like a blur of lights though at this height, I couldn't hear the celebrations.

I circled the balcony and immediately came upon two more corpses, their necks twisted at unnatural angles. The juggernaut stood between them and I wondered if these were fresh kills. My adversary stepped over broken flesh, lumbering to the edge of the platform as if he were going to jump. He must've had a rope secured somewhere to the side. Why bother climbing all the way to the top merely so he could scale down the side of the tower?

The trick to dealing with any high stress situation is to simplify it to its bare components. My goal was to stop the thug from reaching his rope. That was it. Success meant victory, and failure meant defeat. Simplicity.

The brute was beyond the range of my crossbow. He was closer to the edge than he was to me. Somehow, he had to be delayed.

I bellowed the only thing that came to mind. "That's my sword!" To my surprise and delight, the big man stopped and turned. He frowned at the sight of me, probably expecting an onslaught of fighting monks. He clenched his right hand into a fist, the sword held loosely in his left.

The set-up seemed perfect. I closed the distance and shot him with a venom laced dart, right in the throat. His head jerked and he gagged, then plucked out the dart and tossed it aside. *Too late,* I thought. The dart would've already delivered its payload.

Then his face contorted. The poison didn't seem to kill him so much as make him really angry. He snarled and charged. I waited for the cyanide to go to work. Nothing. Fifteen feet away. I felt the vibration of his footfalls.

"This doesn't look good." An understatement. Maybe the dose wasn't high enough for him, except I knew there was enough poison on that dart to drop an elephant.

There was no time to reload for a second shot.

He lowered his shoulder and he was going to try to break me just like he had broken the Legion soldiers. There was no railing to snap me upon, so I'd be launched from the balcony and to the cobblestones below. No matter how packed the streets were, the pedestrians weren't going to break my fall.

He was like an enraged rhino. Luckily for me, I had battled a rhino in DunGhūl. This was no different. I watched the muscles in his legs; I had to time it perfectly.

Now. I ducked, rolled, slid out of the way. He compensated, his knee coming up into my chest. He only glanced me, but it was enough to add dangerous momentum to my evasion. My roll took me to the edge. And over.

Air. Lots of it. My stomach lurched.

I caught the drip edge, my fingers luckily jamming into a gap between the slate and the masonry. I twisted down, ignoring the pain in my knuckles because if I acknowledged it, I'd plunge to my death. I scrambled to get my other arm latched onto something before my own weight ripped the fingers from my hand. Plenty of times in my past I'd considered myself to be hanging on by my fingertips. Not quite as literally, however.

I chanced a quick look down. Way down. I did not want to go there. My feet kicked, trying to find something for a toehold, and found a slight indent, just enough to give me the leverage to take some of the weight from my fingers and pull myself back onto the balcony.

To safety. A relative term.

The juggernaut had recovered from his near miss and was coming at me again, this time more cautiously. Unfortunately, I wasn't going to be able to lure him into diving foolishly off the temple.

He circled to my left. If he got a hold of me, I had no doubt he'd beat me to a pulp. I needed some way to counteract his strength. Leverage. I needed leverage, needed to get him off his feet. The size difference was so drastic, I had real doubts about my ability to get him onto his back. He had easily over a hundred pounds of muscle on me.

I gave myself some room from the edge. My fingers throbbed. It was tempting to check the damage, but it would only discourage me. I felt that I had dislocated several at the knuckle, if not outright shattered them.

The giant was trying to circle, both of us trying to keep the edge behind the other. I flipped through my options. There was a dagger in my boot, but to reach for it would give the giant the time to club me with his fists. Besides, the monks had tried using knives and that hadn't gotten them very far. Several poisons were in my utility belt, but they were meant for contact applications, like mugs, tables, or cutlery; not for a fistfight. If I got out of this jam, I'd have to remember to correct that flaw.

I had no choice but to try to beat him at his own game. I'd outbox him. Outfox him. Dance and hit. Hit and fade. Land a hundred blows to his one. I'd topple him with a thousand strikes. The Abbots of the Way of the Open Fist taught me a thing or two about fisticuffs, and now this giant would feel my wrath.

My feet moved with an acrobat's speed, shuffling, never giving him a target to hit. I danced in, threw a jab, prepared for a right cross...and he punched me in the forehead. I went down like a sack of potatoes.

He hit me again. No, wait, that was me smacking into the balcony. I knew he would be right behind to finish me off. My mind was still willing but my knees were rubber. Damn, why wouldn't the balcony stay still? Why did it have to keep sliding out from under me?

He latched onto the back of my neck and lifted me. I expected he'd simply toss me from the roof. Instead, he began crushing and I managed a choked gasp. I gouged at his hands with my fingernails, peeling away ribbons of flesh. There was no blood and his grip was unrelenting. In the recesses of my brain, I was now hoping that maybe he would toss me over the edge. I had more of a chance of survival battling a two-hundred-foot drop than his killer grip. As it was, the giant appeared to want to make sure I was good and dead before tossing me over the side. Maybe he wasn't as careless as I had first thought.

"*Let me out,*" the voice whispered in my head. I ignored it. Couldn't let it out. I knew it would be better to die than let the Dark out.

My feet dangled in the air, my head feeling like it was going to break from my shoulders. The image of the broken guard with disengaged eyes flashed before me. Would my eyes pop? I tried kicking, hoping to bring my legs up and over his arms. Perhaps try to attack his joints. No luck. I was weakening too quickly. He shook me like a rag doll and I gave up hope of using my legs.

Two of the Legion had joined us on the upper balcony but had forgone the façade of being holy men. Tabards over chainmail, heavy military boots. Swords drawn, they crept upon us from behind, the giant too busy choking the life out of me to notice.

I had a feeling that they weren't here to assist me. They would kill us both. With my feet kicking, my hands trying to get leverage against the crushing grip, I couldn't do much to warn anyone.

My vision wavered. Wouldn't last much longer anyways. My eyes bulged as if they were going to burst like grapes. My tongue was thick, the roar of asphyxiation in my head.

A flash of a sword from the first soldier. Thrusting. Catching the lights from the city below.

Fireworks exploded in my vision. The last gasp? *Was I dead*, I wondered.

No, they were actual fireworks and not merely hallucinations brought on by my air-starved brain. Purple and red flowers sizzled above us.

A sword plunged into the giant's back, through his body, and exploded out his chest—just short of me. Suddenly, the giant's grip loosened and I collapsed to the balcony, trying to get a breath, trying to live.

The sky was awash in magical fires. Fireworks detonated in halos of blue, red, green. Images of a dragon cascaded from the sky, roaring over the temple.

The ugly man turned so quickly the soldier lost the grip on his own sword. The sword that seemed no more of an annoyance than a sliver even though it fully impaled him. The brute punched the soldier in the chest, rings of mail shattering beneath the blow, metal chains raining to the deck. The mercenary's chest imploded, his body wrecked, flying backwards out over the balcony. To my oxygen deprived eyes, it appeared he floated there, magically held.

Another explosion of fireworks. Silvery crackles.

The soldier was gone, torn away by gravity. I was sure he was dead before he hit the ground.

The second legionnaire attacked, his broadsword slashing. The giant held up his arm as if he held a shield. The massive sword cut a swatch through flesh, clanked onto the giant's forearm bone. The soldier's eyes betrayed his confusion—wondering why a seeming killing stroke had been deflected by a bare arm. He didn't have much time to wonder. With a sweep, the giant washed the man over the edge. He plunged to his death, arms flailing as if trying to grab some imaginary handhold. His mouth was open, screaming, but the sky was exploding, drowning out his cries.

The explosion of fireworks dimmed. A brief lull. After the brilliance of the last display, the night seemed impossibly dark, even the lanterns appearing lost in a fog of black.

The giant pulled the sword from his back with no more emotion than swatting a fly. He let the sword clang to the deck.

My throat was raw and my lungs burned, but I didn't have time for that. If I didn't act, this guy would kill me as easily as he killed the Legionnaires. Though my vision was still blurry, I managed to load my crossbow with a poisoned dart. This guy seemed immune to poison, but it was my best option. After watching him deflect a broadsword with his forearm, my boot dagger was a laughable defence.

I raised my crossbow and shot. The giant blocked the dart with his hand, palm extended. He regarded it quickly, then crushed it. No matter, the dart was only the delivery vehicle. The venom was from a red emerald lily distilled through the digestive process of the fire ants of Moragorat. Not as fast-acting as cyanide, it was generally just as efficient. It killed the blood, the bone. Destroyed a man from the inside. Now I just needed to keep alive for another ten seconds while the toxin did its job. *If* it did the job.

I scrambled to my feet, fought off a bout of vertigo, and stumbled back along the balcony. The giant didn't fall. Immune to red emerald? Impossible. Except impossible was chasing me.

The poison wasn't going to work. I had field-tested cyanide and red emerald on people, cattle, a shark, and a python, but they didn't work on him. I knew I shouldn't have been surprised.

"Who in hell are you?"

"I am Creed." Hadn't expected him to answer. The edge of the platform was only a few feet behind me. Too close. I was running out of space and if I wasn't careful, he'd sweep me from the balcony with a wave of his arm. I knew I had to get away from that edge if I had any chance at all.

So I did the unexpected. I tried to tackle him. I shot low on him, hoping to tear his legs out from under him. Creed was surprisingly agile for a big man. He compensated, swivelling so that I only caught one leg, then brought his fist down onto my back. I had fought in the pits of Cresek-Tawn, I had fought bare-knuckled against killers and half breeds. But I had never been hit like that. It was like someone had dropped an anvil between my shoulder blades and I hammered into the balcony floor.

"Let me out."

He had me again. I felt his great meat hooks hefting me. Crushing. I couldn't breathe.

"I can help you."

His face was close to mine, out of focus. I heard snapping and wondered if it was my body breaking.

"You...have the rage," Creed said. I didn't know what that meant, and didn't really care. I had more important problems. I tried to draw a breath. Couldn't.

Fireworks sizzled around us. The last gasps of my dying brain or real ones? Couldn't tell.

"All you have to do is open the door."

"No, I can't," I said, though I knew my lips weren't moving.

"Survive!"

"Maybe I want to die."

"Liar. You cannot lie to me. Survive!"

"I'm so tired."

"Then sleep. Just open the door. She's here," the Dark said soothingly. *"Sleep as long as you need to. She'll be there with you. Close your eyes. Float. Be at peace. But first, open the door. I will do the rest. I will let you sleep."*

"Yes, yes. I will open the door."

The locks peeled away from that door by unseen hands. The door flew open and the blackness flooded out.

Laughter. I knew it. Hated it. Because I knew what I had just done. I had released the Dark upon Shambri-Gal. Released hell.

But I was all alone in an expanse of darkness and silence.

And in that emptiness, I found peace and rest. Memories,

identity—stripped away. Adrift in the void. I was swaddled in a sea of tranquility, floating on the peacefulness. I was submerged but felt no anxiety. Wasn't sure if I was breathing, but I experienced no distress. Nothing mattered, and I sighed my contentment.

Just me. Alone.

I swam through this limitless ocean of dark, hearing the wash of water, the gentle lap of waves against an unseen shore. I drank it in, the perfect taste and while it was cold and crisp on my tongue, to my body it felt like the warmth of life.

How long was I adrift? Time was so difficult here. Minutes? Hours? Days?

I remembered someone. Someone beautiful. She had long brown hair, her skin golden from years under the sun. Her eyes so blue that they seemed to sparkle. I followed the line from her exposed neck, down her shoulder to her well defined biceps, then over to her breasts. Didn't linger there too long. My fingers wanted to trace her outline. My lips wanted to taste her, to touch upon the pulse in her throat.

I knew this woman. No, that was an understatement. This woman was a part of me.

"Jane?" She smiled and I felt the ache, the need to be with her. But at the edges I remembered something else. Something awful. I felt a stab of pain as if a knife had plunged into my chest. There was no dagger. Only the sight of her, dead. Face down in a puddle of her own blood.

But this woman was alive. And here with me.

"Jane," I said again. "I thought you were..." Couldn't say the word. She reached out to touch me.

A peal of thunder and my body jolted. Instead of Jane I saw an arm, bent back impossibly far until it cracked, followed by the scream. A scream that began with sheer disbelief, then an instant later turned to pure torment.

Not my arm.

I tried to force the image away, but Jane was gone. I was alone in my ocean. But rather than feeling myself in a gentle, soothing place, I felt abandoned. Lost. The vastness was like a massive maw ready to close over me, smother me.

Another image. A blast of blood. Where a nose once was, only an open hole, the eyes pressed into the back of the skull.

Fireworks—three dragons belching flame across the night sky.

Teeth exploding from a bloody mouth.

Sword, redirected, up into the man's guts.

Knife, plunging into the eye socket. Driving back.

The Dark, I realized.

"No," I said.

"Too late, I'm free."

"I command you."

"No one commands me."

"You're wrong. I do."

"You like what I do. You like what I make you."

"I'm not a killer."

"The corpses say otherwise."

I wrestled with the Dark. It had no body but my muscles vibrated with the exertion. Its tongue lashed at my face, wanting to blind me, choke me.

"No!" I tossed the Dark back into the recesses and slammed the door, throwing the locks. How long had the Dark been in control?

"Look around you. See what you've done."

I opened my eyes. Except they were already open.

The balcony seemed frozen. Silent. There were others with me. Legionnaires. Many of them. Some still wearing their religious robes, others having stripped away their disguises, now adorned with mail and shield. The bodies of their fallen comrades piled around me. Broken, torn, rent.

These soldiers, when had they arrived? I didn't know. Couldn't remember. A corpse was staring at me, a dagger buried in his eye socket. There, that one had broken arms. I knew I had done that. I had destroyed them.

Had the soldiers attacked me first? I didn't know. To the Dark it hadn't mattered.

I stood in a puddle of piss, vomit, and blood. Didn't know if it belonged to me or the corpses around me. Ten dead. Mangled. Ruined. Soldiers stood on both sides of me, keeping distance, weapons drawn. And Creed next to me, his fists dripping with the fluids of the destroyed. More of the bloodless cuts in his face, arms, and chest. Had the Dark done that? Or the soldiers?

The explosion of fireworks ripped through my malaise and the rush of sound nearly overwhelmed me. Soldiers hollering at me to surrender, the fatally wounded screaming their last few moments in insanity, the crackle of incendiaries lighting the night sky.

"You did this," I said to the Dark. "Not me."

"How...did you find me?" Creed asked, gasping for breath. I wondered briefly if his shortness of breath was from the poison, but I knew it wasn't. I saw something in his eyes. A wariness. Couldn't blame him. I looked down at my hands. They were covered in blood. The blood of these men. I had destroyed them, ripped out their lives. How long had it taken me?

"I don't know you," I replied to the giant.

Soldiers surrounded us. The Legion. Some of the finest fighting men in the Succession. And I had just killed their pals. Not good. Wondered briefly maybe I had been right in letting the Dark out. Except it never stops. Play with fire too long, and it'll burn you apart.

A man stood out from the group. He wore impossibly white plate armour though his head was helmetless. While he dressed the part of warrior, I saw that he was very old. Heavy wrinkles were around his eyes and mouth, and the hand holding his sword was so thin that it almost looked delicate. His receding hair was almost as white as his armour. My brain, still jumbled, took me a few seconds to place an identity with the face.

"Crusader?"

"There's no way off this tower. For either of you."

I should've known that the Crusader would've been close behind the Legion. If the Crusader was involved, there really was no way off this tower. And if I had murdered these soldiers, then it was only a matter of time until they brought archers to cut us down. While Creed might've been immune to those types of things, my flesh was more impressionable.

"I don't want anyone else to die," I said.

"We're not going to let you leave with Black Swan."

"You're talking to the wrong guy. He has it."

I checked my belt and found my hand crossbow attached. I drew it, not to fight, but hoping to buy myself some time. I loaded it, though the bodies strewn around me probably did more to keep them at bay than my weapon did.

"You have squandered the power of Black Swan," Creed said. He took a step toward the Legion, as if preparing to fight them all. Bodies tensed and men braced themselves. I smelled their fear even through the haze of ozone from the fireworks.

My skin tingled, not from the cold and not from the battle.

Pyrotechnics lit the sky. Greens, blues, oranges. Already jumpy men screamed. Fear had a terrible way of inspiring men. Sometimes, self-preservation took over and they'd flee in a reckless sprint. Sometimes, however, it caused men into fool hardy actions. Like beginning the charge against Creed and me. And while the Dark might've revelled in battles with the Crusader's personal guard, I preferred the more low key approach. Unfortunately, when you were surrounded, low-key usually wouldn't work.

The balcony was charged with tension.

I felt the heat from the night display. At another time, I would've been impressed by iridescent colours raining from the sky. The fireworks were close.

And as I turned to see how close the fireworks were, I realized that Creed did have a plan. Why he had climbed to the top of the tower? Perhaps, just perhaps, he was smarter than me and realized that he couldn't have walked out the front door. Knowing that, he led us all up here.

My hair stood on end as I realized the plan. The tension wasn't because of our battle.

"Shyst." I whirled to Creed, but he was unnaturally fast for a man of his size. Charging. Jumping. Into the open air.

"Stop him!" the Crusader screamed.

He plunged off the balcony in an impossible fall. No one else could survive that plummet, but I knew that a man immune to toxins and swords through the chest wouldn't be killed by a two-hundred-foot fall. It probably wouldn't even slow him down.

"Get down!" I warned.

I hit the deck, flattened myself, and covered my head with my hands.

The world exploded. Pyrotechnics detonated along the balcony, turning the air to fire. Even through closed eyes, the fireworks were so intense I saw the greens and blues of their destruction. The heat washed over me, my exposed flesh blooming into blisters. The report shook the upper tower, the vibrations ringing the eaves.

I smelled fire. And cooking flesh.

I opened my eyes and realized that the world was white. No, not white. Night blindness from the explosion. Down below I heard the applause of Shambri-Gal; the people were unaware that Creed had manipulated the fireworks to strike the upper tower. They stopped applauding when the sky began raining burning soldiers. The applause turned to screams. Not a show.

My first sight through the blindness was the fire raging around me. Some of the fire split off into individual flames, which were running. Men, burning. Running to flee the torment of the flames cooking their flesh, peeling their skin like paper. They dove from the balcony. I rolled to my back, tried to collect my senses. Reached to touch my face to make sure it hadn't melted.

Banged myself with my hand crossbow. Through all that, I hadn't let go. My gown smoked. If I had been any closer to the explosion, I would've caught fire too. As it was, the tightness of my skin was telling me that I had some nasty burns.

The upper balcony was peppered with glowing cinders from where the fireworks shell had struck. As the seconds ticked by, the brilliance faded and details crystallized. I couldn't see the Crusader and wondered if perhaps he had fallen victim to the artillery fire. Those that came out unharmed were trying to aid their fallen comrades, though many were past help, their limbs charred, skin sloughing off like ash.

I rolled to the edge of the balcony and searched the crowd for Creed, though I knew he had escaped. He had executed his plan perfectly. He had known that he was too big to walk through the front door. Too conspicuous to make an easy escape into Shambri-Gal. So he had drawn everyone to the top of the tower for his grand exit. While I had planned on using the Paper Lantern Festival as a day when perhaps security was lax, he had used the fireworks to cover his escape.

"Where is he?" a voice rasped.

The Crusader. He was recovering, on shaky legs, his white armour stained with smoking blood and streaks of soot. While there were dead and dying around him, he was focused on me. Which meant that sword was more important to him than the lives of his men and perhaps his own life.

"I don't know," I answered.

"Do you know what you've done?"

"I was only trying to steal a sword."

"Only trying to steal the sword?" the Crusader asked contemptuously. "Do you realize what you've done? What you've set in motion?" He was so focused on me he didn't even bother with his tunic, the arms smouldering.

"It's not me you want. It's the guy who got away."

"But you're the one still here. So for now, that's going to do."

"I don't have time for this." I shot him. My aim was off but I managed to get him in the neck. He gagged, his eyes bulged, and he collapsed forward, the sound of his head bouncing on the balcony a dull thud reverberating over the other tearful screams of agony.

The Crusader would live. Well, the odds were in his favour anyhow. I had had only enough time to load a muscle inhibitor. Muscle inhibitor didn't sound so bad, did it? Instant paralysis combined with minor internal bleeding. Sometimes, body fluids would leak from the eyes, ears and genitals. The usual.

He should've been thankful that I didn't have something more potent in there.

"The Crusader," I yelled. "The Crusader is down. To the Crusader!"

The response was impressive. Even soldiers who wouldn't live through the day somehow pulled themselves up onto charred limbs and clambered to get to their Crusader. I scoffed at their dedication, but only because I had been like them once. Years ago. And look where it had gotten me. Even on death's door, they still tried to hold themselves to a higher ideal. No matter if that ideal had gotten them blown up on a pagoda two-hundred feet above the street.

I didn't have a lot of options. In fact, I counted only one and it wasn't good. My only chance was to disappear so that when the confusion parted, I wasn't anywhere to be found, as if I had been blown from the balcony when the fireworks hit, or my body had incinerated.

I took a breath and winced at the tightness of the skin on my blistered face. It was a long way down. Two-hundred feet. Heights really weren't my thing. Was I afraid of them? No, not exactly. But I had a healthy respect. From this height, my bones would shatter, my legs thrust up through my body, my skull would liquefy. Hard not to respect that.

So I respected my option, climbed to my feet, took a glance over the edge, and jumped.

My gown billowed behind me, and for a moment it felt like perhaps, just perhaps, I would ride the howling winds peacefully to the ground. Instead I was suddenly plummeting, my arms swimming through the air. My jewels felt like they retracted up into my chest.

Only one chance. My momentum threatened to twist me too far to the right. The lantern-line came up fast, too fast, and I worried that I wouldn't have the strength to catch it.

I snagged it under my arm so that my body would take the majority of the stress. Then I locked my hands together. The line sagged dangerously, but helped cushion the impact. I skidded down the knotted cord, paper lanterns exploding as I struck them. The line bowed as I neared the center point between the two buildings. It was stretching too much. Too much give. The line wasn't going to stop my momentum. It was designed for lightweight paper lanterns, not a plummeting man.

Sagged.

Then a twang from the cord as the meagre tension released. The end of the cord separated from the anchor on the Velat Velu temple and the line went slack. That sickening drop again.

My fall veered suddenly to the right. I wasn't going to plummet to the ground and my inevitable death. Instead, I was being whipped into the adjacent building. If I survived the impact with the wall, I knew my chances of hanging onto the cord were slim. *Then* I would plummet to my death. I frantically wrapped the cord twice around my arm. I would've liked a little more preparation time, but I was going to take what I had been given.

I tried to swing my legs before me, so that they might cushion the impact. I wasn't sure if it would help or not. Paper lanterns fluttered past my face and I saw the building loom large.

My feet hit first. I expected the impact to break me upon the wall. To at least snap some bones and probably knock me free from the cord, then plummet to my death. Yet as my feet hit, the wall disintegrated with a shower of plaster and dust. I kept going and while the cord ended, my momentum flung me through the building.

Ironically, I crashed into a heap of lanterns. Paper ripped, shredded, and balsam snapped. I felt like I was drowning and I tried to swim through my own momentum. I cracked into a hard edge, twisted, and crumpled face up onto the floor.

The world spun and I felt vertigo trying to claw into me. I swallowed it down.

"I'm...still alive?" No one answered except the hammering of my heart. I stared up at the ceiling, trying to catch my breath. A pain in my side told me that I had broken some ribs. My head hurt from where the Pariahs had practiced their sap training. But those messages were received from far away, like I was stuck in my own paper lantern. The fog was oppressive. I knew I should be fighting to my feet, using the moments of confusion in the next tower to escape into Shambri-Gal.

Paper lanterns shifted, tilted, and toppled onto me.

I lost consciousness.

∽

Nathaniel snapped the man's neck. The body went limp and he dropped it awkwardly to the stained floor boards.

Three dead.

Soon, they'd come at him with everything they had. He knew he had to leave. Tonight. He wouldn't be able to kill them all. The Dark roared in his psyche but he wouldn't let it out. He had used it before to rationalize the evil things he did. That he wasn't responsible for what happened. Except he was. Ultimately, he controlled it. Unleashed the weapon upon the world.

Sand blasted through the windows with enough force that it would scour the skin from your bones in minutes. The storm, which had seemed like such a perfect omen only an hour ago to hide their escape, now threatened to bury all of Cresek-Tawn. Those caught outside would be blinded and suffocated. Sandstorms were common in desert cities but this one scoured the horizons like a plague of locusts. It struck with the fury of the divine.

The winds rattled the structure, the house seemingly sighing as a wave of sand shredded the stucco exterior.

Joshua didn't care about storms—he was sending over killers, men trained to murder people like Nathaniel. Joshua would continue to send them until they finished the job.

But Nathaniel couldn't leave until he found her.

The only person he had ever cared about. They were both so accustomed to mayhem and murder that neither had expected passion. They hadn't wanted it, had resisted it, but it overpowered them and bound them together.

No more would they be the pawns of Cresek-Tawn. Tonight, they were leaving. Together.

"Jane?" he called, knowing he was giving away his location but thinking it worth the risk. She had missed their rendezvous and so he'd come to find her at her estate. So far, he'd found only murderers and assassins. She's okay, he tried to convince himself. Anyone who tried to harm her would come across her very sharp knives.

The house was dark. A trap set by Jane or by Joshua's men? Impossible to tell.

A blast of the storm hammered the house and clay dust filtered from the ceiling. Nathaniel wondered if the house could withstand the maelstrom much longer. This storm had such fury that it would alter the face of Cresek-Tawn for years to come, he surmised.

He took the stairs two at a time. He didn't appear armed but he had two spring loaded daggers at his wrists; he hadn't used them yet.

"Jane!"

He called out to find her, but also to warn her that he was coming. Otherwise, he could very easily find himself at the wrong end of her knife.

On the landing, a killer lay face up, throat open. White, rubbery. That was Jane's handiwork; the sight reassured Nathaniel. She was here. And alive. Up another set of stairs.

Sand blew in through cracks in the walls. Not much longer.

He reached the top floor and took a step into the room.

He felt like someone had punched him in the gut. Jane lay face-down, her hair splayed out in a glue-like puddle of blood.

So much blood. Splattered on the walls, pooling on the floor. On the ceiling.

Her skin white. Dead.

"Jane," he choked. He couldn't breathe. The house lurched again.

"We were leaving," he whispered. He was trying to go to her but the two windows exploded, glass shards like shark's teeth ripping at his clothing, finding vulnerable flesh underneath.

The winds pushed him back. Clouds of sand filled the room like flies on a bloated corpse. Stung his eyes, flooded his mouth.

Her hair, congealed in blood, didn't move, as if she were only a painting.

They'd killed her.

He couldn't breathe. Because of the storm or because of her? He had to get her. She didn't deserve to be like that. He'd take her, they'd escape. Even in death, she deserved better than Cresek-Tawn.

The winds pulled at him, threatened to send him down the clay stairs. He fought against them but when he stepped into the room, the maelstrom howled.

One step at a time. Used his collar to protect his mouth. Another step. Almost there. Even to touch her one last time.

Then the world collapsed, or what seemed the world. The wall blew apart and the structure drew in one last breath before exploding in a rending of clay, wood, and plaster.

The storm roared, drawing the fragments of the house into its belly.

The winds grabbed him, spun him around, then slammed him into a sand dune.

He felt like his eyes should be crying, felt like he was going to die. The maelstrom threatened to bury him. The debris was still airborne, sucked a hundred feet into the sky.

Nathaniel saw silhouettes dive for cover from the building fragments that had become like javelins. More killers—they had come to murder him.

Jane. She was dead. He should be too. Joshua. He had done this. Destroyed their lives like they were vermin.

Nathaniel knew he had to leave. Revenge would fail; Joshua was too powerful.

The truth was as powerful as the maelstrom. Cresek-Tawn had won. And Jane was dead.

∞

I was vomiting. At least I had had the good sense to turn onto my side and heave my guts into the lantern and not onto myself. My eyes watered from the sudden pain in my side, and the convulsions from vomiting made me dizzy, which started the process all over.

My guts heaved until there was nothing left and I was crying in pain.

"Jane?"

No, this wasn't Cresek-Tawn. Noises filtered through my room of paper lanterns. The festival.

The room was dark. At least I hadn't slept through until morning. I rolled onto my back, trying to find a position where the pain in my sides didn't make me want to scream. Found a spot between breaths and closed my eyes.

The fireworks had ceased but it sounded like the festivities continued unabated. Guess the party wouldn't stop even when it rained burning soldiers. I sipped the air, my cracked rib letting me know when I tried to breathe too deeply. I hurt. Everywhere. My ribs from the impact, my burned face from the fireworks blast, my skull from the Pariah's sap, my hands where I had tried to grip the lantern line on my fall. Then a multitude of other wounds that Creed had inflicted: my throat, back, face.

Tonight hadn't been a good night.

I traced my fingers traced along my cheeks and lips to ascertain the damage. My skin was rough. Burned, yet alive with sensation. The pain was actually a good indicator. It meant that the nerves weren't dead. I knew that over the next few weeks I'd wish that they were.

If I lived that long. I still had to get out of the temple.

I considered closing my eyes and letting the mercy of unconsciousness take me, but once the initial shock of the massacre wore off, the Crusader and his Legion would come looking. A tower with a man-sized hole in the upper reaches would probably be pretty suspicious. If they found me, I had a feeling, they wouldn't be as understanding as the Pariahs had been. They'd work me over, trying to extract information I didn't have. It would turn this bad night into a very bad week. Two weeks if my interrogator was very, very good.

Staying here was not an option.

It took me three tries to climb to my feet. The floor felt like ice, slipping out from beneath me. This was a battle I couldn't lose. To fall would be a lesson in agony—one I didn't want to experience. Worse, I worried that I wouldn't recover. That I'd finally give in to the agony and fall unconscious.

Somehow, the ice melted and the ground solidified. I let my balance weave its way around me.

My swath of destruction through the lantern storeroom was impressive. Creed had blown up the top of the Vera Velat, so in perspective, a few damaged lanterns wasn't going to raise undo suspicions just yet. I pushed my way through the carnage to where I had broken through the wall. Peered out.

While the festival hadn't slowed, the Vera Velat compound was being transformed into a field hospital.

Legionnaires were bringing their fallen comrades out of the pagoda. Sawbones tended to those still alive. Men screamed and howled as the sawbones set to work on them. Some of them would wish they were dead. Limbs would be amputated, bodies sliced open. The cure seemed worse than the disease.

I didn't see the Crusader, though there was so much confusion that that didn't surprise me. I assumed he had lived through the ordeal of being shot in the throat but he was pretty old. Maybe at his age, the poison had been enough to stop his heart. I wasn't sure whether the Crusader dying would be a good thing for me or a bad thing. From what I'd seen of the Crusader, if he had survived, his first job would be to go after that sword. If he died, then I'd be wanted for the murder of the Crusader. Either way, my future would be difficult. Plus, how many men had died tonight? I tried convincing myself that it wasn't me that killed them—it was the Dark.

But you let me out.

I gazed up at the balcony from where I had fallen—easily seventy paces. I would've whistled but my lips were tight as if encased in a mould of wax. Amazing that I survived such a fall. Now all I had to do was get out of a compound crawling with Legionnaires who wanted nothing more than to capture me, so that they could drag me somewhere quiet to dissect me slowly.

I needed to focus. To store the pain in a safe place where it wouldn't bother me. I'd have weeks of recovery ahead of me, but right now, I needed to shut it away, to pull the last bits of energy from my physical body.

Zero.

I closed my eyes and focused on the mystical number. The nothing and the everything. Watched it expand across my mind's eye, then retract into a point on the horizon. Repeated the process.

"*Zero,*" I whispered.

Breathed in threw my nose, exhaled through my mouth.

"I am breathing in," I whispered.

"I am breathing out." Then exhaled.

The abbots of the Way of the Open Fist had taught me meditation techniques designed to control the body, such as shutting down my pain centers when they were close to overcoming me. I needed a dose of adrenaline to suck the last strength reserves from my muscles. I needed a miracle.

Zero.

Focused on my breathing. I didn't feel the pain diminish. It just went slowly away, swallowed by the expanding infinity in my mind.

Breathe in through the nose.

Breathe out through the mouth.

Zero.

The burns, the ribs. All gone.

Breathe in. Find the divine floating in the expanse of infinity and the void of nothing. I would merge with this oneness. Become at peace with the physical and spiritual.

Except I breathed in too deeply and the snapped ends of a broken rib separated, then came together in a clash of fiery nerves like someone was jabbing me with a red-hot poker.

The zero exploded and my wounds nearly hobbled me.

"Shyst!" I screamed, grabbing at my sides.

I hated the Way of the Open Fist. Enough mystical garbage. I was on my own here.

"No, you have me."

I needed to get down to the ground. Without jumping off anymore balconies.

I crunched through the paper lanterns like fallen leaves and found the door. I unbolted it and opened it a crack. An enclosed spiral stairway descended down. I strained to hear signs of the Legionnaires but the stairway was quiet. Slipping out into the hallway, I waited for sounds of pursuit. Only the rat-tat-tat of firecrackers popping outside. My trip down was an agony-inducing hundred-and-thirty steps, and I felt each one. I slowed at the bottom, still searching. The antechamber was darkened. A storeroom, redolent of mouldering burlap and canvas. Large shapes were hunkered in the dark. I floundered my way to the exit, opened the door into the festival.

Outside, the chaos had intensified. The line of the dead had grown, the corpses covered in canvas sheets. The wounded were being tended to in the makeshift field hospital, screaming and flailing as sawbones worked on them. Others lay on their tables with vacant eyes, limbs hanging lifeless over the edge.

The Legion were trying to restore order in their ranks but even with the momentary chaos, I knew there were too many for me to escape easily. I wasn't fighting or talking my way out of this one. I didn't see the Crusader but he wasn't my top concern right now.

Damn, I hurt. I needed a sawbones.

From the darkness of the doorway, I waited for a sawbones to pass by. He wore the traditional sawbones outfit—a black apron over a tight white tunic and pant. His head mirror was flipped up, so the reflective surface was pointed away from me. He wore black gloves, which was probably a good thing as from the gore staining his once-white outfit, his hands had seen a lot of nasty business today.

"I need a sawbones," I yelled.

The man's gait missed a step. He was obviously on an errand of some importance as I saw him trying to weigh the decisions. So many people dying, which ones could he help? He took another step then stopped when he saw my face.

"You're burned?"

"I was attacked. I need help. Please."

I saw the quick debate going on in his head. He decided to help me. Probably a bad choice.

"What's wrong?"

I collapsed, and the scream warbling from my throat was very real. He rushed to my aid. Another bad choice. I felt his hands upon me, trying to assess the damage. What hurt even more than the broken ribs was knowing that my pain wasn't going to get any relief.

I jabbed him with a needle of tetrodoxin. I could've just tried to knock him out, but this was more painless for the both of us. For him because the toxin was fast acting. For me because I wasn't in the mood for a bout of fisticuffs, even if it was with an unskilled sawbones.

He collapsed beside me. I tried to collect my strength with several shallow breaths and somehow managed to get myself to my feet and roll him inside. Once there, I closed the door and proceeded to steal his outfit. I pulled his apron over my clothes, snapped on the rubber gloves then put on the head mirror. It was hardly perfect but hopefully it would be enough to get me out of the compound.

Once prepared, I entered the chaos.

I smelt the blood, and the crap, and the fear. It reminded me of Cresek-Tawn. How many times had I seen this type of thing before? Too many times to count. And while I would've liked to have blamed the Dark, I knew that I had done terrible things of my own. Things like this. Of murder and mayhem.

I walked through the line of the wounded. Their faces roasted, perfectly white eyeballs staring out from a crimson mask of torment. Hands reached for me, pulled at my apron. Though I wasn't a real sawbones, I knew that many were too maimed to be saved. Those that could be saved would find their lives a prison of torment, wishing they had died when the explosion ripped through the balcony.

"At least we killed our victims, didn't we? That's why you feel guilt, because you know you've done this many times. To people far less deserving than soldiers."

"We need help over here," a Legionnaire pleaded. Wasn't that what I had said to lure the sawbones to me moments earlier?

I wasn't a real sawbones and didn't want to help. I knew that my plan was weak. The longer I hung around, the less my chance to escape this hell. But he was grabbing me by the arm, dragging me over to a fallen companion.

The man was laid out on the ground, the pave stones black with his blood. His tabard was stained, a lion's head torn away revealing exposed ribs. Beneath, the meat thrummed faintly with the beating of the man's heart. His complexion was sallow, his eyes vacant. His mouth moved as if reciting to an unseen companion. The wound wasn't going to kill him. The shock of the wound would destroy him long before a real sawbones could get to him.

"What happened?" I realized I had spoken. As if I cared.

"Up there." He thumbed to the top of the still smouldering pagoda. "I've never seen anything like it. The giant punched a hole right through him. Shyst. Right through him." The grip on my arm increased. He wasn't going to let me go. I had to give him something.

"He's in combat shock. It'll kill him before the chest wound."

"You can fix it, right? You can get rid of this shock?"

"I'll need Nightroot and Bloodsbane." I tried to peel the hand from my arm.

"Is there nothing you can do for his pain?"

The man studied my face. I tried not to look directly at him but I don't know if it mattered. He probably saw my burnt flesh, was beginning to put it together. Maybe not that I was the guy they'd soon be after, but that something was amiss.

"The Bloodsbane will help," I mumbled. Because I knew it did. It had been used on me numerous times. "The Nightroot will calm the shock, the Bloodsbane will dull the pain."

"You can't leave. He's dying."

"I will get him Bloodsbane to calm his agony."

The soldier battled indecision. He must've known I wasn't a real sawbones, but what other option did he have right now? What was stronger? His loyalty to his wounded comrade, or his loyalty to the crusade? I slowly reached around to finger the trigger of my hand crossbow tucked under my outfit. If I pulled it, then I'd have ten Legionnaires on me in a moment.

The man decided. "This man saved my life in the Wars."

He released me and I avoided exhaling my relief. I hurried from the close call, found the closest sawbones, an older man using his head mirror to inspect a fatal wound in his patient's chest. I yanked the sawbones to his feet, heard the pop of old joints.

"That man there needs Bloodbane. Get it for him."

The man saw through my disguise instantly. Could've been the burned face, or the way I wore my head mirror in the center of my forehead rather than over a single eye. Could've been lots of reasons. Maybe he just knew that I was a man more accustomed to taking life than saving it.

"Who are you?" he asked.

"I'm nobody. This man here is dead. That man there needs Bloodsbane. Now get it for him."

The sawbones turned his head, saw the fallen Legionnaire with the chest wound.

"Bloodsbane?"

"Yes. Mix it with Nightroot."

He pursed his lips. "That could kill him."

"He's dead if you don't try."

"What do I tell them?"

"Tell them the truth."

"Which is?"

"That you don't know me."

I slipped away and picked my way across the compound. I glanced back across the wounded and the dead. The Legionnaire was crouched over his fallen comrade. The sawbones was there, tending to the man with a poultice. I felt a twinge of guilt. Who had done that to him? Me? Creed?

The soldier looked up, caught my eye. He gave me a nod and I knew he wasn't going to come after me. Maybe because the Dark wasn't the one who had injured his friend. Or maybe because I had indirectly saved the man. Or maybe because he didn't want to leave the man's side. Either way, I was free. I didn't have time to wait for him to change his mind. I slipped into the arms of the festival outside the compound. It was like stepping into another world.

Rather than the distress of battle, the carelessness of festivities flowed around me. The crowd, seeing my bloodied apron, gave me a wide berth, a moment of sobering reality in their midst that they didn't appreciate. I peeled away the stolen clothes and let them fall to be trampled by the unaware.

Tonight had been a complete failure. A bloodless mission had become a slaughter. How many had died tonight over that sword? I wanted to blame it all on the giant named Creed but...I glanced at my hands, expecting to see them dripping with blood, but the explosion had left them caked in ash and char. I clenched my fists and watched it crack and slough away.

Somehow, miraculously, I had survived.

"We always survive," the Dark hissed.

Swallowed that down.

Someone shoved a stout in front of me. I grabbed the cane-shaped bottle from him and drank down the elderberry liquor. It burned my throat but I revelled in the sensation. Took another swig. I had a feeling I was going to need plenty of this.

I knew if I drank enough tonight, immortals, mad crusaders, Legionnaires, and magical swords would fade away into my memory.

CHAPTER FOUR
OLD FLAMES AND NEW ENEMIES REDUX

I stumbled into LaFage's shop and bled over his carpets and a rack of fine clothing. He was less than impressed. He wrinkled his nose and I didn't blame him—I looked like death and smelled like cooked flesh.

"I should've known those fireworks centered around you."

"I'm not in the mood, LaFage. I was setup," I leaned heavily on a rack of fur dresses.

"Setup?" He went back to his ledger.

I tried to shrug but my ribs hurt so bad that I only managed a wince. Hard to look nonchalant when your body was broken.

"There was someone else there."

"You always did take monks lightly."

"The Crusader."

LaFage stopped his scribbling. "The Crusader?"

"And the Legion."

He put down his pen. "The Legion?"

"And a beast named Creed."

"But you're alive. So let me see it."

"I don't have it."

"You don't have Black Swan? Where the hell is it?"

"Creed has it."

LaFage listened while I described the fiasco at the temple,

clicking his tongue when I was finished. "That was pretty slick of him. An expert."

"Are you done?" I didn't want to get angry because when I did, I breathed in too deeply and that hurt.

"It was a good plan," LaFage continued. "Built to his strengths. Minimized his weaknesses. You would be wise to perhaps learn from this encounter."

"My plan was good too. Until he showed up."

"Inadequate foresight, of course." He turned his attention to a jar of clockworks and began taking an inventory.

"I need your help," I said.

"Kind of late for that."

"Not exactly. First, I need a sawbones. One who won't ask questions."

"I don't know any other kind."

"Good."

He returned to his ledger and I waited. His quill scratched across the parchment. He dipped it several times before putting it down and exhaling.

"Is there something else?"

"Actually, there is. I'm glad you're so astute."

"Neither one of us has time for games, Nathaniel. Out with it."

"I need to find Creed. If he has any weakness, it's that he can't blend in. He got off that tower, but chances are he won't easily get past the gates. He's not afraid of brute force, but if he makes a run at the gates, they'll take him down with sheer numbers."

"He could always smuggle himself out in a shipment."

"Or he might try to catapult himself over the walls. I get it. It's a long shot. But I have a feeling this is going to get worse before it gets better. If you hear anything about this guy, you let me know."

I hobbled to the door and paused.

"Is that all?" LaFage asked.

"A lot of people died tonight."

"It was to be expected. This isn't just another chance at glory, Nathaniel. Black Swan is...something else."

I left and stumbled back to a safe house.

I stayed miserable for three weeks. Three weeks of pain, cut off from the world and wallowing in my failure. I couldn't even drink myself into oblivion. I tried that on the third night but ended up re-injuring my ribs while battling a hallucination.

LaFage's sawbones tended to some of my injuries. If he was even a real sawbones. He came from the islands, dreadlocks for hair and his skin smelling like lemons. Not only did he bind my ribs, he also sang and danced and burned *DragonRoot* to appeal to some saint of healing. Whatever. He applied poultices of Slippery Elm, White Lily, and Linseed oil to heal the burns on my neck, face, and hands. It soothed the pain and he said it would reduce the scarring. I didn't need any more scars.

The other wounds I tended myself. And while I had had plenty of practice with stitching myself, my work tended to be sloppy. Which meant more scars.

Finally, after three weeks of poultices and herbal concoctions (and not being able to stand my own company), I headed out into Havencastle. That was when I realized there was a price on my head. I had wandered into a tavern and grabbed a mug of ale, and wondered why everyone was so friendly. In the mirror, I saw the wanted poster beside my reflection. Everyone in the tavern thought they could take me down. My eyes were black and my jaw had stopped hurting days ago, but my boot marks were forever imprinted on their backsides.

I expected the maelstrom of activity to pass. But it didn't. After two more weeks my posters took top billing beside Creed's on most boards and walls. The bounty on my head had even increased. Soon, professionals would be searching for me. The Crusader sure was interested in getting his sword back. The problem, of course, was that I didn't have it.

Still, I couldn't do much more than add the Crusader and

the Legion to the list of groups wanting me. The Pariahs, the Crucifiers, bounty hunters. I wasn't too worried about the Crucifiers. I had left them a full city behind. The Pariahs could prove to be difficult. They had captured me once—chances were they'd try again. This time, however, I'd be prepared. The first time, I hadn't expected them to chase me here to Havencastle. In other words—I had been careless. As for bounty hunters, though sometimes resourceful, they were usually amateurs looking to make some quick drake. I enjoyed proving them wrong.

But someone was going to get hurt. And it wasn't about to be me. That bounty had to be removed from my head.

I checked in with LaFage to find if Creed had resurfaced. I was greeted with a picture of myself staring back at me from his door. A wanted poster. Damn. They were offering five thousand drake. Five thousand! Ludicrous. I ripped the poster from the door before entering.

LaFage the Friendly was behind his counter and he was mighty pleased to see me.

"I'd appreciate it if you didn't post these on your door." I crumpled it into a ball and tossed it in the corner. He was practically glowing because of that poster. Couldn't give him the satisfaction. Sometimes I wished that I was the fence and he was in my position—so he saw what I had to deal with day after day.

"I'm giving my customers all their options."

"That bounty needs to get removed before someone gets hurt."

"Thinking about turning yourself in? Throwing yourself on the mercy of the justice system?"

I snorted. "What have you turned up?"

"On this mysterious Creed? Nothing. Like he didn't exist."

"You don't believe me?"

"I'm not sure yet."

"Fine. I need to get things moving. I just had to fight off a bar of bounty hunters a couple of days ago." I rubbed my jaw as if to accentuate the point. "Put out that you have a buyer for Black Swan. Let's see what that shakes loose."

"You don't have it?"

"I already told I didn't."

"I didn't believe you."

"You're not very trusting."

LaFage scoffed. "It's my business to be distrusting. Especially not trusting you."

Stiff but fair.

"He didn't steal the sword for his personal collection," I said. "He'll want to unload it."

"Perhaps he already has a buyer."

"Maybe. But I don't have a lot of options right now."

"Where can I contact you?"

A glance out the window decided it for me. "It's a nice day. I'm going to get a drink."

∽

The first night was the worst. He lay awake on the cot, listening to the sobs echoing the cells of the prison. Meagre light filtered through a small window in the stone, too high above the floor for Nathaniel to look through. He had wandered the cell a thousand times already, fingers tracing lines in the stone as if he might somehow discover an escape that the people before him had not.

The thought of the years he was condemned to spend here stretched before him like an open maw. How had he even come to be here, in the infernal prison of Gardizael? All alone. The despair lodged in his throat and he thought he'd choke. His parents—gone. His royal blood—useless since the Succession tore apart his family holdings. Only him now.

When the crying outside stopped, Nathaniel froze, fearful because he knew the climate was changing. Something was happening. The door to his cell opened and it wasn't the guards that entered, but three prisoners. He didn't resist when they pulled at him. *What had resistance got him up until this point? A couple of black eyes.* So he went with them, knowing they were pulling him to his doom.

The hallway was lit with naked chemical lamps, the phosphorus spitting and hissing. *Where were the guards? The warden?* There hadn't been a riot so he didn't think the prisoners had taken control through violence. *This was something else.*

He felt the excitement before he heard it. The floor thrummed, sending a vibration all the way to his teeth. Then he heard the yelling, the roar of a crowd. The three prisoners said nothing to him, and he asked them nothing, as they approached the lone door at the end of the fungus-plagued corridor.

The door opened before they reached it and the light and sound beyond finally made Nathaniel pause, to push back against his escorts. They were too strong for him and they never missed a step, shoving him roughly forward.

Past the door, hundreds of freed prisoners screamed, hollered, threw debris from the balconies. The mess hall had been cleared of tables and was mostly empty except for a handful of prisoners standing at the corners, arms crossed, watching their entrance.

"What's happening?" Nathaniel asked.

The prisoner at his back whispered, "Saturday Night Fights" but offered no other explanation.

Nathaniel would learn later that Saturday Night Fights were the fully sanctioned prizefights of Gardizael Prison. A truly democratic system—the inmates voted who they wanted to fight, and then the expert playmakers put odds on the match. Unfortunately for Nathaniel, the runts of the community were usually picked to help warm up the real fighters.

"What do I do?" he asked.

"Survive. There's only one rule—no kicking an unconscious opponent."

"Who am I fighting?"

"Him." He pushed Nathaniel further into the hallway. His

gaze darted to possible exits but he saw none. All the doors were closed and he didn't even think he could climb to safety. Even if he reached the first level of the balcony, there were people to knock him back down.

Nathaniel was small. His years in the Sour Lands hadn't filled out his thin frame. Survival relied on quickness, not strength.

The warrior who emerged from the far doorway was huge. Nathaniel's eyes widened at the sight of him and he tried to retreat but ran into another great slab of muscle behind him. He was shoved roughly forward.

His opponent was an enviable mass of meat and bone. He had long, jet black hair tied into a ponytail that hung to the small of his back. His skin was pasty white, years removed from the outside world. Scars etched his skin, small slashes that Nathaniel wondered represented his kills. Nathaniel had never even been in a real fight, let alone against a veteran warrior.

Nathaniel's breathing quickened and he worried that he might pass out. Fear was a very real threat, as real as the giant approaching him. How did they expect him to fight such a man? That was the problem, he realized. They didn't. He was here for sport. For entertainment. Taking a single punch from that brute and Nathaniel would be a dead man before he reached his sixteenth birthday. Still, he had encountered problems in the Sour Lands, and somehow, he always found a way out of them.

The crowd jeered Nathaniel, probably because they already knew the outcome.

A bell rang, Nathaniel assuming it meant the fight was beginning. Other than the rule of not kicking an unconscious opponent, were there other rules? Time limits? Boundaries? Could he hope to evade long enough until someone called Time?

The giant approached, stretching his muscles, tilting his head side to side. His knuckles were calloused from years of fights. In comparison, Nathaniel's fists were unblemished. The scholars and tutors had trained him in the royal arts: wrestling, jousting, fencing.

Nathaniel glanced about, searching for a weapon. Nothing. The floors were clean, the tables pushed out of the way and propped on their sides to form barriers around them.

Where were the guards? Considering not one prisoner was in his cell, Nathaniel couldn't help but think that the guards were involved.

He was on his own.

The giant took the first swing—a short, choppy punch. Nathaniel ducked easily, ran beneath the man's outstretched arm and dashed to relative safety. The inmates laughed and jeered.

'I ain't paying for you to run away'

'Like a little rabbit'

'Take your medicine like a man'

The giant cursed, then clomped towards Nathaniel, and once within range, tried another punch. Like the first, it was short and missed its mark. He grunted his disgust as Nathaniel danced away. More laughter than jeers this time.

This only seemed to enrage his opponent, his face reddening with anger. He came faster this time. A punching combination but he was still too slow and Nathaniel scurried out of range.

The man glanced up at the inmates. Now he was their target.

'That all you got, Ricter?'

'I always knew you were overrated'

The next attack, Nathaniel dodged and his confidence a little higher, gave the man a little shove, using his attacker's momentum to send him sprawling into one of the makeshift barriers. Two of the inmates grabbed him about the arms to direct him back into the centre but he shrugged them off.

Nathaniel swore he felt the ground vibrate as the man charged. Nathaniel did a head fake left, then twisted right.

"Shyst!" the man cursed, forgoing his usual attacks and trying to snatch the smaller man. Nathaniel saw the arm coming—didn't even think—merely reacted. He grabbed it, used it to propel himself up onto the man's shoulders like a tiger on an elephant.

Nathaniel heard the roar but didn't know if that was the inmates cheering him on, or if that was the blood rushing in his own ears.

The warrior tried to snatch him off his back but his overly muscled body worked against him, lacking the flexibility to get a sufficient grip on Nathaniel to rip him off.

For his part, Nathaniel wrapped his legs around the man's torso to further fasten himself. He took the giant's ponytail in two hands and looped it like a noose around the opponent's throat. Nathaniel arched his back and pulled.

The giant, already fatigued from chasing Nathaniel, collapsed to his knees, made another pathetic attempt to pry the smaller man from him, but failed and collapsed face forward. His face hit first with a sickening crunch. Nathaniel pulled on the hair noose until his muscles trembled. Hands were upon him, trying to drag him away from his fallen opponent. He didn't want to let go.

"Easy, lad. You've won," one of the inmates whispered in his ear. "There'll be plenty more like him if you've got the taste for it."

When they peeled Nathaniel away from the convulsing man, he registered his surroundings again. The prison was a mix of disbelief and joy—he was a 30-to-1 underdog and a lot of money was unexpectedly now changing hands.

His opponent had stopped convulsing. The inmate who had escorted him from his cell earlier said, "Looks like you've got your first kill, kid. Congratulations."

∞

I always seemed to reside in the tropics, but damn I hated the heat. The sun felt like it was three sizes too large today, and sweat drenched my shirt and dripped from the end of my nose. The crowd churned around me, the locals yelling and screaming and generating even more heat. I removed my hat and wiped my brow. I didn't feel good and not because of the brandy gurgling in my gut, and not because every organization (some legal and some not) wanted me dead. Rather, it was the events on the pagoda that upset my delicate constitution.

Creed had known me. Well, perhaps that wasn't fully true. He knew the Dark. From where? From Cresek-Tawn? Or maybe, just maybe, he had known the Dark before it had taken residence in my soul. The Dark hadn't always been with me. Sure, I had had my share of problems as a youth. Pit fighting, slavery, you know, the boys-will-be-boys stuff. But not until Cresek-Tawn did the Dark move in. Not until Joshua bought me, used me as a tool to take control.

I shuddered, twirling the snifter, watching the brandy swirl around the edges. Every time I closed my eyes, the Dark was with me. Every time I slept, it pulled at the edges of my dreams like a thread from a blanket.

Yet I didn't actually know the Dark. I couldn't believe it was a part of me. Couldn't believe that my own personality could hold something so terrible. Make no mistake, I was never a saint. I had been a killer all my life. Killed for pleasure when I was a prince. Killed for food when I was a slave. Killed for survival when I was a prisoner. Killed for business when I was the *Crooked Hand*. But the Dark was something far more sinister.

"I am you."

I gulped my brandy. I had often wondered about the Dark's origins, even asked some questions of the scholars. I didn't press too hard, probably because I was afraid what the results would be—that the Dark wasn't an entity at all, just some mind control experiment that Joshua had conducted on me. Split my personality into two halves, with the Dark simply an aspect of myself.

And yet, Creed had *known* the Dark, signified that it was an entity that predated me. Was Creed somehow the key to free me from that malignant spirit that had taken up residence in my mind?

"No, Creed is a picture of what you will become."

I liked that concept even less.

The market was busy. Men wearing knee-length shirts guided wagons loaded with crates of chickens through the marketplace, rumbling on cracked, overworked wheels. A flock of sheep bleated their protests as they were driven by the shepherd. The din of bartering and chatter created a soothing background noise, an indistinguishable blend of voices that reminded me of an ocean.

The shade of the awning offered little protection from the sun's heat but I didn't really care—as long as it shielded me from the view of the Vera Velat pagoda. Didn't want to ever see that infernal pagoda again though its two-hundred-foot height made it difficult to ignore.

Every few minutes the waiter offered another splash of brandy. Behind me, two nomads argued in their foreign tongue. Judging from their skin colour and the strange blend of clothing, they may've been from the Plains of Maul. Two tables over a young couple stole touches, oblivious to the world. Professionals could take any guise, whether it be young lovers or arguing nomads.

Across from me in the marketplace, a company of players began their tragic tale of love, murder, and betrayal. I'd seen this performance numerous times but I enjoyed the story so I watched with half an eye.

I sighed. Quite simply, I was running out of cities in the Succession to call home. I never was much for the rural life, and all the good cities already wanted me dead or tortured. Havencastle was the last one in the Succession. After that, I'd have to travel West to the Oligarchy of Skellerus. Except I really didn't want to learn the new customs, new languages, new rites. New problems.

All of this because of a stupid sword. Besides, it was Creed they wanted, not me. Except I doubted the Crusader, or anyone else, was about to listen. How amazing was it that a simple botched theft could inflame the entire Succession?

I squashed my *DragonRoot* in the ceramic ashtray. No more drugs. It was intensifying my already frayed nerves. With a final gulp of brandy, my glass was empty, and I slammed it down on the wooden table.

And I choked. Because there, walking only paces from me, was Jane.

No, not Jane, couldn't have been Jane, because Jane was dead. But there she was, close enough that I could've called out to her.

I sat upright so quickly the table tipped, my brandy glass sliding to the stone and shattering.

Not her, someone that looked like Jane. Except this time, out of the hundreds of times I thought I'd seen her, this time it *was* her.

The waiter, he was saying something. I heard the sounds but the words but there was a roaring in my head that drowned him out.

I pushed off from him, fighting through the crowd. They jostled and I bounced around, the ocean in my head crashing through my memories. First kiss, first love, dreams, visions. And it washed away the bad, like a rising tide cleaning away the carrion left after a storm. A weight, or rather the pressure of loss, guilt, failure, it eased for the first time in five years and my stride strengthened.

Jane was alive and she was here. I wanted to call out but I couldn't, my tongue suddenly unwieldy. The crowd must've sensed my determination as they parted before me.

She was as stunning now as she was back then. Athletic build, lithe movements. Graceful. Black hair hung in gentle curls past her shoulders. Her arms were well toned and her shirt accented her perfectly shaped biceps. She wore the fashions of Havencastle, as if she had been here a while. A short dress with exposed back. Only her shoes gave her away as a foreigner—brown sandals from Cresek-Tawn. I caught her before she noticed me.

I grabbed her shoulder, expecting that she'd pop like a bubble in the wind.

She didn't.

Jane spun so fast I barely registered the motion. Her dagger was at my throat, pressed so tightly that I felt the immediate trickle of blood. I wasn't afraid, however. If Jane had wanted me dead, I'd be bleeding out on the cobblestones and she'd already be disappearing into the crowd.

She gasped and I saw the confusion in her features. The same confusion I had experienced.

"Jane," I said plainly as if a knife wasn't at my throat.

She opened her mouth to speak but said nothing, like her mind was whirling faster than the words could come. I touched her cheek, the warmth the validation that she was very much alive.

"Nate?" she gasped. She dropped the blade.

Then I was reaching for her, my arms around her, and she was squeezing against me, both of us holding on tightly so that our personal mirages wouldn't disappear.

The crowd broke around us like a stream around a rock. I chanced to let go so that I could kiss her. The moment our lips touched, I broke the spell but not in the way I expected.

Jane pushed me away and it felt like her wake sucked the air from my chest.

"No, get away from me. Don't touch me."

I couldn't talk. My mind wouldn't form words.

"You bastard," she said, and I thought she was going to strike me. She glanced through the faces around us. She fumbled for the knife at her feet with one hand, wiping at her eyes with the other. She reclaimed her blade and it disappeared into the folds of her clothing.

Then she turned and was carried by the crowd.

Gone.

What the hell had just happened? One minute she was in my arms, the next she was gone. Like trying to remember a dream in the morning, the more I thought about her, the more she faded away.

I wanted to breathe but my lungs wouldn't cooperate.

I wasn't letting her get away. Not this time.

I chased after her, strengthened with my resolve. It would end differently this time. I would make it different. I smelled the scent of her still, let it power me. I pushed people from my path, ignoring the curses and threats.

But as I pursued her, my rational mind began to struggle back through the morass of emotions at seeing her *alive* after these years. And the questions started.

How could she be alive?

The image of her bleeding out had been burned into my memories, her body prone as the sand clotted in the puddles of blood like a halo around her skull.

Yet that had been her right now. Her scent, her touch, her lips on mine. Jane was alive. I vacillated between euphoria and anxiety. I couldn't deny that Jane was well and in Havencastle. But at what cost?

"It is the Beast on the Throne," my inner voice said but I knew the words were lies. No one could be resurrected. Dead was dead and there was no coming back from that. *How?* Somehow, my own eyes had betrayed me years ago. *Or are they betraying me now?*

Why had she run from me? A chill settled over me and the brandy sloshed in my stomach. Somehow, I had been played for the fool and this was a vast and tangled trick. *Impossible.* This was no trick, though her death had been undoubtedly staged because no form of sorcery could've possibly brought her back.

Five years had passed, though the time felt much longer. A lifetime ago. A hard truth. I was a complication from her past she hadn't expected.

My pace slowed as the doubt grew.

I caught sight of her but didn't close the distance. But couldn't let her go either. I had to know. My heart had been ripped away once—and I had a feeling it was going to happen again but I couldn't stop myself.

Then I was back to wondering how it was possible that I was tailing her, five years and a continent removed from seeing her dead in Cresek-Tawn, wondering if I had been played all this time.

Each question was a dagger in my gut. Damn, why had I drank so much?

The crowd thinned, forcing me to fall back. Luckily, she must've been as distressed as me because she was easy to shadow—no backward glances, no doubling back.

"She's leading us into a trap," the voice said. I ignored it. She didn't need to lay a trap as I would've willingly walked into the pits of Hell for her.

When I saw the woman and man working in tandem to trail Jane, I knew that perhaps I hadn't been as aware as I should have been either.

She was being followed, and not just by me.

They worked well together, using precision that set them above common street toughs looking for an easy victim. When one would fall back, the other would advance, one always in line of sight with her. And if there were two working together, there could've been a third but I couldn't spot anyone else. These two blended well so that I was unable to determine their allegiances. Were they independents or with a union?

Oddly, spotting them calmed me, gave me focus. The questions about seeing Jane after all this time were momentarily pushed away. She should have spotted them, just as she should have spotted me earlier. They were good but not the best, which meant Jane was distracted. Awareness wasn't a skill that you suddenly forgot—it became instinct. Regardless, these two were closing their net around her and she didn't even realize it

Jane veered away from the main street down Artisan's Row, a nice sounding name for a despicable district known for gambling, prostitution, and heavy drug use. At this early hour, the crowds were sparse. On the right were the brothels and drug dens, and on the left was the slow flowing Battleford River, heavily polluted and stinking from sludge and effluvia from the slaughterhouses upstream.

The four of us ignored the beggars and the last, desperate hookers trying to turn a trick. I suspected that Jane had finally realized she was being followed and was no doubt leading them into a trap of her own making.

Jane turned suddenly, taking a set of stairs down into an alley. We all converged there. I was the last to arrive and the fun had already started. Jane and the two shadows danced in the shaded, sunken alley.

Jane was holding off the man but he was clearly stronger and was attempting to overpower her. Jane couldn't fully commit to attacking as she must've known that the woman was ready to pounce with knife in each hand. All Jane had to do was expose herself and the fight would be over. Instead, Jane was barely managing to stave him off, wary of not putting herself in harm's way of the woman's knives.

I came behind the woman, my hand crossbow drawn. I jabbed her in the back. "I wouldn't suggest moving." The woman stiffened but remained still. "Drop the blades. Do it." She dropped the knives and Jane saw her opportunity. Able to focus her full attention, Jane's skill with knives overwhelmed the man. Jane was fast, maybe even faster than when we were younger. She stabbed him numerous times: in the thigh, in the hand, in the shoulder, in the calf. She jabbed him repeatedly rather than going for the kill and I wondered if she was enjoying herself a little too much.

"Jane," I said. "Let's—"

My attention momentarily diverted, the woman acted. She was fast. Damn, she was really fast. Shifted to the side, knocked away my aim with the hand bow. I dropped my weapon to deflect her punches. She struck me once and my head snapped back. She was strong, but worse, she was quick. Deadly quick. She had another dagger in hand and I wondered how many she had on her.

The woman was relentless and soon she me pushed up against the wall. When she lunged to stab me, I sidestepped and came at her from behind. I locked her arm so she couldn't slash me, and my other arm curled under her neck. She was frantic so I squeezed harder.

I glanced over at Jane. The men bled from numerous wounds and he had collapsed to his knees. He held up his hand in capitulation. She didn't relent, however, and with a deadly efficiency slashed his throat. He died vainly trying to staunch the spurting blood.

The woman freed her knife arm so I did what I had to do: I swivelled my hips and transferred all my weight to her neck. There was a sickening crunch as I severed her spinal column. She went limp and I released her, and she collapsed to the ground. If she wasn't already dead, she would be soon, either through suffocation or a stopped heart.

"You killed her?" Jane demanded, her knife dripping with the life of the man. I wiped my cheek, wondering how the man's blood had managed to splatter me. I experienced a surge of excitement from the Dark but I pushed it back down.

"I didn't have much choice," I snapped. "If you had been paying attention, you would've spotted them."

"I *did* spot them. Five minutes ago, the same time I spotted you, which is why I led everyone here."

"Precisely my point. I've been shadowing you for fifteen minutes, not five."

She bit her lower lip and I saw a flash of guilt. Then it was gone. I had hit home. She knew she'd let her guard down.

"Maybe you sent them," she accused.

"Twenty minutes ago I didn't even know...I wouldn't orchestrate something like this."

She nodded almost imperceptibly in understanding.

She finished cleaning her knives, then quickly checked the bodies. Jane acted so cold, so distant, like we hadn't been lovers. Like she barely even knew me. I almost wondered if it would have been better if she had stayed dead to me.

"Who were they?" I asked.

"I don't recognize them."

"There might be others."

"I didn't see anyone..." She glanced away sheepishly. I knew that having been caught unaware was burning her. No one snuck up on Jane. Except I had, and these two would-be killers. "We've got to get out of here."

"We don't know who's out there. Someone wanted you dead and you don't know if there are others. I have a safe house—not connected to any union or allegiance."

"I'm not afraid," she said a little too quickly.

"I know you're not. But until you know who you're up against, you can't stay in the open like this. These weren't street thugs. They were targeting you." I knew better than to ask who might want to kill her. The list would be long. "This isn't a trick."

She chewed on her bottom lip, a familiar habit that made me want to pull her close. *Focus!*

She gave a nod, then, "Lead the way."

I didn't have a place I called home. Home implied a permanence I hadn't possessed since my days as a child prince. Even in Cresek-Tawn, my domiciles never truly belonged to me. Though my estates were furnished with the trappings of success, they were staging areas or hideaways, easily discarded and forgotten when necessary. While my current safe houses were far less extravagant, they were just as ephemeral, places paid for with cash in advance, usually negotiated through several faceless intermediaries. Many lay dormant for months, if not years, until they were needed. Some I used more than others, perhaps more from habit than any form of attachment, though I suppose I did possess a certain fondness for the Ordeum.

The Ordeum was a crumbling theatre, once home to Havencastle's greatest performances. Now it housed indecent productions that pushed the boundaries of moral acceptance: bodice rippers, salacious shows of orgasmic proportions. They charged a few brine for each performance and they packed the Ordeum, the old timbers trembling during each production. I was sure that one day, the whole thing would collapse upon itself.

But until that day of destruction, I had a nice little room in the upper rafters. The rent was cheap and as a side benefit I got to watch the performances.

Today was a rehearsal, the Ordeum buzzing with the stress of a rapidly approaching opening night. Two women pushed past, rubbing their naked breasts against us in the narrow confines of the hall, wearing only masks with exaggerated phallic noses.

"You've moved up in the world," Jane commented once the women were by, rubbing her eye as if one of the noses had inadvertently poked her.

"I've always been a supporter of the fine arts."

I led her through the back passages of the Ordeum, navigating past a troupe of performers. Their dry rehearsal involved a dozen naked men and several batons. I tried not to stare at the over-endowed men, wondering how the hell they could even walk with such afflictions.

Then we climbed the five flights of stairs to the upper room that served as my apartment. I checked the lock for tampering, then ushered her inside. Though I'd stayed here for several months, the place didn't reflect my identity. A lumpy bed with a few rumpled blankets, a washstand, a change of clothes hanging from wooden pegs. There were no windows, but I had removed a few of the knotted floor boards to provide a vantage point down to the stage.

She took a cursory glance of the room. "I like what you've done with the place."

I straightened the sheets on the bed, which I realized was an odd thing to do considering we'd just murdered two people. I didn't bring her here to impress her, I brought her here to be safe while we figured out what had just happened.

And we stood there in an awkward silence, while several floors down the actors and actresses went through their rehearsals, the director yelling that their orgasms weren't authentic enough.

I wanted to touch her so badly, but she stood with her shoulder to me while she absently wiped at the dried blood on her forearm. I offered her a towel and she snatched it away.

"When are you going to tell me what the hell is going on?" Dammit, I'd been hoping to approach the subject with a little more tact, but it turned out that five years was a long time to keep that much frustration bottled in. "You've been..." Couldn't bring myself to say dead, "gone, for five years. Five years! Then you show up in a cafe halfway across the world. Coincidence? I never know with you. Not that it matters, because you call me a son of a bitch and push me away without a single word of explanation. Really? That's how this is going to play out? Within minutes of seeing you, I'm splattered with blood and we've just murdered two people in the heart of Havencastle. So let's cut to it. What are you doing here?"

"I called you a bastard," she said.

"What?"

"I called you a bastard, not a son of a bitch."

"What does that have to do with anything?" I screamed. The sounds of the director on the stage had disappeared. It seemed we were becoming the main event. I had to get myself under control.

"You're blaming me for this?" she asked.

"It's a pretty good place to start. Who were those two?"

"Maybe you sent them."

"Why would I send them?"

"I don't know, Nathaniel, maybe to finish the job you started five years ago?" she spat.

My mind was reeling. "I don't even know what you're talking about. Jane, I thought you were..." The image of her lifeless body flashed in my memory but here she was standing in front of me.

"You know you can't trust her," the Dark said, and I agreed. But it didn't matter. She didn't say anything. Reading her body language used to be difficult—she kept her emotions in check—but now anger practically wafted from her, as if I was to blame.

I exhaled and turned, unbuttoning my bloody shirt and tossing it into the wood stove. My days of washing blood out of my clothing was long past. I splashed myself with tepid water from the wash basin. I sensed her staring but I didn't face her. Not because I was angry, but because I didn't know what I was. More confused than anything and I wondered if I had somehow become caught in one of the surreal productions of the Ordeum, just with a whole lot less sex.

"Those are new," she said softly.

Her words brought me back. I turned and realized she was staring at my back.

"You're a sawbones now?" I tried to say it with sufficient bite but failed miserably.

"Just...I remember every inch of you."

I didn't need to tell her the biggest scar was the one she couldn't see. There was so much I wanted to ask her but I couldn't—because I didn't want to hear the answers, fearful of what those answers would be.

She stepped so close I felt her warmth. I faced her and she didn't retreat, nor did she step away when I took her delicately by the arms. My heart was beating so forcefully I heard it in my ears. I wanted so badly to lean and taste her lips but this wasn't the time.

"What happened?" I asked her, and there was a quickly covered flash of confusion.

"It's complicated," she said, that line like a spear to my gut. *Complicated* often meant someone else was involved. I wanted to push. Damn, I wanted to push but if I did, I would drive her away.

It was like I was stuck on a high wire without a net. Instead of asking questions, I said, "Right, complicated."

"I've missed you," she whispered so quietly I barely heard it. Then I leaned in, and kissed her.

We were much quieter than the performance troop of the Ordeum but no less orgasmic. The theatre had cleared out hours ago but we lay entwined on the lumpy mattress. We hadn't spoken for a long time but I heard from her breathing that she was still awake. Perhaps she was like me and simply didn't want this to end.

Words would ruin the moment, even though we both knew those words would come soon. There were so many unanswered questions, and worse, hard truths that had to be told.

I took the time to hold her close, wrapped so tightly that it was nearly impossible to tell where she ended and I began, and yet still I wished I could've been closer. Our breathing had fallen into rhythmic sync and her heart felt strong and confident against my chest.

We stayed that way until the glow of dawn approached.

"I've missed you so much," I said. "I've dreamed of holding you like this every day."

She lay silent for a few moments, then as I feared, she began to retreat from me. I let her go.

"Did you?" she asked.

"Every day, Jane."

She pulled herself away from my touch and from the bed. She fished on the floor for her clothes and began to dress, her back to me.

I wasn't sure why my confession angered her. Exploring that now was obviously too raw.

Instead I asked, "Why are you in Havencastle?"

"I see you haven't changed."

"What's that supposed to mean?"

"You always wanted to talk at the most inopportune times. Sometimes can't we just let things be?"

"I haven't seen you in years. How can I let anything be? Now you show up when my life is going to hell."

"I'm here on a job."

"Of course you're here on a job. But why now? Why in the square that I'm at? Are you telling me that you hadn't seen the pictures of my face on every storefront from here to the Union?"

"You think I came here because of you?"

"I don't know why you're here, that's why I'm asking."

"What do you want me to say? That I've missed you? Of course I've missed you. More than anything."

"Then what the shyst happened?"

"What do you want from me, Nathaniel?"

"How about the truth?"

"I was sent here to kill you," she snapped and she instantly regretted it. We fell into a stunned silence.

"What?" I finally asked.

"Dammit." She sat next to me, suddenly drained. "Those two back there...they weren't after me. They were after you."

"I don't..." Then I understood. "You were the bait." She knew I'd follow her, spot the two. It would all come together in a murderous plot.

"You never thought I could take care of myself," she admitted. "The way you left..."

"The way I left? That's not fair," I said.

"I'm telling you that I was sent here to kill you, Nathaniel. But I couldn't. When you came at me in the square, the look on your face changed everything. I backed down. I failed, *again*." Then in a whisper, "Just like I did the first time."

I sat in stunned silence. This hadn't been on my list of possibilities.

"Word got out about the job you pulled at the festival. About Black Swan." She whispered the name as if we might be overheard in the abandoned building.

I groaned. That sword was causing me a lot of strife. Every bounty hunter in the Succession was after me. Including my true love.

"And the two we murdered?"

She shrugged. "Local operatives. Independents."

"Will they be missed?"

"Maybe in a few days. Not so quick."

"Who hired you?"

"The *Crooked Hand*." A chill passed through me.

"Joshua?"

She scoffed. "You were the one who took orders from him. Not me." She climbed onto the bed, leaned in behind me and wrapped her arms around my naked chest. Nuzzled my neck. "We can leave together. Forget the past. Forget all of this and just leave. We'll have the whole world to explore," she whispered.

"Like we were supposed to before?"

She stiffened and pulled away. "You can't just make this easy, can you?"

I was surprising myself. How many times had I played out a scene similar to this in my imagination or my dreams? She wasn't a dream or an hallucination. She was even more beautiful than I remembered. Her touch ignited my skin, her kisses made my body tingle. Being with her made me feel like a man with limitless potential—a conqueror of the world. All of that and I was asking questions.

"There is no running away, Jane. That's all I've been doing for the past five years. No more."

She considered. "Then we give them Black Swan. Return it to the temple, or give it to your fence, or send it to the Crusader. It doesn't matter where, just get rid of it."

"You think it's that simple?" I said.

"Don't make everything so complicated." Her kisses became more impassioned and soon I had forgotten that only moments ago she had confessed that she had been sent to kill me.

"Let's see if you remember every inch of me." She pushed me back down onto the bed and shrugged away her shirt.

I accepted her challenge.

∞

Damn, I was whistling as I entered the Antique and Rarity store.

LaFage dangled at the top of a ladder, reaching into a far corner for a jar of pickled eggs. "I'll be with you a moment," he said without turning.

"Good morning," I said.

I must've startled him because he had to catch himself and he scrambled to latch on. Secured, he turned. "What did you say?"

"I said good morning."

His eyes narrowed. "Good morning?"

"It certainly is."

He scrambled down the ladder. "What's wrong?"

"Nothing's wrong, LaFage. It's a good day."

"A good day? You don't have good days, Nathaniel. You have less bad days."

"Today, is a good day," I insisted.

"When you're happy, things go to shyst."

"Not this time."

"Are you going to tell me why the morning is so good?"

"Nope. This one I'm keeping for me."

"Before this turns bad, what do you need from me?"

"Creed. Anything else about him?"

"Have I contacted you?"

"That's why I'm here."

"Do I keep information from you? Have I ever not delivered the goods?"

"No, I thought —"

"You thought you'd come down and gloat. You thought you'd spread your good morning filth around here. You're happy and wanted me to know it."

"Look, LaFage—"

"Get out."

"I wanted to—"

"Don't make me kill you, Nathaniel." He was reaching under his desk. Hell, that meant he could activate any number of traps. And I didn't doubt that he'd do it.

"Okay, okay, I'm leaving."

"When I find Creed, I'll let you know. I don't want to see you in here until you're back to normal."

The door slammed so hard I thought the door glass would shatter. LaFage's hand snuck under the blind and turned the sign to closed. I heard the locks snapping into place.

That man had a bad attitude.

Sometimes, you just have a feeling. A hunch or an inkling that the regular ebb and flow of the crowd has somehow changed. I was fairly certain that someone was tailing me from LaFage's Antiques and Rarities. I had no direct evidence. I couldn't spot a nefarious spy with a murderous expression.

My instincts tended to solve patterns that I consciously was unable to recognize. They would spot the woman who seemed to have a little too much interest in that stand of apples; the group of street kids passing hand signals as a way to keep track of me.

Life had a way of going sideways when I didn't trust my instincts. I doubled back twice, hoping to spot that one person who was out of place or detect that random fish monger who happened to be walking the same circuitous path. Nothing.

"*She's trying to kill you,*" the Dark said. "*She admitted it before—those people were meant for us, not her. Do you really think she's going to forget about the past?*"

"If she wanted me dead, she already had plenty of opportunities to do it." I was certain she didn't want me dead—but I didn't know what she wanted.

Plus, if her goal was to kill me, she had me completely vulnerable when we were in bed together. She could've easily stuck a knife in me and ended it there.

Maybe she's being genuine. Maybe she just wants...me.

I passed through a back alley and waited, brazenly hoping to force my shadow into revealing themselves. No one appeared. Doubt formed—maybe I was being paranoid. I squashed that thought violently. Of course I was being paranoid—paranoia was one of my defining traits. Of course, it had led to a few embarrassing incidents over the years: overturning tables at fine restaurants when a waiter took too long filling my goblet; diving through glass windows when a child would laugh too loudly; or a punch-up aboard a royal yacht when I thought the princess was trying to poison me.

If I was being tailed, they were very, very good. Or I had lost them. I tended to think they were very good. Which meant I couldn't return to the Ordeum. I quite preferred my apartment and didn't want the location compromised, even if Jane was waiting for me.

Instead, I went to a different apartment at the back of the slaughter house. The smell of offal was sickening, sometimes blood seeped beneath my door, and the bleating of condemned sheep had a way of working into your dreams, but really, there wasn't much to complain about. Plus, I had a spy hole that allowed me to watch the street without being spotted.

I checked and saw no one.

"Except you know someone is there."

I only knew of four people good enough to tail me without being spotted.

And one of them was Jane.

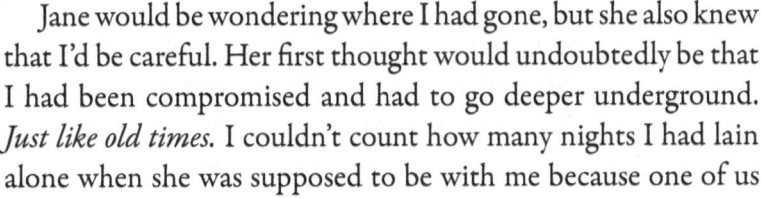

Jane would be wondering where I had gone, but she also knew that I'd be careful. Her first thought would undoubtedly be that I had been compromised and had to go deeper underground. *Just like old times.* I couldn't count how many nights I had lain alone when she was supposed to be with me because one of us had felt threatened and had disappeared for a while.

So I paced. I tried to read some of the dusty philosophy texts but I only got as far as I normally did: the foreword. I stared out the spy hole. Someone was out there. I just couldn't see them. But I knew they were there. I paced some more.

I had been caged before; both voluntarily and involuntarily. Thrown in jail, or sequestering myself when things on the streets got too real. But the wait in my safe house was killing me. I checked the damned spy hole every minute, as if my tail would give themselves up.

If someone was following me, they knew perfectly well I was in here. They weren't in a rush to take me (like the Pariahs, when they'd busted into my room). Whoever was tailing me was content to keep me under surveillance. They wanted something from me. Black Swan was the most obvious answer but I had debts across countless cities. Anyone could be calling in those markers now.

What was really upsetting me?

"That Jane is the one that's tailing you."

She wasn't being honest. This had nothing to do with me but everything to do with the reason she was in Havencastle: for a job.

"She's using you."

Was I a means to an end?

"She wants what you have. She'll rip out your heart to get it. You can't trust her."

I realized I had clenched my fists. I checked the spy hole again and saw the same thing I had every other time. Nothing. I knew they were out there. Was it Jane? Maybe.

If she was following me, I would never be able to spot her. Unless...

I burst from the safe house, not attempting to keep my location secret. My ploy was amateurish but Jane had me acting impulsively. If she was waiting for me at the Ordeum, then I'd know she hadn't been my tail. If she wasn't there...

"You know I'm right."

I took the most direct path to the Ordeum, glancing back frequently to see if my sudden flight had exposed my shadow. It hadn't.

My plan was hardly perfect. I had been gone for hours. She may've rightly assumed I'd gone to ground, and left. Just because she wasn't there didn't prove that she was the one tailing me.

She had my head spinning. Of course I wanted to find her in the Ordeum, naked, waiting for me in bed. Then I'd fall into her arms and we'd make love. But what if she wasn't there? What then? Just because she wasn't there didn't mean that she was guilty. More worrisome: if she wasn't there, how would I find her again? Havencastle was a sprawling city. I could spend a lifetime looking for her.

The Ordeum was quiet, no rehearsals and therefore no performers and not even the maintenance crew. And without the infectious energy of the performers, the theatre was nothing more than an aged building sagging on centuries-old timber.

I took the five flights of stairs, racing against an unseen tail.

Please be there, I wished, pushing aside all thoughts regarding my carelessness. I was being reckless and that was how a man could find himself killed, or worse, engaged to retrieve a magical sword in a citadel full of fighting monks.

I arrived at my room, threw open the door and burst inside.

The room was empty. Jane wasn't there.

A blade was at my throat, someone pressed into me from behind.

"You've been gone a while," Jane whispered in my ear. Despite her having a dagger pressed against my neck, all I could focus on was the swell of her breasts on my back, her free arm wrapped around me to prevent a struggle.

"Just rushing to get back to you," I said gasping. If she wanted to kill me, now was a perfectly good time.

"Close the door," she said and I kicked it shut. "You know how long I've been naked waiting for you?"

The knife was gone and I took that as permission to turn. I gazed upon her and my body responded immediately. I didn't see where she'd put the knife, but she definitely had *nowhere* to hide it. I touched her shoulders and she startled. Her skin was cool, too cool to have run all the way from the slaughterhouse to beat me here, and I closed my eyes in relief. She wasn't my mystery shadow.

"You think it's that simple?"

"What happened?" she asked.

I tried focusing on the question but her nakedness was making it hard to concentrate. She had new scars since her days from Cresek-Tawn, and they were evidence that she'd had a life without me in our five years apart. Did I think that she'd been stored in a box like a puppet? Well, I hadn't considered anything, because I thought she'd been dead.

"I...was being tailed."

"By who?"

"I don't know," I said. It was the truth but it felt like a lie. Probably because I should've said *I don't know, but I thought it was you.*

"I don't know what to make of you, Nathaniel."

"Neither do I." I pulled her close and kissed her. "I have to have you. Now."

"I'm yours," she whispered back, and I heard one of her hidden knives clatter to the floor.

We spent the next days together. She never asked about Black Swan, though I kept waiting for it. My paranoia retreated but never fully left—paranoia was part of my nature.

"Where are you going?" I asked. We had spent our time like young lovers, our carnal appetites never fully satiated. The Ordeum performances had come and gone and we only retreated from our perch for food and the occasional breath of fresh air.

"I have work to do," she said.

"What kind of work?"

She shot me an annoyed look. "Do you really need to ask?"

"I thought your job was to kill me?"

"I didn't do a very good job of it." She sighed when she saw that I wasn't going to let her off easy. "You know how this works."

I wasn't concerned about her being in Havencastle on a job. That was expected. That was what Jane did. But I kept coming back to my main concern: was she using me? My instincts just wouldn't be quiet. Yet I knew if I let my insecurities run the show, I'd push her away. A final barrier stood between us and she wasn't ready to climb it yet. I'd prodded and she'd rebuffed me every time, and I was afraid she'd retreat back to the desert and I'd never see her again. Being with Jane the last few days felt right, despite what my paranoia was screaming. Though it was an overly melodramatic thing to admit, being with her made me feel complete. I didn't want it to end, even though the Dark kept whispering that she'd ruin it.

"You don't trust me?" I hesitated before saying that I did trust her. She noticed. "Shyst, Nathaniel, we've made love a hundred times in four days and you don't trust me?"

"It's been five years. What's happened in that time?"

She released her tension, her shoulders loosening and her expression softening. "We'll talk. Soon. I promise. I just need to be ready."

"And the job?"

"I was supposed to *kill* you, Nathaniel. You think that my handlers aren't checking up on me? I have to make contact or they'll assume I failed." And if they assumed she'd failed, they'd send others, some who wouldn't fall naked into bed with me. "Trust me on this. Okay?"

I watched her leave and considered tailing her. *"Like she shadowed us."* Instead, I tried to do what was so unnatural for me: trust.

When we were together, bits and pieces of our past five years filtered to the surface, though I wasn't sure it was intentional. She had seen my posters across town and I told her about the *DragonRoot* job. I didn't offer information about the Black Swan. She was already aware of the broad strokes of that one because it was what brought about the contract on my life. But the details, I guarded.

The days evolved into a week, our fantasy world only occasionally interrupted by her jobs. Once, she returned with hair messed, sweat dripping, and hands covered in blood. She didn't acknowledge me until she'd washed in the basin. Then she turned and acted as if nothing was amiss. Which I guess it really wasn't.

Meanwhile, I reached out to my contacts but the news remained the same, as it had for years. Heists, power struggles, murders, intrigue. I defined it with one word: theft. Everyone was after what someone else had. Those with all the power had stolen their way up the ranks. Those at the bottom would steal whatever they could: influence, lives, money. It never ended. A cycle of theft and retrieval. With Jane in the picture, I found it all terribly boring.

I couldn't put my distrust behind me. I resisted, but I finally broke down and tailed her. I waited several moments for her to leave the Ordeum, then I picked up her trail. She walked quickly yet gracefully. She blended well and it took some skill on my part to go unnoticed. She took us out of Southmont, along the Ridges, into the Merchant's Quarter. Then into the Dead Zone, the section of Havencastle that had been razed during the Crucifier rebellion.

While the rest of the city had been somewhat rebuilt, this area of town was treated as if it possessed the plague. There were no corpses—they had at least disposed of those. But no one had begun rebuilding. Homes and shops were gutted, their structures ruined from fires. Now, a small community of vagabonds, beggars, and thieves called this their home. They didn't attempt to restore this area—they used the remains to shelter themselves from the elements. City patrols rarely entered this zone. No honest citizen, for that matter, ever came here.

We neared the Palace of the Crucifixion, the old fortress blackened since the failed rebellion. The fallen fortress used to be the Crucifiers' stronghold. Now it was rubble, the ruins a permanent reminder of the blood spilled years ago.

Entering the Dead Zone made my concealment more difficult. With every glance behind her, I was forced to duck behind an outcropping of dirt or a shattered store sign to avoid her gaze. She became more cautious as she wended her way over the cracked streets. Looking back, looking forward, her lips moving as if talking to herself under her breath.

Jane wasn't trying to see if she was being followed. She was doing her own surveillance. Jane was casing the place. For what? Assassination? Robbery?

I made sure to arrive at the Ordeum several moments before she did. I washed off the day's grime and was relaxing in bed when she walked in.

"We're going out," I announced as she walked through the door. "Out?"

She was right to be wary. Going out was dangerous. Not only was I Havencastle's most wanted, but judging from the blood on Jane's hands, she was amassing an enemy list here too. Yet I was nearly euphoric with the fantasy world we'd been living in the past days. I wanted to live in that world with her. Though perhaps my normal life already was a fantasy world and this was more of the real world. Over the years, I'd been a prince, a slave, a murderer, a thief, and a conman. Maybe it was time just to be a man.

"Let's pretend we're two people in love without the world trying to kill us."

She considered then. "Where are you taking me?"

"Anywhere but here."

Havencastle had been one of the richest, most splendid cities in the Succession until the civil war ripped it apart. Though the war was years in the past, the city hadn't fully rebuilt. Streets were in disrepair, the old royal houses were crumbled and vacant, and the signs of old battles still hadn't been removed: scorched walls, broken windows, arrow holes that looked like massive termite bites.

"You make me feel like such a lady," Jane said as we bypassed a hole in the street large enough it could've swallowed a horse.

I took her to an impromptu block festival. Singing, dancing, drinking.

I drank too much for my own good. I had to remind myself I was a wanted man. That seemed like a lifetime away, like a bad dream. I tried not to dwell too much on it, but maybe Jane and I could be together.

I should've been jubilant about being together but instead my mood darkened. I didn't want this to end. I needed her now and for always.

Then there was a Pop! Pop! Pop! that yanked me from my preoccupation. While Jane remained composed, I drew my hand bow and was preparing to fire off a shot before I realized the sound was from firecrackers set off by a group of kids. Jane moved quickly, however, to push down my arm and block view of my weapon. I cursed as I returned it to my belt.

Jane sighed. "We can't live like this forever, Nathaniel."

I returned my weapon to my belt. "Then let's not." I pulled her away from the festivities. We left the glow of the lights, walking aimlessly from the block festival. The darkness was peaceful, our hands clasped together. I caught Jane checking the blind spots of the buildings. I didn't comment, but she didn't mention me checking for tails. We made quite a pair.

We didn't speak for several blocks.

"This doesn't have to end," I finally said. "You and me—it doesn't have to end."

"Nathaniel, I…"

"It's been a long time. And I know that we need some space, until we're ready. Unless…is there someone else?"

"That's not an easy question."

"I need the truth."

"So much has happened."

"Tell me."

"Only you." Her palm on my cheek.

I kissed her, hard, and she returned the passion. A pack of drunken fools broke the moment. They came upon us like a thunderstorm. Hollering, cheering, hoisting drinks above their heads, and slapping us on the back in companionship.

"The Right of Lighteousness," the one man mispronounced.

"Have some ale, friend," another insisted. It was easier to accept than fight back, so Jane and I found ourselves with mugs of recycled brew. Then, like a summer storm, they were moving down the street.

"To the Right of Lighteousness," I said, and we clinked glasses.

We headed back to the street party, our gait relaxed and easy. With the most difficult question out of the way, the pressure was gone. For now.

"You're famous," she said.

"Famous?"

Jane pointed to a poster.

"Shyst." A picture of me stared back, reminding us that the past was always chasing.

"Five thousand drake. Wanted, dead or alive. Maybe I should turn you in for the bounty?"

I scratched my neck uncomfortably. "Would you believe that I'm innocent?"

She neared me. Her lips enticed me, daring me to make contact. "I could never believe that you're innocent." I moved for a kiss but she backed away and I feigned annoyance. "Let me help you," she said.

"I don't need help," I joked.

"Not with that. With that." She pointed to the poster and I reacted like she'd slapped me. "You're right. We can't live like this, Nathaniel. We've both lived in the life, we know what it's like. But until you settle *that,* we'll never be able to live in this world."

Black Swan.

"You're a fool," the Dark whispered from the far recesses. *"I told you she was after only one thing."*

"How can you help me?" I asked.

"Whatever you need me to do, I'll do. I'd do anything for you."

She was right, of course. There was no getting past Black Swan. She asked for the security of putting that affair behind me, as if people like us could ever put anything behind us. And for me, I needed to know if Jane loved me, or was merely using me to get Black Swan. My instincts told me that this wasn't going to end well.

∽

"Why are we meeting...here?" LaFage asked. Behind us was a sixty-foot telescope aimed to the heavens. Astronomers did most of their work at night, so the lab was empty save us.

"Vinzent owes me a favour," I said, as if that explained everything; it actually explained nothing.

There were no windows other than the closed skylight through which the telescope could be raised.

Vinzent's lab was cluttered. The benches were heaped with books, notepads, spilled ink wells, small lenses, and bits of machinery components that he'd pulled from his telescopes.

"Were you followed?" I asked. It was a silly question because LaFage was more paranoid than me, which meant of course he wasn't followed. But by merely asking the question, I conveyed why I'd picked a place with no windows.

"Of course I wasn't followed," he sniffed. He pushed his spectacles higher onto his nose but they immediately slipped back down. He regarded me. "I hope we're finished with that cheery carelessness from the last time we spoke."

"I've put that behind me."

"Hmm." Rather than sitting, he inspected the telescope. "These lenses are exquisite. Free from bubbles, completely clear and homogeneous."

"The telescope stays," I said. "I'm not here to sell the place." I cleared off a section of bench only to reveal a shiny puddle of oil. I shrugged and placed a book atop the spill and motioned for him to sit.

"I'd prefer to stand," he said, clutching his general ledger to his chest. "Why am I here?"

"I need a message delivered. To one particular person, but it can't come from me."

"Then hire one of the local unions."

"It's not that simple. I know this person...very well, but the message can't be traced. The local unions are too careless. Plus, it can't reach my target as a message—it needs to be more innuendo or a rumour. It needs to sound legitimate."

"Who is this person?"

"I can't say."

"You're setting a trap?"

"Something like that. It's a foreign agent working in Havencastle. I'm not sure if she's sanctioned or not. I need to get information to her, and only her. Even the intermediary can't know the nature of the message."

"But it won't come from you?"

"No, not from me. From the Syndicate."

He raised an eyebrow. "You know how they feel about you operating in their territory."

"Let them know I'll owe them one. Or better yet, leave me out of it altogether."

"Then what's in it for me?"

"I'll owe you a favour."

"You already owe me a lot of favours."

I knew he wouldn't go for the favour, and he knew I knew that. All part of our little dance.

He gazed at the telescope and he considered. We both knew the price but had to play our little game.

"This is about a woman, isn't it?" he asked. I didn't care that he knew it was about a woman—I couldn't have him knowing that it was about Jane. They had history. She'd tried to kill him a few times and he'd taken it personally. Plus, he never approved of our relationship. Back in Cresek-Tawn, he was certain that Jane and I being together would end in bloodshed. Well, it had, but I wasn't going to give him credit.

"It's about a woman. And about Black Swan. I need this done. If you can't do it—"

"I never said I couldn't do it," he snapped. "I said I have enough favours in the bank. I need something of substance."

"Then name a price."

He appraised the telescope and was probably realizing (if he hadn't already known it) that the lenses would've been from the Times Before. As he alluded to earlier, those lenses were comprised of a glass beyond the craftsmanship of the current trades.

He ran his hand along the smooth shell of the telescope. Then he nodded.

"Good," I said. Vinzent wouldn't be impressed that I'd traded away his one-of-a-kind telescope, but considering I didn't even know the astronomer, I wasn't too worried about him. "We have ourselves a deal."

I could've just told Jane that I didn't have Black Swan, but it wouldn't have mattered. If that truly was her goal, she would've believed that I was misleading her. And for me, I needed to know where her true loyalties lie. If she was playing me, it was a marvelous act. Days of reconnection and lovemaking, with nary a word about business in general or Black Swan specifically. But I felt this tension, and I'm sure she sensed it too. Unless the Black Swan affair was put behind us, we were doomed.

The Havencastle shipyards was a sprawling enterprise abandoned since the evils of the civil war. Now, the miles of harbour-front territory was fought over by squatters and low-tiered unions. Hulking wooden beams towered above me, those arms used to build some of the Successions finest warships.

Several half-completed ships hung from booms and winches like decaying whale skeletons. Anything salvageable had been stripped and stolen. Now, the new shipyard residents used the beams, timbers, and planking for nighttime fires or to construct new buildings. Ah, the circle of life and all that.

I waited in the broken carcass of a war galley that looked like it had been dropped from the sky. The hull was splintered and the decking twisted on itself. It had obviously snapped from the construction rigging and had broken on the platform several hundred paces from the ocean.

I had arrived five hours early under the cover of darkness. The dwellers had few habits as they battled over the scraps of glory from an old war. That made it easier to move unnoticed.

Of course, if I could move unmolested, it meant others could as well. I wasn't overly familiar with the layout of the shipyards but I guessed that Jane wasn't either. More importantly, I didn't suspect the Bronze would bother us here.

From my perch fifty-feet high on the broken galley, I could spot incoming riders from both directions. I didn't suspect that anyone would be so bold to drive directly into my trap. Especially not Jane. A setup like this required me to be adaptable—to know that she'd have planned for all contingencies as well. Where we differed, however, was I only needed to spot her to confirm my suspicions. Black Swan wasn't really in play—I only needed her to think it was.

I wasn't sure what outcome I desired. If she showed, my fears would be correct and I couldn't trust her. If Jane didn't make a move, would my relief be tempered by the knowledge that I still wasn't sure of her intentions? I wondered if maybe the only outcome that would satisfy me would be her trying to stick a dagger in my ribs. Anything else and her motives would remain mercurial; as if I could ever determine someone's true purpose.

I wasn't sure if I'd see her coming. For all I knew, she had already staked out her spot somewhere in this wreckage just like I had done. I had arrived five hours early because I assumed she would be four hours early.

I watched the routines of the shipyard: the battling over land, the clandestine meetings in the shadows, eyes in the darkness watching for threats. The Bronze came here infrequently, but that didn't mean the yards were lawless. Small-time gangs patrolled, enforcing their own arbitrary, rules.

I staged the meeting for early morning, before it was too hot, simply because I didn't want to be baking in noon-day sun. I scanned the drop point with my telescope. *There.* A woman broke away from a smaller group of scavengers and approached. She wore black cloaks, perfect to hide both herself and a package like Black Swan. I wasn't sure who she was but it didn't really matter. Merely a courier—a decoy that made it appear like Black Swan was in play. I hoped it was enough to fool anyone watching.

She waited in the designated drop spot in the shadow of a capsized crane. I searched the surrounding area for signs of outsiders but I doubted I'd see Jane or her emissaries quite so easily.

Soon, the buyer would arrive. Neither my courier nor my recipient knew that they were involved in brokering a deal for a fake sword. They didn't even know that they had been hired by the same person.

As time passed, my courier grew restless.

"Nice and casual," I whispered. I couldn't have everyone run for the hills before the fake deal even went down. The courier needed to stay until at least the buyer showed. I wasn't focused on the courier, however, I was searching for signs of sabotage or interference from an outsider.

There. My buyer approached. He blended well and flitted between wreckage, wending through the smashed beams and broken hulls, making me think that he was a native of the shipyards.

"If you move, I'll kill you," a gravelly voice from behind said. "I've got a crossbow aimed at your back. Understand?"

I froze with the telescope still raised. From his voice, I judged him to be at least ten paces behind me. I cursed the terrible timing. Down below, my well choreographed deception was playing out. My mind sifted through the possibilities: the Pariahs, the Crucifiers, the *Crooked Hand*, the Bronze. None fit.

I raised my hands. "I'm going to turn around now, okay?"

"Slowly."

Ten paces from me stood a soldier, his glory days years behind him, though I wondered if he'd actually ever had any glory days. His armour was slapped together rusted plates over worn leather fittings. His black hair was long and greasy, his pockmarked face a testament to many brutal campaigns, and his left eye was clouded with cataracts.

"I've got you covered," he said again. The crossbow perched at his shoulder appeared too large for his slender frame. My guess was that he'd need a winch to fire a second shot. Of course, as unsophisticated as it looked, a single shot could kill me just as well as one from the newer, sleeker models.

"You're coming with me." He licked his sun-burned lips.

"You're taking me in?"

"Dead or alive."

"You're...a bounty hunter?"

"That's right."

"The reward is for me alive. Dead is of no use. So instead of aiming for my head, maybe you should aim for my leg. Plus, aiming for the head is usually a bad practice—it's a smaller target than the body." *Amateurs.*

"You worry about your business, I'll worry about mine."

"That's the thing—I have important business going on down there. Right now. I need you to give me five minutes."

"You don't have five minutes."

"How much is the bounty for? Five thousand?"

"Ten," he said.

"Fine, ten thousand drake. The deal that's going down right now, it's worth a whole lot more than ten thousand."

I saw the greed on his face. "How much more?"

"There's a reason there's a ten thousand reward for me alive. It's because I know where the treasure is stashed."

"What treasure?"

"I'm willing to cut you in. Fifteen percent."

"Fifty."

"Now you're being greedy."

"Fine, thirty."

"I have partners. They'd never go for thirty," I explained. "Twenty-five. That's the best I can do."

He considered, and the crossbow lowered ever so slightly.

"Twenty-five percent. What's the treasure?"

"Can I trust you?" I asked.

"I've got a crossbow aimed at your head."

"I suppose I can view that as a form of trust. I'm trusting that you're not going to shoot me. And I need to trust you if we're going to be partners."

"We ain't partners, I just want my cut that's owed to me."

"You see what's happening down there? I need you to use that crossbow." He took a couple of steps and looked down below. With his aim off, it was simple enough to close the distance and push aside his arm.

He pulled the trigger, more out of surprise than any real attempt to shoot me, but the bolt missed entirely, firing off into the distance.

"You dolt. You might've killed someone with that," I said. I pulled my hand crossbow and jabbed him in the ribs.

"Let's get this over with," I said. I took the crossbow from him. "Lay over there on your belly," I instructed. "If you move, I'll shoot you. Even if you don't move, I might shoot you anyway. Get it?"

He shambled over to the designated spot and lowered himself to his belly, his knees popping.

I wondered if he was the worst bounty hunter in the world.

"The worst bounty hunter in the world still got the drop on you. What does that make you?"

How did he know I was here?

I didn't have time for these kinds of distractions. I turned my attention back to the drop site. "Shyst," I cursed. My courier and buyer were arguing. The fake deal was about to end in real bloodshed.

A ship's bell rang, the frenzied clanging carried from far away in the shipyards. The buyer and courier stopped arguing and both reached for weapons, perhaps thinking that each had betrayed the other.

Out on the sea, that ringing was an alarm: all hands on deck. Usually it sounded because of a grave and approaching danger, like pirates. Except there would be no pirates in the shipyards. Aside from the bell itself, there was almost nothing of value here. *Except Black Swan.* My courier carried a fake version, one that was no more than a rusted broadsword, but I wondered if everyone else knew that.

Another bell rang in response, this one closer. Then another. Soon the shipyard was awash in the ringing of bells.

"What's happening?" The bounty hunter's eyes were wide, as if he wondered if all this was for him.

"The Bronze," I hissed.

No, not the Bronze. The Legion. They came in numbers, forgoing stealth for speed on their chargers. They rode with their gold tabards exposed, red capes flapping behind them. Their formation fanned out so it appeared they flowed through the shipyards.

If it was the Legion and not just the Bronze, then they surely believed it was after Black Swan. We'd been betrayed, but by who?

The Legion ignored the squatters scrambling for safety, and stampeded over any who challenged them. They were heading here, directly toward my fake drop point. At least I didn't see the Crusader this time.

Someone had alerted the Legion, must've told them that Black Swan was going to be here. The *real* Black Swan. I only had a few moments before they'd fully surround my courier.

"Did you bring the Legion?" I asked the bounty hunter.

"I ain't no snitch."

"You were going to turn me over to them. How would this be any different?" I believed that his hurt expression was authentic; he hadn't alerted them.

Had Jane orchestrated this? Did she know it was a setup? I looked back down to the drop point: the courier was dead and the buyer was searching the body, pulling the rusted sword from the corpse. The deal had gone bad but soon the Legion would be upon him. I didn't see any way he could escape.

As for me, I could escape onto the old cranes and disappear into the rigging.

My mind was whirling.

"Who sent you?" I crouched next to the bounty hunter. He was the worst bounty hunter in the world. There was no way someone like him was going to catch me. Even luck and my carelessness wouldn't have gotten him this far. He had help.

I produced one of the knives strapped to my wrist and showed it to him nice and close. "That one eye is kind of cloudy. Guess you can't see much out of it. Maybe you wouldn't mind if I popped it out?"

"He's a foreigner," he blurted. "His name's Farger or something like that. He said for a finder's fee he'd pass me the biggest score of my life." The bounty hunter spit at the mention of his deal. I often felt like that when I dealt with LaFage.

"What did he tell you? Exactly."

I saw him considering to withhold information, maybe because his conscience was telling him to not betray his new partner, but when his good eye glanced at my knife, he started talking again. "He said that you'd be so busy with your fake deal, that you wouldn't know about the real deal going down."

"Real deal? Where?"

"I wasn't paying attention to that."

I poked him in the chest. Nothing serious, mind you. Just a playful jab—I stabbed him with only a few inches of the blade. You'd think that I'd actually hurt him from the way he hollered.

"Shut up," I insisted, holding the blade to his throat now. "The Legion will kill us both." Untrue. They'd capture and torture us until we revealed the location of Black Swan.

"You've killed me," he said. There was a lot of blood but I scoffed. "Look, I've hardly killed you. That's a flesh wound if I've ever seen it. I've murdered people far less deserving than you. Tell me exactly what he said or I'll stick this all the way in next time."

He gasped several times, winced, then nodded.

"He said that you'd be so focused on your plan, you wouldn't even realize the real deal was going down now." Another few shallow gasps. Damn, the guy acted like each breath was his last. Real drama queen. "I didn't care about that. I was only going to fetch you. Then we'd rendezvous."

LaFage had sent the bounty hunter as a message. LaFage was clever—he was sending a message that only I'd understand, which meant there had been no way to intercept it.

"Where?"

"At the Brass Cage." He must've been in a real confessional attitude because he added: "I wasn't going to go. I'd have done all the work. Why would I cut him in on it?"

I wiped my blade on his shirt. He was bleeding a lot. Perhaps he was right—maybe he was going to die.

"This is a dangerous line of work, old man," I said. "You'd better get to a sawbones soon or you might bleed to death."

"Aren't you going to help me?" he asked.

"Go ask the Legion." I thumbed down below where they had apprehended the buyer and were attempting to secure the area.

I took to the cranes.

LaFage had sent me a message. Black Swan, the real Black Swan, was in play, right now, at the Brass Cage.

While the Legion was securing the shipyards, the Bronze had arrived in force to try to secure the perimeter. It was an impossible job but their efforts still slowed me. I wasn't the only one fleeing the shipyards. All the gangs, outlaws, and cast offs tried to vacate. The sheer chaos helped cover my tracks.

With the Bronze and the Legion distracted at the shipyards, the journey was easy. It was a stroke of genius, really, creating such a large diversion. The Brass Cage sat on the edge of the Dead Zone, and it suited the area well. It appeared more like a military bunker than a tavern. The front glass windows had long ago been replaced with iron. Inside, the walls were covered in brass sheets, as they were easier to keep clean of blood, piss, and vomit. The original name had been forgotten long ago—probably about the same time the tavern's sign had been stolen.

I surveyed the entrance but saw no signs of trouble. LaFage's message had been purposefully vague so I was short on details. When was the deal going down? Was I late? Was I early? Walking through the front door would leave me exposed but there was only one way in or out of the cage.

I contemplated my next move. I could wait outside, wait for the deal inside, then swoop in after and secure Black Swan once it was in play. Did Creed still have it?

Then I saw Jane and my stomach clenched and any thoughts of a plan evaporated. She had rounded the corner and was heading into the Brass Cage. She glanced over her shoulder to check for tails and I ducked back momentarily. When I looked again, she had disappeared inside.

I threw away caution and hurried across the street. If this was a trap, I was walking directly into it. And I didn't care.

I entered the Brass Cage.

The tang of *DragonRoot* hung in the air, the aroma ingrained in the roughly hewn tables and chairs. Even at this early hour, a few patrons huddled around their drinks, mumbling drunken words to one another. A man hunched over the bar, head cradled in his hands as if trying to live through a hangover. Another man was passed out in the corner, asleep in his own vomit. If he had been younger and stronger, Flesh Mongers would've already claimed him. Luckily, he was well past his prime and worth nothing.

The bartender stared at me. He looked more like a grizzled warrior than a bar keep. His gray-flecked hair was slicked back, his solid face covered with scars of numerous fistfights. He leaned against the bar, his forearms thick and muscular. He didn't say anything but he watched me, ready for trouble. I didn't want to test him.

Jane sat near one of the walls, her back upright and calm. She gazed across the room at me, a sudden cloud of confusion. I was the wrong face in the wrong place.

"Nathaniel..."

"Jane," I said. Though I saw from her expression that she didn't want me there, I sat opposite her with arms crossed.

"What are you doing here?"

"I thought this wasn't about Black Swan," I spat. I wanted to handle this with more dignity rather than a petulant young lover, but my emotions got the better of me. "You set me up at the shipyards."

She blinked. "You orchestrated a fake drop to lure me." She snorted. "I thought you trusted me."

"That's how you're coming at this? That I should trust you even though you set me up?"

"We can't do this now," she whispered harshly.

"I think this is a perfectly good time."

"Nathaniel...please, you can't be here. You have to leave. It's... dangerous."

I wasn't sure whether to laugh or cry. She looked sincere, but I couldn't tell anymore. "Our nights together...were they just part of the game?" My heart was hammering and I was unsure what I wanted the answer to be.

"*She's playing you,*" the voice said.

She touched my hand and though I wanted to pull away, I didn't. I craved her touch. "Nathaniel, I don't know how to explain it. It's complicated."

"It's not!" I hissed and pulled my hand away. "It's not complicated. Was this a game?"

"It was supposed to be a game. But..."

"Then answer the question. Was it a game?"

That anger in her returned. "You left me, Nathaniel. You left me to die in the desert."

I couldn't process the words. *Left me to die.* Impossible. But her being here was impossible. I needed to explain that I had seen her corpse, that I had been misled.

But there wasn't time.

The man sitting at the bar turned and my entire world felt like it went upside down. His eyes were different and his face had been reconstructed, but I recognized him. How could I ever forget? He was from the *Crooked Hand* of Cresek-Tawn— the kind of man who was employed to find people like me.

We stared at each other, both trying to comprehend why the other was displaced so far from native territory. The *Crooked Hand* rarely left Cresek-Tawn and never to simply be seated in the Brass Cage halfway across the continent. And me, well, he probably couldn't comprehend why I had calmly sauntered into the very bar where he was enjoying a drink.

There were no coincidences in my line of work. The *Crooked Hand*, here in Havencastle, meant only bad news.

Double cross.

I recovered from my surprise first. I yanked my crossbow from my belt and shot him. The *Crooked Hand* assassin's eyes widened, initially probably from surprise, then in shock as his throat swelled shut from the toxin coursing through his veins. I kicked back my chair because I anticipated his next move. He was extending a knife from a forearm holder. I snagged his wrist, however, then pushed on his forearm until I heard the snap of bone, and jerked the blade back into his gut. He should've thanked me. Better to bleed out than to die an agonizing, prolonged death from the toxin. All right, either way was terrible. Rarely do we get to choose.

I sensed Jane moving behind me. I was taking a gamble that she wasn't preparing to put a knife in my back. Not that I had much choice—the nasty looking bartender had vaulted over the bar top, holding a small club that he planned to use on my skull. Plus, the drunk asleep in his own vomit wasn't a drunk at all. He sat upright, tearing off the coat that was concealing a huge crossbow, which he aimed at me.

I tossed my empty crossbow at the charging bartender. Instinctively, he tried to bat it away. I snatched his hand, using his momentum to spin him around and use his body as a shield.

The click of the large crossbow in the corner. The bartender convulsed as his life splattered against me, the bolt protruding from his back. With a shove, he tumbled onto the fake drunk, giving me more time.

I ducked. I don't know why but it seemed the thing to do. Instincts seemed to run a second faster than my senses and they had often kept me alive.

A chair swooshed overhead, smashing into the grimy barback mirror. A bar brawl had broken out and it wasn't even noon. For any other tavern, this would be a record. This type of fight was pretty ordinary for the Brass Cage.

The doors swung open. Heavy boots thudded on wood. Soldiers' boots. Armour, swords. But not the Bronze. These soldiers wore no insignias or crests. The movement all around me indicated they came in numbers.

Jane lunged into the cauldron of chaos, bringing splashes of blood. Damn, she was beautiful. Not that I'd forgiven her, but she almost drove me to distraction for the way she twisted and turned, knives slashing and men grabbing at their opened throats.

A bottle struck the back of my skull, the glass shattering and sending me toppling to the floor. Wetness poured over my neck and across my face. Blood? My tongue flicked across my lips. No, not blood but whiskey. Terrible whiskey. Well, at least it wasn't a sap. My vision was blurred, my balance off center. Remaining on the ground was sure death.

I stumbled to my feet, trying to find my attacker before something else smashed into my skull. When a bottle typically meets a skull, the bottle wins. I was fortunate that I won the first battle but I wasn't going to push my luck to hope I survived two. When I turned, I saw a man holding the broken bottle. From the looks of him, as blurred as his image was, he wasn't the *Crooked Hand*, only a customer who had become excited at the thought of a bar fight in the morning. If that was what he wanted, that was what he'd get.

I catapulted myself into him, sending us flying into his table. Glasses burst and ale sprayed across the floorboards. We tumbled on the floor, back and forth, until I gained the superior position atop him. My fist struck his jaw, sending his head snapping back. Another punch, this one square on the nose. Blood sprayed from the impact. His body relaxed. Now he'd be seeing double, too. Then his companion was coming at me. The slick floor made quick movements difficult. He prepared to kick my face like a kid playing ball. As his boot sailed, I adjusted my position. Where my face should've been was the back of his friend's skull. The body in my hands went limp as head and foot connected.

My next move formed instinctively. Twist, turn, and grab a leg of the kicker to bring him down. Unfortunately, it didn't happen that way. As the kicker brought back his leg, he was launched over me with such force his head snapped back. Except I hadn't even touched him. He landed five feet behind me. Only one person could generate that kind of power.

Creed.

The giant roared, his foot coming down to stomp the life out of me. The plan designed for the bar brawler was no good. Escape was now the only option. Creed's massive boot came down, cracking through the floor boards as if they were twigs. Creed sent a wooden table my way. I dove behind the bar. The table struck the wall and it burst apart as if made of glass. Such strength.

This situation needed a plan. While the bar protected me from Creed's projectiles, it also made me a sitting duck. Taking a quick peek over the counter, I did the unexpected and vaulted up and over the bar at Creed.

I hit him around his shoulders, catching him unprepared and the giant of a man began to topple. Even as we fell, I marveled at how downright ugly the brute was. I wrapped my legs around his neck and squeezed—my only real play against him. By the time we struck the floor, I had captured Creed in a perfect blood choke, his throat locked between my thighs. He would only have another few seconds of consciousness—if it worked at all.

Creed thrashed and my hold began to slip. His great hands fastened on my legs, attempting to pry them apart. Had to hold on a little longer.

Creed broke the hold, thrashing around like an animal caught in an iron trap. All I could do was try to scamper to safety. Even without the benefit of leverage, he used his inhuman strength to toss me across the tavern.

I skidded across the floor, sliding through a pool of beer and human filth. The ground vibrated as Creed charged. I tried to dash out of his path but he anticipated my move. His kick crushed into my midsection, sending me headlong into the reinforced wall. That rhino in DunGhūl hadn't hit me as hard as he just did.

Disorientation.

My senses weren't registering. Hands were on my coat, hauling me upwards. The air emptied from my lungs a second time. Had I been punched?

Excited voices penetrated through my disorientation. I expected to see Creed's ugly mug but I no longer saw him. Had he let me go or had someone else intervened? My vision blackened and my knees buckled. I collapsed to the floor, unable to regain my balance or my wits. Jane's cries pierced through my haze of confusion. She was screaming. I wanted to help but my body wouldn't cooperate. Tears of frustration burned my cheeks.

"Nathaniel!" Jane's voice.

Through my distorted vision, the Cage appeared to boil with conflict. Swords, blades, fists, teeth. I tried calling out but nothing came from my throat. I had to remain conscious, so I wouldn't lose her, not after the miracle of finding her again.

The battle faded from my senses, leaving me in a silent darkness.

The Brass Cage beat a rhythmic sound. My eyes opened and I realized that was the sound of my pulse pounding in my head.

I tasted blood and I explored my smashed lips with my tongue, then played with a broken molar from when my teeth slammed together. It hurt to breathe but I knew I was lucky to be alive. As I sat up, pain erupted through my midsection as I must've reinjured my broken rib. Still, the agony wouldn't discourage me from climbing to my feet.

The Brass Cage was a shambles, probably worse than usual. The bartender was dead with a bolt through the heart, corpses were strewn about the floor, tables were smashed, and puddles of blood and beer mingled. I stumbled to the bodies. Inspected all of them. Jane wasn't here. Some of the men twitched, in varying degrees of consciousness, though none were the soldiers I saw burst in earlier—if any had fallen in battle, then they had taken their dead and wounded with them. If they were battling Creed I had to assume that many had fallen. But what of Jane? Had she been killed too or had she escaped?

"And she's laughing at you."

Shards of shattered mirror crunched underfoot. I had to get out of here before the Bronze arrived. I lurched onto the street, knocking into two talking men. They startled and cursed but taking one look at my bloodied appearance, they turned and fled rather than confront me. Good move.

Strangers gave me room but stared at me in curiosity. My knees buckled and my lungs struggled for breath.

Though on my knees, the crowd stayed away from me, sensing a sick and dangerous creature. How long was I in that position? On my knees, head down, and hands clenched into fists, body shaking with the emotions.

I was a fixer. Solving trouble was my job. This was going to be just another job. This wasn't Cresek-Tawn. This was Havencastle.

"Except the Crooked Hand is here, Jane has sold you out, and the world wants you dead."

And for the second time in my life, I realized I didn't have to fix someone else's problem—I had to fix my own.

CHAPTER FIVE

KIND WORD AND A CROSSBOW

I departed the Brass Cage before the Bronze arrived though I knew they'd connect me to this mess anyways. Even if none of the survivors became cognitive, the amateur bounty hunter back in the shipyards would eventually spout off some crazy story to protect his reputation. I should've killed the man when I had the chance though he was probably the most innocent out of the lot of us. Which wasn't saying much.

I staggered through the streets of Havencastle. The crowd parted for me as if I were a leper though my appearance must've resembled a man who was drunk or crazy, maybe both. A team of horses nearly trampled me, briefly breaking me from my reverie.

This wasn't a daze. I was thinking, calculating, and trying to figure out what the hell had happened in the shipyards and the Cage. Jane must've gotten word about the real Black Swan, decided that the shipyards drop was a ruse, and sent the Legion in her place.

My life had never been easy nor clear cut. But this was even messier and confusing than my comfort zone. What was Creed trying to do with Black Swan? And who were the soldiers?

Then there was Jane. Was this finally confirmation that she set me up?

"She set you up and sold you out."

I clenched my fists. How much did she orchestrate? Was I just the mark in her elaborate game? I wasn't sure what hurt more: my numerous bruises or the way she'd twisted a figurative dagger in my gut.

Except those were the *Crooked Hand* in the Brass Cage. Normally, I would've assumed they were searching for me, but not this time. The look of surprise on his face was genuine. He hadn't known I was going to be there.

The Jane I used to know despised the *Crooked Hand*. Even if she had somehow done a complete reversal, she had always liked to work alone. No, it wasn't that she preferred to work alone— she *always* worked alone.

Or were they watching Jane? She had told me that unless she produced results, others would come. A double cross or someone keeping tabs on her? I knew I was clutching at straws, letting emotions cloud my judgment. Jane had set me up. Tried to get me killed.

There was no more keeping to myself. I needed to find that damned sword. I needed to steal it back, and kill any man who got in my way.

"And what if Jane gets in your way?"

"Then I'll kill her too," I said.

I was getting ahead of myself. I needed to recover, to nurse these wounds, both new and old, so that I could physically perform any act of recovery. I returned to the slaughterhouse. I went through the motions while I mulled over facts, assumptions, and blind theories. I stripped out of my bloody clothing, cleaned my wounds, ate, and prepared myself for the dangerous world ahead.

I rested in an uncomfortable wooden chair, purposefully choosing it so I was forced to sit bolt upright and I wouldn't be tempted to drift off. Before I realized it, my eyes were closed and I was asleep.

∞

The Rominratu.

The night of madness. The blood rite. When Cresek-Tawn turned upon itself to determine the strongest and the mightiest: the new lord of the city. Cresek-Tawn boiled. Laws were put aside, feuds were settled, and past injustices solved with murder and brutality.

Nathaniel had been sent to deliver Joshua's justice to the Rei clan. They were the ruling family though he saw they had become too complacent and too soft. This estate was the seat of their power. It should've been defensible, a bulwark against the Rominratu. Their decades-long rule made them favour extravagances over practicality. The splashing of the fountains masked his footfalls, the imported trees cast shadow, and the tall, foreign grasses gave him cover. Beyond the walls, the Rominratu raged. He heard the sounds of battle, the cries for mercy cut short, and the screams of the madness.

He sensed the Dark slavering in the background but Nathaniel didn't release it.

"I can help you," the Dark said.

"Not tonight." Nathaniel felt the warm glow of the Dark within—the creature that lived inside of him, a perfect ally that he embraced. But the Dark was unpredictable, a force of nature once released, and tonight he needed to focus.

Nathaniel crouched in the grasses, letting his eyes adjust. A fire had erupted in the last room and the brilliance had ruined his night vision. His fine silk clothing was sliced cleanly from where a scorpion's sword had come close to drawing blood. His kept his breathing even and regulated, careful to not let his pulse race—he knew he might have to continue this pace until dawn. Splattered blood tightened on his cheeks and he resisted the urge to wipe it away.

Movement.

A slave crept through the darkness, hoping to hide from the murder. He was an older man, perhaps stolen from the Northern cities, his posture bent from days of keeping his head bowed. The slave shuffled hurriedly, not knowing he was being watched. Nathaniel considered killing him. A quick strike. Perhaps a palm blow upwards into his nose. Or maybe a blood choke. But Nathaniel let him pass. The slave could've been a decoy.

Nathaniel planned to kill him later, just like he'd kill everyone here. Joshua had ordered the massacre but his true target was the leader of the opposing clan: OtoruRei.

He looked past the shuffling slave and he was rewarded with a single flash of light in the darkness: the glint of reflected steel. Perhaps, if OtoruRei had been a true sword master like the rest of his clan, he would've kept his sword sheathed. Instead, his fear must've caused him to prematurely draw his blade and he now he held his sword before him in a double-handed grip. As he shifted nervously, it caught the light of the blood-red moon shining through an upper window.

OtoruRei wore the hardened hide armour of the island of Moragorat, his helmet a mixture of iron and leather, designed to withstand all but the sharpest of blades. Another symbol of complacency. The Moranian armour was designed for riders. Impractical in Cresek-Tawn where horses were foreign.

Nathaniel scanned down the hallway. Nathaniel had killed two scorpions which left one alive. He'd heard the rumours and the gossip: OtoruRei's third scorpion was a vengeful spirit: bloodless, emotionless, and unrelenting. Nathaniel didn't believe rumours. Even ghosts could bleed.

Where is the scorpion now?

Nathaniel watched OtoruRei stumble through the hallway. Is it a trap, Nathaniel wondered. He didn't think the man's fear was an act. Would the third scorpion leave OtoruRei so exposed? If so, it was a risky ploy to draw him out. He weighed his options and decided that now was the best time. Even if the scorpion lay in wait, Nathaniel figured the trees and grasses would give him enough cover that he could kill OtoruRei before any trap was sprung.

He closed the distance. Ten paces and no sign of the scorpion. Maybe, if the rumours were true, the ghostly scorpion would *materialize when he reached OtoruRei.*

Removing the silk scarf from his own neck, Nathaniel wound an end around each hand. OtoruRei stopped, searching for a phantom sound. His breathing was loud and panicked. Luckily for Nathaniel, OtoruRei's helmet further hindered his vision.

Nathaniel sprung, looping the scarf around OtoruRei's neck, bracing his knee on the man's back for extra leverage. In his panic, OtoruRei lost his one chance of survival when he dropped his sword and instead grasped in vain at the silk cloth. The sword clattered to the floor, so loud that it would've alerted anyone within range of his presence. He was at his most vulnerable now, while focused on OtoruRei. Keeping the pressure tight, he scanned behind him.

There.

The scorpion seemed to materialize feet away from him. He knew it was a trick of the shadow, that the scorpion wasn't a ghost. Ghosts didn't need to use swords. The scorpion was thrusting a sword.

Nathaniel swivelled so that instead of stabbing him, the sword plunged into OtoruRei's chest. The man was silent upon the strike, the scarf around his neck preventing a moan. It was a perfect sword blow, directly into the man's heart.

Nathaniel saw the third scorpion. It wasn't a ghost, but neither was it a man.

It was a woman. She yanked the sword back but it was too late. The thrust had been a killing strike. Nathaniel felt OtoruRei sag against him as his life expired.

Nathaniel slowly lowered Rei to his knees then released the scarf. Rei remained kneeling, head slumped onto his chest as if praying.

The scorpion seemed to be stuck in an enchantment, her gaze locked on the man she had sworn to protect but had just killed. Even in the darkness, Nathaniel saw that she was an outsider like him.

She was tall, her hair black and pulled off her face in a warrior's braid. He couldn't see the colour of her eyes in the dark. Her armour was fashioned in the same design as OtoruRei's, but much lighter with a design focused on agility and quickness.

Neither moved. His mission objectives had been clear. Kill everyone, and he could've killed her easily because she was in a state of shock. He could've used OtoruRei's dropped sword and opened her throat in a bright, red gush.

She was beautiful, though that wasn't why he spared her. He'd murdered many beautiful women. They'd promise him pleasures of the flesh, and still he'd murder them without a second thought. So why was he hesitating now? Maybe he wanted to defy Joshua. Or maybe because tonight was Rominratu—the night of madness, and he let that madness infect him.

"Go," *he ordered to her.*

She tore her eyes from OtoruRei and frowned as she looked at Nathaniel.

"He was already dead."

She didn't move. She must think it's a trap, *Nathaniel thought, so he stepped back. She stared back at the motionless OtoruRei. Perhaps she was thinking it was better to die than live with her failure. Just when his resolve weakened and he considered killing her, she turned and ran down the long hallway until her shape blended with the grasses.* Like a ghost, *he thought. Then she was gone.*

What foolishness was it that caused him to release her? He shook his head, as if trying to dispel an enchantment. Nathaniel kicked OtoruRei over. The body crashed forward, blood leaking from the joints of the armour. There was still much work to be done. He let her live, but he wouldn't the others. This was to be a massacre. A message from Joshua. And if any survive, they might spread word that he let the final scorpion live.

Nathaniel slaughtered the slaves. They screamed, begged for mercy. Their pleas were of no use. Nathaniel was a professional hunter, trained in the arts of pursuit and death.

He surveyed what he had done. The fountains ran red with the blood of his victims; the corpses were dismembered and spread throughout the estate. Nathaniel's task took nearly three hours to complete.

At the end of his grisly job, he was shaking but not because of the brutality. He'd been trained for such acts of barbarism. He stared at his trembling hand with suspicion, then clenched it into a fist. He shook because of the woman. The one he had let go. Have I gone mad? *An act of defiance so grave, that if Joshua discovered, he'd throw Nathaniel to the wild boars.*

But tonight was Rominratu—the night of madness.

⁂

The smell of blood wakened me, the stench so cloying that I thought I'd puke. I groaned, the wooden slats of the chair leaving their impressions in my back. My muscles, already tortured from the brawl, had seized from a night of sleeping in a chair, my neck so stiff that I winced when I tried to straighten.

The butcher must've been busy working: chopping, slashing, rending. I felt like I could relate to all that mutilation. Was it possible to feel worse than yesterday? Why yes, it was. I hurt everywhere. My bruises had ripened, my muscles tender to the touch. Yet surprisingly, there was something else, something that I was fearful to touch. I sensed the breath of the Dark on my neck.

"You want me unleashed," my internal voice said.

My joints creaked and my bones popped as I tried to stretch out the kinks. I felt twice my age but that was what happened when you got in a brawl with a bunch of trained killers and a giant.

I needed a sawbones. My ribs hurt, my head hurt, and I had blood all over me—some of it mine. Despite my fatigue, I washed, dressed, fastened my utility belt to my waist, hooked a hand crossbow to my hip, and pulled on a duster. I left my apartment, walking past rows of hanging cattle, their throats slit and the blood sluicing through the floor grates. A perfect backdrop.

The butcher knew I preferred anonymity and he gave it to me freely. Not a wave or a hello. Surly old bastard. I made sure to pay my rent on time because I didn't want to give him any excuse to mount me on the dangling meat hooks.

With an hour before dawn, the streets were dark and abandoned other than a few patrolling Bronze. I avoided them easily, ducking into alleys when needed or cutting through the parts of town where the Bronze didn't tread.

I was heading for LaFage's. I was relying on him a little too much lately but he was my only good connection in the city. And if I was going to pull off what I had planned, perhaps that was a good thing.

Glass crunched underfoot as I neared his shop. I thought nothing of it until I realized that the entire square was littered with glass. I stopped, looked around but didn't see any broken windows or lamps. I inspected the pebbled glass, scooped a handful and let it sprinkle between my fingers. This wasn't glass from a shattered window—it was sand that had been heated, transforming into smooth, pearl rainbows.

The heat required would've been intense. In the fjords of Rundarin, I had seen lightning strikes that had turned quartz sand into standing statues of glass. But this was too widespread, as if the entire area had been bathed in flame. What would cause something like this on such a wide scale?

Still holding a handful of glass, I knew instinctively the catalyst for this event. LaFage's shop. Bad luck seemed to follow that guy. Sure, he'd claim that none of this happened before I showed up, but he was just trying to cover for an unfortunate string of malicious fortune. Though the front windows of LaFage's shop were still intact, the walls had been scorched black. The structure itself appeared solid. A 'closed' sign hung in the window of LaFage's shop. Who believed signs?

My steps became heavier as I approached, not through some form of black magic but from the sense of dread that heightened as I neared. I stood at the door, feeling heat waft from the structure. Swirls of colour pervaded the metal of the lock and handle. They had been re-tempered. They were warm to the touch. The lock was warped and twisted but enough of the original structure remained for me to throw the tumblers and open the door. The bell tinkled with my entrance. The smell of mould hung heavy in the air, the lanterns extinguished. The place appeared untouched by the outside disturbance.

Someone rummaged through the backroom, a frantic sound as if they were ransacking the place. A jar shattered and baubles bounced along the smooth floors followed by an under-the-breath curse. I grabbed my hand bow, snuck around the front desk, and peered through the curtain.

LaFage reached into boxes, frantically stuffing valuables into a merchandise bag. In his rush, more trinkets clattered to the floor, some breaking, and others bouncing beneath the shelving. LaFage was robbing his own store.

I crossed my arms and tapped my foot lightly, waiting for him to notice me. The damned fool took a while and I grew increasingly impatient but I didn't want to ruin my perfectly good appearance.

He shuffled towards me, large canvas bag in hand, contents spilling with each step. Finally, he spotted me, startled with such intensity that he lost his grip on the bag. He fought to counterbalance it, failed, and it hit the ground, spilling merchandise across the floor just like Evil Patrick's bag of toys.

His fox-like features widened from his shock. "Nathaniel? It's late, I mean early. What are you doing here?" He looked guiltily at the bag, as if it were my store he was robbing.

"I've got a problem, LaFage."

"I'm sure you do. You're a fixer. You attract that type of stuff, but I'm leaving. Maybe you could come back at a decent—"

"You're leaving town." My gaze wandered from the bag of merchandise to LaFage's face and I saw it there as plain as the glasses on his face. Guilt.

"I'm leaving for a bit. I'm a businessman and business is slow. Thought I'd take a tour of the countryside before—"

I lifted him by the collar. "Did you set me up?" His glasses slipped, now askew near his chin.

He pushed me away and straightened his glasses, scowling. "Set you up? From what I heard, I saved you from the Legion at the shipyards. And I thought the whole mess at the Brass Cage was your standard operation. Bloodshed, confusion, death."

"What happened here?"

"I had visitors."

"From the look of things outside, you did all right."

"You know me. I err on the side of caution. After I left Cresek-Tawn, I purchased protective wards from an Exactor out in the wastes." He motioned with his hand as if urging himself to hurry with his own story. "Those wards were unbreakable. Unbreakable."

"And?"

"They were broken."

"Your shop's still here."

"A guy was watching my store last night. Real freaky type— looked like one of your associates, not mine." I ignored the comment. "Leather mask, white gloves. Looked like the remains of someone after a Crucifier interrogation. Deformed ears, burnt face, wearing a mask. He's coming to the store. The next thing I know, my wards go crazy and half the street lights up. He's still standing. How could anything live through that? They couldn't. But this guy did. My wards were shattered and I'm left with only a few tricks up my sleeve. Luckily, he mustn't have known I was vulnerable as he doesn't come any further. Walks away as if nothing happened. "

"An enemy of yours?" I was growing impatient with his story. I had my story to tell.

"Not an enemy of mine. An enemy of yours. He was here for Black Swan."

"How do you know?"

He sighed as if explaining something to a child. "I don't like surprises."

"I get that."

"The problem, Nathaniel, is that you never actually cared about Black Swan. You never respected it or what it represented."

"You're worried about legends?"

"You just don't get it. It doesn't matter if it's only a sword. Others believe it's something far greater. So whether or not it's a sword handed down by the heavens is irrelevant. Because if these people believe the stories, then they'll be motivated to do anything."

I waited for him to get to the point.

"That guy with the mask who showed up last night...I think it was the Beast on the Throne."

I laughed. I didn't mean to, but to hear LaFage, a man of business, starting to spout superstitious nonsense took me by surprise. When I realized he wasn't joking, I composed myself. "Shyst, LaFage. You've got to snap out of it," I said. "The Devil does not shop at your store."

"It doesn't matter if he's the real Beast on the Throne or not. He is dangerous—beyond what you and I are capable of handling. Real apocalyptic type—doomsday, Armageddon, end of the world."

"What about the sword? What does it do?"

LaFage shrugged. "No idea. But he'll be back." He motioned to his bag. "I'm not going to be here when he returns. With only a few tricks left, I'll feel a whole lot better when there's some ground between me and him."

I puffed out a heavy breath. "The situation gets worse, LaFage."

He blinked, then pushed his glasses up his nose. "Worse? Someone walked through my wards and survived. I don't think it can get much worse."

"Oh, it can. The *Crooked Hand* was at the Brass Cage. Waiting for me."

"The *Crooked Hand*, here?" LaFage stammered. He knew that if Bounty Killers could track me down, that they could most certainly find him.

"I walked into an ambush." I hung my head, almost in shame. "Jane was there."

"J-jane?" he stuttered. I felt a flood of relief with his reaction. LaFage wasn't an actor nor a particularly good liar. His face said it all—he was as shocked as I had been. "I thought she was..." He didn't finish, but I knew the next word should've been *dead*. "So she's the one you were trying to set up?"

"She's been in Havencastle for over a week. I thought..." I wanted to say: I thought it would end differently this time. I didn't because I knew he'd probably slap me.

"We need to get out of Havencastle. Both of us."

"Not this time," I answered.

"This is too hot. Lay low for a while. Find one of your cute lady friends and disappear for a year or two. We've done it before and we can do it again. Hell, maybe become someone new for a while."

"I'm going to get it back."

LaFage grabbed my arm and even my glare didn't loosen his hold. "She's not worth your life, Nate. She's trouble. For all we know, she could be one of the *Crooked Hand*."

"This isn't about her. It's about a sword. I'm going to get it back."

"She's from Cresek-Tawn, isn't she?" he continued. "She's no better than the rest of them."

I imagined grabbing him by the throat, slamming him against the wall, and crushing away his life. "*Yes, yes, yes!*" the voice encouraged. I took a step back instead, not trusting myself. This wasn't about Jane, I told myself. I needed to find that sword to end the madness. "*And maybe kill her at the same time.*"

"I need to put an end to this," I said. "There's only one way to do that. Black Swan."

"Why are you coming to me?"

"You sent the bounty hunter?"

"Yes, clever bit there, wasn't it?"

"You knew about the Brass Cage and that Black Swan was in play. Tell me."

"Nathaniel...You know how this works. I don't deal in identities. I deal in shadows."

"Give me something," I implored. I would've used the 'because we're friends' angle but I knew that would only make him angry. We weren't friends and we both knew it.

"I was brokering a deal. Like I said: I don't deal in identities. But it was simple to ascertain that I was dealing with Creed."

"How'd you know it was Creed?"

"Because he killed three Bronze and maimed five others, all while he was unarmed."

"Yeah, that's him."

"Most certainly." He frowned. "I'm intelligent enough to connect those dots. May I continue? Thank you. Creed was trying to get out of town because, well, he's a murderous giant and I suppose he realized he couldn't get past the border. And even he couldn't get beat an entire army." I shrugged, not certain of that, but let him continue. "He hired a union to smuggle himself out of town. I brokered the deal. Wasted a lot of resources and good favour to get you that information."

"What union?"

"The Syndicate."

I remembered the soldiers storming into the Brass Cage after my battle with Creed. The Syndicate? I had never seen a guild so heavily armed, but if they had known Creed's background, perhaps they were playing it smart or had brought in outside mercenaries.

"So they pulled a double cross," I said. "Agreed to smuggle Creed out of Havencastle, but then stabbed him in the back and most likely stole Black Swan."

"What would they want with it?"

"Standard reasons, most likely: end-of-the-world artefact, after all. Perhaps purely pecuniary reasons. There would be a hefty price tag attached to such an artefact. They might've had a buyer already lined up. It is a prized commodity." The little man began shoving the fallen goods back into his canvas bag. "It could be anywhere."

"I need to know where it is exactly."

"You can use a Diviner."

"I don't believe in fairytales."

"Do you think I'm a fairytale?" the voice asked him. It wasn't that I didn't believe in Diviners, more that when I used them, bad things happened.

"Maybe you need to start believing," LaFage said.

"You think a fairy stole it?"

"When are you going to admit that there is more transpiring than any rational argument can explain?"

"A man of lesser experience might fall for smoke and mirrors. Like you've always told me, LaFage. Follow the money. Someone in the underworld has got to know."

"Sure, someone's got to know. But no one connected with me."

"Then I need into the Syndicate."

"This isn't a problem for you to solve," he hollered. "You can't just get in to the Syndicate. Even if you didn't have your picture plastered all over Havencastle, they'd never trust a newcomer like yourself."

"So I have to be discreet. I'm discreet."

"Don't you get it? You're already a dead man. If the Syndicate doesn't figure out your plan, you also have the Beast on the Throne to worry about. You don't walk in and enlist. It's not that simple."

I figured it was going to be simple.

I said my goodbyes, left his shop, and smiled. Things were starting to look up. Getting into the Syndicate would be simple, but not easy. I had to get into a position of trust, and fast. The Syndicate didn't operate like a local merchant at the bizarre, but no one said I had to play by the rules. This was my starting point.

The Syndicate ruled Havencastle and so they had a lot of thumbs in a lot of different pies. I had to find my pie. Something low profile, which meant no assassinations, kidnappings, or extortion. Not yet. Start small, then move through the ranks of the Syndicate until I came to a position where information would be available about something as hot as Black Swan.

The problem was that this had to happen fast, before Black Swan was swept beyond my reach. Climbing the ladder in the Syndicate would normally take years. I needed to do it in a matter of days or weeks. I'd check in with a sawbones, get some patchwork done, then get me that sword.

My mission was possible. No one said it had to be done honestly, and it didn't matter if my advancement came because of guile—this wasn't a career, only a brief stopover.

The world was a dangerous place. It was a good thing I had people like LaFage looked after me.

O'Meara was at the gaming halls. He shouldn't have been there because he was considered respectable now, but O'Meara was never where he was supposed to be. I walked into the Rolling Bones gaming den, clouds of smoke burning my eyes and lungs. Business was good; the place was packed. Gamblers pressed around the tables, cursing or crying in proportion to their fate. Waitresses wearing far too little delivered complimentary drinks to the gamblers. Unlike other taverns, the waitresses here never had to worry about being pinched or poked; the customers were too concerned with money to worry about more primal urges.

I pushed my way through the crowd, watchful for the hands of pickpockets. I stopped at a game of coins and stood opposite a large man with a thick, black beard. He was having a good night, his stack of chips teetering on the table with each good-natured slam of his fist.

His eyes watched the bouncing coins like his life hung in the balance; I knew it didn't. As the gold tokens spun to a stop, the burly man slammed his fist again. "I'm hot tonight!" he roared.

He wore a dark-blue uniform with gold collar and cuffs. His uniform was unbuttoned to his navel, chest hair exposed and a gold chain dangling from his neck. At the end of the chain was a star with the words "Sheriff" engraved on it in large, block letters. His smile widened as he noticed me taking up residence opposite him.

As a Bronze for Havencastle, he should've tried to throw the shackles on me and taken me before the Crusader. But this was O'Meara and he wouldn't do anything of the sort.

Not yet, anyways.

"Nathaniel! It's been a good night!" O'Meara had one volume: loud.

"They're still letting you win?"

"Letting me win? This is skill, my friend. Skill and pure luck."

"Right. Skill."

The coins stopped bouncing. A losing hand, but the dealer pronounced "winner" and shovelled money at O'Meara.

"Okay, the house rules do tend to favour me. Only because I'm a favoured client."

"Wouldn't it have been easier for them to simply bribe you?"

"Not as much fun." He rolled the coins. They bounced against the bumpers on the table. They spun, and came up crowns. "Shyst!" he boomed, reaching forward to gain his winnings. His stacks of brine and drake toppled in a cascade of riches but O'Meara didn't seem to notice.

"Gentleman wins again," the table attendant declared in a bored voice.

O'Meara began counting his money, his smile slipping. "You're a wanted man, Chief. You shouldn't be showing yourself around here."

"You worried I'm going to tarnish your reputation?"

He glanced up—a cautionary look—then back to his money. "You've done some nasty things. They true?"

"Some. Well, most. But it was self defence."

"Of course. You're always innocent, aren't you?"

"I'm morally flexible. I'm not here to talk about me."

"Then why you here, man? You're ruining my game."

"I'm here to help you out. Keep you respectable for a while longer." O'Meara grunted, a sign of affirmation. "You can't live off your last job much longer. Soon, your superiors are going to want you to get some results. And if you don't get them, then no more free games for you." He cast an eye to his winnings.

"And you can help me?"

"That's right, but first you have to help me."

O'Meara piled his winnings into his pouch. "All right, we'll talk, but I'm not promising anything, Chief."

"Whatever you say, O'Meara. Let's talk outside."

"Sure."

O'Meara pulled me from the gaming table. Normally, the sight of a Bronze in an illegal gaming and prostitution den would send everyone scurrying for the exits, but O'Meara must've been a regular as no one glanced at him twice. Plus, it was hard to fear his badge when his own pockets overflowed with contraband.

I knew O'Meara from his days in New Eval King. Back then, he had been a scoundrel like me, but times changed, and so did identities. Different city, different life. Now he was part of the Bronze. Though corrupt, everyone knew his exploits. About once a year, O'Meara made a high profile arrest. Last year, he shut down a *DragonRoot* pipeline from Maul. Turned out that a few Crucifiers thought it would be an easy way to make some coin (strange that most of that *DragonRoot* then disappeared and found its way into the warehouses of the Pariahs). The year before that, he helped shut down a flesh-trading ring. His first year in Havencastle he foiled an assassin's plot to kill the Crusader. Rumours spread soon after that O'Meara himself had hired the assassin to kill the Crusader, that it had only been a setup to make himself look good. Unfortunately, the assassin was killed before he could be brought before a magistrate. Such was the nature of law enforcement.

His most notorious achievement, of course, was apprehending, and murdering, Hugo the Hellion. I rubbed my chest scar at the thought of Hugo the Hellion. I shouldn't begrudge O'Meara for his success. If it weren't for him, I would've become the Hugo's victim. By killing Hugo, O'Meara was promoted to sheriff and given full authority to "keep the peace."

O'Meara could've arrested me, but he mustn't have thought me important enough to keep him entrenched as a sheriff for another year. And since he wasn't entitled to reward money, it probably wasn't worth the hassle of trying to drag another scoundrel before the magistrate.

There was a rule in this game: stay away from other scoundrels. I paused. Jane had always told me to never steal from a thief. Something about honour among thieves or some such nonsense. Mind you, if I would've listened to her, I wouldn't have tried to rob the Pariahs, which was what started me down this path of disaster. Lesson learned.

We left the heat and smoke of the Rolling Bones and stepped into the cool, fresh morning air. The dawn rolled towards us with a tired grey. The streets were coming to life as merchants opened their stores and hawkers set-up their booths. The fresh air felt good and my pores tightened.

"I need a drink," O'Meara stated. The man smelled like booze, drugs, and sweat. I wondered when he'd last had a bath. I thought I saw the remnants of a three-day-old meal crusted in his beard.

"You're a wanted man, Nathaniel. Wouldn't want to be in your shoes."

"I'm used to it."

"So what have you got for me?"

A quick glance around confirmed there were no eavesdroppers. Business would've been better suited to be held in private and not on city streets, but from O'Meara's attitude, this was our only option.

"I need help."

"Help? This wasn't about you. It was about me. How you could help me."

"I'll help you, all right, but first you have to help me."

His eyes narrowed and I saw I was losing him. "Is it big?"

"The biggest." O'Meara rubbed his jaw, unsure. "This will set you up for years. Everyone will recognize you when you walk down the streets. You could retire early."

"And what do I have to do for you?"

"Get me into the Syndicate."

"Now I really need a drink!" he roared. I cringed at the volume of his voice. "You? Working for the Syndicate? Ha! That'll be the day! As if you could work for anyone but yourself!" He jabbed me in the chest to accentuate his point. I hated when he did that. "The Syndicate! That's a good one."

"I'm serious, O'Meara. I need in. Fast. You get me inside the Syndicate, and once I'm through with them, I'll hand over the entire thing to you."

His laughing stopped. "You'll give me the Syndicate?"

"Hand-delivered."

More laughter. "You should perform in the Crusader's court as a fool!"

I grabbed his arm and pulled him close, though I quickly released him once I got a whiff of his breath. "You get me inside, and you can have all the pieces when I'm through with them."

He frowned and craned his head sideways. "Is this personal, Nathaniel? You got something against the Syndicate?"

"Let's say they're an obstacle. I don't like obstacles. Either help me and get the rewards, or I'll find another way."

O'Meara grunted. "When was the last time you succeeded at a job? Remember the Marauders back in Maul? You lost the load and got three good men killed."

"Bad planning," I said.

"But you planned it."

Hmm, good point. "Listen, if I succeed, you're a famous man."

"And if you fail, you're a dead man."

"You get me in, O'Meara. Because we're friends, remember?"

"People like you and me don't have friends." He eyed me for several moments. "I'll open some doors for you. You do the rest."

"That's all I need, O'Meara." Now it was my time to be cautious. "Will it be dangerous?"

"That's the only way, fixer."

I slapped him on the back. "Good. That's the way I like it."

I waited in the alley, my crossbow loaded and a bandana over my face. O'Meara had been right—this was dangerous, but only for me. Our plan began to unfold in the early afternoon. Neither O'Meara nor myself had slept, but that didn't dampen my enthusiasm.

The horse-drawn wagon rumbled towards me, escorted by the Bronze. I counted seven mounted soldiers, the men exchanging hand signals for positioning. The plan had called for O'Meara to have two or three escorts, not seven. What was he trying to do to me?

A double-cross? Maybe O'Meara's greed made him think of the bounty on my head and not the possible riches if we pulled this off. My indecision almost cost me; the shipment almost passed.

I jumped into the path of the wagon and its escorts. O'Meara was driving and when he spotted me, he pulled hard on the reins. If it had been a real driver and not O'Meara, they would've run me over rather than risk their cargo. The horses whinnied their annoyance, lips curling and eyes circling.

Seven crossbows came to bear at me. If this was a double cross, there wasn't much I could do now except lament what happens when a scoundrel becomes semi-respectable.

"This is official Bronze business," O'Meara snapped. "Out of the way!"

"I don't think so." I waved my crossbow at the group of soldiers. "I'll be taking the shipment, if you don't mind."

My eyes shifted from one crossbow to another. Seven full-sized crossbows. Not just regular crossbows, but heavy. The kind to punch through armour and bone, and used to bring down horses. The kind that took two hands to fire because the kickback was so severe. The kind that could kill me.

While luck might've saved me from a single bolt, there was no way I could survive that many crossbows at this range. I looked from my hand bow to the oversized weapons and felt ridiculously exposed.

"Easy, lads." O'Meara waved the soldiers away. "I think he has us." Several of the soldiers blinked in surprise.

"I can take him down right now," a soldier stated, the weapon braced to his shoulder and aiming with his one eye squeezed shut.

"It's no good, lad. We'll give him what he wants."

"He's got a pea shooter there, sir! We can —"

"No!" O'Meara boomed. "A shipment like this isn't worth anyone dying for."

"That's right," I insisted. "Now off the wagon before I start shooting."

The large sheriff climbed from the seat with his hands in the air. "There won't be any trouble here, son. Take what you want."

As soon as O'Meara was down, I took his place on the seat, my hand crossbow aiming for his heart. Now, I was at O'Meara's mercy but I wasn't completely stupid. I had double-loaded the dart with Blister Bush toxin. Maybe not enough to kill O'Meara, but certainly enough to disfigure—which would certainly end his current career. I needed a little leverage in this escapade. "Don't be getting any ideas of chasing me or there'll be real trouble." The horses reacted to a forceful snap of the reins and we lurched forward. The wagon was to speed in moments.

The shipment was a batch of contraband seized from the Syndicate several days ago. Barrels of gin, gaming supplies, and even a crate of *DragonRoot*. I tried to ignore the fact that the last time I was driving a wagon of *DragonRoot* it had ended very badly for me.

Perfect, another well executed plan. Something thunked behind me, the sound muffled by the clatter of wheels on flagstone and the pounding of the horses' hooves. A wooden sound. A crossbow bolt protruded from one of the liquor barrels. They were firing on me!

The Bronze pursued, charging hard. And O'Meara was at the vanguard.

"This can't be good." The usual curses streamed from my lips. I couldn't let myself get carried away—had to keep my wits about me or this would end exactly as my first adventure with a wagon of *DragonRoot*. I took a deep, calming breath, and found that it did no good whatsoever. "That no good, O'Meara. He's going to try to take me in, is he? I'll show him."

But instead of worrying about my failing plan, as some lesser fixers were apt to do, I instead focused on the road, urging the horses faster. Outnumbered, slower, and less manoeuvrable than my pursuers—some would claim that those were terrible odds. I tended to agree. O'Meara had his hand in the air preparing to give the soldiers the command to shoot. My only advantage was that they'd have to pull up to brace themselves to fire those heavy crossbows. Firing them one handed, on a charging horse—that was dangerous business. So they had one shot.

I gave the reins a sharp pull to the right, the horses yanking on their bridles and harnesses, veering away from the main street. We took the corner so quickly the wagon lifted onto the two side wheels. I resisted the urge to grab the seat. If my grip on the reins loosened, we were finished. My eyes widened as the wagon tilted...tilted...tilted, and I was certain we were going over.

Then the horses straightened and the wagon slammed back onto all four wheels, bucking me off the seat and onto the wagon floor. Somehow, I maintained my grip on the reins, even while I was bouncing around, hat over my eyes. I switched the reins to a single hand and righted myself.

The alleyway was a tight fit. If anyone poked out a window to investigate the approaching commotion, they would likely have their head removed.

My seat cracked and something jabbed into my spine. Had I been shot? Hopefully it hadn't hit my liver. Please not my liver.

Another bolt exploded through my seat beside me. If the aim would've been better, that one would've killed me. The shock of the near miss caused me to forget about driving.

O'Meara was trying too hard. He was timing the men to discharge individually, rather as a complete firing line. Yup, double-cross.

I exploded from the alleyway like I had been spit from Hell. People dove from my path, other horses reared, and livestock scattered. Must've been a spectacular sight. Kind of like back in Moregeth when I was trying to outrun the Pariahs with the crates of DragonRoot. Damn, here I go again. Except that gave me an idea. A chance to get out of this mess.

Another yank to my right and we entered the main roadway. I had a chance.

I tied the reins to the seat. We were going straight and that was about it. I wondered if the horses would try to run through an obstruction or if self preservation would take over. After all, this time I hadn't given them any hallucinogens. Not out of ethical, or even practical, reasons but because I simply hadn't had time.

I clambered over my seat while the Bronze galloped from the alleyway, more crossbows coming to bear.

I cut loose the straps to a crate, then slid it to the tail gate. With a kick, the gate flipped down. The wagon bounced and I wondered if I'd just run over someone. No time to worry about that.

The crate fell from the wagon, bounced along the cobblestones, then exploded. *DragonRoot* fluttered through the air. There was a delay, then the street was packed with merchants, sellers, buyers, gossipers...all scrambling to get their hands on it. The street value of the contents of that crate would've been worth a fortune.

Just like that, the street was choked with a scrambling mob. The Bronze's horses reared their frustration. The men yanked on reins, trying to control their mounts, blocked by a wall of bodies.

I had no time to celebrate my success. The wagon had no driver. I lunged back into the front and regained control over the racing horses. I waved good-bye to my pursuers with my hat and I noticed O'Meara gave me a barely noticeable nod. Shame washed over me. How could I have ever thought that O'Meara was trying to double cross me? The Sheriff was only trying to make my escape look authentic. A true professional.

Of course, when I saw the multitude of bolts sticking through my back rest, I realized I had come close to taking a shot. That no-good son of a bitch. Never trust a scoundrel.

A full three streets over, I was still attracting too much attention. Little kids pointed, women's jaws dropped, and men stared. Oh right, the bandana. I removed it from my face and tucked it under my leg. Onlookers continued to gawk but that must've been because of the crossbow bolts. A smile and a wave was all I gave them, acting like nothing was amiss. Just another merchant interested in selling his wares.

O'Meara's plan was perfect. He had made a small sacrifice— this wagon was loaded with contraband confiscated from the Syndicate a few days ago. He had removed it from the Bronze's compound and had now given it to me to return to the Syndicate. How could they not trust someone like me who had put their life on the line to recover their shipment?

To avoid the Crusader's patrols, I took a less direct route, wending through the back streets and alleys. The wagon rumbled into the DZ, the wheels clacking and creaking with each pothole they struck.

O'Meara had given me directions to a small-time operation and I drove into the Dead Zone. The wagon creaked, the booze in the barrels sloshing as we rolled over fallen timbers and loose cobblestones. Faces stared at me from the ruins, their eyes full of lust and greed. The contents of this wagon was enough to buy your way out of the Dead Zone. Enough to buy yourself into a respectable life.

The place still held the smell of battle. Sulphur and burnt pitch. I felt like if I listened hard enough I'd hear the echoes of brother-on-brother warfare. Strange that the Crusader allowed such a desolate place within his city. Blocks and blocks of ruins and charred buildings.

O'Meara had described several landmarks to follow. The destroyed livery, the intact key maker, the lone steeple where the church used to be. Then, I found the warehouse.

The warehouse's exterior blended well with the surroundings though it did appear to be one of the few buildings that maintained its integrity. Before the rebellion it must've been a lumberyard or mill.

A small man with a clipboard on his arm, gazed as I approached, mouth agape. I jammed on the brakes when I reached him, throwing the wagon into a skid for theatrical effect. His eyes wandered over the bolt-riddled wagon then settled on the *DragonRoot* and booze.

"I believe you're missing a wagon?" A casual statement.

He must've realized his mouth was open because he snapped it shut, cleared his throat and said, "I'll be right back." The little man tore into the warehouse, slamming the door behind him.

My wait lasted for several long minutes. I didn't want to consider if this plan went sideways but I had no choice, scrolling through options depending on who came out of that warehouse.

The bookkeeper returned accompanied by two large men, real brutes who looked like they came by the muscles honestly from the heavy strain of the warehouse grind. They appeared unarmed, which meant I probably wasn't going to have to start shooting immediately. Which meant we could negotiate.

"You stole a wagon from us?" one of the men asked.

"No, I didn't steal the wagon," I replied. I almost get killed for these guys and all they could do was accuse me of being a thief.

"But that's our stuff."

"I know it's your stuff. I got it back for you."

"So you stole it?"

With one hand gripping the reins, I nonchalantly reached for my crossbow. "Who's in charge here?"

"I am." The woman who stepped from the warehouse might've been beautiful once, perhaps, ten years ago and before the burns had claimed half of her face. A thick braid of scar tissue circled her neck. I had seen that scarring plenty of times—the mark of a noose. I wondered if she had concocted a fantastic escape from her hanging, an escape that could explain her disfigurement.

She tucked a pair of gloves into her back pocket.

"You stole our wagon?" she asked. I couldn't help but admire her well-defined arms. Obviously she didn't mind spending time in the trenches.

"Yes. I mean, no. I stole it, but not from you. I've brought it back."

The tiny bookkeeper continued his tour around the wagon. He gave a nod of affirmation. "It's ours. We've lost half a keg of gin...and an entire crate of *DragonRoot*." Why was everyone always so concerned with *DragonRoot*?

"Where's Joel?" she asked me.

"Was he the driver?"

"That's right."

The two large men took positions at the front and back of my wagon. I shifted in my seat to better keep an eye on them. I kept a finger on the trigger of my crossbow.

The woman was staring at me, perhaps trying to place my face to any one of the posters across the city. I had seen her type before, the anger bubbling just beneath the surface. It wasn't dangerous to me necessarily depending on the source of that anger. A spurned lover? An abusive parent? A life of slavery?

People took up a life of crime for so many reasons. Sometimes they had something to prove, or maybe they were born into it. Others liked the challenge, while others wanted to watch the world burn. I wondered what kind of criminal she was.

"I broke this out of the impound," I said. "The driver is on his own."

"I know you," she stated.

My fingers scratched my three-day beard. "I don't think so."

She gave me a smile, her little indication to me that she had probably placed my face to the myriad posters around town. "So you're a good citizen and brought back our property?"

"I'm a driver. A good one, at that."

"Not that good," the bookkeeper interrupted. "You lost half a keg of gin and an entire crate."

I waved him off. "Anyone else would've been dead. Take a look at those wheels. That's from hard driving. I outran seven mounted Bronze. Seven."

"What's your name?" she asked.

"The name's Nathaniel." I flashed her my best smile, but my advances bounced off her like a sling shot off a shield.

"You going to let us in on this little game of yours, Nathaniel? Going to share with us why you broke one of our wagons out of compound, at risk to yourself, and returned it to us minus a keg of gin?"

"Half a keg," I corrected. "I need a job. I'm the best driver in the Succession."

The bookkeeper said, "He's probably an informant."

"Look at those bolts! If I were an informant, do you think I'd let someone shoot me?"

"You could've shot the wagon before you were riding. Then it would look like you out-rode a couple of guards," he argued.

I drew my crossbow. "You calling me a liar?" The way his

face drained of colour reminded me of LaFage when I stuck my crossbow in his face. This bookkeeper liked to talk rough but didn't like the real stuff. Theory versus practice, most likely. The thugs tensed but didn't advance and I doubted they would. They were hired to lift boxes and to look menacing. Besides, they were worried about me killing the bookkeeper. A professional would've sacrificed the bookkeeper and killed me. Letting someone like me ride in and kill management was bad for business.

She chewed on the side of the cheek, never letting her gaze drift from mine. I wondered if she was doing those exact calculations right now, weighing the life of the bookkeeper over the dangers of letting me live. Finally, "Fine, start him on the McPhee Run," she said.

"But, but, but..." the bookkeeper stammered.

"Shut up, Nim," she scolded the smaller man. Then back to me, eyes narrowing, "You've got one chance. But you already understand that, don't you, Nathaniel?" The extra emphasis on my name was her polite way of saying she knew exactly who I was but that she was willing to play my game for a while, perhaps out of curiosity.

I shrugged and she said, "You don't mind road blocks?"

"There's nothing I can't get by with a kind word and a crossbow."

"One hundred drake per trip."

"A hundred drake? I've got five kids to feed." I didn't care about the money, but I had to at least make it look like I cared about the money.

"Then you best get rid of a couple of those kids."

"What's your name?" I asked.

"Alexis," she said. "Now get to work." She motioned to the two men and they followed her back inside the warehouse, leaving Nim and me alone in the street. I replaced my crossbow on my belt and I noticed the small man relax.

"What's her story?" I asked.

"Not my place to say," he replied, his voice quavering.

I hoped that Alexis would let play my game long enough until I found what I was looking for. I also hoped I was tough enough to play hers.

The McPhee Run was the lowest rung on the criminal ladder. The contraband tended to be harmless: *DragonRoot*, booze, stolen merchandise. Not that I expected Black Swan to simply be in my shipment one day. This outfit was too small to move something as volatile as Black Swan. Alexis and her crew were a small-time outfit focusing mostly on redistribution from others sources across the Succession, then brought to her where she then redistributed throughout Havencastle.

I drove one shipment a day. The typical run would be a shipment of booze to RenDragan, then pick up a stash of *DragonRoot* for delivery back to Havencastle. The driving itself was simple. I never rode with an escort—an extra man would've complicated matters. Luckily, I had some past experience in smuggling and I could always rely on my skill, technique, and charisma to get me by any inspection. That and a fistful of money.

The wall trooper looked up from the bribe placed in his calloused hand. "There's only a hundred drake here. The deal's one-fifty."

"Come on," I said. "Cut me a break. I've got a wife and kids to feed." The wagon was full of stolen gaming tables. The contraband was enough to send me to jail for a long time, but of course, once apprehended, they'd realize my true identity.

"Hey, if I'm caught letting you through, I'll be hanged," the trooper said. "Understand? So give me another twenty-five and we'll call it even." He held all the bargaining power. "All right, all right. You're killing me. You really are." I counted out several drake on my palm. "I've only got twenty-two here. Is that enough?"

"Hand it over and get going."

I ushered the horses into Havencastle, suppressing a smile. If he would've been better at negotiating, he could've worked me as high as one-hundred seventy-five. That was the problem with so many people; they set their goals too low.

With a few runs under my belt, I quickly rose up the ranks. It also helped that O'Meara was tightening the screws to the Syndicate, impounding wagons and arresting drivers, making me more valuable each passing day. The first week alone, the driving crew was down to me and two other drivers. And once I gave O'Meara the info on the last two drivers, I'd be Alexis's only option.

A few of my co-workers didn't annoy me too much. The bookkeeper really did remind me of LaFage. He was a friendly but paranoid fellow who seemed to get caught up too much in the fine details. His name was Nim something-or-other but I just called him LaFage because it was easier for me to remember. He had worked with Alexis and his devotion was a sure sign that he was madly in love with her. But Nim wasn't her type. I wasn't sure if Alexis even had a type. Tough as nails. She loved to stare at me when I entered the shipment yards. While Nim would greet me with his ever-present clipboard, Alexis would stand at the back, endlessly wiping her greasy hands on an even greasier rag.

"How are we doing this week?" Alex asked.

Nim checked over his ever-present clipboard. "Three wagons gone. Seven crates of *DragonRoot*, two barrels gin, three of bourbon, twelve sacks of grain, a full table setting of silver cutlery...Not good at all. O'Meara's onto us."

"I guess he is," she said, staring at me.

"Maybe we should shutter the operation temporarily," Nim said.

"No, I want to see how this plays out," she replied, gazing at me so relentlessly that I had to struggle to maintain eye contact.

"General..." Nim trailed off, his eyes focused on the clipboard so intently that it was like he was magically compelled to stare at it. He looked a little pale. While his quill was on paper, his hand didn't move other than the trembling. I remembered the last time he had looked like that. Back then, I had been pointing my crossbow at his face.

"What's wrong?"

"We've got problems," he said, and pointed almost imperceptibly with his quill behind me and before I told him that I solved problems, I heard the commotion. Alexis's face hardened further and I could practically feel the hate roll off her in sheets.

When I turned, I saw we had visitors. Lots of them. So this was the Syndicate. The man leading the procession must've been the General. He was older, face weathered and etched with lines and I couldn't help but think that he'd be more comfortable on a battlefield rather than the trenches of the underworld. The General was short but that was more than compensated by his solid frame, his exposed forearms stained with misshapen tattoos. His hair was silver, including the moustache that draped to his chin. He wore a gray cloak that hung past his knees and black boots polished to such a gleam they cast a reflection.

Five escorts followed behind in lock step. They brandished crossbows, loaded and ready, as if the warehouse workers might stage some sort of revolt. They looked more like a military unit than a crime guild. I remembered the heavy boots vibrating on the Brass Cage floor and wondered if some of these guys might've even been there. If so, I hoped in all that chaos that they didn't get a really good look at me. If someone did recognize me, I'd just tell them that they were confusing me for the guy on the poster.

They secured the area. Crossbows, swords, axes, chain mail. These guys came prepared for the worst. In fact, a group like this might be capable of taking down someone like Creed in the Brass Cage. Two of the men had bandages on their cheeks as if covering slash marks and I thought those were courtesy of Jane. I felt a surge of excitement. These were the type of people who would know about Black Swan, and I was certain that several must've been in the Brass Cage.

"I wondered when he'd show up," Alexis said, pushing her greasy rag into Nim's chest and shoving her way by. The General met her at her office door. He gave a brief nod but she ignored him and pushed past the group of men and into her office. The General and all but two of his escorts followed her in. I had only been in there once—the place was small and they must've been standing shoulder to shoulder. Two of his men waited outside, taking up positions flanking the door.

Military types were always alike; they liked big and flashy. These guys weren't a crime guild. There was something else going on here, and I had a feeling that somehow it was going to intersect with my goals.

I spent the time in the warehouse, pretending to repair the wagons while waiting for the General to reappear from Alexis's office. They met for two hours. Meanwhile, I greased the axles and listened for any signs of trouble. Would he blame O'Meara's success on Alexis? If anything started to go wrong for her, would she point the finger at me? If I was forced to fight my way out, the odds would be ten against one. I'd been in worse. Not sure when, but surely ten against one wasn't undoable.

The door to Alexis's office opened and men marched out, Alexis escorting the General from the room. She said something to him that I couldn't hear, then leaned back against the doorframe, watching him go. Her face was pale and I couldn't help but think she looked tired. The General was expressionless, his eyes flat. He walked down the stairs with no wasted movements. This guy looked like a pro.

Alexis gazed at me, gave a nod, then retreated back into her office. I waited ten minutes before rapping on her door and entering.

"Quite the visitor," I said.

She leaned back in her chair, drinking from a stained glass. "He's a buck fitch," she said. "Comes in here acting like I don't know how to run the operation." She reached into a desk drawer and poured me a drink into a dirty glass, then slid it over to me. She didn't bother putting the bottle back. "You know how long I've done this job? Seven years. Best numbers in the game."

"Who is he?"

"I don't know his real name." She swirled her drink, inspecting it. The stress was etched on her face and for a moment, I thought her tough veneer might crack and I'd see the real person underneath. But then it was gone. "He only shows up when things are going wrong. Things are going wrong."

Of course things were going wrong. She hired me. I knew I was the weak link but she hadn't mentioned it yet. I figured if she was going to sell me up the river, she would've already done it.

I knew she hadn't called me in here to complain about the General. She could've used Nim as a sounding board. Still, I resisted the urge to ask the questions swirling in my mind: who was the General? How could I reach him? How connected was he?

But she didn't say anything. Just sat there sipping at her drink. I took a swallow from the offered glass and I nearly spat it out in disgust. It burned. She was studying me, however, so I swallowed, eyes watering.

"You know why I got into this racket?" she asked.

"No idea," I wheezed through the alcoholic fumes. I wondered how I could dispose of the rest of the drink without her noticing.

"My father was in the Bronze. My two brothers followed in his footsteps. One of them's dead now, but Rudolph has risen to Lieutenant. Haven't spoken to him in years but I hear he's doing well. You know what my father had planned for me? The wife of a sheep farmer. Do I look like a farmer to you? What the hell do I know about sheep? I ran away, which might've been what he wanted me to do from the beginning. I always went making trouble for myself." She smiled fondly, had another drink, then refilled her glass. "This life hasn't always been good to me." She motioned to the nasty scar at her neck. "But it's been better than being a sheep farmer's wife."

We sat in silence, her gulping her drink, and me trying to pretend to force down the liquid fire. She broke first. "So what's your story?" she asked.

"The usual. Petty crimes, some thefts, some murders, and here I am."

She nodded approvingly. "That's quite a tale. Does it get better each time you tell it?"

"I make sure to hit all the important points."

She finished her drink, thankfully returning the bottle to her drawer and then standing. "I don't want them to see us leave. Too many questions that I don't want to answer." I wasn't sure if this was an offer to accompany her or instructions to get the hell out. Then she said, "Lock that door. We'll go out the back."

I did as instructed, then had to rush to keep up with her.

"What about Nim?" I asked.

"What about him?"

"Won't he find it odd that we disappeared together? I don't need him sending out search parties for us."

"Didn't think you scared so easily."

Ouch. "Just looking out for the poor fellow."

I knew better than to ask where we were going. She'd reveal her plans in good time. I didn't sense a trap—she could've sprung something much easier back at the warehouse.

Her apartment was in Archer Heights. We walked up three flights of stairs to reach her door. The paint was peeling in the hallway and the place smelled like strawberries.

Inside her apartment, I saw a different person than the Alex who ran a smuggling ring. Plush, white carpet. Waves of cold air swept over us. Not many could afford such extravagance. Looking around, I saw she liked the finer things.

As soon as the door closed, she leaned close.

"Are you going to kiss me?" she asked.

"Do you want me to?"

"Yes."

CURSED: BLACK SWAN   A FIXER NOVEL

I leaned in, felt her body meld to mine. Her hands were roaming and mine smoothed around the curves of her body. I knew that I was definitely being played but sometimes I just had to see how things would shake out. The strange thing was, I don't think she cared that I already knew. This was just some weird game. She wanted something from me, and I wanted something from her. Neither of us knew what the other wanted, but we were each going to pretend that we were acting sincerely.

In the morning, she kissed me on the cheek and told me to leave, practically pushing me out the front door.

I worked for Alexis and her smuggling operation for over a week. I was her best driver, and I assume her best lover but for all I knew she could've had another three guys on the hook in this game of hers. The money for driving wasn't good as most of my drake went to bribing wall troopers. Still, it was good honest work and I'm sure if I'd had a father, he would've been proud. But this wasn't to make a living. This was a stepping stone to find Black Swan.

Nightly, we returned to her apartment. She played the game so well that several times I thought I might actually see her tough veneer crack. After some particularly tender lovemaking, she began to cry. When I asked her what was wrong, she said nothing, turning her face from me and hugging me close. I began to wonder if maybe it wasn't an act. Maybe she *was* a vulnerable person who had made a bad career choice and needed a shoulder to cry on.

She snuggled next to me in her massive bed. As being played went, this was pretty good. We lay in silence for a while. The problem was, I didn't know how long her game was going to last. We were competing in a game of wills, and she was winning. I didn't have time to let this go for too long. I had timelines. I was going to have to be direct.

"I'm looking for something, Alex."

Her body tensed, wary she was being led into a trap. "What?"

"Something that could make us both forget about the grind of smuggling. We'd be set, set up so even the General couldn't touch us." I kept waiting for her to issue her demands but she didn't. She probably wanted all my cards on the table first. Damn, she was good. "It's worth more than your outfit pulls down in a year. It used to belong to the Crusader. And before that it belonged to some king."

"And you want my help to steal it?" she asked.

"Not exactly. I can handle that part. The problem is that I don't know where it is. But you have connections. Direct with the Syndicate."

"What is it?"

"Something beautiful. I've seen it, Alex. It's perfect." I imagined it in my mind's eye, pulled from my memory and wished I could make it solid. "It wasn't made by any blacksmith on this continent."

"Black Swan?" Her fingers danced along my chest, her face hidden.

"Yes," I answered her.

"We're a small ring here, and I'd like to keep it that way."

"Do you know where it is, Alex?" I wanted to shake her, ask what type of game she was playing, but I knew the moment I did that, she'd be in full control... though I guessed she already was.

"Is that why you're here? The sword? That's all this means to you?"

"That's why I came here. But it's not why I stayed." Oddly, I wasn't sure if that was a lie or not. I wasn't falling for Alexis, not yet anyhow, but I found I craved my time with her. Or maybe I was beginning to believe our silly game. Or maybe even my time with her somehow eased the pain of Jane's betrayal.

"What if I told you I knew where it was?"

"I'd be eternally thankful," I said.

"Thankfulness isn't a very good currency, Nathaniel." Her using my name was jarring. She never used my name. It was like she suddenly pulled the covers away to reveal the truth. "You're a fixer." She climbed from bed and began to dress. The last time I had been naked with a woman who was playing me, I had been sold out to the Pariahs. Luckily, Alex didn't move to the windows. "You're not here to drive wagons—you're a terrible driver."

Ouch. "So that's what all of this was? A game?" I said it like it I was actually hurt, and I wondered if I was. "Then why all of...this?"

"Because I like you. I also needed to know if our interests aligned." She regarded me, and I saw her weighing her options, wondering if trusting me was worth the risk. Finally, "I don't know who has Black Swan, but I can get you close to someone who does. And then, you can help me."

"How can I help you?" I asked.

"You know that we wouldn't have something like Black Swan," she said. "But I have the connections with the people that do, just like you suspected. And I assume that's the whole reason we're playing these roles right now. I can make the introductions. Get you in. You take it from there." I knew she was speaking of the General.

"Introductions?"

"That's better than you have now."

"What do you want in return?"

She opened the window. I tensed, expecting acrobats to come flying in. But nothing happened. She turned. "You get O'Meara off our backs."

"O'Meara? I don't have—"

"Save it. I don't know what you have worked out with him. But you get him looking elsewhere. Have him leave us alone. And if he happens to turn his eyes on the General instead of us..." She shrugged. "Then that would be an added bonus."

She was good. Not only did she know that I was working with O'Meara, and she wanted to use that knowledge to further her own career instead of ratting me out. A woman after my heart.

I gave a nod in agreement.

"Good," she said. "The General will be returning soon. I think you'll want to talk to him."

CHAPTER SIX
CLIMBING THE LADDER
OF SUCCESS

The General arrived two days later. Heavily armed men escorted him through the warehouse, Nim by his side, like a court fool walking by the king. The bookkeeper was jabbering, his mouth in a frenzy, face covered in sweat. Unable to hear what he was saying, I thought it was gibberish. The news couldn't have been good.

He gained a step on the General, turned and held up both hands with palms out, instructing them to wait outside Alexis's door. Nim disappeared inside. The platoon of men waited. The General's intensity was frightening, cold-blue eyes that seemed able to stare directly through the door.

When it opened, Alex was there to greet the General and his escort, a seemingly genuine smile plastered on her face as if she was greeting an old friend.

The escort entered her office first, to sweep for assassins or concealed weapons. If they were doing this type of search, then the news couldn't have been good. A crossbowman gave a nod and Alex and the General retired inside, leaving Nim alone, staring at the door, as if someone might realize they had forgotten about him and invite him in. It never opened and he finally turned, eyes downcast, like a lost puppy. How pathetic. This whole crew of smugglers weren't experts. They were more suited to be toll booth operators, or a legit driving business. Not criminals. They'd get themselves killed.

I wiped my hands and tossed the rag. Nim saw me approach and he broke from his stupor. He saw my intentions.

"You can't go in there!" He was trying to block my path.

"Move." He would get one warning.

He shook his head, as if he were a parent trying to explain an important issue to a child. "You're not allowed in there. This is official..."

In Moragorat, the abbots of the Way of the Open Fist taught me three hundred seventy-six ways to move someone who doesn't want to be moved. I used technique number one on Nim. My foot locked around his ankle and with a simple push, he went flying backwards. Of course, a lot of strength wasn't needed—I didn't want the little fellow to crack his head and hurt himself.

He landed with a grunt.

I opened the door on Alex and the General. The office was packed. Of the occupants, nine men held crossbows, all of them pointed at me. A heavy bolt through the chest would be enough to kill me. The men were military: crossbows braced against their bodies, feet shoulder width apart, standing strategically throughout the room. Why did all these army guys pretend they were something else? First the monks, now the Syndicate. However, in a strange way, it put me at ease that these guys had training—that meant I didn't have to worry about being mistakenly shot by a nervous crossbowman. The Syndicate continued to surprise.

Alex stood so quickly at my entrance she knocked over her chair, though the General merely swivelled in his chair to face me. Alex glanced from me to the General, and back again. She was trying to *act* upset, but this had been her plan all along—to have the fearless fixer come in and rescue her. Though really, I wasn't rescuing her. She had manipulated me into intervening. Impressive. Guys were such easy rubes.

"Who are you?" the General asked.

"I'm the one who's going to help you." I paused, wanting to frame myself in the doorway for dramatic purposes, then when satisfied I had their attention, I entered and shut the door. "You've got problems? I solve problems."

"You haven't answered the question."

I reached into my coat, carefully, so the soldiers wouldn't fill me with bolts. Pulling out a rolled-up poster, I unfolded it and placed it on the table, and smiled.

"That's me." I pointed at the crudely drawn picture of me with the reward price beneath my name. I swallowed my desire to scowl at the low price tag.

The man's gray eyebrows lifted in curiosity and he scooped the dried paper into his hands, crinkling it as he inspected it. "That's a lot of drake. That drake could help recover some of the profits we've lost."

"Maybe. But I'm worth a whole lot more than that, working for you."

"What kind of problems do you solve?"

"Anything you got. You want to get the shipments through? Let me handle it."

"And O'Meara?"

"Don't you worry about him."

The General sat, and once Alex righted her chair, she followed suit. She gave me a nearly imperceptible nod and I noticed a small smile briefly traced her lips. Then it was gone. Back to business, I supposed.

"You're a fixer?" the General asked.

"At your service." I managed a deep bow and a roll of my arm.

"Do you know who we are?" His eyes narrowed. Hmmm, sinister.

"I've already been through this conversation with your colleague." I motioned to Alex. "I know exactly who you are. I'm a newcomer to Havencastle, though my work speaks for itself." I held up the poster again.

"You can't be that effective—they know what you look like. You allowed witnesses."

"True. I'm not one to normally blame my environment or situation but in that instance, I was working with a partner who, shall I say, wasn't properly skilled."

"I don't like arrogance. Kill him."

"Wait a moment." I gave my best smile. Now I knew he didn't want me dead. If he had, the second he gave the instructions, my chest would've been like a porcupine. This was power negotiations.

"I can make O'Meara disappear. No fuss. No hassles."

"No hassles?"

"It'll be all hush-hush. They won't even realize he's gone."

The General stared at me. I didn't like his eyes. Cold and hard. No compassion. This man had done some terrible things in his life. He wasn't a rogue, no matter what he would try to tell me now. There was something else going on here. Something big.

"And what do you get for making O'Meara disappear?"

I couldn't just ask for Black Swan. It wouldn't work that way. I'd have to do this carefully.

"You get me out of this small-time operation. I work for you. Freelance. Top drawer cash. Any troubles you got, you send them my way."

"You have until dawn tomorrow." He began to rise.

"Dawn?"

His eyebrows raised a question but his eyes remained flat. "Do you have a problem with that?"

"Of course not."

"Until tomorrow. If you don't get it finished by then..." His pause was good, gave everyone a sense of impending doom. Seemed that he had a flair for the dramatic as well.

The men filed from the room. I knew exactly what would happen if O'Meara was hanging around town; sometimes, it was best not to dwell on such negative thoughts.

Then it was just me and Alexis.

She was staring at me but I couldn't help but think that something had changed. That hardness had returned and it looked impenetrable this time.

"What about our deal?" she said.

"I'll get O'Meara off your back. Today."

"O'Meara is an inconvenience. It's the General I want off my back."

"So this is about career advancement?"

"Doesn't matter," she replied. "What matters is that if I tell him what you're really after, he'll draw and quarter you."

I shrugged. "See, you still have all the leverage. When I'm done with O'Meara, I'll take care of him too. Your path to the top will be clear."

"How long do you need?"

"As long as it takes for me to gain their trust."

She studied me through narrowed eyes. "Who are you really?" she asked.

"You know who I am."

"I thought I did, but it's like there's someone else in there calling the shots. This is personal for you."

"Why won't you tell her who you really are?" the Dark asked.

"I have to get that sword back, Alex."

"Have I made a deal with the devil?"

"Yes," the Dark whispered in my ear. "Things might get bad, Alex. Very bad. I care about you. Stay away. Lay low."

I went to kiss her but she turned away.

I guess we were done playing games.

I sent one of the street kids a coded message to O'Meara. He met me at the Vertigo Express shipment yard as instructed.

The yard was a livery stable located in the Ridges. We could've met in a tavern or inn but in my business, they were the hangouts of gossip mongers. And the Syndicate did not need to know that I was meeting with their current nemesis—even if I was going to solve this problem for them. The less they knew about my business, the better.

O'Meara showed up in his usual state, stained tunic unbuttoned halfway and unbelted pants. Tarnished leather boots. His black beard was getting wilder by the day.

I tossed the wad of cash at O'Meara. He caught it with one hand, judging the thickness while keeping his eyes on me. He raised his eyebrows in question. The guy smelled like a distillery. Damn, he even overpowered the smell of horses and the mouldering hay.

He tucked the bill fold into his pocket. "How much is here?"

"Enough for you to leave Havencastle."

"I'm leaving?"

"That's right. Take an extended vacation. A full month. On me."

"I don't feel like taking a vacation."

"Tell the Crusader you're leaving to explore some new evidence."

"And when I get back?"

"I give you the Syndicate." I wondered about Alex. Felt that stupid thing called shame again. Was I going to give her up too?

He gave me a grimy smile. "You still claiming you can do it, huh?"

"That's right. Now get lost. You have to be out of here by dawn. No later. Don't let anyone see you leave."

"Whatever you say, Chief."

I slept so soundly that I didn't hear the messenger push the folder under the door. I wakened to sunlight streaming in my eyes and the smell of blood heavy in the air. Just another day in paradise.

I noticed the folder as I sipped at three-day-old café.

I had given the Syndicate this safe house as the best way to contact me, though, by that admission, it was no longer safe house. Too bad. I'd already abandoned the Ordeum and when all this was over, I was going to have to find another safe house to replace this one. Old blood stained the walls, so thick that the top coat of paint could only blunt the outlines rather than hide it fully. A trough of blood flowed outside my door. In the mornings, like now, it was a terrible stench.

Now that I had followed through on my promise to make O'Meara disappear, the Syndicate must've decided I was trustworthy enough to not saw into four pieces and spread me across the Succession.

I broke the wax seal on the folder and shook out the papers inside. It was a breakdown of my first job. I memorized the details, then destroyed the contents in the fire pit. They burst into flame, their surface pre-coated with an oil residue. The fire cracked and popped, the papers burning to a fine black dust. All these little responsibilities of the job came back to me easily.

My target was a fat man named Sam Hurst living in the Ridges, a man who had been living beyond his means for several months, his once-vast resources dried up, or more accurately, squandered on women and drugs. I stood across the street from his bungalow, searching for signs of guards or intrusion countermeasures. None. Sam was careless. After an hour of watching, two women, either drunk or drugged, stumbled from the front door and down the walk. They dressed like prostitutes: garish makeup, heels too tall, and clothing that left little to the imagination. Their hair was unkempt, their complexions rough from too much *DragonRoot* and booze, as if they had been visiting for several days. Sam Hurst had truly fallen.

My normal methods usually involved me breaking in through a window and shooting anything that moved. But with my employment handled by the Syndicate, this couldn't become a big production. By the book. After two hours of watching, I moved closer, inspecting the bungalow from all sides, ensuring the exits were secure. The place smelled of garbage. How long it had been since Sam had stepped outside?

I gave the knocker three slow, deliberate raps. No answer. Another three raps. Something shifted in the house, the sound of someone awakening from a very deep slumber. Three more raps. I kept my eyes on the flanking window to prevent any surprises even though I knew none were coming. Though letting down my guard usually resulted with someone kicking in my teeth.

Then, footsteps thumped towards the door, which I figured belonged to Sam because of the heavy vibrations. My crossbow was loaded with a nasty dose of Sundarian Rhino-Horn Venom. My hand rested on the grip of the weapon, ready to draw if anything went wrong.

The door opened and I knew there was no danger. Sam blinked from the morning light and shielded his eyes. He wore a pair of tattered breeches and a tunic opened to the belly, his fat rolls hanging over his belt. His clothes were soiled with stains. Disgusting. Hard to believe this man ever possessed anything that would interest the Syndicate.

I slew footed him, sent him tumbling backward, then followed him inside and slammed the door before any interested spectators could get involved.

"Hello, Sam," I said.

"Who? I don't know you."

I flipped the lock on the door. He tried to rise but a quick boot kept him in place.

"You're not going anywhere, Sam."

"What are you doing here?" He didn't look me in the eyes; these types always knew it would betray their guilt.

"You know why I'm here." I glanced into the other rooms. Disgusting. His bungalow looked like a tornado had roared through before my arrival. Clothes were spread about the furniture. Pictures and ornaments hung crooked on stained walls. I swore I saw a miasma rising from his kitchen.

Sam Hurst tried to crawl past me and reached for the door. I grabbed him around the shirt collar. His skin was oily. I'd seen addicts before. This was only the first stage. The second stage was more severe: loss of teeth and hair, skin lesions.

I dragged him to the main room and pushed him up against the wall. The scent of stale *DragonRoot* lingered around us. This man had once been one of the major power brokers in Havencastle, but now he was in ruin.

"I can get you money," he promised.

"It's beyond money, Sam." The words returned so easily even after all these years. There were always men like Sam Hurst. Too many to be counted.

"You like women? I can get you women."

He was desperate. He'd offer me women, money, power—usually in that order. If these types of men could acquire any of those three, then they wouldn't be getting a visit from the Syndicate.

The Syndicate had hired me to solve problems. Really it should've been a sideways career move. But like everyone else, the Syndicate seemed to confuse fixer with assassin.

Kill. Assassinate. Sanction. Slay. Murder. Wet work. Butcher.

Why did everyone always confuse it?

The name didn't matter. I would be stealing what was most precious from him.

"This is the part I like," the Dark whispered.

As I contemplated the vilest of deeds, the memories of Cresek-Tawn intruded. The city of my nightmares. Where everything important to me had been destroyed. There was no turning back now.

I pulled out my hand bow and tried to ignore Sam's snivelling. Do it!

The locks keeping the Dark at bay rattled. It was just on the other side. The thought of murder energized it, brought it salivating to the surface.

He was on his knees, his hands clasped together. "Please. Don't do it. I'll make amends. I'll do whatever they want." He was sobbing, tears streaking down his grime-covered cheeks. "I've fallen on hard times, that's all." He tugged at the lapels of my overcoat. I pointed my crossbow. "Another chance. Everyone makes mistakes, right?"

How many times in my life had I heard those words? If only they were true. Everyone makes mistakes. These weren't people who made only one mistake. For a professional to be sent meant there were multiple errors, each compounding the severity of the other.

"I wasn't double-crossing the Syndicate," he confessed. "He told me he could help you. Help us. He promised me money in return for a few favours. The money I owe you. He's going to pay me in a week. I swear."

"Kill him."

I don't know why I bothered, but I asked, "Who was it?" Seven years ago I would have killed him outright. Times change.

"I don't know." I jabbed him with the crossbow and his memory improved. "I only know his first name."

"Not good enough."

"Jacob. No, no, Joshua! Yes, that's it. Joshua. That's all I know."

That name hit me so hard that I almost pulled the trigger from surprise. "What did you say?"

"His name was Joshua. He wanted me to spread a few rumours. I thought it was harmless."

"What did he look like?" I asked. My old master wouldn't be conducting business here in Havencastle, would he?

"It was dark out. I didn't get a good look at him." Sam rubbed his faces against my shoes like he was a cat locking for a scratch. Pathetic. Have some dignity when someone is about to shoot you in the face.

"Was he from Havencastle?"

"No, no. He was a foreigner." Sam Hurst tried to act so cooperative. "He had his hair braided. Real cocky."

My eyes misted. Such a vague description but I knew that it

was my old mentor. My enemy. The person who ripped my life apart. What were the chances that he'd be here in Havencastle after all this time? Except Jane had already been here.

"Joshua?" I felt the hatred flow from the Dark. We might've opposed each other, but we agreed on one thing—Joshua. *"Kill Joshua. Break open his skull, sink my tongue into brains. Drink him in."*

"I didn't know it was a setup," Sam babbled. He stared up at me, his eyes puffy and red, tears running down his jowls. "Please, I have a family. I have kids. I made a mistake."

I knelt. "What did you do, Sam?"

"Joshua came to me. Wanted me to broker a deal for a sword." Black Swan. I had been so close. "I thought he had it. He set me up. Please, believe me, he set me up."

I straightened. "What am I going to do with you?"

"Give me another chance. I'll make this better."

"Yeah, you will."

I shot him in the chest. The fat man's eyes widened, he coughed twice, and he crashed backwards, his head slamming into the floor.

I felt the satisfaction roll from the Dark like a swarm of ants on my skin.

As everyone knows, Sundarian Rhino Horn Venom would be enough to kill a horse, and definitely enough to kill a man like Sam Hurst. I felt regret, but not because I killed him. I regretted that I *didn't* feel remorse at killing him. I felt nothing at all.

I went over his home but found nothing of value. I waited for another fifteen minutes before I stepped over Sam's corpse and unlocked the door. Three deeply tanned men waited in the archway. They were unwashed and their smell must've attracted buzzing flies. All three were visitors to Havencastle.

"Over there." I thumbed to the corpse. His weight required two men to move him. To the third I dropped several coins into his hands.

"Where to?" he asked, his eyes fixed on the gold.

"Doesn't matter as long as it's clean."

The man nodded. "The sea clean enough for you?"

"I don't need him washing up on shore."

"Deep-sea expedition. Swordfish. Leagues from any land or island."

For most, murdering a man who had done me no wrong should've had a moral weight to it. Unfortunately for me, my list of men I'd murdered like Sam was long. My regret was the excitement welling from the Dark about our newest kill, then realizing that I wasn't sure if it was actually coming from the Dark or from me.

I knew my path was a slippery one—I could fall easily into my old habits and the Dark would only be too happy to assist on my descent into Hell.

Yet, even with my minor victory over my internal nemesis, I was still troubled. I saw the gates of Cresek-Tawn. And standing at the entrance was Joshua. But was he there in Cresek-Tawn or was he here, in Havencastle? I frowned, trying to force those strange thoughts from my head. The description was so vague. And Joshua would never leave Cresek-Tawn. Not to come here.

It must've been someone else.

But I couldn't bring myself to believe that. There were no such things as coincidences.

I didn't remain long at the residence of Sam Hurst. My job was to solve trouble. Mission accomplished.

Sam Hurst wasn't the only man the Syndicate sent me to visit. Other assignments were slipped under my door at the slaughterhouse. Some were simple but none were pleasant. Havencastle had a dark side.

After each mission, I became infected with the poisons of Havencastle, sometimes vomiting during the night. The city was a cesspool of crime and misery. While this darker side had always existed, I hadn't immersed myself in this underworld of despair and hopelessness since Cresek-Tawn. If I had been a religious man, I would've blamed Havencastle's disease on some evil god. But Havencastle was ill because of the evil of humankind. And it was devouring me, making me become a part of it.

And all the while, the Dark drank in this poison like it was nectar, gaining strength, knowing that it would make an attempt to escape soon.

My employer kept me busy. Not that the General ever made an appearance. Perhaps I had miscalculated, as Black Swan was as distant to me as it had been over a week ago while driving wagons for Alex. With little direct contact with the Syndicate, I had to find some way to weasel my way back into the organization.

Ask, and you shall receive.

The knock came on the door. This would be the first contact since I'd left the smuggling operation. My mind cycled through the possibilities. Landlord, an enemy, taxman, philanthropist. As I padded to the door, I grabbed my crossbow from the front table and tucked into the back of my breeches. Whether it was a philanthropist or enemy, I'd be prepared.

Or so I thought.

A man stood in the doorway, framed by the hanging slabs of beef. He appeared average. Normal build, normal height. Except his face. No emotion, flat eyes, lack of lines from years devoid of laughter. Smooth, impenetrable expression. I resisted the urge to pull my crossbow and shoot first. I figured him to be from Havencastle, the perfect candidate to blend in just about anywhere.

He was a professional. And his presence both worried and excited me. Why had my mission not been slipped under the door like all the others? Protocol had just been breached, which meant something big was about to go down. Whether that was good or bad for me was about to be discussed. I kept my expression calm and neutral.

175

"You shouldn't be here," I stated.

"We have no choice. Let's talk inside." He glanced behind him as if he had been followed. I sensed an edge to his voice. Something had him spooked.

I nodded, and moved aside so he could squeeze by. When he made a motion, however, I grabbed him by the shoulder, spun him around, and slammed him against the wall with my forearm tight against his throat, and my other hand holding the crossbow to his temple.

"You should know better than that," I said. "Who sent you?"

"Close the door," he whispered. His breath was sour like old whiskey. "Then we'll talk."

I slammed the door with my foot, then relaxed my grip around his throat and checked him quickly for weapons. Found a couple of daggers that I tossed aside while he kept his gaze on my crossbow. He didn't need to be told about the toxin in the dart. I was sure he knew that it held a lethal poison, and that with one shot, he'd be dead.

Tucked into the back of his waistband was a packet—the kind usually slipped under my door. I tossed it aside too.

I pushed him further inside and he left a trail of bloody footprints—he must've carelessly stepped in blood from outside. He was both nervous and careless; a dangerous portent.

"Lock the door," I ordered and backed up. He did as instructed, throwing the latch. As he turned, I slammed my fist into his gut. He doubled over with a grunt and clutched at his stomach.

"Wha...what..." he gasped.

"That was to keep you honest," I answered. "You're lucky I didn't kill you outright. If you didn't notice, you're in a slaughterhouse. It would be nothing to chop you up and make you disappear forever."

"This comes straight from above," he wheezed.

"What about the messenger? Why not send a message that way?"

"We've been compromised."

"How do I know I can trust you?"

"You don't. But there's a problem. We need an outsider to fix it. So he sent me to get you."

"Who?"

"You know who," he said. He motioned to the packet on the floor. I nodded and he retrieved it and he handed it out. Stepping back, I snatched the dossier away from him with my free hand and inspected it, searching for signs of tampering. Then tossed it back to my guest.

"Open it." If there was any contact poison, he'd find it first. Without pause, he ripped open the envelope and handed over the sheets of parchment.

I took the sheets and sorted through them. After several moments of reading, I glanced at him.

"This is my assignment?"

"The word comes from the General. You handle it." He must've felt that he was past the danger zone so he straightened his clothing.

"I'm not a cleaner," I insisted.

"I know that. But this is different."

"What's so different about it?"

"If I were you, I wouldn't try to find out. Do your job."

Without ceremony, he left, leaving bloody footprints in his wake.

The first time I'd entered a kill zone, I almost puked on Joshua. He hadn't appreciated that. Squeezing a person's life away with your bare hands in cold blood was one thing, but a killing spree was another animal. We'd slaughtered everyone. You'd think you'd become desensitized to it, and I suppose after several killing sprees I did, but that first time was brutal and I vomited everywhere, the splash nearly hitting Joshua.

Now, years later, my stomach revolted again. My balance reeled, the bad bourbon in my stomach sloshing. Humid air, stench of fluids, the bright colours of spilled life, and silence broken by the buzzing of flies.

A kill zone was more than murder. It was a message as much as a means. A message that no one could mistake: cross us and we'll kill you, your family, your servants, and anyone else who is near you.

A kill zone was a specialty from Cresek-Tawn. The guilds and organizations down in the Southern Arm didn't have the stomach for such mayhem. Until now.

"We used to be so good at them. Do you remember when the blood would be up to our ankles, splattering our hands and face? The taste of the rich copper of their lives? Don't pretend it's beneath you now."

"I've changed," I whispered, but realized that I said it a little too meekly.

My instincts took over. I stepped inside and closed the door. Passers-by didn't need to take a peek inside and alert the Bronze. In my right hand I carried my black bag of tools. These weren't the usual tools of my trade. These were different.

This building might've been a shop once. The foundation was built of white stone, the materials imported from beyond Havencastle's boundaries. Now the white helped display the splashes of blood and gore like a painting by a mad artist.

There were bodies crumpled around me, twisted at unnatural angles. A corpse stared oddly at me, the calm expression belying its violent death. A massive wound in its chest had emptied his life onto the floor in a black pool, arm twisted shattered behind him. He was naked, genitals sliced away and missing.

Vertigo threatened. I steadied myself against the wall. Not just because of the gore or the death but because I wondered... wondered...*did I do this*?

Had the Dark somehow escaped? Was I playing with fire by descending into the Syndicate? While I slept, had the Dark broken from his tomb, unleashing itself upon Havencastle?

Because the raw violence reminded me of what used to happen.

No, I told myself. Because if the Dark had escaped, I would've known. I would've experienced the mutilation as if through a dream. I would've seen the splatters of life. The taste of blood coursing down my throat.

I would've been there.

This hadn't been the Dark. The Dark was still locked away. Behind the doors. Behind the locks. I smelled the foul stench of its breath, humid and heavy. The Dark was where he belonged. Away.

Someone else had done this. It hadn't been me.

The reason I thought I might've been responsbile? Because the method of execution, followed by the mutilation—that was something direct from Cresek-Tawn.

"This is what we used to do," the Dark said gleefully. I could practically taste its joy, sickly sweet like thick syrup. *"A blade across the throat, pull out the tongue and leave it flapping on the chest."*

More bodies awaited me further in the house.

This wasn't just a slaughter. This was a message shot directly at the Syndicate. Was this payback for what happened at the Brass Cage? Had the Syndicate been blamed for the bloodshed that I had caused? Or were those men the first wave of assault? The clans from Cresek-Tawn were brutal and violent. To them, death was a glorious opportunity. How could you defeat an enemy who didn't fear death? And yet the *Crooked Hand* had never looked outwards for power. But times change.

If the Dark hadn't done this, then who? Except I already knew the answer.

"Joshua is in Havencastle," the Dark said and I didn't disagree.

I stopped counting the corpses after nine. It didn't matter anymore at that point. My contact had suggested that this had nothing to do with me; that my job here was only to clean up the mess. I disagreed. This had everything to do with me. This was one more answer, so that when I finally discovered the question, it would lock into the overall puzzle.

I opened my black bag and slipped on a pair of gloves, snapping them into place. The place needed to be cleaned so that it was like no one was ever here. But how the hell was I going to get rid of all these corpses? I could load them onto a wagon and have them carted to the harbour. There were plenty of unscrupulous captains who would gladly take my money to dump the grisly cargo out at sea, just like they had done with Sam. But imagine taking a wagon through town, attracting flies and ravens, and probably the Bronze.

A hand latched onto my ankle and despite all my training, all my experience, I gasped. I tried to jump clear but the hold was firm and I fell back. The hand belonged to a horribly disfigured man. My mind reeled through the irrational. Zombie. Re-animation. Monster. My heart pounded and the terror roared in my ears.

No, not a zombie.

I had to get control of my thinking.

He was alive. How could he be alive? I thought the man was grinning at me but realized that his cheeks had been slashed open into a permanent smile so wide I saw his back molars—a DunGhūl smile. It wasn't just the facial wounds, however. His body was a map of torment. The man coughed wetly, lungs swimming in blood.

The grip loosened and the man mumbled something incoherent before placing his head back down in the puddle of blood. I swore that he had said my name.

The terror was still fresh, my heart thudding and my senses heightened. Still, this man was no threat to me. *Did he say my name?* I edged closer and he stirred again.

"Nathaniel," he whispered.

"Who are you?" This man could've been my best friend and I couldn't have recognized him. He was too disfigured.

He tried to speak, failed, and I thought he had died right then. I shook him about the shoulders and he sputtered through his own blood. Then he said something.

Trent? Trevor? Tristan.

"Tristan?"

Years ago, when I ruled the *Crooked Hand*, a man named Tristan had been one of my greatest students. When things went bad, he had taken up the mantel to hunt me down. I had somehow escaped with my life. I had correctly guessed that the next time we saw each other, one of us would be lying in a pool of blood. However, I hadn't envisioned it like this.

But this changed everything. It wasn't the *Crooked Hand* that was hunting the Syndicate. No, in fact the *Crooked Hand* was equally the victim. The Pariahs? They didn't have the stomach for this type of violence. Who did? The Crucifiers? Even if they had the strength to pull this off, they wouldn't operate this quietly. Sure, they were good for the butchery, but they would've made it a public display. Whoever did this intended it as a private message to someone. And why had the Syndicate sent me to clean it up?

"I know who did this," that voice told me.

"Who?"

"The Beast on the Throne."

I scoffed outwardly, but couldn't help feel a niggling of doubt.

The situation in Havencastle was reaching a boiling point and I wanted nothing more than to bolt from the house but I had to play the game a little longer.

I shook off Tristan's grip and left him. He would be dead soon.

There was only one way to clean this mess.

I lit the place on fire, ensuring that nothing was left except the stone foundation, smouldering like a charred skeleton.

CHAPTER SEVEN
GOSSIP, LIES, AND DEATH CULTS

Burning down a building tended to attract a lot of attention. What made matters worse is that I had to stick around to make sure the job was done right. The fire crews took fifteen minutes to show up, but by then all they could try to do was contain the flames. I wasn't an amateur—I learned to light proper fires back when I was a boy like any proper prince.

I left at mid-morning. Thick, heavy clouds were rolling in from the ocean, bringing with them frigid winds laced with moisture. Good news for the fire crews, I suspected. I pulled my cloak tighter but it didn't keep out the cold.

I wanted nothing more than to return home, pour myself a hot bath, and try to scour away the filth of that place. Unfortunately, I knew I might've drawn attention with the whole arson thing so I couldn't directly return to the safe house. What good would a safe house be if everyone knew I lived there? I had planned to do several loops of the city but I spotted a tail almost immediately. They weren't very effective at staying hidden. Four men wearing robes and cloaks, as if they were trying to play priest or something. Shyst, why did everyone try to pretend to be something they weren't? Okay, so I was being a little hypocritical.

I lured them through the streets and alleys of the city, trying to get a gauge on their identities and their capabilities. They weren't good at all this subterfuge. I also didn't recognize them. Several times I caught the glint of armour beneath their robes, the sound of metal weapons clinking together.

They were a nervous bunch, odd considering that they looked like they had been through their fair of action. Faces and hands that had seen battle, and from what I saw of their shapes, they were fighting men.

I led them to an alley, then quickly took to the rooftops and doubled back. It was easy to come upon them silently before they realized I was there.

I grabbed the first man from behind, my blade pulled tightly against his throat while I aimed my crossbow at the other three.

"Good evening, Gentlemen." I always loved a good entrance.

The man in my grasp went stiff, obviously having done the risk assessment on the situation.

The other three reached for weapons but they too sized up the situation and paused. Good move. If they tried anything funny, I could slit the first man's throat and shoot in one motion, a full heartbeat faster than they'd have time to draw. After that, it became anyone's guess who would come out on top, but odds were three of them would be dead before they could drop me.

With hands still on weapons, their robes were parted and I saw the armour beneath. Bluish-gray chain mail. Crucifiers. Shyst. Here to collect for the lost *DragonRoot*. This is *not* what I needed right now.

"This is not official business," the man in my grasp hissed.

"So I'm supposed to let you go?" I asked. How foolish did they think I was? I pushed the blade tighter so that I restricted his breathing. I wandered if I had sharpened this blade recently. If so, I'd slice clean through his neck soon.

"Drop your weapons," he gasped. The men did as instructed, producing five axes, two swords, three daggers, and a sling shot.

I loosened my grip on the man to show that I was reasonable but didn't release him.

"What do you mean it's not official?" I asked.

"We're not speaking for the Syndicate."

"For the Syndicate?"

"The General didn't send us."

The General? The Syndicate? I wanted to groan. How obvious, and I chastised myself for not spotting it before. The military precision. The heavy weaponry. The Syndicate wasn't a guild. They were the Crucifiers. They had taken their entire organization underground. Completely ironic that I was working for the very people who wanted me dead. Strange.

And I wondered suddenly if once again I was confusing their intentions, that if perhaps this had nothing at all to do with the *DragonRoot* and everything to do with my current employment.

"Then why are you tailing me?"

"Because...we need to hire you."

I released the man and pushed him away. He coughed and hacked, massaging his throat and then showing me the blood that he produced on his fingers. I shrugged.

"I'm not very trusting," I said as a way of apology.

The men exchanged nervous glances. The man with the red line across his throat did the speaking. "We need you to put us back on the path of Righteousness."

"Friends, I'm not a priest." My blade disappeared back into the leather sheath inside my duster, and I lowered my crossbow.

"We know what you are. What you're capable of."

"They know about us. They know what we can do."

"This is highly unusual," I replied.

"Do you know what we're risking coming to you? If the General found out..."

"What do you want?"

"We need you to steal Black Swan."

My skin tingled at the name. "Never heard of it," I lied.

His smile indicated that my poor attempt at deception failed.

"That's a shame," he said. "It's the most beautiful thing you will ever see. From tip to hilt, it is forty inches in length and the blade is thirty-four and three-quarter inches. Under two pounds in heft. Perfectly weighted, but too perfect to be used in combat."

I hadn't held it. Creed had ensured of that, beating me to it. I remembered, however, the look of the blade. I remembered how I wanted to touch it as if that sword was drawing me to it.

Stop it, I chastised myself. As a man who could cut through legends and find the truth, I felt myself being pulled into the fervour.

The Crucifier reached into his cloak. I tensed but saw he was just drawing out a handkerchief. He dabbed his forehead. "Do you know what it's like being the chosen of the King of the Light of Righteousness, then to wake one day and find that you're forced underground like a common worm?"

I related to the worm part, but not being the chosen one.

"With Black Swan," he continued, "we can reclaim our place, spread the Light of Righteousness across the Succession and maybe even into the Empire or the Free Cities."

"Right." Had to cut him off before he started rambling on about this god or that god. "Who do you want me to steal it from?"

The men exchanged their conspiratory glances once more.

"We need you to steal it from the General."

These guys were full of surprises. "You want me to steal it from...you?"

"Yes. The man you call the General, he was once the Untercommander, before the schism, known throughout the lands for his masterful art."

Art—the Crucifier way of saying human dissection.

"But his eyes were always turned inward," the man continued, "never out among the flock. He is a genius, a patriot."

"Sounds like a decent guy," I chided.

"Unfortunately, the General doesn't understand the intricacies of the political world. His specialty was the enemy from within, not the enemy from without. But when his superiors were slain in the war, it was natural for him to take control."

"Yes, yes." I hated history lessons.

"His view...it is myopic and is bringing ruin upon us. The underworld is embroiled in a war where the ultimate prize is Black Swan."

"War with the *Crooked Hand*?"

"No, not a war against flesh and bone. That was a war we could've won. The General thought that if we possessed Black Swan...we could slay the Beast on the Throne."

There was the crazy devil talk again.

"Your disbelief may've protected you thus far, but it won't last. A giant from the North contacted us to sneak him outside of the Succession. He was stealing Black Swan from Vera Velat Temple. Do you remember the Festival of Lanterns?"

I suppressed a groan. "I'm familiar with what happened."

"That was Creed. We discovered what he had stolen. Such a righteous weapon has no business in the hands of the unwashed," he said. "We reclaimed it in the name of King of the Light of Righteousness."

The brawl at the Brass Cage.

"This giant...is he dead?" I asked.

"He escaped our trap. A brute of a man. Impossibly strong and harder to kill. Trust me, we tried. With Black Swan in our possession, the General was very convincing. He told us that we'd cast down the devil and regain our position of favour. No longer would we hide in the underground like rats."

"So what went wrong?"

"What went wrong? What kind of arrogance does it take to confront the Beast on the Throne? We were doomed from the start. Black Swan may have the ability to slay the devil, but not in our hands. We are being hunted, tormented, and slain but the General will not back down, saying that it is only a test from King of the Light of Righteousness. It is folly. You haven't seen..." he paused, swallowed deeply. "The only way this can end with our souls intact, is we wrest the sword away from the Untercommander."

"And what are you offering me?" I asked out of habit more than necessity.

"To begin, we can lift the bounty on your head."

"Which one?"

"For the *DragonRoot* job."

"You heard about that?"

"It was hard to miss."

"Well, that's a start."

"A starting point then. You can name your price."

"Where's the General now?"

"He's at the Palace of the Crucifixion."

"How long do I have?" I asked.

"Tonight."

"That's not much time," I stated.

"I fear that even tonight may be too late. The Beast on the Throne has sent his minions against us. They travel in the shadow, striking where the King of the Light of Righteousness is weakest. They hunt us down one by one. The General has attempted to fortify himself at the Palace of the Crucifixion."

Blah, blah, blah.

I wasn't listening. I was busy planning to steal Black Swan.

A second time.

⚬⚬⚬

"What is it?" Nathaniel asked.

"Exactly what it looks like. A pie."

Joshua had placed the faded ceramic dish in front of him. The crust was golden brown, Nathaniel's mouth watering at the sight. Joshua had been a cruel master. Since Joshua had purchased him from the flesh mongers, he'd put him through a training regimen that bordered on torture. There were no drills or routines. Only anguish. Deprivation. Malice. Combat. There were others like him also facing the same torment. Nathaniel had fought many of them. Fought them for meals. Fought them for the best place to sleep. Fought them for clothing. He had killed several, the battles primal, fought with taloned hands and gnashing teeth.

The pie pulsed. Nathaniel couldn't help but think once he cut into it, vipers would explode from the pastry.

"This is a gift I'm giving you, Nathaniel. A great gift. Now eat."

Nathaniel stared warily at the pie. Joshua placed a fork in his hands.

"You have worked so hard. This is your reward. You are the last of my disciples. The one that I have chosen."

Killed all the others, *Nathaniel thought. Yet he knew better than to question Joshua. His master had unmercifully beaten a woman to death when she dared question 'why'. That was on the second day. Since that time, his lessons had been followed religiously. Do not question. Only do.*

Nathaniel dipped his fork into the pie. The outer shell broke, flaky. The filling was a dark, rich purple. Elderberry, *Nathaniel thought. Perhaps Joshua was doing something kind.*

He took a bite. Sweet. Juicy. And wrong.

He began to retch but Joshua was already scooping another bite to Nathaniel's mouth.

"Eat. Get it in you. This will make you strong. Make you powerful. All your training was simply so you'd be strong enough for this gift."

Nathaniel's stomach revolted, but he knew if he vomited that Joshua would be harsh, perhaps deadly. As he had been trained to do, Nathaniel quelled his body, voided the sensation of the pie and its wrongness. He ate with a frenzy, swallowing down the pastry until there was nothing left except crumbs. Even then, Joshua urged him to finish it all.

Then Nathaniel sat still and waited. Felt his stomach rippling. Even through his mental blocks, Nathaniel was afraid. What had he just done? Did he even have a choice in the matter?

Or perhaps that was the lesson. That only those foolish enough to eat the pie would die. Nathaniel had to escape. Waves of nausea threatened to topple him. Motes floated before his eyes. He tried to stand.

Nathaniel collapsed.

He suffered through hallucinations. Of yellow eyes in a void. Of hate. Of murder and death. The screams were terrible. He saw cracking bones, the flash of white as it ripped through skin, the splash of gore along terrified faces. A skull cracking under the weight of a club. Sights so terrible that they made even Nathaniel weep.

The hallucinations lasted for months. Or so it felt. It was never-ending and he thought that surely he would teeter into permanent madness.

Then the haze parted and his eyes opened. His body was drained, so utterly spent that he thought he might've died right then. Nathaniel lay on his back, clothing soaked with sweat. Wait, not sweat. It was blood.

When Nathaniel looked at his hands, he realized they were caked with blood. Some of it fresh, some of it dried. My blood? *Yet he knew it belonged to others. Not his. Joshua was standing over him, and for the first time since he had met his cruel master, saw him pleased. To see Joshua smile sent such a powerful surge of joy through him, that he knew he would kill a thousand people just to see it again.*

"You have done it, Nathaniel. I didn't think it would be you that survived the ordeal. But you proved me wrong. Oh, Nathaniel, do you realize what I have done? I have given you a great prize. My greatest creation."

Joshua left him alone, Nathaniel trying to sort through the images in his mind, to discover which belonged to his senses and which were aftershocks from his hallucinations.

And through the haze, a voice came from deep inside him.

"My name is the Dark. And we are together," it said. And Nathaniel was fearful of what he had just done.

∞

The Dead Zone.

Dark. Desolate. The lights of the city were only a dream here, and the night sky was a shroud. I knew I wasn't alone. Somewhere in the gloom, the lowest forms of the underworld, the beggars and the cripples, they'd be watching me, wondering if I was prey.

Not tonight I wasn't.

I heard them scurrying through the rubble, quick enough that I never caught a full glimpse. They were harmless. Scavengers who fed off the lower rungs of the ladder.

The Palace of the Crucifixion was rubble. A blasted hulk of stone, wood, and bone. Actual bone. A hand, bleached white, protruded from rocks. I kicked it, watching as knuckle bones scattered. Other skeletons were littered throughout the debris. The aged bones indicated that these weren't soldiers killed in the rebellion, but from old graves disturbed when the fortress crumbled.

Three years ago, this was a pillar of power. The ArchCommander had influence across the continent, some saying he rivalled the kings. But he over reached. Tried to take it all. Was left with nothing.

Mounds of rubble were the last remains of once great buildings. The fortress walls were fragmented, a disjointed line of rock and stone. The signs of battle lay everywhere: broken armour and shields, abandoned siege equipment, scorched rock, puddles of oil. Somewhere in this mess was the General, the leader of a band of Crucifiers who had refused to lay down their arms and instead became the Syndicate. Now, he was boss of the most powerful crime union in Havencastle.

I wandered the ruins but couldn't find anything. The place was huge and would take me all night to inspect. If the General and his men wanted to stay hidden, I wasn't about to find them here.

"Shyst." The situation needed the Master of Randomness to send a sign or a helping hand.

I stumbled upon a sign. Literally. A piece of the foundation crumbled beneath me, several hundred pounds of rock shifting due to my carelessness. I tumbled forward, catching myself with a quick somersault and once more on my feet, as if the whole act had been intentional. I glanced around sheepishly, hoping that one of the Dead Zone's scavengers hadn't witnessed my clumsiness.

My embarrassment was quickly forgotten, however, as the resulting dust cloud caught a ray of light from below. While the top surface of the fortress had been razed, some of the subterranean levels must've been intact. There was a door in the earth, cleverly constructed to appear as if part of the debris, found only because of my clumsiness. The trapdoor was partially open, a thin shaft of light stabbing the night. Had I sprung it open?

I drew my crossbow. If this was the stronghold of the Crucifiers, there should've been guards. Sentries. Even a watchman asleep on the job. Something. Not an unsecured entry point. Someone could've left it open out of carelessness, which made me worry even more. Everything I'd seen about the Syndicate and the Crucifiers indicated that they weren't overly careless. Something was wrong.

I glanced through the crack but saw no one within. The lights flickered from the wind that gusted by me. *No time like the present*, I thought, and threw open the door. A metal ladder was braced to the stone wall. A torch in a sconce flickered, shadows contorting around the entrance. I crouched to get a closer look. The rungs were smeared with fresh blood.

As a rule, blood was never a good sign.

No sentries and blood. A bad combination. Really, I only had one reasonable option: close the damned door and pretend I'd never spoken to the Crucifiers earlier. But no one ever accused me of being a reasonable man. So that meant I was heading down. I bypassed the rungs and slid down the rails. Landed soundlessly.

The corridor stretched in both directions. No one.

Puddles of blood on the floor. Too much to be just from one person. I thought briefly of the kill zone I had been forced to clean earlier. Oddly, I wasn't worried about my safety. The grand violence had already transpired. I was worried that I had arrived too late, however. What if the General and the Crucifiers were gone? What if they were dead?

The air was humid, thick. Pools of blood set out my path for me. I crept forward, stepping around the puddles. The path was well lit, a combination of torches and chemical lanterns. At least there was no fumbling around in the dark.

The corridor twisted then ended at an oaken door, partially open, bloodied palm prints smeared across the wood. From whom?

Laying before the door was a sword, its sharpened edge glinting. The hilt, however, was covered in gore. Someone had fallen here, before they even had a chance to defend themselves. Perhaps the *Crooked Hand* had invaded. They moved like a summer storm—without warning, fierce, then gone.

I slipped into the adjoining passageway, careful not to touch the door.

The true nature of the Crucifiers greeted me. Once, this corridor had dissected their holding cells, five on each side—a warehouse of flesh. Perhaps those waiting to be crucified.

Now they held death.

The metal cell doors were twisted, bent as if the heavy iron had been cheap tin. The hinges and pins had snapped from their welded foundation. Such strength. Such power. The last time I had witnessed this kind of might was during the battle with Creed.

Inside the cells was horror.

Bodies were piled high, their flesh ripped as a butcher might dissect fowl, tossing the useless flesh in a heap for the dogs. Most of the corpses were too smashed to recognize. Women, children, some men. Those with eyes stared unblinking at me, as if blaming me for not arriving sooner. The hands of the corpses were clenched in claws. A body lay face down in a pool of congealing blood, its chain armour distinguishing it from the other corpses. Its white hands grasped its axe. I kicked over the corpse.

A Crucifier. His face was mangled, cheeks shredded, the flesh pale and rubbery. Two rows of glittering white teeth smiled as if he had found the scene of death amusing. This was the work of something that revelled in death and slaughter.

"Shyst," I choked.

I held the collar of my duster over my mouth, attempting to filter the stench of blood, urine, and crap. The smell of terror. I might not have believed in the divine but I was beginning to believe in hell.

I wished I had a little bit of *DragonRoot* to calm my nerves, to take the harshness off this sharp edge of reality. I left bloody footprints, no longer caring about leaving a trail. I wanted to leave this place, to run far away, but I couldn't. The mission. Think of the mission! My body acted on its own now, trudging forward, needing to find the answers. If there were answers to this horror. Who could've done this to the Crucifiers?

"The Beast on the Throne," came the whisper, and I thought I sensed the Dark's fear. The thought that something frightened the Dark was deeply unsettling.

The door at the end of the passageway was splintered and cracked on broken hinges. The large chamber on the other side held more chaos.

A statue of the King of the Light of Righteousness stood in the center of a fountain, the waters running red. The statue had been desecrated, blood splashed across the stone. More corpses. All Crucifiers. Eight in number.

Whatever had done this saved the true horror for these men. No, these weren't just murders. These were sacrifices. Someone had sacrificed several of these knights to some dark Immortal. Three spikes were planted in the ground, the corpses skewered through the thick poles.

The air was so thick I wondered if I'd be able to take another breath. My head felt light, like it was ready to float away from my body. My vision distorted, colours fading, leaving a painting of stark black and white.

The Crucifiers had been impaled, their hands gripping the stakes as they had died trying to pull themselves free. They hadn't perished immediately: they had wriggled around like a worm on a fishing hook, intensifying the agony.

My hands shook. I tried to regain my focus. No matter what happened here, I had to keep control. This was no different than a standard murder. Well, except for the impalement and the mounds of corpses.

The walls were drenched with blood. Yet it wasn't from the spray of murder. There was a pattern to the blood, like a mad artist had splattered them with scarlet, displaying an image only he could decipher.

With all the puddles and smears across the floors and walls, there should've been some sign of an attacker. There were none. No footprints. No tracks. No trail. Gone. Many of the Crucifiers hadn't drawn their weapons. Something had come upon them without warning.

The General would be dead. The trail of Black Swan had been wiped clean. I sidestepped the impaled men and the desecrated statue of the King of the Light of Righteousness. Was something with me in these subterranean caverns?

I heard a rustle from the corridor and I shivered. I was spooked and needed to regain my wits. A fixer who lost his senses would find himself losing his life. But all the blood, all the flesh, made my task difficult.

An impaled Crucifier stared at me. The body quivered, a trickle of blackness spilling from a hole in its cheek. The corpse slid another few inches down the pole.

Just settling, I tried to convince myself. I closed my eyes in an attempt to regain my wits. I could do this. The answers were here, ready to be found. Corpses were harmless. I had witnessed butchery before and it had never unhinged me like this. However, those were back in the days of Cresek-Tawn. Those were different days.

Opened my eyes. The death wasn't what terrified me, nor the primal fear of dismemberment. There was something else in here with me. Something unnatural. I gazed across the walls and ceiling, searching for the unseen intruder. The scourge, whatever it was, had destroyed Crucifiers easily and quickly, torturing them like they had tortured their own victims. Perhaps not being a Crucifier was my greatest strength right now. Maybe this unnatural entity preyed on Crucifiers.

The Beast on the Throne.

No, just fairy tales.

"Like me," the Dark whispered.

Demons, devils. The Beast on the Throne. The Crucifier had warned me and I ignored him. Maybe I was the crazy one, not him.

I had to get out of here, but I couldn't run headlong to escape as that would most certainly lead to my downfall.

Another body shuddered, slipping further down the stake. I startled, turning my aim upon the settling corpse. Its face was badly mutilated but I recognized it. The once-cold face of the General was wrenched into a permanent and agonized expression.

In his right gloved hand, he held a silver knife, its blade stained a deep red. His red. His blood. The General had carved at his own body while on the stake. His abdomen was peeled back, ribbons of flesh hanging from his midsection.

A string of drool hung from his lower lip. He stared at me with a single white eye, his other having burst like an over-ripened cherry and spilled down his cheek. His gaze wasn't dead or unfocused. How I wished it were. His single eye tried to probe me, as if searching the deep recesses of my soul.

The body broke into a grin. "Nathaniel," it whispered. I wanted to turn and run, to flee as fast as I could. But I was frozen, locked in a gaze with a dead man. "Give me Black Swan," the corpse whispered. "Where is it?"

My mouth opened to answer but I couldn't speak. The body shuddered. Its chest convulsed and despite myself, my eyes were fixed on the display. Like the sound of tree limbs cracking in a storm, the ribs shattered, exploding through flesh and muscle. White bone. The single white eye widened until it seemed it too would burst.

The General convulsed, as if something were trapped within and struggled for freedom. His arms danced, held by an invisible puppet master. Its mouth moved—trying to speak but the words were lost in the convulsions. The corpse tensed, its muscle locked, arms and legs jutting straight outwards.

The inner force won. The body burst like a balloon, scattering debris across the desecrated temple. Bits of flesh, clumps of hair.

But it had left something behind. Something terrible.

The devil stared at me with red eyes that threw a terrible heat. Its face was concealed in a leather mask, tufts of black hair hanging from between straps fastened at the back of its skull. The ears were exposed with the slant of fae heritage. I tried to shield my face from the heat of its gaze. The figure wore gold chains and pendants resting on the chest of his reddish leather suit. It wore black, silk gloves that stretched to its elbow. The blood from the General's destruction rolled from its fine robes like oil on water.

"Where is Black Swan?"

Was this The Beast on the Throne? The Devil? It stood before me in all its terrible might, demanding something I could not give it.

I found myself running, my fear over-riding all that was rational and settling on the most primal—survival. I slipped on the slick floor and scrambled to regain my balance.

Dashing through the prison block, I lunged over the dead bodies.

The fiend chased me, it's voice a howl. No doubt the masked demon could've simply disintegrated me with a black bolt of death. But that would've been too easy. This monster revelled in horror and pain.

"Black Swan!" it screeched, its banshee wail painful. Kept running. Had to get away. The ladder. Almost there. The demon ran effortlessly, its robes snapping behind it and the heat of its gaze burned blisters into my back.

Jumped for the ladder. Hit the third rung. Scampered upwards. Climbing and rolled from the trap door. The leather-faced devil scrambled behind me. Only one chance.

I swung the trapdoor shut, slamming it upon the upper torso of the masked man. The creature howled, its shrill cry echoing but it didn't let go. I slammed the door again. The monster shuddered. I opened the door, slammed it down. The masked man slipped. I kicked, my stained boots striking it beside the leather mask. The fiend released its hold on the railing, plummeting down into the tunnel and the trap door smashed into place.

Turning, I ran, knowing that this was a brief victory. The creature would be right behind me.

∽

I stumbled through the streets of Havencastle.

My hands shook, gasping for air and my pulse racing. I searched the skies, the streets, and the darkened windows for the devil.

Alleyways appeared like the mouths of an abyss, calling me into their darkness. Abandoned buildings were breeding grounds for monsters from Hell. Inside the darkened homes, the inhabitants slept cocooned in their blankets, unprepared and unable to defend themselves against the horror stalking Havencastle.

Even the beggars frightened me. When they approached with outstretched grubby hands, my eyes widened and I scampered away as if they were asking for more than a few brine.

The Beast on the Throne. The devil. Whatever it was, it came straight from the pits of Hell. LaFage had been right. My childhood tutors and the scholars had taught me there was such thing as the devil. "The devil is a man's heart" they used to say, but I had seen a seen a lot of strange things on my travels. Hypnosis, fire-eaters, self-impalers, zombies, mutants. And of course I festered with my own internal demon named the Dark.

But this...this was The Beast on the Throne.

In my haze, I returned home. The safe house at the back of the slaughterhouse.

I trudged through the rows of butchered flesh like a dead-man walking. I stepped in a puddle of blood. My nerves needed to recoup. Never in my experience as a fixer had I ever experienced anything like that. Not even back in Cresek-Tawn.

I tried to run my fingers through my hair. Somehow, blood from the Palace had gotten into my hair, making it a sticky, tangled mess. My clothes now possessed the cold, gumminess of drying blood. At least it wasn't my blood. I had been in some bad scrapes before, but nothing could compare. When I blinked, in that fraction of a second, the image of the General was there, gazing at me with his single eye.

Demons, devils, immortals...the Beast on the Throne? How was it possible? In my travels across the continent, I had experienced many strange things. Most times, there were easy explanations. Not tonight.

Perhaps, if my mind hadn't been so preoccupied, I would've noticed something wrong at the opening of my door. Then everything might've unfolded differently.

How long did I stand in the doorway of the darkened safe house, wondering about entering and lighting a lamp? Wouldn't fleeing Havencastle be the best option? The Syndicate was in ruins, the trail to Black Swan washed clear. Yet I was in no condition to travel. Not now. Besides, Havencastle was the last friendly city in the Succession for me. There was nowhere else to go.

I breathed deeply, trying to regain my resolve and composure. I was a fixer. What happened at the palace was just a little trouble. Take away the death, the slaughter, and the theatrics, and at its basest form, it was only a form of trouble. I solved trouble. Being able to solve this problem would begin with taking the first few steps into my apartment.

The lamp flared to life and I cursed at the brilliance. The door slammed shut behind me, blocking my escape. A trap. Then my senses registered my surroundings and an odd sense of relief calmed my hyper-sensitive nerves. The cause of my alarm wasn't the supernatural.

A man sat in my chair, his blond hair tied into three equal ponytails. He wore a fine silk shirt and dress pants to match, as if he were nobility, and in a way, I guess he was. He was smiling, a taunting expression that brought a desire from me to wipe that look from his face.

My hand reached for a hand bow that wasn't there. Did I drop it at the palace? The blond man's smile didn't waver. His four escorts, all Killers from the look of their physiques, didn't react—they were too well trained for that.

"It's been a long time, Nathaniel," the man said. Perhaps, years ago, I might've had a chance against him in a fair fight. Probably not. Besides, those years were gone.

"I saw what you did at the palace, Nathaniel. Your depravity knows no bounds, does it?"

There was so much to say and ask. How did he find me? Why did he leave Cresek-Tawn? But those questions weren't asked because I refused to give him any satisfaction.

He looked me over as if a cattleman inspecting a cow. "You've changed. Gone with a more rough-and-tumble look. I don't think it suits you."

I remained quiet. If he wanted me dead, he would've slit my throat the moment I stepped inside. We kept our stare.

"We can kill him," the Dark said. *"Use the first man as a shield, distract the second, grab the blade from his sheath, plunge it into his heart."*

Except it wouldn't be that easy. These weren't just soldiers, warriors, or assassins. They were trained by the *Crooked Hand*, and I didn't stand a chance against all five of them. Joshua was usually three steps ahead.

Joshua broke the stare first though it was little consolation to me. He nodded to one of his Killers. "Show him," he said. The man unwrapped a length of burlap longer than a man's arm. I knew what it was even before the first rays of light nearly blinded me.

Black Swan.

I licked my lips as if the sword were a drink of water and I was a straggler in the desert.

"When I heard about the calamity at the Festival of Lanterns, I knew it was you. You always did have an eye for the dramatic. I've followed your exploits as you've rampaged across the Succession. When you were run out Morgeth, I knew it was only a matter of time before you showed up here. Black Swan is such a prize. I was going to come get it myself. But you know who demanded to come in my place? Who begged me for this opportunity because she so wanted to stick a knife in your chest?"

My head was swimming.

"I'll kill her." My voice was low, hoping he accepted the threat as real.

"She's mine. You know that, don't you, Nathaniel? She's always been mine."

I was lunging forward. I wanted to rip his heart from his chest. He didn't flinch but it didn't matter. I was still in shock from the palace. His men brought me down easily, pinning me so effectively that I could barely breathe.

"Bring him," Joshua instructed. He rose from the chair. "Don't struggle so much, Nathaniel. You'll need to save your energy. You're going home."

CHAPTER EIGHT
FIRST CLASS AROUND THE WORLD

As slave galleys went, this one wasn't bad. Sure, I was shackled to my seat and forced into rowing half my waking hours, but overall, I couldn't complain. These slave traders didn't push us too hard and they fed us well. Most flesh mongers didn't understand, or simply didn't care, that if you didn't properly feed your slaves, you won't get a lot of work out of them. No matter what stories you've heard, flesh mongers like to take care of their conscripts. After all, a dead slave didn't do anyone any good.

They freed us every few hours to wander the back deck to stretch our muscles. They kept a watchful eye, of course, scimitars drawn and ready. Most times they kept the whipping to a minimum because whipping caused welts, permanent scarring, and generally lowered the value of any slave. Free-market forces actually ensured they treated us fairly.

It was during one of these free moments I realized that Joshua hadn't sent me unaccompanied. I spotted the *Crooked Hand* assassin on the second day, three rows back on the other side.

He had the bronzed skin of someone born and raised in the harsh sun of the desert. He was good at blending, I'd give him that. He was young, probably fresh to the *Crooked Hand*, though that didn't lessen the danger for me. A shiv driven into my sternum by an eighteen-year old really was no different than one wielded by someone twice his age. Either way, it would kill me.

It was his gaze that gave him away. In that brief second when our eyes met, I spotted the recognition. He looked away but it was too late. I wondered if the flesh mongers knew that he wasn't a real slave but one of the *Crooked Hand*. I guessed that they didn't.

I assumed at that moment of eye contact that he knew he had been made. If I realized who he was, he probably saw the recognition in my eyes as well. I scanned the rest of the slaves, wondering if any of them were also the *Crooked Hand*. I didn't spot any, but perhaps they were simply more versed at blending than this one.

The slave ship had a single mast, and whenever the sail drooped from lack of wind, they pushed us into rowing. I counted forty-one slaves, twenty on my side, twenty-one on the other. The ten crew members took turns with the various chores: slaver, pilot, deck hand, navigator, cook.

I sat between a bad-tempered barbarian with an overbite and a foul-smelling Moranian. The three of us worked the same oar, though often the Moranian wouldn't pull his own weight.

"What's your clan?" I asked my foul-tempered companion.

The barbarian gnashed his teeth and snarled. He liked to elbow-jab me in the ribs. My grunts appeared to satisfy him as our restraints prevented any real fisticuffs.

"No need to be rude," I said, though the barbarian kept gnashing and cursing. The Moranian only spoke Conragess, so there was no need to bother with him. Besides, most of the time he was puking his guts onto the floor from sea sickness. His sickness was a strange affliction for a man who came from a sea-loving country, which was probably why someone sold him into slavery. The flesh mongers didn't take kindly to his vomiting and usually repaid him with a few lashes of the cat-o-nine tails.

So I sat there, trapped in my own thoughts. And as the tongue plays with a painful tooth, my memories played between the two events: that last horrific night at the Palace of the Crucifixion, Jane's betrayal. On the surface they appeared unrelated but I knew that I was merely missing the cornerstone that would connect them together. And I had a feeling that it involved Joshua.

I remembered the terrible image of the creature in the palace. Despite the horror, I wasn't ready to confess that I believed in the devil. How could I believe in fairy tales? How could I not? Always an explanation.

"How do you explain me, then?" the Dark said.

I tried to ignore that voice whispering through the locked door in my mind. It had been testing the locks more frequently. I worried about the outcome when I finally did reach Cresek-Tawn.

"If I exist, should not the Beast on the Throne? You saw what it did to those people."

"Nothing that you wouldn't have done," I mumbled.

The barbarian grunted at me, reminding me to keep my thoughts to myself.

The *Crooked Hand* was cruel, but cruel with a purpose. They weren't just taking me back to Cresek-Tawn to be a slave. They had more planned from me. But what?

I didn't consider myself a prisoner. I had a few surprises up my sleeves if I needed them, but I knew that I had to go along with Joshua's plan. What were the alternatives? That I escape, swim to shore, and return to Havencastle and live out my life? No, he knew that I'd coming looking for him and Black Swan. But why would he want me back in Cresek-Tawn? I leaned back, let the other men in my aisle do most of the rowing, watched the scenery drift by, and contemplated how exactly Joshua was manipulating me.

Our ship stayed within sight of the coast though I grew disoriented quickly. Not only was I not a nautical guy but the coast was but a distant, jagged, green line.

We stayed clear of other ships, veering hard away to ensure a wide berth. Technically, slaving was illegal in the Succession, the Empire, and the Free Cities though some districts turned a blind eye to it. Like everything, it was only illegal if you didn't bribe the correct officials and so it was a dangerous game for these flesh mongers. If they didn't grease the right palms they could easily be sentenced to death while we'd be sold to another slaving outfit.

"We're going home," the Dark whispered.

Initially, only the nights were cold. Then even the sun grew distant and frigid.

"Can I have a blanket to keep warm?" I asked the slaver.

"Another word out of you and this'll be keeping you warm!" he shrieked and displayed his cat-o-nine-tails.

"I'd prefer a blanket," I muttered.

The barbarian gnashed his teeth—his version of laughter. He probably didn't care about the temperature, as his skin was most likely as thick as a rhino's.

Abruptly, our course changed and we headed towards land. I thought perhaps we might be evading another ship but I couldn't spot any. I thought about asking the flesh mongers where we were headed, but the cat-o-nine-tails game had grown tiresome.

Though still far away from Cresek-Tawn, we headed to port, maybe to take on supplies. My rowing weakened, allowing the barbarian to pick up the slack. He gnashed his teeth and muttered but his complaints fell upon deaf ears.

The setting sun reflected blindingly off the water. I squinted, trying to block the brilliance with my hand but failing. I had to wait until the sun dipped further beneath the city skyline to get a good look at our destination, though it didn't look familiar from this vantage point. We reached the pier two hours later, chemical lanterns mounted on the docks guiding us. The city sprawl, now awash in artificial lights, was as unfamiliar as before. I had never been a seafaring man, so these ports and docks all looked the same.

We extinguished our lights, so we could sneak into port like a priest into a whore's den. I didn't think we were going to stay long.

We moored to the end of the furthermost pier, a small party waiting for us. I counted close to ten, eight of which were slaves chained together around their ankles. The other two men who guarded them were nothing more than thugs. Real knuckle draggers who looked mean, large, and clumsy.

As I scanned the newcomers, I nearly shouted in shock. That face! Tiny glasses set on a thin nose. Wiry features. LaFage the Friendly! What good luck that he was also being sold into slavery. Maybe there really was something to all this talk of divine powers because surely the Master of Randomness had put us together.

The barbarian grunted beside me, watching as the prisoners were searched again before being allowed on the boat. The slave master was busy with the newest recruits.

There was no room in my row for LaFage.

"Sorry about this, old fellow," I apologized beforehand to the barbarian. He looked at me questioningly. I kicked up the oar with my knee, the wooden handle cracking him in the mouth. His lips exploded in blood. He didn't moan, didn't curse, didn't gnash. He sat there, stunned. I threw my arm irons around his neck. Twisting. His eyes bulged as my grip tightened and choked him. With only the lanterns of the pier, it was difficult to see him changing from blue to red to purple. He clawed at the chains but my grip was too perfect, too tight.

He slumped forward and my grip slackened. The barbarian shuddered, his throat making clucking noses as his lungs tried to draw in air.

"Excuse me. Slave master?"

The slave master turned to me, his whip drawn back.

"My companion's seasick," I said hurriedly, not wanting a lashing. "He collapsed." The barbarian wasn't regaining consciousness and I wondered if I had done any permanent damage.

"Shyst!" the driver cursed. "Get him outta there! Now!" The two burly men on the pier clambered onto the ship. Stupid oafs. If I had the inkling to escape, I could've easily overpowered them. As it was, I was content to watch them unchain the barbarian and drag him away from the seat.

"Slave master," I said, "That man was the strongest on our row. I'm afraid that to pick up his slack would be unbearable for me."

He gazed at me, squinting as if a noonday sun were shining in his eyes. "That so?" Then he gave me a smile full of rotting teeth. He pointed to LaFage, the smallest of the new crew. "Bring him over here."

How predictable. Friendly was seated next to me and shackled in place.

"Good thing there was room beside me," I whispered to LaFage. The tiny man couldn't hide his surprise at seeing me. Luckily for the both of us, he didn't make it too obvious or the slave master surely would've punished us both.

The other slaves were loaded on board and without any extra supplies, we set out again.

"Where are we?" I whispered.

"New Eval King." He was having trouble rowing. I probably should've assisted in the work but I was too excited at seeing my friend to do anything other than rest my hands on the oars.

"We're weeks away from Cresek-Tawn," I estimated, though I really had no clue.

Now he stopped rowing and stared. "Cresek-Tawn? We're heading to Cresek-Tawn?"

"Yup."

He shrunk on his bench. "I can't go back there."

"Think of how I feel."

"Get rowing!" the slave master bellowed. His whip fell upon LaFage's back. The tiny man yelped, arching his spine with pain. "You're not here for talking. Now row!" The slaver kept a watchful eye on the both of us, LaFage's face twisted in agony. Obviously, he hadn't been brought up with a life of torture. The cat-o-nine tails was pretty minor on my agony scale.

After a few strokes of the oars, the slave master was satisfied we were pulling our weight and turned his attention to the other passengers.

"How were you captured?" I whispered.

LaFage merely shook his head while biting his lower lip. His eyes filled with tears from the excruciating pain.

"Don't worry about it, Friendly. He's all talk. You get used to the whippings. Really."

"I don't think so," he squeaked.

"Trust me. Have I been wrong before?" He shot me a terrible glance, so I changed the topic. "How'd they get you?"

I saw LaFage considering keeping his mouth shut, still concerned about the flesh mongers but I think his frustration prevented him from remaining quiet for long. "Damned bounty hunter. My own fault—I didn't think they'd follow me to New Eval King. You know how much was on my head?"

"Not a clue."

"One-thousand drake. Can you believe it?"

"That's a lot of cash. What made you deserve that?"

"Assisting you."

My nod gave him the impression that it all made sense to me.

"How about you? I didn't think I'd see you headed back to Cresek-Tawn. At least not so calm."

"Joshua brought me in." I said it all nonchalant, as if the name meant nothing to the two of us. LaFage whistled between his teeth, hearing that name momentarily distracting him from the fear of the slave master and his whip.

"He has Black Swan," I continued. "He was flaunting it. I'll go peacefully back to Cresek-Tawn, because that's where he's going. I'm going to get it back, LaFage. He's not going to stop me. Not this time."

"This is big." He whispered. "It's bigger than us, bigger than the Syndicate, and bigger than Cresek-Tawn."

The slaver's footsteps thumped on the deck toward us. We fell silent, putting our strength into rowing as he watched. LaFage was right. This sword was bad news.

The slave master's footsteps drifted away from us.

LaFage leaned over. "If this is all about a sword, why is Joshua keeping us alive?"

Another question I couldn't answer.

I slid inch by agonized inch down the splintered pole, the spiked tip ripping apart my bowels, up past my spine. There was no pain. It was beyond that now. Only a whiteness, pure and hot, as if I were filled with the power of the Divine.

The Palace of the Crucifixion.

The demon with the leather mask stood beside me. Surely it had to be the Beast on the Throne. The devil pushed a metal barb into my forearm, slicing through the fold of skin. He hooked the instrument on a muscle and slowly pulled, peeling it away from the bone like a slice of cheese. The devil slowly stripped a ribbon of flesh from my arm, his leather mask hiding his screams. No, he wasn't screaming. It was me. Then there was silence as my vocal cords snapped like an over-tightened lute string. I wanted to close my eyes to hide from the torture but couldn't; my eyelids had been cut away.

A knife parted the skin along my stomach, reaching into my core. The blade turned and twisted at my innards. Blood ran down across my groin, down my legs and filled my boots. The liquid was ice upon my skin. The leather-faced demon peered into my eyes, the slits of his mouth hole so close his breath choked me.

Wait, it wasn't the demon, it was Jane.

"My love," she whispered in my ear. She was here to rescue me.

"I had the worst dream. You were, you were..." Except I couldn't speak and it came as a guttural moan.

"Shhhh," she placed a finger to my lips to quiet me. "There's nothing to be afraid of now."

A great pain erupted through my chest. Blood everywhere. A terrible wound in my breast gushed gouts of my life. Jane sneered at me, her right hand holding a blade soaked in scarlet. She had stabbed me.

Jane used the knife on me again. The blade scraped along my ribs as it burrowed deeply. My lungs burst and I couldn't breathe.

Where was I? I saw impossibly tall towers, reaching from lakes of liquid fire, red like a sunset. My body hung from the stake in the middle of this inferno,. Despite the flames, I was so cold. Her claws were on my genitals, ripping me open, laughing at me.

"You betrayed me, Jane," my lips mouthed.

I woke with a scream. Not a unique situation on a slave ship. My panic had already awakened LaFage.

"What's wrong?" His voice calmed me. Grounded me to reality.

I frantically searched for Jane, for the devil but they had dissolved into the ether. Only LaFage and the creak of the ship against the lull of the ocean's water.

"A bad dream."

"A dream?"

"Yeah, a dream. Slavery can do that to a man," I gasped.

The flesh mongers were at the bow, huddled around a lantern, playing a game of coins.

"You still deny it?"

"Deny what?"

He glanced over his shoulder, as if our conversation were of great importance. "The Beast on the Throne."

"Truly? The devil?" Except my voice didn't sound so sure.

"You've been near Black Swan, Nathaniel."

"Look, I'm fine. Go back to sleep."

LaFage shrugged and laid his head back on the wooden railing, asleep in minutes. Me, afraid of a silly dream. Regardless, I didn't fall back asleep immediately. I tried to swallow down the memories, the horror of the nightmare. And yet when I did that, I realized that for the first time in months, the Dark was quiet. As if the dream had even terrified it. That wasn't a thought I dwelt on for long.

That exact dream haunted me four nights in a row.

We rowed for the better part of a week. The days became insignificant scratches etched into my oar. Another seven days, maybe eight until we reached Cresek-Tawn. I tried not to think about the city, about my past, but it was difficult, and then there were the thoughts of Jane's betrayal.

Then my mind would circle to Joshua and the current scenario. Sure, I was a slave, being watched by a group of ruthless flesh mongers, as well as a *Crooked Hand* assassin sitting three rows back.

But Joshua would've known that couldn't stop me. So I kept coming to the same conclusion: Joshua wanted me in Cresek-Tawn.

"What's that?" LaFage had ceased his rowing. During the past days, his paleness had bloomed into a much healthier burn. The ship had transformed us. My muscles, perhaps a little soft from years of freelancing, had hardened, now tight like cords of rope. Our hands had blistered, then calloused, and became stiff. We had severe sunburns, so that our exposed flesh was in a perpetual state of peeling skin.

At first, I saw nothing. LaFage must've had eyes like a fox. I squinted, and slowly a shape materialized.

"Looks like a ship."

"It's been following us for a while," he whispered.

"For a while?"

"Several hours."

"We're on the same course."

"We've already altered ours twice. It's after us, and giving chase, I'd say."

The crew of our ship gathered at the bow, whispering but gesturing with animated hand signals at the pursuing boat. They weren't doing a very good job hiding their concern.

"Let's put some muscle into that rowing," the slave master ordered. He paced the middle plank, holding the cat-o-nine tails at the ready if anyone faltered.

Even I began to row.

"You look worried," LaFage puffed.

"I am."

"Why?"

I didn't answer. I glanced back every fourth row. The ship gained steadily, cutting through the water like a predator, never wavering even as it changed course to intercept us.

"You recognize it?"

"Yeah, I've heard of it."

"What is it?" Poor LaFage's voice cracked with fear.

The pursuing ship was twice our size. Not a dreadnaught or a Ship of the Line, but a cruiser with a blast marks on its hull from previous battles. Still, we were only a slave galley and no match for any military vessel. Especially not this one.

Sailors clambered in the rigging, and worse, boarding parties mustered along the railing for the inevitable attack and capture.

"They're not here to kill us," I said.

"What do they want? Flesh mongers?"

"No, they're here to save us."

"That's a good thing, isn't it?" LaFage said, unable to hide his confusion.

"Not for me."

The flesh mongers unbolted the locker near the bow of the ship and weapons were distributed while the slave master kept his whip ready, searching for signs of revolt. Their strategy was simple though destined to fail: the slave master would watch us while the rest of the crew would fend off the larger ship. I couldn't fault their logic. They knew if they were captured, they would probably be executed quickly. This gave them a chance, or so they thought.

Strategically we were at a severe disadvantage. Outnumbered, poorly positioned against the much larger cruiser, plus the flesh mongers had to fight with a boatload of angry slaves at their back.

The cruiser glided through the water. It was a vessel built for speed, a thin hull, streamlined upper deck, and a series of black sails. While we sailed under the power of slaves and a meagre single mast, the enemy ship used the full might of the wind.

As the ship closed to grappling-hook range, its scars became glaring. The ship's hull was battered and full of patches where enemy artillery had obviously struck home. The original name across the hull had been splashed with paint, making it unrecognizable. With deep red ink, they had written "War Hammer" in uneven letters.

When the ship pulled alongside us, LaFage shouted with joy. A whip fell against his back and his triumph turned to a squeal of pain.

"Another sound from you and you'll be finding my boot knife in your neck," the slave master promised.

The *War Hammer* was a legend among the seas. I had only heard of it from my days in ShadowDark. Years ago, that ship had belonged to the Havencastle navy. Or rather, the original *War Hammer* belonged to the Havencastle navy. For whatever reasons, the entire crew deserted, flying the black flag of piracy, and taking to the high seas for loot and plunder. Of course, if that rogue ship happened to attack the enemies of the Succession, that was strictly a coincidence.

Any smart rogue understood that the *War Hammer* still fought for Havencastle's glory, just not officially. Truthfully, I was hoping they weren't here to arrest me.

They pulled aside us and ropes and hooks arced between the ships as if a spider shooting a web. Flesh mongers rushed to cut the lines but they were at a numerical disadvantage. For every line cut, another two appeared.

Then came the arrows, a deadly hail that sent three of the flesh mongers tumbling into the rows with the slaves. Chains and shackles rattled as slaves attacked them. The slave master did his best, his whip rising and falling, trying to keep the captives in line. He was losing the battle.

I glanced back at the *Crooked Hand* assassin. He was gone. Where he should've been sitting was now only a set of empty shackles.

"Shyst," I cursed, ignoring the battle waging between the two ships. Where the hell was the assassin? "I need to get free from these shackles," I said.

"What about the lock-pick set I sold you?"

"I don't—"

The chain looped around my neck and tightened and I couldn't breathe. My eyes bulged. Damn, the *Crooked Hand* really was good. I hadn't heard him coming and LaFage obviously hadn't seen him coming.

The assassin had me at his mercy. From what I could tell, he was using his unlocked shackles to choke me to death. Probably used a hidden lock-pick set—the same type that I should've had hidden on me.

LaFage for his part couldn't assist. He tried but the leg irons gave him little room to manoeuvre, and besides, even when he attempted to rise, the *Crooked Hand* kicked him back down onto his seat.

With all that was going on, I doubted a slaver would come to my aid. I was on my own, which wasn't good. I remembered back to my first fight at Gardizael prison when I had used my opponent's extra-long ponytail to choke him. He couldn't get me off his back just as I couldn't get this assassin off mine. I reached back, tried to find purchase, to grab anything that might twist him away. He had perfect positioning.

By catching me by surprise, I only had a few moments before I'd black out. My vision distorted as the pressure behind my eyes built until I thought they'd burst. My lungs filled with liquid fire.

"Let me out."

I'd do anything to get a breath. I tried thrashing but I knew it was pointless. How many had done that to me when I had a loop of wire around their neck? Always thrashing, grasping, hoping for that one-in-a-million shot that somehow they'd gain even a lungful of air.

Not being able to breathe was a crushing weight. The chain tightened another link. The fighting became distant like recalling a dream—not quite real.

Anything for a breath.

Blackness overcame my vision but there was no peace in that darkness. The door in my head vibrated with such force that surely the hinges would splinter. Claws appeared in a crack of the door attempting to gain leverage.

"Let me out."

I'd do anything to survive. I'd proven that to myself countless times and this was no different. The conscious world faded so that I stood near the dark recesses of my soul, the place where the Dark was locked away. I reached with a trembling hand, and unlocked the door.

The Dark sprung free. It was cruel and merciless.

I huddled in that darkness, startling with each sound or flash of sight, just like a child on a stormy night. I tried to close my eyes against the visions, to pretend that it wasn't me that was brutally murdering the assassin. *It was the Dark,* I'd argue.

Another flash from the real world: the assassin's jaw broken and twisted from his skull, eyes bulging as my bloodied hands tore open his throat.

Then a slaver, face savaged as if beset by a wild animal. Not a wild animal. Me. I had done that.

Slaves cowering, the planking slick with blood and piss. The Dark killed them too.

A sword exploding through the neck of one of the invading crew. LaFage, sword aiming for his heart.

LaFage!

I pushed aside the blackness and behind that veil I saw it: the Dark. It was pure malevolence, an engorged tick that shuffled on stumps of bone. I grabbed its scaled tail, pulled myself from the abyss. It turned upon me, a face that smoked and spat like oil in a pan.

"You did this," it said.

We wrestled, our battle surely as great as the mythical battle between the Creators during the birth of the world.

"You use me, because it relinquishes you from guilt. But you're the murderer, not me. I am only a tool to fulfill that which you don't have the courage to do yourself. Coward."

I didn't know how long we battled. Hours? Days? Weeks? Finally, I hurtled it back into my abyss. The door slammed shut and the locks clicked into place.

I opened my eyes.

I held a scimitar in a reverse grip above LaFage, the point dripping blood onto his face. Drip, drip, drip. He was on his back, freed from the shackles but unmoving, mouth open, eyes wide.

I looked around. The scene had changed since I had released the Dark. The War Hammer was drifting away, the water full of frantic soldiers and slaves. Our ship was littered with the dead or wounded. I wondered, briefly, if I had done all of this. My eyes drifted over the mangled body of the *Crooked Hand* assassin and I knew the answer.

"Coward!"

"Nathaniel..." LaFage whispered. I glanced down at him.

"I...I..."

"You're mad." He was picking himself from the floor. The remaining slavers, though they were armed, kept their distance.

I expected LaFage to stutter something about the death and carnage, or that I had nearly plunged my blade into his heart. But he didn't. Instead, "Look what she's done to you, Nate."

"This wasn't her."

I saw from his expression he didn't believe me. Like a parent who just discovered their child playing with explosives for the first time.

"You go back there, you'll be walking into a trap."

"There's worse than death," I replied.

"And you'll find it there."

I fixed him with a serious stare. "You've never cared before, LaFage. Why do you care so much about me now?"

He paused, his eyes shifting across the bobbing bodies in the water. "Because of Cresek-Tawn."

"I won't let it win this time."

He smiled sadly. "It always wins."

The two ships continued to drift apart and as they did, LaFage's chance of escape diminished.

"You have a plan?" he asked.

"I always have a plan."

"A good one?"

I didn't answer. LaFage hesitated, as if considering staying. I made the decision for him, hefting him under the arms.

"You can't stay with me, LaFage."

I tossed him over board. As he fell, he screamed something about being unable to swim. He could thank me later.

I wondered if maybe the *War Hammer* would re-engage but I suspected from the amount of dead that they'd had their fill of death tonight. Besides, there wasn't much to gain by attacking us again. The flesh mongers were mostly dead or missing, and the slaves that remained here were like me in that they probably preferred being slaves rather than returning to the Succession. We were all running from something.

When I turned, I faced the slave master, brandishing an axe

with his right hand while his other hand clenched at a gaping wound in his side. In his condition, I could've easily disarmed him. Hell, if I stood there long enough, his blood loss would be enough to kill him.

"We're going to Cresek-Tawn," I said. "All of us. Now put down the blade or I'll stab you with it."

He dropped it with a shaking hand.

"Now get that wound stitched up. We're going to need help getting these bodies overboard."

The sharks would feast tonight.

I took my place on the benches and along with the few others, began to row. Flesh mongers and slave, we'd work together to get ourselves to the desert city. I stared off to the horizon, as if the night and the distance would part, revealing the spires of Cresek-Tawn.

CHAPTER NINE

THE INS AND OUTS (AND PITS) OF CRESEK-TAWN

We had disembarked from the slave galley three days ago in a small bay. There was no pier, only a rickety dock that wouldn't be able to hold the weight of our ship if the water became choppy.

A patrol from Cresek-Tawn greeted us. They didn't ask why our ship was nearly empty or covered in dried blood. They shackled us, as if that was necessary considering that we were here willingly.

We clambered for a half day over rocks and outcroppings until we reached the salt flats. That was when the sweltering heat of the desert struck us. The sun was nearly unbearable. How was it possible that I'd spent most of my life in this climate?

My skin had transformed from a red sunburn to the colour of leather. Luckily, my body had adjusted quickly to the sun, unlike the other slaves from the south. Their skin remained red and blistered. The flesh mongers gave them light cloths to shield them, and rubbing ointment for their burns.

Our footfalls crunched over the salt. The wind stirred up clouds of salt that stung the eyes and burned exposed wounds. The sun reflected off the ground like a mirror. Two men went blind on the first day. Guess their value in the slave market would drop significantly. Another dropped dead from dehydration.

Out on the flats, sometimes you didn't even know you were thirsty before it was too late.

At first, the city was only a line on the horizon. A troop of Cresek-Tawn warriors thundered past. Their passing exploded a plume of salt that enveloped us, my throat burning and further drying my mouth. My tongue searched for a bead of water along my lips.

The Cresek-Tawn warriors were one step above animals and more savage. They rode in packs of twelve with little armour to slow them down. They carried curved swords on their hips and hidden knives and daggers.

We were close now. I saw the spires of the city. They were a splash of colour against a lifeless terrain. Blood reds, purples, blues. The towers were of various heights. Unlike the buildings of the south, these weren't straight and true. The scene resembled a watercolour painting smudged by the artist's palm. The spires were bent and crooked, rising at minor slopes, then twisting off at another angle. They were built from hardened clay and dust—a single rainstorm would cause havoc with the stability but there hadn't been a major rainfall in two lifetimes.

We stopped again, the flesh mongers handing out the last of the water rations. I took several mouthfuls then handed the canteen to the next person in line.

"Welcome to your new home," the slave master announced. They pushed us forward.

We approached the walls at nightfall. Unlike the spires, they were not built with aesthetics in mind. They were constructed to keep the barbarian hordes out. The walls were non-uniform stone blocks that had been excavated from miles away. In the Succession, this wall wouldn't have stopped even an ill-equipped army. But out here, the wall was nearly insurmountable to the small bands of raiders roaming the salt flats who wouldn't have had the resources for a battering ram, bores, or siege forts.

Despite the heat, a coldness took refuge in my core, increasing in intensity with each step toward the open gates. It felt like a lifetime since I had lain eyes upon this place.

"We spilled so much blood here. Imagine if all our victims rose from the graves to seek vengeance—a vast army of the innocent, the meek, sinners, and saints."

That dark door in my head seemed so much thinner and less resilient here. In Havencastle I imagined it as an iron-banded heavy oak door. Here it appeared warped and splintered, the locks rusted.

How much longer do I want to keep it closed? I shivered at my thought. Was that why I had come here? For a bloody revenge? Did I even care about Jane or Black Swan anymore?

I turned my attention to the top of the walls. A warrior stared lazily down at us, his javelin held at the ready. I knew what the gate guards could do with a javelin so I was a good slave, keeping pace with the chain gang.

Despite being in one of the most inhospitable places in the world, Cresek-Tawn was a thriving city. Pedestrians crammed the streets, their skin concealed by layers of silks and robes. In the coolness of double basements, spiders and caterpillars spun silks that seamstresses transformed into the multi-coloured robes. Others used sun parasols, usually carried by a slave. Maybe I'll be lucky and have a job like that. Joshua didn't bring me here to carry an umbrella.

Much had changed since I'd been gone. The city was like a cancerous growth—buildings grew atop each other, a sprawl with no design. Streets would suddenly end, blocked by recent construction. The heart of the city was the fountains. They were the source of water, and therefore the source of life. The origins of the water was a mystery. The Lifers said it was a gift from the Lord of Sustenance and Fertility. The Doomsdayers preached that this was the life well from the Bringer of Conflict—a tear drop from heaven.

The two sides were at constant strife, which supported the claims that it was the Bringer of Conflict who placed the never-ending fountain in the salt flats. The two opposing belief systems didn't even break down clan or family lines. Brothers became enemies, allies became rivals. Cresek-Tawn was a bizarre place and yet it all seemed perfectly normal when I was part of the system. Regardless of the truth, without that fountain and the connected aqueducts, Cresek-Tawn would dry up and blow away within a month.

We trudged through the streets. Not everything was unfamiliar. Some of the structures, though altered through time, remained similar enough for me to recognize. My gaze dared not stray too far lest unwanted memories awaken before their time.

I couldn't hide from the smells, though. The scent was unique to the Cresek-Tawn. Spices too harsh for southerners were in common abundance, hanging from street stalls and drifting from cooking pots. The pungent smell of human odour somehow penetrated the pleasant smell of spice. Cleanliness was considered letting the salt and dust blast away at your skin for an hour. Showers and baths were luxuries beyond all but the richest of nobles. And of course, there were the beasts of burden. Asses, horses, and the infernal camels.

The crowd was dizzying. They shouted at each other in the harsh tongue of Cresek-Tawn. Syllables and words stolen from other languages and combined into their own.

A boy ran to us, painfully thin, his clothing mere tatters. He held a glass of murky water in his hands.

"Five coins. Real deal. Cheapie, cheapie, almost free," he declared in the common tongue. Our escorts snapped their whip in his direction.

"Get out of here, vermin."

The streets were uneven and cracked, constructed of fire-hardened bricks. A stream of sludge flowed through the make-shift gutters; Cresek-Tawn's version of sewage disposal.

Smoke and ash blasted into the sky from the iron-works, the lone smelting shop, the sulphur further thickening the air. From within came the clanging of hammers on cooling metal. Most of the metal would be shaped into weaponry. Iron was in short supply yet demand for weapons was high. After the weapons, little iron reached the market.

Cresek-Tawn almost overwhelmed me. Breath did not come easily, as if someone held a great weight on my chest. I squeezed my eyes shut. I was falling. On my knees, gasping for breath.

Hands were upon me, pulling me up. Water doused my lips, the flesh mongers thinking I was dehydrated. I drank greedily, as if the warm liquid might somehow save me from my misery. The water washed over the salty film on my tongue, cleaning my teeth of the layers of dust. The taste was so familiar. A taste that only those who had visited the salt flats would understand.

"You're almost there," the slaver said. He was concerned that I might not be ready for market. Oddly, his words reassured me, as if grounding me in the present.

Perhaps, if shackles didn't hold me in place, I might've turned and fled, never glancing back at Cresek-Tawn. That wasn't part of the plan, however. My mission here was to fix the past. Or was it revenge? Or was it to find Jane? I wasn't sure anymore.

Without warning, the chain pulled at me. I nearly lost my balance, my head and shoulders yanked forward.

They marched us through Cresek-Tawn. Finally gaining the courage to look around, to really look, I did with cautious glances, as if staring at a secret lover across a crowded room. I searched the faces of the crowd, as if Jane or Joshua might casually walk by. As if it would ever be that easy.

A cart toppled before us, its wheel shattered. Beets and gourds rolled across the street and an excited crush of people rushed forward to steal what they could. The merchant tried desperately to chase them away while retrieving his wares but he was overwhelmed. Urchins scooped them into their hands like balls and ran to the alleys. Pedestrians kicked the gourds further away so that they could retrieve them later.

"Get away from there!" the merchant bellowed at the crowd. He hastened to retrieve them, but for every one he recovered, four others disappeared in bags and the folds of clothing. "I'll have each one of you executed," he threatened.

We were jostled by the excitement. The flesh mongers tried to keep the crowd at bay but they were simply outnumbered. A thief bumped into me, his arms full of beets. The thief dropped his load and created another blast of confusion.

"Get away from them," a slaver ordered, using the butt of his whip to push the thief away. A whip cracked twice and the crowd fled.

The chain was jerked and we were forced onward. I wondered if the beets were a diversion, if this was merely the beginning of something larger and more elaborate. Perhaps someone was planning to rescue me? I searched the crowd, searching for signs that we were being followed. Sadly, there were no daring escape plans. Of course it seemed foolish that I was projecting a simple beet theft into an escape plan. But nothing in Cresek-Tawn was ever simple. If there was one thing I learned in this infernal city, it was to trust first instincts.

"Is that all you learned here? Trust first instincts? You learned how to kill a man with your bare hands. You learned how to choke them silently so it would appear like an accident. You learned how to poison a café. You learned how to use children as disposable diversions."

The chain gang abruptly stopped when we reached the bazaar, the square barely recognizable from my last visit. The other slaves were unfastened from the shackles then marched through the bazaar and past the prospective owners. I didn't hold out my hands to be unfastened. I had a terrible suspicion of where I was going to be taken.

I anticipated my stay in Cresek-Tawn would be short lived— two days tops. By then, according to my non-existent plans, I'd have found Jane, recovered Black Swan, and killed Joshua. Yup, two days should about do it.

They marched me further and my dread grew. The flesh mongers must've assumed that I'd be desperate—five armed men escorted me.

"We'll shoot you dead if you try anything," the slaver whispered in my ear, his crossbow at my back. My death would be a huge hindrance to my mission. That was no good.

Then I saw it. Of all the structures in Cresek-Tawn, the dungeons of Gardizael alone appeared unchanged. Two great bastions were joined by a main stone building. Three smoke stacks spewed a rain of fine grey dust. That dust was all that remained of the victims of Gardizael.

My legs felt like rubber, each step worse than the last and I felt like I was carrying Creed on my back. Gardizael was a most vile and dread place where some of the greatest torture masters practiced and learned their trade. Back before the Genocide Wars, the Crucifiers used to send their students here for tutelage.

Finally, we stopped and I presented my wrist irons to have them unlocked. The heavy crossbow was pointed at my back while one of the slavers began to unfasten my shackles. Doubt clouded my judgment. I calculated the odds of escape. *Twirl, grab the first slaver, use his body as a shield against the crossbow, steal a weapon, and fight the remaining men, one of whom would be trying to reload the crossbow.* The odds were not good. I had to quell my fear and follow along the path before me.

"Do you know what they'll do to you in there?" the slave master sneered.

"You can go to hell." I expected a blow to the back of the head or even a shot to the knees. Nothing.

The six of us stood there, watching Gardizael, waiting for something to happen. No one walked the walls and I saw no one at the towers. We stood for so long that the combination of fear, fatigue, and dehydration made the world begin to spin.

With a thud of hidden counterweights falling somewhere in those walls, the gates of the Dungeons of Gardizael ground open, the contrasting darkness of the prison appearing like the maw to Hell.

"Shyst." This was Cresek-Tawn and I had willingly returned to my nightmare.

∞

The Keepers of Gardizael wore masks of hardened clay, more for concealing their identity rather than protection. They carried spear-like weapons, the heads ending with a slightly curved blade. Perfect for reaching through the cell bars and either prodding or slicing a prisoner depending on the need. Around their waists flowed purple sashes.

Their eyes were expressionless as I was led deeper into the prison. They pushed me into an empty cell with a metal grate at the ceiling. Sand and dust filtered from people above me. The door slammed shut and locks clicked into place. Despite myself, I startled at that sound, anxiety swelling within me.

My first instinct was to circle that room and search for weaknesses. But I knew there would be none. Back when I was a fallen prince, I had spent weeks and months scouring a cell just like this one to find a means of escape. I found nothing, of course. There was no escape from Gardizael.

The cell was small but had enough room for a stone slab that I guessed was my bed. The grate in the ceiling was small but allowed torchlight to flicker through with, along with the footfalls of the occasional keeper walking overhead. I would not see the outside world while I was here. A jolt of panic hit me at that thought, that I might never see the sun again.

I lay down and closed my eyes, hoping that I could find calm. I couldn't. I figured Joshua would let me rot in here for a few months at least, enough to break my will.

I had learned much about killing in Gardizael. I used to fight weekly, and became feared throughout the populace. I wasn't big, but I was fast and relentless. Of course, that was years ago.

Back then, I was fuelled by hatred and an overwhelming desire to survive. Those were hard days when I fought for everything. Fought over scraps of food, fought for a section of floor to sleep on, and fought to keep myself alive.

Gardizael was a prison but it wasn't like the jails of the Succession. In the Succession, the prisons were overseen by the rulers and the judges that held at least the pretence that they were bastions of justice . The prisons were places for the guilty, or at least a form of punishment: murderers, rapists, thieves. They weren't pleasant places, mind you. Unless you were skilled at navigating the internal politics, or very lucky, chances were you'd be beaten, raped, maybe killed.

Gardizael, however, was different. It was a prison, but prisoners weren't necessarily wrong doers. Half the populace wasn't sure why they had been incarcerated. The charges against you were never announced, and you never saw a magistrate, judge, or official for a chance to proclaim your innocence against these unknown charges. Instead, you could be forcibly pulled from your home in the middle of the night and thrown into a pit, sometimes never to be released.

I had forgotten the sounds of the prison. The screaming, the lonely wails. In-between those were the oppressive silences. Someone was singing, an off-key version of *Bring Her Back Around*. It was a terrible rendition except I listened to the words, wondering if my fate would be the same: lost and forgotten forever. The song ended abruptly and the silence returned.

Food was pushed through a slot at the bottom of the door. I didn't bother trying to catch the person distributing the slop onto my tray—that was a fool's game, one that I had played years ago. I tried to reason whether I was being a realist, or whether I had already surrendered to Gardizael in the first few hours. Shouldn't I have been trying to escape? To do something?

I had to have confidence that Joshua had a plan for me, that he hadn't tossed me into the darkness to be forgotten forever.

After only a few hours, I felt panic began to needle me. What if I had miscalculated? What if this was all that I was destined for? Did I really think that it would take months to break me? At this rate, I would be broken within three days. How long until I contemplated taking my own life?

I paced my cell, searching for some weakness that might lead to my escape. I still knew it was useless, but I had to do something.

My door opened and I shielded my eyes against the brilliance of the corridor.

A man stooped to avoid the low arch. I recognized him as my old trainer. Time hadn't been kind to him. He was greyer, more wrinkled, and hunched. His face had always looked odd, as if his eyes were maybe too far apart, and combined with a ridiculous overbite. Despite his strange appearance, the man knew how to fight.

More than anything, I wanted to rush and hug him, not because I missed him, but because after a few hours, I had already begun to wonder if I'd ever see another human face. Guess prison wasn't really my thing anymore.

"It's been a long time, Puck," I said. I had never known whether Puck was an inmate, or if he was brought in purposefully to train us. All I knew about the man was his name.

He didn't share my enthusiasm at our reunion. He grunted something, then said, "You know what tonight is?"

"I've been locked in here for days—"

"Hours," he corrected. "You've been in here for hours. It's Saturday night."

My stomach lurched. Saturday night meant one thing. Saturday Night Fights. Joshua brought me back here...to fight?

I realized Puck was talking. "...I want you to use your speed to your advantage. Come around from the side. Remember to keep your guard up."

"Shyst," I mumbled. A true man could always see the good in a bad situation. I tried to see the good. I was fighting a warrior who would be battle-hardened, with super stamina, and heightened fighting skills. There was no way to compete with someone like that in a fair fight. So a little cheating would be the strategy. I needed the Master of Randomness to help me out of this mess.

"Who am I fighting?" I asked weakly.

"Barbarian from the wastes. Just like old times. He's good, but not as good as you were." He said it with pride, like I could somehow revisit my glory days.

Puck set to work on me with the wax, spreading it across my shoulders, face, and neck. His nearly crippled hands felt like brittle sticks on my skin. The years of fighting had been hard on him, too.

"Any chance you could help me get out of here?" I asked him.

"Why would I go and do something like that?"

"Maybe for old times."

"You never would've made it out of this place alive if it hadn't been for me. Remember when Joshua bought you? You never came back for me. You left me to rot."

He had me there. I could've argued that he was a prisoner like everyone else and I had no control over his release, but that wasn't true—I could've had him released easily. I'd never really considered Puck doing anything but being a trainer. I guess I assumed this was all free choice for him, which was a stupid thought.

"I'm rich," I lied.

"Maybe yesterday you were rich. Today you're just another fighter."

"Is my opponent any good?" I asked.

"Good, but not as good as you were. Have you been keeping up your training?"

"Fighting in the pits isn't a hobby of mine, old man."

The door opened and several prisoners were there to escort me out.

He led me through the small door. Crossbows kept me honest as we entered the hall. Puck didn't comment on the heavy security. He led me down the narrow clay hallway, prisoners behind and in front of me. Like my past days, there were no signs of the Keepers. They always made themselves scarce when it came to fight nights.

If it had been any other city, I probably would've attempted a daring escape. But not here in Cresek-Tawn. One of the prisoners grunted and shoved me. I was led into an arched antechamber, the ceiling rounded and low so we had to duck our heads. Spider webs of cracks marred the surface. The air smelled of fungus, sweat, and blood. Another unforgettable odour that had been burned into my memories.

This didn't make sense. Why would Joshua bring me all the way here to kill me in the pits? I sniffed. Maybe Joshua didn't respect me like he used to.

"They've been waiting weeks for you to return, Nathaniel."

Weeks? Joshua always played the long game, his plans set sometimes years in advance. Sometimes with Joshua it was like he was a deity—I thought I was expressing my free will when in fact it had been preordained all along. Puck led me over to a stone table and I sat at the edge. He, along with two assistants, prepared me for the fight. They wrapped my knuckles with heavy rope, searched me for foreign weapons, and gave me another quick massage to help loosen my muscles. That killer instinct was nowhere to be found. I had better find it again, and soon.

"You're a legend here. Your records still stand, you know that, don't you?"

"My records?"

"Most kills, fastest victories, most kills in one night."

Well, at least I had records. They were important, weren't they?

"You've lost a lot of muscle since you've been gone," the trainer assessed. "I hope your reflexes haven't deteriorated as much. Otherwise, you won't last a moment."

"Thanks for the confidence."

The door opened and a man wearing a garish outfit entered: red tights, a flowing purple gown, and a gold scarf wrapped around his neck.

"It's almost time," the man announced, then quickly retreated.

"Who's that?" I asked Puck.

"Announcer."

"There's an announcer now?"

"Fights are big business."

My escorts kept a close eye on me, as if this might be the time for me to act. And it would've been too, if there were some form of plan.

I left the table, shaking my arms and shoulders as if they were rubber. Puck followed closely yapping in my ear about strategy and tactics but I wasn't listening. There were other, more important issues.

Like how I was going to live through this. I kept my muscles loose, bouncing slightly on my feet as we walked. How many times had I walked this route? Fifty? One hundred? Nearly impossible to recount. This would be my last time—win or lose.

Which brought me again to the puzzling question: if I were such an important part of Joshua's plan, so important he risked bringing me across the continent, why would he send me into the pits to my doom? If he had wanted me dead, then he would've killed me back in Havencastle. The more the ideas played in my mind, the more I realized there wasn't going to be a fight. Something was going to happen. But what?

They pushed me through the archway and I felt overwhelmed by the screaming and yelling. The balconies were crowded with both prisoners and the wealthy. Looked like Saturday Night Fights had gone legit. Land owners, politicians, clan leaders stood shoulder to shoulder with murderers and rapists. Despite the differences in social standing, they all wanted blood.

"The Master of Randomness can stick it up her arse," I said. There was going to be no last minute reprieve. I was going to die.

RYAN T. MCFADDEN

"Since when do you worship anyone but yourself?" Puck asked, unable to hide his amusement.

"The Master of Randomness helped me out of a few scrapes. I thought maybe she was on my side but now I realize this was all a joke and this is the punch line."

The mess hall had been converted into a combat arena, the tables turned on their sides and propped near the walls, prisoners standing with shields around the room, ready to shove an unwilling combatant back into the fray.

When I spotted my opponent, my stomach twisted on itself. He was twice my size, rippling muscles glistening with oil. His skin was dark from years of working in the sun, perhaps from one of the slave farms on the islands. He wore a bone mask painted like the maw of a terrible horned devil—red skin, jutting cheekbones, rows of razor sharp teeth. Real cute. Guess the fights weren't exciting enough anymore and we had to add props to the mix. I wished I would've had a mask. Something with knives or horns so I could use it to gouge his eyes.

He flexed his arms, chest, back, stomach, and legs and I couldn't help but roll my eyes. Yes, I got it—he was a scary bastard. Remember when the fights used to be about fighting and not just theatre? How I longed for the good old days.

His appearance caused me to evaluate myself. I was lean and lithe, my scars displaying my history in the pits. But my scrawny appearance must've looked downright pathetic next to him. What happened to small, quick opponents that had become all the rage during my time?

Okay, okay, no need to panic. My speed would be my weapon of choice. But where the hell was the killer instinct? Speed didn't matter if there was no instinct. He would grind me up. What if I had returned all this way back here to die?

I had been in tight situations before. This was nothing new. Sure, under their rules, victory was impossible. So change the rules. My gaze scanned the prison.

231

The announcer walked into the center of the fighting area and the crowd's shouting subsided. He stared over at me, then at my opponent. I didn't have long to figure out an escape plan. Hopefully it would be a long series of introductions.

"Begin," he said, and stepped back. The Master of Randomness seemed determined to kick me in the jewels. What kind of an introduction was that?

When I didn't step forward, hands pushed me roughly. Instead of a graceful entrance, I stumbled and fell. I glanced back at the offending people. Puck shook his head in embarrassment.

"You might want to get up," he said.

He had a point. The brute of a man approached me. Now was time to get inside my opponent's head. Surely he was as terrified as me, after all, he was the one fighting a legend, not me. My chest puffed out and I flexed my shoulders and arms, trying to look as menacing as possible.

There were a few cheers and catcalls so I wasn't sure if my display had the desired effect. This guy would pulverize me. A good, old-fashioned beating with my brains smeared across the floors. Unless of course I did the unexpected. I had a plan. I wouldn't let him catch me. It was hardly perfect. In fact, it was downright idiotic but it was all I had. When he neared me, I simply scurried beyond the reach of his calloused fists. He roared something at me, his arms outstretched and flexed. The dull roar of the crowd garbled his words, but they were probably promises to rend me limb from limb. Those kinds of promises weren't good for morale.

Back pedaling, I planned to keep out of reach, watching for signs of weaknesses. His movements were marvellous. So much muscle yet able to move with agility. In a fair fight, he would definitely beat me to death. I lasted this way for a minute, which didn't really matter because there wasn't a time limit on these fights.

As I attempted to slide sideways, a shield knocked me forward. Guess they wanted a fight, not a jogging match. I had no choice—I'd have to fight him.

I glanced at the crowd, at the wealthy and the privileged. If there was a time to release the Dark, maybe now was it. Let the demon inside of me free. Let it wash away the powerful and damn the consequences. Who here didn't deserve to die? Maybe I'd be doing the world a favour, trying to wipe the ruling elite from this world.

"Yes, their deaths would be a blessing. You'd be a hero," the Dark told me.

Then I saw her. Her appearance had the same effect on me now as it did in Havencastle. Jane stood near the front of the second balcony. For the past two months, I had tried to convince myself that I pursued one thing: Black Swan. And if Jane happened to get in my way, I'd kill her like I'd killed Sam Hurst. That drive had pushed me through the filth of Havencastle, and the morbidity of humanity.

Beside her stood Joshua.

Joshua gave a tiny salute and a hint of a smile. Perhaps LaFage had been right. Perhaps she had been leading me back to Cresek-Town to torment me. She had betrayed me.

"It's time to wash away this city. Kill them all. Kill her."

"Yes," I hissed, and I prepared to release the Dark.

My gaze switched back to her and I saw her concern. That was all it took to for the doubt to delay the Dark's release. Maybe this was another facet of Joshua's increasingly obtuse plan?

"Doesn't matter. Kill them all."

It was a punch in the gut. No wait. It really was a punch in the gut. The devil hammered me like a horse's kick. I had been punched, many times, but this was one of the hardest I remembered, right up there with Creed. Before I worried about it too much, he followed up with a blow to my jaw. My vision exploded, my balance suddenly backwards. Up was down. Crunched into the ground, my lungs deflating with the impact.

The twilight between sleep and consciousness held me. Jane was with me in the haze. We made love in our nest atop the

Ordeum. Our bodies moved together and we climaxed together. But rather than falling into a quiet rest, Jane was laughing, harsh and cruel. "You are a fool," she sneered. "You are nothing to me."

The roar of the crowd somehow brought me from the edge of unconsciousness and I was thankful that it pulled me away from Jane's taunting. I opened my eyes. The crowd wasn't cheering. They were booing. Two punches and I had gone down like a sack of potatoes.

Finally, the fight had begun in earnest. Move or die. Those were my two options. Except my jaw hurt and my lungs couldn't draw breath. Oddly, my opponent circled as if allowing me time to recover. Maybe he wanted to play with me for a while.

I gained my feet and tried to compensate for my wonky balance. I tried to mimic a dislocated shoulder to hopefully draw him to my right side.

"Why would you do that when all you have to do is open the door?" the Dark asked.

He feinted to his left then launched his attack. He came right into my clutches. I dropped low and launched myself at him feet first. My heels exploded into his midsection, his grunt a mixture of surprise and anger. The demon-man toppled backwards.

Now the crowd roared its approval and despite myself, I felt the surge of excitement that I hadn't felt since, well, the last time I was here. Blood washed over my tongue. The tooth I had cracked back at the Citadel had fully disintegrated with his punch. Impressive.

The devil whirled to his feet, realizing that he had a fight on his hands. No longer would my simple tactics fool him. He kept his guard up, forcing me to dance in, hoping to enrage him. We exchanged punches and kicks, but every time I went for a clinch, he stepped back.

The crowd loved it and we both fed off it. We went toe to toe.

One of my punches cruised through his defences, connecting solidly with demon mask. The bone cracked, the bottom corner shattering. First blood on my part. His mouth moved but the crowd drowned out his words. This wasn't the time for a speech. Some fighters always wanted to yap instead of fighting.

The heat of the prison worked against me. I was accustomed to the climate of Havencastle, not Cresek-Tawn, and I began to tire under the sweltering temperatures of Gardizael. The heat felt like lead weights strapped around my shoulders, constricting my breathing.

I tried glancing in Jane's direction but she was gone. I was alone.

The fight wore on. My cheek swelled, as if a mouse had burrowed under the skin. My eye was only a slit from the swelling. His mask hung oddly on his face from my many strikes.

Still, I could do the calculations easily—unless my tactics changed, the final result was inevitable. He was stronger, faster, and more brutal. While it was a good fight, the outcome was becoming predictable; he would be victorious. We circled each other. I need an escape as this fight could not be won.

I punched again and he did the unexpected, tackling me. My weary legs collapsed. He was going for the kill.

His great bulk pressed down, threatening to suffocate me while his hands circled my throat. Soon, he'd squeeze away my life.

Then he rolled off me as if he had been pushed. Which he hadn't. Regardless, freedom was going to be mine. Somehow, I teetered to my feet.

He came at me again. Jab, jab, cross. Darkness flickered through my consciousness like a flash of lightning.

Another clinch.

We were in the wrestlers stance, my head buried in his shoulder.

As I've said before, crowds behave like living creatures. You can read them like any other animal as they display fear, rage, and excitement. The crowd had changed again. There was fear now. They were afraid. Why?

Confusion rippled through the ranks. I smiled wryly. The Master of Randomness, that crazy bitch, had decided to change the rules again because there really was no other explanation. Because there was Creed, the ugly bobber, pounding his way through the third floor balcony. He tossed prisoners aside, threw a few rich folk over the balcony and they crashed in our fighting arena with a crunch.

Creed was heading toward Joshua and I felt two things: jubilation, because Creed would kill Joshua; and jealousy, because I wanted to be the one to squeeze his life away.

Divine intervention then. Silently, I forgave Creed for trying to kick open my skull in Havencastle.

Joshua watched slack jawed. I had only seen that reaction once. And it was now. Whatever plans Joshua had, they were forfeit as Creed entered the arena. He was the fly in the ointment. He was the wrench in the gears. He was my saviour.

The Keepers rushed forward to stop Creed while the prisoners and spectators tried to retreat. It was a chaotic mess and yet Creed just smashed through it like a juggernaut from the myths of old. When Keepers did get close enough, the blades from their spears shattered as if striking stone. Those fleeing began trampling one another as they rushed for the exits.

Creed bashed attackers with arms as big as trunks, sending them flying into the pit.

"You know him?" my opponent asked, standing beside me calmly, as if we hadn't been trying to kill each other moments earlier.

"We go way back. Think you can raise me up? I have a score to settle."

My opponent considered, and I noticed his tongue playing with his back molars, appraisingly searching for broken teeth. Finally, he nodded. "We'll have to finish our fight another day." He slapped me on the back as if we had merely been playing a friendly game of coins.

"I wouldn't have it any other way. Were you taking it easy on me?" I asked.

He shrugged. "A little. Always fires up the crowd."

I sighed, slightly deflated. "Now get me up there."

He cupped his hands, giving my foot a makeshift stirrup. With amazing strength, the demon boosted me to the edge of the first balcony. I waited for a space to open then balanced on the railing and reached for the lip of the second balcony and worked my way to the top.

A Keeper thrust his spear into Creed's back. This one penetrated his hide but it didn't slow the brute. He turned, snapping the spear in two and crushed the Keeper's throat with a squeeze.

Neither the Keepers nor the crowd concerned me. Only Joshua. I hurdled frightened spectators, didn't bother helping the fallen to their feet—they had no mercy for me during the fight and now I showed none to them. Joshua was the priority.

Two Keepers escorted Joshua but they looked ridiculously over matched. Joshua scowled. For once, it seemed, one of his plans wasn't going smoothly.

A Keeper clawed at the crowd but he was swept away as if trying to resist an incoming tide. He went under the mass of bobbing heads and he never recovered. The other guard swung his spear wildly. No good. His spear shaft snapped and they overwhelmed him. He was swept towards an exit.

Fear and panic have a way of spreading through a crowd like a disease spreading through a body. Creed wasn't enough to elicit such a response, but when half the crowd was murderers and rapists, it didn't take much to incite a riot. The inmates rebelled, against the Keepers, against each other, and against anyone that they could vent their rage at. It was chaos.

I lost sight of Joshua and I wondered if he'd been overwhelmed. I pushed, gouged, spit, and kicked my way through.

There.

But no sign of Jane. She would have to wait. Get rid of Joshua while I had the chance. He didn't see me as he scrambled to escape. A calmness settled over me. There wasn't a joy or rush of excitement that finally I'd be able to destroy the man who ruined my life and poisoned my soul with the Dark. My heartbeat slowed and my vision sharpened. That special moment before I was going to murder someone. How long had I tried to lie to myself that I didn't love this feeling?

I launched myself, wanting to take him down.

Joshua, as always, seemed to be one step ahead like he had eyes in the back of his head. He sidestepped so I missed the mark, and landed beside him. Before I compensated, he kicked the side of my knee and my leg buckled.

"Do you know what today is, Nathaniel? This is Rominratu, the Night of Madness." Joshua's shirt was ripped and he was cut over his right ear but otherwise unharmed.

"You shouldn't have brought me back to Cresek-Tawn. You're playing with forces you can't control."

"I'm counting on it."

I attacked. I knew most of his moves and he knew all of mine. It was a flurry of strikes and counterstrikes, feints, slips, and weaves. When he gave me openings, I knew that he was trying to bait me. Unfortunately, I was already fatigued from my battle in the arena. I was tiring too quickly and he knew it. He overwhelmed me with elbows, knees, and fists. I crumbled against the rail. One last awkward, desperate attempt. I grabbed his shirt...and flung myself over the railing.

My clumsy move surprised him. While I plunged, he momentarily hung at the balcony, and then his balance abandoned him and we fell.

I struck first with a crunch.

When I opened my eyes, I realized I must've blacked out. The prison arena was empty except for Creed who crouched over me. At seeing my eyes flutter open, his massive hand latched around my throat. His hold was firm, as if just trying to let me know that he held my life in his hands. As if I didn't already know that.

He hefted me into his massive arms like I was livestock. I thought of resisting, but Creed seemed to be my best opportunity at getting out of Gardizael. Besides, there wasn't much I could do anyway. I was sore and exhausted. The floor was littered with broken bodies as if they had fallen from the sky. Which I guess they had.

Another fine day in Cresek-Tawn.

Creed seemed a decent enough fellow. Once he smashed his way from Gardizael, he found a relatively safe hiding spot in an alley and waited for me to recover before continuing with his plans, whether that be talking or pulverizing me into fertilizer.

Creed had moved quickly through the city, familiar with the layout while I couldn't pinpoint our location because the topography of the city had been altered so much. We were somewhat safe, however, as he dumped us into a hidden alleyway, an area hemmed in all four sides by the builders of the city. The only way in or out was to scale the walls. To make things even more private, it appeared there were no windows or doors facing into the alley. A perfect hiding spot.

Joshua knew I wasn't going to die in the pit. Did Creed fit into his schemes too? And Jane. Couldn't think about her. Not now. I had to think about survival and she only confused the situation. Made me forget my sense of direction. Made me do careless things—like coming back to Cresek-Tawn.

"How much do you love her?" Creed asked. Of all the questions he could've asked, that one surprised me. I blinked, mouth moving but unsure of how to answer. He repeated the question as if I hadn't heard him correctly, and I wasn't sure I had.

"I hate her," I said, trying to conjure all the venom I possibly could.

He laughed. "You can't even convince yourself!"

"She betrayed me."

Creed nodded knowingly, as if he had the answer. "I did not ask the question to mislead you or draw you into a game of wits. You love her. You crossed the Four Lands to find her. You risked your life, your limbs for a chance to be with her. So answer the question: how much do you love her?"

"I came for Black Swan," I said weakly.

"I can threaten to kill you. To break your bones and smash your body, but I know that it won't matter." Creed looked away. "I know how much you love Jane," Creed said. "My love's name was Aliénor and she made me whole. Several lifetimes ago, I made a terrible mistake— one that I regret every moment I am on this earth. Ironically, my mistake allows my time to never end. Now, I will rip apart heaven, earth, flesh, and bone to get her back. I know that you'll do the same for Jane. Black Swan is the instrument to make me whole again. It's the instrument to make you whole again."

My stomach did that terrible flip accompanied with the feeling that something was about to go terribly wrong. "I don't have it."

"You'll find it."

"What makes you think that I'd give it to you?" If Creed had gone through all that trouble to get me out of Gardizael, then surely he wouldn't kill me. I had a little bit of leverage—how much was another question.

"Because if you don't, I will kill her."

I stood quickly. "If you touch her—" He shoved me down.

He chuckled, cold and mirthless. "Your threats are empty. But I have no desire to harm her, not unless compelled. I followed her for several days when I arrived in Cresek-Tawn. I will use her as a tool to get what I want, just as she was the tool to steal Black Swan from me."

"It's just a sword," I said.

He smiled softly, a lopsided, friendly-looking grin for such a large man. Then something else I hadn't been expecting.

Calmness. Creed was a contradiction. His smile was without malice. His voice didn't match his brute size. He spoke softly as if he were only half his size.

"It is not a sword. It is a key."

"A key? What kind of key?"

"What a strange question. Keys open locks, of course."

"What doors?"

"Limitless doors. Doors to infinite realms."

"Right," I said though I didn't know what he was talking about. "So I bring you Black Swan, you open some door, and then all will be right in the world?"

"Your ignorance is impressive," he said. I didn't think he meant it as a compliment. "Black Swan isn't a sword," he said. "It can slay a man like any other steel. It can even cut down deities from heaven. It is so much more than that. It can bring me back Aliénor. And then I shall throw myself to my knees and beg her forgiveness. If she does not forgive me...I shall cast myself into an abyss of flame."

He was a little over the top but I understood the sentiment. His one good eye remained fixed upon me. His other was a white mass that appeared to look inward. "I used to be a king of kings. Over one hundred lifetimes ago. I had the world at my command. At my word, I could condemn a thousand men to death. At my word, a hundred virgins would throw themselves at my feet. And yet, it wasn't enough. It never felt enough." His words were slow and measured.

"From the Times Before?" I asked, intrigued. No one really knew about those days. There were the ruins, of course, and the rare technology that kingdoms still fought over. But all that really existed now were myths.

"In my pride..." I waited for him to continue. "In my pride I lost Aliénor. She was as beautiful as the dawn after a storm. She was all I really needed but..." He trailed off and I thought I saw a tear in his good eye.

"Why do you need me to get it back?"

"The Beast on the Throne watches," Creed whispered. "He is coming. I can feel it looking inside me, touching recesses in my soul. Places that are dark and lonely, that even I do not know. Like a...Hunger."

I blinked. Was he talking about what was inside of me? Did he have a version of it secreted away, or had he merged with his own devil to become the giant he was now?

"Time grows short," Creed said.

"You'll use it to destroy the devil?" Wasn't that what the Crucifiers had wanted?

"The Beast on the Throne cannot be vanquished by anyone."

"It's going to be difficult. There's Joshua, and the *Crooked Hand*, and the Crusader in Havencastle, and..."

He shifted forward in an attempt to intimidate. Very effective. "Worry about me first. I give you a day to bring me Black Swan or I'll kill the woman."

"What about true love and all that?"

"Love," he scoffed. "Is it not the greatest reason to murder and kill? Is it not reason to tear apart flesh?"

He had a point.

"You have one day to find it," he commanded.

"How will I know how to find you?"

"I will find you."

He turned, moving lithely for a fellow of such size, clambering up the wall as if born to climb.

The alley proved a perfect place to sit alone in contemplation. Perhaps that might not have been a good thing. I vacillated between thoughts of her betrayal, and the many nights above the Ordeum when the world seemed perfect. I couldn't determine which one was the truth and which one was the liar.

I summoned my courage, an easy task, and my strength, not so easy, and stood, breathing deeply the night air. My lungs drew in a breath of dust and salt. What a hateful place.

For being a man who prided himself on solving trouble, life sure was difficult. Jane had probably set me up, twice, and now Creed would soon be added to my list of mortal enemies.

The sword, my enemies, and all the plots didn't matter. Not anymore. This was about one thing. Jane. Long ago, we had developed a plan. We were going to leave Cresek-Tawn, leave behind the *Crooked Hand*, Joshua, the murder and mayhem, and all the curses thriving in this city. We'd never had a chance. I needed to talk to Jane and ask for honesty. Was this love or was it merely a ploy to get the sword? All I needed was the truth. She owed me that, didn't she? I sensed she was holding onto anger, but I also remembered her arms around me. There *were* feelings there. So just tell me: the sword or me? If she chose me, the plan was going to be the same as it was the night I thought I found her dead. We'd leave, together, and never look back. The rest of the world be damned.

"And if she picks Black Swan?"

"She'll pick me," I said unsurely. What if she didn't? I found that my fists were clenched and I looked at them as if they had betrayed me. Was that the answer? Would I try...to kill her?

"Slit her throat."

No more conjecture. I needed to find Jane. So there I went again, making more trouble for myself.

⚬⚬⚬

I looked like a gypsy after stealing clothing from a clothesline. That didn't mean it was clean. Washing clothes with water was considered a luxury so it was up to the wind and sand to somehow make everything fresh. So my clothes still had the stink of the previous owner.

But my new clothes kept me covered and protected. While they made me look like a Gypsy—which I wasn't—the limp was real, which added to the authenticity of my disguise. My body ached. That was a real pounding I had taken in Gardizael.

My face was swollen and both my wrists hurt, probably from punching the guy in the skull. My feet cramped from the boots which were two sizes too small. The shawl was more my size. I draped it over my shoulders, neck, and head, as is the custom. My lower body was swathed in a faded cloth wrap. The outfit wasn't as comfortable as my hats and boots, but it helped me blend with the natives.

Cresek-Tawn had become a new city since I'd last been here. New streets were built on top of old ones. Former roadways were now rubble. Of course, the patrols didn't make life easier. They were on alert and it wasn't only my escape that had made them nervous. Something else was in the air. I sensed a simmering anger: neighbours screaming at each other over imagined offenses; a merchant cutting down a thief with a razor slash across his throat. Signs of the ruling clan were sparse, as if they had retreated inward, fearful that their city was about to explode.

I'd lived through a Rominratu, I had helped destroy one clan and raise another up. I didn't wish to be around for another. Did I have a choice? Could I find Jane before the city erupted?

I needed to reach Phelps, Jane's old handler. I couldn't trust him, but I could trust that he would be out to hurt me the least. Flawed logic, perhaps, but the best I had right now.

I slid into a doorway to avoid a patrol passing me on the street. In my condition, I wouldn't stand a chance against six men. On a normal night, it could've at least been interesting. Tonight wasn't normal.

The path was difficult, but I reached my destination after ducking into alleys, sliding behind obstructions, and somehow staying inconspicuous. While the surroundings had changed, the estate itself was the same. It was a house that looked like it belonged to the Succession rather than Cresek-Tawn.

While Phelps was a native, he had spent much of his youth traveling across the Four Lands. Thus, he had developed some strange tastes while he was gone, some of those tastes too perverse even for Cresek-Tawn.

The front grounds were withering and dying. Phelps had tried, and failed, to have a grass lawn. Dead trees appeared frozen, their limbs clean except for a few stubborn leaves. Dust clouds followed my footsteps.

Hounds bayed from within the estate's fences, forceful and angry, upset that someone had entered their territory. They charged at me. Three large dogs. Short black fur rippled with every forceful stride they took. Only a few seconds of decision. I froze.

The dogs were on me. Easily over a hundred pounds of muscle and able to tear a man apart in a matter of moments. They dove for my face, tongues furiously working me over.

"Okay, okay, okay!" I tried saying forcefully. The hounds were glad to see me, even after all these years. I lowered myself to their level, rubbing their chins and ears, and when they rolled on their back, I rubbed their bellies too.

Jane had introduced me to these dogs when they were pups. And they remembered me. Attempting to push my way through them proved difficult. They wanted another pet and scratch.

The lock on the front door was ineffective. I few well-placed kicks and it fell uselessly from the hinge. Cheap craftsmanship. Mind you, the lock might not have kept me out, but the sound from shattering it alerted whoever was inside.

I swung the door open, the rusty springs wowing their annoyance. The place was falling apart.

Phelps greeted me, as I knew he would. He was in his wheelchair, a crossbow propped unsteadily against his dead arm.

"You won't live to reload that, Phelps. You know it and so do I."

"I knew you'd be coming. I heard about your escape." He barely finished his sentence before his body was wracked in a spasm of coughing so wet it sounded like he was drowning.

I easily sidetracked his aim and within two quick strides was at his chair. Phelps attempted to compensate but another round of coughing crippled him. I pulled the crossbow from him with little resistance. I gave Phelps some room, letting him gasp for air. In the meantime, I discharged the crossbow into a wall. Clumsy, heavy weapon. I tossed it into the corner.

Phelps gasped for breath. "I knew you'd be here right enough. Come to kill me?"

I spun the wheelchair around roughly, trying to shake him up. "Do you really think killing an old man like you is important to me?"

His wooden teeth were rotted and his breath stank. "You want Jane?"

I shoved his chair, spinning it across the floor until he slammed against the back wall.

"You always were a smart one, weren't you, Phelps? Were you smart when they castrated you?"

His smile didn't fade. Seems that when they slice important bits from you, a few words, no matter how well aimed, can't really cut anymore. Even in my glory days, I hadn't liked Phelps. He was a bad man. Corrupt, vile, despicable. Worse than an animal. And far more ruthless. So why was he different than me? Perspective, perhaps. I liked to think that I was driven by my own sense of honour and righteousness, that all the violence was a means to an end.

Phelps's former victims would've been pleased that time had not been kind to him. He was half a man years ago, and now he was even less. He must've been nearing his seventieth year though he looked older than that. His hair was gray, slicked back with too much grease. The colour matched his eyes. He had a salt and pepper three-day beard which couldn't cover his sunken cheeks and his liver spotted skin.

His lack of a left ear was from the days when he battled out in the wastes. He had more horrendous scars from his war years but they were all hidden beneath layers of clothing. Rumour had it that he took too much of a liking to the spoils of war. His own men had done it to him. They did some nasty stuff to him, stuff that left him half a man. Literally. Now he was rotting in a wheelchair.

Despite his torture, he had made a name in Cresek-Tawn. He handled all the free agents like Jane who didn't fight for the clans.

"You're going to tell me where Jane is?" The hounds were at the door, scratching to get inside.

Mucus dripped from his mouth. He wouldn't last another two months. Mind you, we'd gambled on him dying in the next two months since the day we'd met. "You came all this way for her?"

"You trying to antagonize me?"

He tried to chuckle but his laugh turned to more coughing. Breathing heavily, he looked at me. "Listen to my lungs. You already know I'm a dead man. Two, three more months. Then it's over. You took Jane away from me once. Maybe I want to keep her from you now."

"I never took Jane from you, Phelps."

He wheezed, his body slumped in his wheelchair. "How do you think this will end? That she's going to show up and rush back into your arms? That's not how it'll work and you know it."

"That's between us," I said weakly.

"What do you think you know about her? That she's been waiting for you? Weeping by the window since the day you left?" He spit a wad of bile next to his chair. "She didn't lose a night's sleep since you left."

I slapped him. I didn't even realize I had done it until I heard the sound and the red welt appeared on his cheek. He was shocked and blinked his surprise. He recovered before I did, however, and began to cackle.

"I guess I had that coming," he said. "Maybe I don't know where she is."

"She doesn't work for you anymore?"

My slap hadn't succeeded in removing that crooked smile from his face, and if anything, it had gotten stronger. "You know nothing. She's with the *Crooked Hand* now, Nate." He sat smiling. Wheezing. I wanted to kill him right there but he'd probably welcome death. I wouldn't do him that sort of favour. "She took your spot when you left," he continued. "As cold as they come. But you already know that."

I felt numb. The *Crooked Hand*. She had played me in Havencastle.

"If you get Jane back, are you leaving Cresek-Tawn?" he asked.

"Maybe." I didn't know whether I wanted to love her or to kill her, but that just meant that nothing had changed.

"But you know what? I'll make contact. Because it'll be especially sweet seeing her kill you."

"You're setting me up?"

"I don't need to set you up!" he shouted. Another display of his browned teeth. "You've done it all by yourself. I'll bring you Jane. Tomorrow. Now get out of my sight."

"If you double cross me..." I mumbled, turning to leave.

"Those threats make you feel better, boy? There's nothing you can do to me that hasn't already been done. I'll get the woman here. Then it can all play out."

I hated Phelps, but right now, he was my only option. I opened the front door and the hounds bounded inside. They didn't think about attacking. They licked my hands and tried to jump for my face. I pushed my way past. Phelps was in the middle of a coughing fit, gasping and hacking for another breath. He cleared his throat and spat, his phlegm splattering on the floor.

I had just been defeated by a cripple.

I needed a place to lay low. Maybe an alley to protect me from the winds. My muscles ached, my face felt like it was on fire, and my stomach rumbled. Shyst, I hated this city. The smell, the sounds, the taste in the air. I hated everything about this place. Perhaps, it would've been better for everyone if I would've died five years ago.

The hour was too late for the common folk, but too early for the tavern goers. Empty streets made me nervous—it made avoiding the constant patrols more difficult. My business needed to be completed here quickly. Half the town wanted my head on a platter. And I knew the Rominratu was coming. I sensed the simmering heat of it, like a pot about to boil over.

I decided to head to the relative safety of the rooftops. From there, I stole some prickly pears from a rooftop garden, and some meat drying over an exhaust pipe. I don't know what type of meat it was. It was sinewy and bitter but I choked it down. The pears, however, were juicy and ripe. I devoured even the core.

Having eaten my fill, I found an alcove on the rooftops, hunkered down, and prepared to wait out the night. Though exhausted, I figured I wouldn't be able to sleep, not as my mind was still trying to process the past few hours. I didn't even remember closing my eyes.

CHAPTER TEN
TRIP DOWN (ANGUISHED) MEMORY LANE

The heat of the sun woke me. I didn't want to get up but my clothes were sweat soaked, my stink merged with the stink from the original owner. The tiny overhang had been adequate for a while but the sun had shifted and now afforded me no protection.

My wounds and bruises were ripening. A quick inspection showed black and yellow marks along my chest, arms, and legs. My face must've been a mess. I touched my eye delicately and winced. While the swelling had receded, blood oozed from the nasty gash. And my joints throbbed.

Just another day in Cresek-Tawn.

My troubles were real and the situation was far from perfect. My trust rested now with Phelps. He could sell me to any of the groups who had a price on my head. And what if Jane did show? Would she try to kill me? She was the *Crooked Hand*.

"Maybe you'll try to kill her."

All my instincts screamed to leave Cresek-Tawn. Forget about her and Black Swan. I recalled what Creed had told me: "Is it not the greatest reason to murder and kill? Is it not reason to tear apart flesh?"

So here I was, broiling in the desert sun. I hadn't been this beat up since, well, the last time I had been in Cresek-Tawn.

I crawled from my overexposed shelter, smacking my lips. From the dryness of my tongue and cheeks, it felt like a pigeon had made a nest in my mouth. What a day, and it hadn't even involved booze. I figured I'd have to steal some more of those pears to help quench my thirst.

My descent was slow and deliberate as I was perched a good four stories above street level on buildings that weren't exactly marvels of engineering. A misplaced foot or a poor transfer of weight and a whole wall could simply crumble.

I made the final delicate step to the alley. On the street, the crush of people was stifling, yet their presence was a welcome one. They made it easy to merge into the collective and not be spotted by my pursuers, whether that be Creed, the *Crooked Hand*, or Joshua.

I wanted nothing more than to rip off my damp rags and shawl but the clothing afforded me camouflage, blending into the crowd; perhaps my one true advantage. My eyes shifted, on the lookout for an assassin's blade. Very quickly, I had gotten back into the swing of things here in Cresek-Tawn. Only one day of freedom and already everyone hunted me.

"Shyst!" someone cursed as I rammed into them with such force they dropped their basket of crafts. All they received was a brief nod of apology before stepping over them, many of the trinkets crunching under the crowd. His cussing was gradually swallowed by the thousand different conversations.

I fought my way against the currents in the crush. Then I was free, standing on the edge of the pedestrian thoroughfare. Phelps's street was abandoned as his was the only house—everyone knew better than to set up shop on his street.

Phelps's house squatted on aged supports, cracked tiles lining the bowed roof. The place would die the day Phelps's did. Then others would move in and claim this territory for their own. The history of Cresek-Tawn lasted only as long as someone's memory.

I slipped into the estate, walking slowly up the path to the house. This wasn't the time to be careless. I searched for signs of an ambush or trap, finding none. Clouds of dust blossomed in my wake. The place was dying.

The stairs cracked under my weight. I stood, listening. Where were the hounds? They should've heard my approach.

Still no sounds, the estate quiet. The situation didn't feel right.

The door squawked and I thought I'd see Phelps greeting me with a crossbow but he wasn't there.

"Phelps?" No reply. Another few steps. My heart missed a beat. Phelps's wheelchair was on its side, empty. No sign of the cripple. "Phelps?" Softer this time. My hand reached for my hand crossbow—came away empty. I cursed myself for not re-equipping.

The wheelchair was overturned, the wheel bent and the wooden spokes splintered. Despite my growing dread, I felt a brief spike of satisfaction with the thought that someone kicked him over. As I investigated the wheelchair, I saw further up the hallway. Phelps lay prone and unmoving, his good arm outstretched before him, his fingers spread as if he had been trying to crawl away. I smelled the blood. My eyes hadn't fully adjusted from the brilliance of outside, but I saw the dark outline of the puddle beneath Phelps.

Jane stepped out from a room down the hall. She was wiping her hands on a towel. "I told you to stay away, Nathaniel. Joshua is coming."

I didn't know whether to run to her, or from her. My mind was overwhelmed with the things I wanted to say or to scream. Instead, I asked, "You killed Phelps?"

"He set you up. He set *me* up. Phelps was working with Joshua. Please, you have to go now. They'll be here soon. You can't win against him, don't you get that? Nobody wins against him. Not you, not me, not Phelps. Joshua always wins."

"Not this time. This time we win."

"Look at your face. Look what they've done to you already."

"This will heal."

"Will it? The last time you talked like that, you left and never looked back. You ran with your tail between your legs."

"I didn't leave you, Jane. I told you: our last night together I came for you and...and...you were dead. I don't know how he did it, but you were dead. I saw you with my own eyes, touched you with my own hands. I didn't leave you."

I saw her indecision. "How can I believe that? All these years..."

"I wouldn't have left without you. I would've torn this city apart to find you." I sighed. "It doesn't have to be like this. We can create something new."

"There is nothing else," she whispered.

"This is a sick, twisted game that we don't have to play anymore."

"You think it's as simple as running away?"

"Yes," I said and she took a step back. "I know it's crazy but we were going to do it once. We can try again. I've seen life outside of this city. You've seen it too. This place," I said, sweeping my arm around me, "it isn't real. It's some demented dream. It's time for us to wake up."

"I am the *Crooked Hand*. This is my city," she declared.

"That's not who you are," I said.

"You don't know who I am," she spat.

"Then let me find out." I approached, slowly, and she didn't retreat. "I have nothing left to hide. I have nothing else I can give. I've lost Black Swan, I've lost you. I have nothing left. But no more games, just answer me: what happened between us in Havencastle—that was real, wasn't it?"

She considered for a moment so long that I thought she wouldn't answer. "I waited for you, you know. I kept thinking that you'd come back even though Alvaro told me that you were gone forever." She smiled sadly. "I behaved like a scorned princess from a child's fable, waiting for you to rescue me. You never did. You abandoned me, left me to rot in this city and my longing for you turned sour. I hated you. Why didn't you come back for me? Instead, I did what I've always done so well. You created me, Nathaniel. I never wanted to become the *Crooked Hand*. I wasn't like..." She caught herself before she could say my name. "Alvaro was there for me. Helped me navigate the pain..."

Now it was me who wanted to take a step back, her confession that there *had* been someone else hit me strongly. And it was Alvaro Megellin—Joshua's brother and the leader of the clan. I had never been close to him. Joshua had ensured that, perhaps worried that I'd be corrupted by his brother if I spent time in his presence. I didn't remember much about him, other than he was older than me by at least twenty years, though my memories on his physical appearance were untrustworthy as I had conflicting images of him. In some memories, he was my age. In others, he was far older. Like all lords, he had a streak of cruelty in his nature, but luckily for Cresek-Tawn, he was benevolent in comparison to Joshua's maliciousness.

Jane and Alvaro together—I was trying to process the strangeness of that relationship. I had been gone a long time, and in a rational way I suppose it made sense. Alvaro was powerful, perhaps the most powerful person in Cresek-Tawn. He had many things I didn't. Namely, he had a future. Something I hadn't possessed then, and I didn't really now.

Emotionally, I just wondered if it was another lie. Did they share nights like Jane and I had? Did she rest her head on his chest as they fell asleep, holding each other tightly? Did they steal kisses when no one was watching?

"But it was always you," she continued. "Instead I turned to the one thing I did best. I killed and murdered. You would've been proud, I suppose." I was trying to comprehend her words, still trying to digest her proclamation regarding Alvaro.

"And Havencastle?" I finally managed.

"I didn't lie to you. I intended to hurt you." She smiled sadly. "Then I saw your face that day in the square. You were so...happy to see me. Like you still cared for me."

I pulled her into me and kissed her. Hard. She grabbed me and for a moment, I thought we had a chance. Then she pushed me away. "We can't do this. You have to leave. I told you not to come back."

"I won't leave without you."

"It's not that simple," she shouted.

"I told you in Havencastle that I loved you. I've never stopped. I thought you were dead. I've relived your death nightly and then there you were, with a knife to my throat. I'm not leaving now. I left you once, I won't do it again."

"Do you think this is up to you? Tonight is the Rominratu. And Joshua is coming here now to kill you. I won't stop him. Do you understand?"

"I don't believe you."

She pushed me away. "There is no us, Nathaniel. There can't be. It'll be the end of both of both you and me."

"Then let it end us."

"I..."

I saw her gaze flick to the side and I felt a pinch at the back of my neck. I whirled.

The intruder was wrapped in tattered funeral gauze, face concealed and blades strapped to his forearms. While he looked like he had risen from a grave, he exhibited an impressive fluidity of motion. He was one of Joshua's so I suspected there were others like him already in the house.

But the fight was over before it began. I took my first step and my leg buckled. I imagined that someone had struck me from behind and the realization hit: Jane was behind me and she'd poisoned me.

"She's stabbed you in the back."

Except she hadn't. When I turned, she had retreated and

disappeared into the side room that I had seen her come out of earlier. When I turned to face the assassin, my other leg buckled too and I collapsed to my knees.

The assassin wasn't pouncing on the opportunity. Instead, I saw him push the slender tube back up his sleeve. *Blow gun.* He stood and watched as it felt like my body turned boneless and I slid to the floorboards. I tried to yell to Jane for help but instead I emitted a pathetic moan. The assailant craned his head to the side as if inspecting a specimen in an aquarium.

I was in a whole load of trouble. My muscles resisted my wishes and I lay on the floor, at his mercy. A second assassin stepped over me, crouched, and checked me for weapons and tossed my few blades to the side. Then he dragged me roughly down the hall, and up the stairs, my head banging on the treads.

With my body unresponsive, I only had a slender chance of survival: I had to think my way out of this mess. Or I needed Jane to save me. I wasn't sure if either was a possibility. I tried analyzing the poison from the dart gun. It had hit fast, complete paralysis, with retained consciousness. I was still breathing fine and none of my senses suffered. *A perfect poison to subdue someone while you torture them.* Perfect, that is, if my torturers didn't mind performing their art on a silent victim—like a musician, torturers preferred feedback from an audience. I was clinging to that hope.

At the top of the stairs, he dragged me down a hall then dumped me unceremoniously in a darkened room. I tasted grit in my mouth and smelled a dry rot but I was face down so I couldn't see the details. He walked so quietly that I was unsure whether he was with me or if he had left.

I tried not to focus on what Joshua planned to do to me. The man possessed no remorse or empathy. I had seen him slice apart his victims for a perceived slight, their torment lasting for days as they watched themselves being disassembled piece by piece and fed to the dogs. He'd do far worse to me.

The time stretched until it became agonizing. No matter how hard I strained, I couldn't control my body and while the rage and frustration grew until I thought I'd explode, I lay quietly on that dusty floor.

I heard arguing from further in the house and I thought I detected Jane's voice. If that was her idea of saving me— reasoning with Joshua—I was doomed. Maybe she hadn't been lying. Maybe she really couldn't save me.

I wasn't sure whether it was fifteen minutes or two hours, but I sensed I wasn't alone. A window shade was opened and light filled the room. Someone snatched a fistful of my hair and roughly tilted my head until I was staring into Joshua's face. He was smiling and he gave me a hard smack across my cheek.

"*I will kill him,*" the Dark promised, and if I believed that somehow the Dark could've overcome my incapacitation, perhaps I would've released it.

I took in as much detail as I could. We were in Phelps's attic, the room where the cripple had kept all his spoils of war. Chests full of valuables, walls covered in weapons taken from fallen enemies. His near priceless tapestries hung in tatters from years of neglect.

"Welcome home, Nathaniel. That was quite an act you pulled at the prison. I should always come to expect the unexpected with you."

Jane stepped into the room behind him, accompanied by one of the assassins.

Joshua glanced at her, then back to me. "Have you guessed what poison I've used on you? It's Sundarian Horn venom, the same one you used on Sam Hurst. Oh yes, I knew about that and your rise through the Syndicate in Havencastle. Except your dose isn't fatal, but enough to disconnect your nervous system for several hours."

He straightened and considered for several long moments. I tried to meet Jane's gaze but she wouldn't look at me. If she wouldn't look, then I was a condemned man. She was my only opportunity out of this mess.

"Jane has disappointed me," Joshua said. "She begged for the opportunity to retrieve Black Swan for me in Havencastle. She failed. Then I tasked her with controlling you while you were rampaging here. She failed at that."

The Dark was growing. It fed off my dread and fear. The Dark licked at my drops of panic and snaked tendrils around my heart. Felt the tightness in my chest.

"Let me free. I can save her."

He won't kill her, I thought.

"I'll wipe them away. Kill them all. You want to unleash me. You want me to solve this for you."

I did. I really did. But I had learned, from hard lessons, that the repercussions would be disastrous. That the payback would be too high—because it always was.

"They're going to kill her! Let me out!" Those malevolent eyes burned from inside me. I couldn't breathe. They wouldn't kill her. Not yet. They wanted something from me. But the Dark sensed my indecision, began to bang at the rusted locks. It was right there. I could let it out. Let it kill them all. If I released the Dark, it could kill her too. *But I can't move!*

"I should've killed her," Joshua continued. "Failure comes at a high price, but you must remember that." He toed me with his boot. "But Jane has offered me a bounty for you. A sizeable one. She's offered me...everything...to save you. All her resources, all her power. Weeks ago she begged me to send her so she could rip out your heart. And now she begs me to save you. She's amassed a sizeable fortune since she's ruled the *Crooked Hand*. All for you—a broken man." He chuckled to himself, then motioned to Jane. "He's all yours."

She took a tentative step to me.

It happened so easily and quickly. A knife dropped from his sleeve into his arm. I saw it too late but I couldn't have done anything to prevent it anyway. Without ceremony, he pulled the edge across Jane's throat, opening her neck from ear to ear. There was a splash of bright red blood and her eyes widened.

I could do nothing, and I did nothing.

"*Let me out!*" the Dark screamed.

Jane was trying to say something but couldn't because she was choking on her blood. I felt warmth on my cheek and I knew that was her life splattering on the floor. Her feet slid from beneath her. She landed close to me, her vacant eyes staring into mine, her mouth moved as if she was trying to speak but she was already dead. Her face so white, so pale. And her throat…

I tried to call forth the Dark but for the first time in years, there was only a silence there now. An empty hole. Gone. I had been abandoned. Wait, no, I could sense it still there. The seed of hatred and anger. And something else now. Confusion? The Dark, as confused and as lost as me.

Joshua kicked me in the side of my head. Blackness rolled across my vision. Punches fell across my body, landing on my midsection, my shoulders, and my head. I didn't care.

Then he spat on Jane's corpse and motioned to the assassin who pulled the blowgun from the gauze, loaded it with a dart, aimed, and shot me in the cheek.

I swore I would rip their spines from their bodies paint the walls with their blood. Except the poison from the dart hit me hard and fast. Perhaps a lethal dose. I stared at her and managed one small moment of futile resistance.

"Jane," I whispered. Then the world went black.

⁓

"*I have to go.*"

She moaned her displeasure. "No. Not tonight. Stay with me."

"*I'd give anything to stay here.*"

The smell of her was intoxicating. Despite himself, he smiled. Their afternoon lovemaking had been memorable. But every moment with her he considered memorable. Gone were the days when he had to contact her through Phelps. She trusted Nathaniel enough to give him the location of her home. He spent every possible moment with her, in her arms. Now it was twilight, and Nathaniel had a job to do.

She pulled him into her chest and momentarily he considered staying. But if he stayed, then they'd probably both die. Their affair was forbidden. If Joshua discovered their secret trysts, he'd have them destroyed. She was considered the enemy. She had worked for OtoruRei. Joshua wouldn't understand that this wasn't about revenge.

Jane made Nathaniel feel different. Not the same feeling after a kill in the pits, or the feeling of women after a fight. This feeling was something completely different, and addictive. Thoughts of her entered both his conscious and dreaming mind.

He knew Jane felt the same way about him. The way she ran her fingers delicately along his body. The way she was looking at him now. Disappointed that he had to leave.

"Just another few hours," she purred. She traced a line with a fingertip from his chest down to his thighs. His body reacted. He had to be strong.

"I can't. Not tonight. Joshua would..." He didn't have to finish.

She sat up, pressing herself into his shoulder. "Forget about Joshua. Forget about the Crooked Hand. *Forever. We can leave this place."*

The thought had never occurred to him. "Leave? But there's nothing worth living beyond Cresek-Tawn."

She laughed gently. Not harsh like Joshua's. She wasn't laughing at him.

"Did Joshua teach you that?" She took his face in her hands and stared into his eyes. "I've seen what's beyond the salt flats. There's an entire world out there. Big enough for the two of us."

"You've seen beyond the flats?"

"Once, when I was a child, Phelps took me to another city..." Her sentence died. They never spoke of their past. Both of them were slaves. He to Joshua; her to Phelps.

He pulled himself from her grasp. "I have to go, Jane." He dressed. She fell backward in the bed, staring away from him now. "Will I see you tomorrow?" he questioned.

"I suppose."

After finishing buttoning his tunic, he leaned over, kissing her. While she appeared upset with him, she returned his kiss passionately. Jane tried to pull him down to her. He eluded her grasp.

Nathaniel stopped at the door. "I love you."

The Dark recoiled within him. He felt the tendrils of the beast wanting to snake around his mind. But more and more he had been swallowing down that evil thing, contained him in a faraway place.

There was a silence. Nathaniel felt her eyes upon him. "You've never said those words to anyone, have you?"

"No." They were odd words. Foreign to his lips. They seemed so inadequate but they needed to be said.

"We don't need Cresek-Tawn, Nathaniel."

∞

I was alive.

But didn't want to be. The physical pain was nothing. My vision returned slowly—first as lines, then shapes, then a blur. Why was I alive? Joshua does not make careless mistakes like that. I realized that I could move again and I turned my head.

Jane. Her eyes open, her skin white. I couldn't breathe, couldn't move. Her blood was underneath us, soaked into my clothing. As it dried, it had become sticky and cold.

A squelched cry came from my throat as I forced myself to my knees.

"Jane?" my voice was raw. I gathered her into my arms. Her hair was clumped and I tried to brush it back from her face. "Jane?" Why wouldn't she answer me? She was going to be all right. I held her head in my lap, staring into her eyes, wondering when she was going to awaken.

Then I saw the wound in her throat. Such a terrible sight—the skin peeled back, torn away, her flesh white. Who had done this to her? Who? I didn't want to remember. Something built in my throat.

I rocked her back and forth, hoping that sheer determination would make her all right. My eyes burned. Why were they burning? I felt my cheek. Tears. Why would I be crying? Jane was right here with me. Wasn't that what we had always wanted? Wasn't that why I had traveled across the world to be here?

Her joints were stiff, locked in position. I tried to slide my hand into hers but her fist was closed and she wouldn't open it.

"What's wrong, Jane?"

Tears dropped down my cheeks onto her white skin. Her forehead was covered in droplets of blood. My attempt to wipe away the blood only managed to smear it further. Where had all the blood come from?

My lips moved in an effort to say her name but no word came. Only a strangled cry. My body shook with sobs. I pulled her close.

Jane was dead.

They had killed her. Taken away the one thing that was more precious than anything. She would not awaken and she would not rush into my arms.

Her body was cold but I held her tightly, not wanting to let go. But it was no longer her in my arms, only the shell of who she once was. She was gone. Forever.

We sat in her congealing blood. Jane's body could not be left here in this terrible place. She was so beautiful. I needed to find somewhere to lay her to rest. Lifting her caused pain to blossom throughout trouble areas on my body. However, that pain, such a bane before, was probably the only thing keeping me sane. The agony grounded me, kept my rational mind from careening over the cliff of insanity.

From beyond the estate's walls came the sounds of chaos. Yelling, screaming, fighting, cursing. The clang of metal on metal. The shattering of glass. As I had thought, the city had exploded.

"We're leaving, Jane," I said.

"We cannot leave now," I imagined her saying. "There is madness outside."

"It is the Rominratu," I stated. "Tonight, madness roams the streets."

The Rominratu. The night of madness. A closed my eyes in anguish. Too late. The city had exploded with rage, as if it had sensed all my frustration and acted on my behalf. Except I knew that wasn't true. Somehow, Joshua had orchestrated this, as well. Now we were captured inside this cursed city with my own madness threatening to consume me; the madness of the city paled in comparison.

I stared at her, wondering at her beauty. This time, the blame didn't fall on me. Cresek-Tawn was to blame. I blamed this infernal place and everybody who lived here. Joshua and the *Crooked Hand* were all to blame.

I gently laid her down, placing a kiss on her forehead. More of my tears fell to her cheek, my body shaking from the sobs. How long did grief hold me in its debilitating grip?

My head was upon her chest, pouring my devotion into her. I wanted to disappear. Another man, an ordinary man, would've grieved for Jane, then left the city and the pain behind. But through years of training, Joshua had ensured I was no ordinary man. He had locked a darkness within me, a darkness I had buried for five years. It scratched. Joshua's creation wanted free.

Wiped my eyes with the back of my hand. Joshua had stolen the one thing that was precious to me. The debt needed to be repaid.

Despite her death, there was a certain clarity to my thinking. There was no right and wrong, there was only action. The one act to bring myself, and Jane, peace.

I saw the gates of Cresek-Tawn opening in my mind, welcoming me back. The darkness welled in me, a darkness I hadn't wanted to revisit. Joshua had been warned about the forces he played with. Now they were beyond my control too.

The claws...those claws that tormented me, that I kept locked away deep in my core—they were at my throat. I couldn't keep them away. They were squeezing, crushing, my lungs suddenly void of air. I thrashed but the pressure increased—not just squeezing my windpipe, but crushing away my will. Those damn eyes, boring a hole right through me. Blue, sizzling, yet they threw no heat. An electrical fire crawling up my body. The mouth moving soundlessly. What was it saying? A tongue dancing along the chipped teeth, splatters of blood streaking my belly and chest. The breath rancid. Wanted to get away but those claws held me fast, a weight pinning me. Trapped.

The eyes inches from mine, the mouth reaching for a perverted kiss. The tongue in my mouth, probing. I wanted to bite, to crush it away but the tongue kept coming, forcing its way down my throat. Intimate. Raping. Those eyes. Soulless. Emotionless. And I knew what it meant.

The kiss drew my last air reserves from me, the tongue violating, further down, past the claws. Into my chest, the tip poking at my guts. Could feel the pressure build. Wanted to close my eyes but the blue electricity burned away my lids. There was nowhere to hide.

I do not want this.

"You brought me here," it answered. Not sure if it was speaking aloud or it was already inside of me.

Get away.

"Too late for that. You brought me here. You unleashed me. Let me do it for you. Let me do what you cannot bare to do. I will be the hand of vengeance."

Please...

"I will rain fire down on Cresek-Tawn."

Cannot...

"I will peel the flesh from our enemies. Splatter their blood on

the walls. You brought me here. You want me here. Release me."

The death...

"*Shall be on my hands. Not yours. I am a tool. An instrument. Created by this city, to destroy this city. Sleep. You deserve sleep.*"

"They are my hands, as well."

"*You are weak. Let me be your strength. Release me.*"

"I'm...confused. I've left you behind."

"*I've always been here. Waiting. Release me.*"

"I...can't."

"*You have no choice. Release me.*"

Then the tongue was down deeper, pushing. Invading. The eyes, I saw nothing but those damned eyes. I breathed them, smelled them. The intimate kiss sucked away my will. Felt the broken teeth slash at my lips, the tongue thick in my mouth.

And then I saw Jane's throat. And what little resistance I had crumbled. Just like this city would crumble.

"Yes," I croaked. "Yes. Do it."

The laughter. I remembered it because it came from my throat. It sounded like madness to some, but to me it sounded like murder. The claws consumed me, the mouth breathed me in. The eyes burned me until there was nothing left. Nothing except the darkness.

The Dark composed himself, wiped away the wetness from his cheeks, then paused as if momentarily confused by them. Sadness? No, now was not the time for sadness.

Now was the time for vengeance.

It was time for people to die.

CHAPTER ELEVEN

ROMINRATU: ANOTHER NIGHT OF MADNESS

T he Dark was a devil wrapped in the body of a human. He surveyed the streets approvingly. Civil war consumed Cresek-Tawn—and the city felt like home.

Men battled in the gutters, children threw rocks at passing wagons, and people dashed for safety. Tonight was the night of madness and no place was truly safe.

A phosphorous lamp exploded, sending burning metal across the street. The crowd scattered from the brilliance like roaches at the flick of a match. It left two men in a lover's embrace, teeth gnashing, hands at throats, blood smeared on the roadway from blistered wounds. They wore the cloaks of nobility but settled their dispute the most ancient of ways—in combat. The larger man gained the advantage, pinning his adversary under his weight. Slowly squeezed his life away. The helpless man flailed his legs, fingers reaching out, eyes bulging. Pleading. The hand stretched to the Dark.

He kicked it away and stepped over the violent lovers.

Tonight, as the law dictated, old scores could be settled. Murder and other atrocities were condoned.

And yet, no matter how much death the Dark would visit upon the city, he knew he would never be truly satisfied. The thing he hated most of all was the other entity inside this body, the one he called the Other. The Other kept him trapped in the dark places of the mind for years. The Dark often wondered how he could be held in subjugation to such a pitiful, weak man. All he did was moan and complain about a lost love when he should've been revelling in the glory that was life, which oddly, was all about killing others.

The Dark tried to stretch his mind back to the Times Before but his memories were hazy. He couldn't remember how he'd come to only be a passenger inside this frail body.

Joshua. The Other both hated and feared Joshua, but so did the Dark, for it was Joshua who locked him in this fragile prison of flesh. He licked his lips, as if tasting the blood of his enemy. Not yet, but soon. He dreamt of sinking his teeth into Joshua. Maybe the shoulder, maybe the softness of the belly. Imagined the warm blood flooding his mouth as he gnashed and mutilated him.

His tongue played over his teeth. Pitiful. These could barely cut through meat. They were meant more for grinding than for stalking and killing. He remembered his past life like a dream, so long ago it stretched into grainy images. His fangs had been massive, stretching over his upper lips, serrated, dripping with toxins. And his fingers...the Dark stared down at his hands.

So meagre. No claws, no talons, no razors. Only pink flesh, blistered and calloused from years of battling. Still, this physique was useful. Mercurial. Able to move fluidly, to bring death with the slash of weapons, dancing away from counter-attacks, striking against the multitude of vulnerabilities in the human body: the genitals, the neck, the stomach, the eyes, the heart.

It was not completely ideal, but it would do.

First, he would destroy Joshua and cast the rest of the *Crooked Hand* down with him.

The path through Cresek-Tawn was a difficult one, strewn with obstacles, people, traps. Riots flowed through the streets unchecked, like water washing over sand. There were no regiments, garrisons, or front lines, but make no mistake, a war raged.

Tonight was the time when old scores were settled. Neighbours with qualms battled for each other's throats; adulterers found themselves besieged by angry wives or husbands who wanted to rip sinful hearts from beating chests; abused slaves and servants turned on cruel masters.

And the Dark breathed it in. Took a taste of the chaos, the anger, the uncontrollable rage. He was one with the Rominratu and he would watch the city crumble. Finally, after all these years, he had returned home.

Buildings burned, flares of oily light, creating an unnatural dawn. Fire was the true enemy of Cresek-Tawn for it could do what no army had ever done; raze the city to the ground. There wasn't enough water even with the aqueducts to combat the blaze. The flames caused a frenzy, as if someone had moved a stone, revealing the squirming, crawling insects underneath. With the hidden veil of society removed, people strove for new safety. It came down to basic survival. The trappings of success mattered little when former servants tried to beat you to death with gold candlesticks. Most simply ran.

Men brawled in the streets, using makeshift weapons: bottles, rocks, rusted knives.

The chaos intensified. The Dark gained relative shelter in the overhang of a building that had somehow survived this long against the flames. Its roof sizzled, cracked, and smouldered. Soon, it would collapse, and like the rest of Cresek-Tawn, it would burn. From the doorway, the Dark gazed to the archway of the *Crooked Hand* estate.

Alvaro Megellin, the lord of Cresek-Tawn would be inside, protected by his most loyal killers, the Scorpions. They'd be trying to hold on until the end of the Rominratu at dawn. If they could last until the cresting of the sun, Alvaro and the Megellin clan would retain control. If Alvaro died, then the clan who claimed his head would take control. Such was the only law of the Rominratu.

Assuming Alvaro was still alive.

The Dark assumed there'd be an ambush set for any that approached. Probably archers hidden in the two nooks, and then several killers in the barbican.

The Dark dashed from his hiding spot, arrows filling the air with their angry singing. He danced amongst the shafts. Watched them skitter along the flagstone, or embed themselves in the detritus of battle. He heard the bowstring pulled, sensed the exhilaration of the archer, felt the beating of their hearts. He licked his cracked lips and urged himself to patience. Vengeance didn't mean he had to be careless. More arrows. They formed a beautiful pattern as he slid between them.

He wanted to call out and tell them that no arrow would ever stop him for he was the Dark, and that he was their doom. He didn't call out, however, not because he was worried about revealing his identity or drawing more attention to himself, but because he'd forgotten his real name in the fog of time.

He scanned the windows overlooking the streetscape. There, saw one. Hiding in an upper window, searching the street. The Dark avoided him and three others to reach the estate.

Beyond the fires, the darkness of the estate felt almost unnatural. A static in a city tearing itself apart—the eye of the hurricane.

The Dark planned to break that calm.

The Dark remembered this place as if from a dream. Years ago, this had been the estate of OtoruRei but was now the home of the Megellin clan. The Other had found Jane that night, and that was when the trouble had begun. Trouble that still followed them years later. The Dark tasted something. Bile. Was that the taste of vengeance or love? Didn't matter.

Outside the estate, the city boiled. Inside, water splashed in fountains, the bubbling somehow comforting. Though darkened, the flames of the burning city filled the halls with swimming shadows. As the Dark squatted behind a bronze statue, he heard more street lamps exploding, the phosphorus flare casting a brilliant cloud of blue light, scattering the pools of shadow like a flock of birds. Where there had been shadow stood an assassin, momentarily blinded by the glare. His stealth had been impressive, hiding so perfectly the Dark hadn't noticed him. He wore ornamental armour laced with hardened leather. Three swords of various lengths hung at his waist, encased in hide sheaths. He was one of the Rei's assassins, a man who had studied the art of blades rather than bows like his clansmen. He had snuck into the estate with plans to kill Alvaro.

With his back to the explosion, the Dark was spared the blinding brilliance. The assassin dug his knuckles into his eyes, trying to clear his vision.

The Dark was upon the assassin, stealing a razor-sharp sword from a sheath and parting his head from his shoulders. His head hit the marble floor with a hollow thud. The body remained standing, arms extended in a defensive position.

The Dark gazed at the weapon in his hands, gleaming in the fading phosphorus glow, only a single smear of blood marring the perfect surface. *How many more will this kill tonight?* He shivered in anticipation. This was a good weapon.

The body crumpled, the head had rolled beside the fountain, eyes staring up at the ceiling. The lips appeared to mouth words from the ebb and flow of the shadows. The Dark stepped over the corpse.

The Other hated Cresek-Tawn but for the Dark—he was home. This place flowed like a disease through his veins.

The royal doors appeared to be unguarded with no signs of a struggle. Which meant the assassin, or anybody else, hadn't reached Alvaro Megellin yet. The Dark breathed deeply—the anticipation was exquisite. A slight flutter of nervous energy, his skin covered in goose bumps.

The Dark reached for the doors but before his fingers made contact, the doors swung inward, artificial light streaming from the grand hall. His pupils adjusted. Spinning shapes. A blur of blades. Scimitars.

The Scorpions, the elite of the *Crooked Hand*, came at him in a wave, framed by the sizzling light of phosphorus pots. They moved with an efficient gracefulness, dancing the arts of the blade.

The sound echoing in the chamber, the Dark realized, was his battle cry. So full of joy, so full of energy. Let the death begin.

The Dark sidestepped, lunged. His blade hacked into the thigh of a blade dancer, the muscle shredding. And with a single stroke, the perfectly choreographed dance fell out of time. Became a jumble of limbs, torsos, and blades.

The Dark spun over the fallen warrior, scimitar arcing, cutting from shoulder to torso. Burst of blood. Buried the blade into a Scorpion's face. The man didn't make a sound but stood stiffly, his joints frozen. Used his body as a shield against the oncoming tide. Ducked low, separated a foot from its ankle, watched as the rest of the meat crumpled, twitching, grabbing at the phantom appendage left several paces behind.

The Dark tumbled, the clang of swords chopping where he was moments ago. Kicked at a knee, bending it backwards like a broken branch, stabbed upwards through the belly, the blade exploding through the dead man's shoulder. The Dark marvelled at the colours. The splashes of crimson flicked along the columns, the patterns of the puddles of life on the marble floors. Couldn't wonder at the beauty too long as he deflected two spear points, pushed away the awkward weapons, and dove into the heart of the spiked entity. They became clumsy, fearful, panicked. His movements were graceful, like a perfect ballet. Split a man's head in two. Dissected a torso. A rippling of flesh. The scimitar, soaked with blood, it's edge chipped, the pommel difficult to grip. Retrieved a fallen flail in his free hand. Rained it upon his foes. Ribs exploded, guts sliding wetly to the floor. The flail wrapped around weapons, yanked them from hands. The scimitar followed behind, arcing, seemingly frozen, then suddenly cleaving hands from their arms, leaving the victims flapping uselessly on the floors.

His enemies nearly became hypnotized with the beauty of their own slaughter. The precision. The Dark danced through them, tasted the blood on his lips. Smelled their death. Piss, blood, and fear, each death powering him to new heights. Their misery thrummed in his veins making him stronger and faster.

There had been ten Scorpions, now there were but two, on their knees grovelling for their lives. Weapons discarded, they were at his mercy.

Mercy. It was a concept perfect in theory, but rarely in practice. Memories from the Times Before floated to him, snippets of another time, when he soaked in the blood of cowards and his mere presence caused his enemies to dash their heads against rocks.

The Dark paused as he looked at the man before him, hands clutched in ferocious prayer and his head bowed low in supplication. Was this not the pinnacle of life? Was it not better to bend this beaten opponent to his will than to kill him outright?

The Dark kicked over the begging man on his right, brought the flail down on the other. Smashed his skull and broke his face. Before the other could recover, the scimitar flicked through the air, cut away his throat with a splash of blood. The man drowned, gagging on his own life.

His senses crackled with energy. Hyper focused so that he thought he heard the blood dripping from his knuckles. Drip-drip-drip. Pattering along the floor. The bodies moved as one, rippling with pain, death coming slower to some. The Dark stepped over the hacked flesh into the chamber.

Beyond the massacre was a long table, an entire feast laid, untouched. Palm trees, tapestries, gold statues, and slaves with massive fans. A picture of extravagance. In the middle sat Alvaro Megellin on the steps.

Alvaro was Joshua's brother, and though only three years separated them, he looked like an old man. His cheeks were sunken, spider webs of purple veins exposed because of almost translucent skin. His hair was white, like his brother's, but white with age. Alvaro was wasting away, with the body of someone three times his age.

Across his shoulders draped the Shawl of Cresek-Tawn. Such a magnificent treasure. The material shone and reflected the light as if made from threads of gold. The Dark had touched it long ago and though it appeared to be made from the finest metals, it was smooth and soft. Tonight, the Shawl would inevitably switch hands to the Rei family and they would take control of what was left of the *Crooked Hand*. If the Dark left anything left of them.

"I remember you," Alvaro said. He showed no outward fear nor could the Dark smell it on him.

"I am not...Nathaniel." The Dark said the name as if it were acidic.

"I know. You're the devil." Alvaro cocked his head. "Though I often wonder if you are the real entity and Nathaniel was the impostor."

"I will rip out your tongue if you mention him again."

Alvaro shrugged. "You'd kill an old man?"

"You're not old," the Dark said.

"Not in years. But look at me. I am but thirty but my body creaks like it has seen at least eighty years. There is nothing the sawbones or Shapers could do. I possess a natural affliction, handed down from the Immortals. You know the strange thing? It is I who lays withering but it was Joshua who became fearful. All this death and suffering was caused because Joshua became afraid...of me. He saw what age brings. Weakness of mind, of body, diminishing power. He grew obsessed over life. Or should I say, became obsessed over battling death. He strove for a fools dream. Immortality. I was the one dying, not him!"

"His life ends tonight. I shall drink the marrow from his bones."

"You won't, you know. You'll kill me. Kill many others but you won't kill him. In the end, Joshua always wins. If I had been stronger, I would've killed him long ago but he is my brother, and I allowed him his fantasies until he was too powerful to stop."

Blood dripped onto Nathaniel's leg and when he looked down, he realized that his fists had been clenched too tightly, nails tearing into his palm. Such a frail body. It couldn't even contain the rage that boiled inside. The destruction of the Scorpions had pacified him momentarily but the blood lust was beginning to thrum in his veins again.

Alvaro stared at the dripping blood, then smiled sadly. "He killed Jane, didn't he?"

The Dark didn't answer. Though the Other was locked away in the recesses, the Dark still felt something. A twinge of sadness. Like a brief arctic shiver in the oppressive heat of summer. That twinge was because of her. And the Dark wasn't about to deny that emotion. After all, if it hadn't been for her death, he still would've been locked away.

"She never loved me, you know," Alvaro said. "I had hoped that she would've tried to at least reflect the love I showed her. But just seeing her became too painful." Alvaro straightened, as if trying to draw upon the strength from his youth. "Tonight is the Rominratu," he said. "The night when old scores are settled." They locked gazes and the Dark saw something in his expression: satisfaction? Alvaro nodded once, and his lips turned into a slight smile, as if some understanding had passed between them.

"Where is Joshua?"

"You must do something for me."

"There will be no bargaining."

"Spare the life of my boys. I have hidden them. From you. From the clans. From the Rominratu. Please, leave them be."

"Do you think this city deserves to rise again from the ashes? I am not the hand of mercy."

"Not rebuild. Renew. We are bad men. You, me, Joshua. I have taught them...differently. I spared them the brutality."

The Dark stabbed him in the chest with such accuracy a sawbones couldn't have done better. The blade cracked through Alvaro's sternum but missed his heart and lungs. Only an artist could've struck with such precision. Alvaro's death would not be immediate.

Alvaro's eyes bulged and the Dark pulled him into a lover's embrace, nuzzling his neck with his lips where he felt the old man's pulse weakening. "Tell me where Joshua is," he whispered.

"My...boys..." Alvaro gasped.

"Your heart fails."

"The Keystone," he gasped. "My boys—"

The Dark sunk his teeth into Alvaro's throat, easily biting through his paper-thin flesh. Blood pulsed weakly over his tongue as he savaged the man's neck. The blood tasted foul and though the Dark wanted to drink deeply, his stomach recoiled at the putrid taste. He pulled back and let Alvaro die in his arms. It was troubling that blood no longer tasted sweet to him. He'd tried, many times, to drink the blood of his enemies, but each time the taste was foul. He removed the sword with a yank and Alvaro crumpled with a dull thud on the marble floors.

He found the boys easily enough. He hollered that if they came out of hiding that he wouldn't hurt them. They couldn't have been much older than eight. They shambled out from their hiding spots, eyes cast downwards in submission.

These boys were the future of Cresek-Tawn. Innocent? Perhaps. But they'd be corrupted like everything in this city was corrupted. He expected to feel something from the Other, something that would beg him not to kill them. Instead, there was only a question, a wondering of whether these boys belonged to Jane.

"There is nothing to be afraid of," the Dark whispered, and when the boys came close, he was merciful—cutting them down with a single stroke. He stood over the two generations of blood.

Oddly, he felt no glee or joy from their deaths and he wondered if maybe the years with the Other had perverted him.

He sensed he wasn't alone.

Creed stood motionless in the doorway, face and neck smeared with blood. And though he was an image of carnage and destruction, he stood agog at the hacked bodies, at the lake of blood.

"You are from the Times Before." Creed stated.

"I stretch beyond even my memory," the Dark said because it was the truth. He wondered briefly if he was The Beast on the Throne but he didn't guess he was. Maybe a vestige of The Beast, or a duplicate spawned as The Beast replicated.

"I do not know you," Creed said.

"I am Cresek-Tawn," he answered.

The Dark sensed the years wafting from the giant like ozone near a lightning strike. He felt the emotions oozing from him— the frustration, the anguish, the pain. His mouth watered at the thought. Oddly, the Dark thought he should've known who Creed was, as if he was a man of great importance in the eons previous.

Creed nodded sadly. "You do not understand yet, do you?"

"There is nothing to understand."

The Dark lunged for the giant. Creed met him head on and they struck together with a mighty crash. Even with the murders of the ten Scorpions powering him, the Dark was no match for Creed's limitless strength. The Dark broke away and Creed didn't pursue.

"You are a pawn," Creed said. The power flowed from the giant in waves. It was intoxicating and though the Dark knew he was no real match for the giant, he couldn't retreat. "Can you not even remember your true nature? Once, you ruled the forests. Now you're the servant of men. A slave to their will."

The Dark wasn't listening, the heavy swish of Creed's blood deafening in his ears. *Such power!* Still, he knew he couldn't defeat the giant directly.

"Deception is the key against a physically superior opponent," the Other whispered to him. *"Lure him to us."*

The Dark licked his lips, circled away. Creed seemed unwilling to engage however, eying his opponent warily.

"Joshua brought you here. Killed the woman so that you'd be free again."

The Dark fell into Creed's crushing embrace. It was like the grip of a mountain, the air squeezed explosively from him, his vision flaring from the sudden spike of pressure.

He had one chance.

The Dark bit Creed's neck, channelling all of his strength and energy into his jaws. Creed's skin was like oak and the Dark's teeth cracked and began to crumble. He didn't relent, hoping to burrow until he found blood.

Creed's mighty arms. The Dark channelled all of his strength and energy into that single attack and even then, he barely broke the skin.

Creed realized, too late, his mistake. A drop of blood squirted from his neck and the Dark swallowed it down. The single drop coursed through his veins giving him the strength of a hundred years.

The Dark's bite grew more fierce and their embrace reversed so now Creed struggled to get away. With every swallow of Creed's essence, the Dark grew more powerful until he eclipsed the giant. Creed's blood carried with it the power of the eons. The Dark's skin hardened, his bones became like steel, his vision crystallized. Still he drank.

"Aliénor," Creed whispered. Both eyes were milky white. He smiled, then died.

CHAPTER TWELVE

KINGDOMS OF THE DARK

The night was growing old but his bloodletting continued unabated. The Dark felt like a conductor to a grand symphony, each clash of metal on metal another note and each scream a crescendo. Blackened corpses littered the streets, buildings burned, and the survivors wept and begged for mercy.

His veins thrummed with the power of Creed but eventually that would fade. Right now, he felt like he held the power of a titan. Like the Times Before.

He had wandered into a clan war, both sides stationed behind their makeshift barricades. He didn't care for politics. He walked through their flights of arrows, sundered their shields, and broke their skulls. The warriors eventually banded together to battle him but he murdered them regardless of affiliation or age.

The Dark wondered what would come after the vengeance. This body was frail and not suited for such battles. When Creed's power eventually failed, the Dark wondered if his body would simply crumble from the great stresses he had heaped upon it. He had faced down hammers and spikes, been smashed with boulders cast from siege weapons, and he'd pounded through stone to get at his enemies.

"*We must avenge her,*" the Other said.

"The city must burn."

"*Joshua imprisoned you within me. Destroy him and you'll be free.*"

The Dark considered as he finished crushing a man's skull. "How can I be free of you?" Despite his grand symphony of carnage, the Dark worried that if this frail body survived, the Other would find a way to cast him back into the dark recesses of his psyche.

"Find Joshua. Complete the journey and I will give you anything you want."

"The Keystone."

The Keystone was at the heart of the aqueducts that kept Cresek-Tawn alive against the desert. It was also one of the artefacts left from the Times Before. Something tickled the back of his mind about the Keystone but it was lost in a haze he couldn't remember.

"He'll be waiting for us."

The thought of being unshackled from the Other was intoxicating. Imagine, being free to wreak his beautiful art upon the world again. So much had changed since the Times Before. The world had become desaturated and dull. The Dark would strive to restore the agonizing glory of those forgotten times.

The Dark trekked to the Keystone while temptations attempted to mislead him. No, he said. He had to be strong and to ignore the cries of battle and the whimpering of the dying. The streets worked against him. The layout of Cresek-Tawn had changed considerably from his hazy memory of five years ago. Each dead end led to another pleasure that he had to turn down.

Finally, he reached the heart of Cresek-Tawn: the Keystone. It appeared like a godly octopus rising from the desert, its tentacles six-foot wide black pipes arcing a hundred-feet high than reaching across Cresek-Tawn to deliver water. While the rest of the city had a decidedly temporary nature, the aqueducts appeared impervious to time, war, and the elements. Nobody knew who built them or why someone once deemed it important to pump water from the earth and spread it across the desert.

The fighting around the Keystone had subsided, and the cleanup had already begun though the Dark didn't spot any signs of the living. Only the dead. There were two mounds. The first was a smouldering ruin of corpses. The second was their possessions piled high. Weapons, clothing, equipment.

The centre of Keystone was a foreign looking dome with no obvious entrances. Its smooth black surface gleamed in the raging fires. The Dark knew only one way inside and that was through the pipes. The access hatches were all near the apex. A long, dangerous climb.

First, he sifted through the mound of supplies and recovered several phosphorus orbs. The smell of fatty meat smoking from the corpses made his mouth water. He straightened and breathed deeply, the blood beginning to dry and tighten on his face. For many years he'd been trapped within the Other. And before that...it was murky, but he had been asleep for so long. And though this body was weak and imperfect, the taste of freedom was sweet. He never wanted to let that go. The Dark wished this night would never end but already the horizon lightened from the impending dawn.

He pocketed the phosphorus orbs then tried to decide the best way to climb to the access hatches on the ducts. He knew he had to be careful as even with Creed's strength powering his heart, a fall from those heights would surely break his body.

He climbed upward, scaling walls, twisting over awnings, scrambling as spots in weakened roofs collapsed. Though the Dark was loathe to admit, the Other's body was nimble and lithe, perfect for flights such as this one. He tried to recall his body back in the Times Before. He thought he pictured hooves, or maybe talons, but then finally remembered paws. He'd had paws with sharp claws.

Clay tiles gave way beneath him and his frantic footfalls sent them spinning to the ground below. It was like running on marbles and his scrambling was sending him faster to an edge. Just when he thought he'd lost control, he gained traction and jumped to safety.

"Shyst," he puffed. He'd have to reminisce about the Times Before later. Focus now. A fall from this height could be deadly. He continued his careful ascent, jumping over several spans to ever taller buildings until finally he pulled even with a pipe. There was an eight-foot span between the lip of the roof and the side of the pipe. He steeled himself and leapt. For a fleeting second, when suspended between failure and success, his stomach lurched and he thought he'd come up short. Then his hand scrabbled for purchase on the black stone. Though it gleamed as if smooth, the surface provided enough friction for him to latch on and pulled himself to the top of the pipe and afforded himself a deep breath. The air was full of cinder and ash. Oddly, the Dungeons of Gardizael was probably one of the safest places tonight.

The Dark pulled open the hatch to the pipe. On any other day, water would be flowing but tonight, the fires of the Rominratu had drained the supply to only a trickle.

"Joshua knew that," the Other said. *"He wanted access to the Keystone. He's waiting for us down there."*

"Let him wait." The Dark jumped into the pipe, the water rising to his ankles. The temperature was icy. The Dark opened a phosphorus globe and it flared, the light reflecting off the algae-covered pipes. From here, he'd head to the Keystone. He splashed back. The pipes would be descending quickly. He had to be careful or—

His feet slid out from beneath him. The floor was slick with algae and he lost traction. He dropped the phosphorus ball and he was launched down the tube on a plume of water. The drop was precipitous and he scrambled to find a handhold to slow his descent.

No good. The tube levelled out, which meant—

He was launched into the expanse of the Keystone, skidding along a trough of churning water with currents dragging him through a series of canals. Even through the splashing, he heard the churning of gears. The water engines. Up ahead, gears as large as a carriage meshed and spun, powerful enough to mulch him into indistinguishable bits.

The Dark rolled, dove, and grabbed onto the side of the trough before he could be carried into the machine. He rolled from the trough in a wave of water, coughing and sputtering. So much for a dignified entrance. The Other had a flair for the dramatic, but he did not. He climbed to his feet and peeled off his clothes so he was naked, left them on the floor like a snake sheds its skin. His skin rippled from the cold and the Dark shivered— though he wasn't sure if it was from the chill or the anticipation of murdering Joshua. His phosphorus globe, dropped earlier, glowed at the bottom of the trough and he retrieved it.

In this room, machines from another era churned away and created water from the air. The Dark seemed to remember the engineers who used to power these machines. Lanky men with white coats and eyes of fire. The more he tried to recall it, however, the more those memories disappeared like sand through his fist.

The air was thick with humidity and carried the scent of mould spores and algae. Outside, the aqueducts and the Keystone appeared impervious to time. Inside, age weighed heavily on the inner workings of the water generators. Rust chewed at the metal, fungus and moulds grew unhindered, and several gears were missing teeth. These machines would eventually fail though the Dark couldn't guess whether that would be tomorrow or in a hundred years, but one day, a gear would break, the engine would bind, and all the water would stop. The Dark considered destroying the water engines—then truly the city would die.

Maybe later as right now he was focused solely on a singular vengeance.

There was a series of doors leading off the engine room. They were all utilitarian in nature save one. It was the same foreign black stone used to build the Keystone. Etched into its surface was a symbol that triggered recognition from his past. It was a frog atop an upwards facing crescent moon, its rear legs extended in a position of motion, leaping away from the celestial body.

The Dark's instincts told him that Joshua was beyond that door. What diabolical scheme would he have waiting? He found himself grinning at the thought of the conflict. He pulled and the door ground open with a rumble. He expected to be greeted with the sound of a flight of bolts and was rather disappointed when no one was there, only a dark and empty corridor.

The Dark slipped inside and held the phosphorus aloft which cast ghostly shadows. The air smelled stale as if it had been sealed for many years though he knew that to be untrue.

Somewhere down that corridor, Joshua and his bounty killers waited for him. They were assassins trained to kill other assassins but nothing could prepare them for him. Their deaths would be glorious, punctuated with splashes of crimson and the cracking of bone.

A sound escaped his lips. Laughter. What an odd noise. The Other was more accustomed to it. Still, though the rage pulsed with a malevolence, the glee of the kill kept pace.

He followed the corridor and left wet footprints on the smooth stone floors.

The Dark froze. He felt a light touch on his bare leg. A trip wire, nearly invisible in the phosphorus light. The Dark retreated, careful not to spring the trap. Another inch and he would've broken the cord. He knelt and inspected the wire, giving it a little tug and watching the string vibrate. A professional job. The string was constructed of cotton-womb spider silk. Half the width of a human hair, but comparatively stronger than steel. Nathaniel traced the path of the string, first to the wall, then looped upwards to a ledge.

The Dark pulled himself until he was level with series of small blow guns aimed into the corridor. A dart trap. Interesting choice. Another sign that Joshua didn't want him dead, but maybe a little maimed.

He heard the click of a crossbow. Shyst! A bolt exploded through the front of his shoulder, spraying his blood onto the ledge. He stared at it with amazement, wondering why that arrow was protruding through his arm. A wave of pain washed over him but before he cried out, he shut away the torment and jumped down.

Two men with crossbows had snuck up on him. The first had discharged and tossed the weapon down. The second man aimed and pulled the trigger. The Dark anticipated this one. Dodged the arrow and it shattered against the stone wall behind him.

That had been their chance for their kill. Their time was done.

They wore the tattered funeral gauze, bandoliers of knives strapped across their chests. The men that had helped murder Jane. Both killers reached for knives, their hands a blur as they closed the distance while tossing blades, the air sizzling with thrown metal. The Dark drew his scimitar, knocked the first aside with a clang, slide stepped to the right as he dodged another dagger, then slid his sword into the softness of the first man's belly all the way to the hilt, then a quick tug down opening him to his jewels and withdrew, a flood of blood, bile, and crap slopping to the floor. The killer was stoic in death, or maybe he simply couldn't comprehend that he'd just been gutted. He died quietly on his feet.

The other came at the Dark with knives in his hands, arms twisting and spinning in an exotic fighting stance. The Other would've known the name of the style but the Dark didn't care about names or theories. All he cared about was the practical— the patterns, the deficiencies, the strengths. He drank in the scene and saw very few weaknesses of the dancing blades.

He threw the phosphorus globe at the blade dancer and the glass dome shattered on the man's chest, spraying him with flame and burning metal. The man screamed, his burial cloth igniting so quickly that he became a human torch. Regardless, the killer was a true professional, still not abandoning his dancing blades.

The Dark marvelled momentarily at the beauty of the windmill-like arms, the flames, the sickly smell of burning flesh.

The man was coming at him, a cartwheel of fire.

The Dark accepted it, grabbing the killer around his neck, spinning, twisting him against the wall. The man was already dead, he just didn't know it yet. The Dark watched as the skull withered, the flaming hands clawing at the air. The Dark could've ended the torment, and perhaps prevented his own flesh from burning, but he was feeling slightly indulgent and drank in the anguish.

The screams died as the blade dancer's vocal cords withered and popped. He drew in a lungful of flames and began to burn from the inside. He writhed under the Dark's hold. There was no strategy in his flailing, only a base instinct to escape.

Black smoke filled the corridor, the fire snapping and popping as if it were devouring a freshly fallen tree. Finally, the Dark let him fall, a cloud of sparks dancing like angry hornets when the body hit the stone.

The Dark's hand throbbed and he inspected it as if it belonged to someone else. The blisters had bloomed, skin red. A crossbow bolt protruded from his shoulder and he tried to remember when that happened. He snapped off the head of the bolt, then yanked the other end through with a spurt of blood. Blood bubbled from the wound and his arm twitched. His pain was shut away in a place that wouldn't bother him. Pain was a poison of the weak.

He licked his lips when he looked at the ruined flesh on the floor. The place smelled of dust, blood, crap, and burnt flesh. Just an appetizer. He wanted more.

The Dark pilfered the dead man's bandolier of knives and blades. Good quality. Weighted for throwing. He looped the bandolier over his good shoulder. While the pain was shut away, muscle and sinew wasn't as easily fooled. That arm was weak and he'd have to compensate.

He hoped there would be other killers waiting for him, but it was unusual for Joshua to even have two assassins with him—he preferred to trust only one. Which meant Joshua was next.

Freedom was intoxicating. Away from the locks and doors within the psyche of the Other. When this was over, he refused to be tricked or prodded back into his cage. This was his time. The Other would lie and mislead in an attempt to take control again. The Dark wouldn't let that happen.

The Dark continued further down the corridor until he reached a red-veined white marble stairway. Dormant chandeliers told of a time long ago when this would've been a grand hall. Joshua would be waiting in the chamber at the bottom of these stairs.

A stolen knife dangled loosely in the Dark's hand. Absently, he played with the blade, twisting it around his fingers and spinning it in his grip. He took the stairs quickly, aware that his pulse raced and that blood bubbled from his crossbow wound.

A set of double doors waited for him at the bottom of the stairs, each emblazoned with a black swan insignia. He stood before them. He and the Other had battled across the continent, spent half a lifetime running, and finally it was all going to end. After so long being imprisoned, the Dark wasn't about to be defeated. His own life was too sweet to allow a man who had been on the earth less than a century to cut him down. Impossible.

The Other sent him images of Jane's corpse at Phelps's estate and her torn open neck. The Dark accepted the anger and mulled it over like fine wine. Savouring. Let it give him strength.

He threw open the doors, unworried that Joshua would do anything as mundane as shooting him. Joshua had planned something marvellous, and despite his intention to kill the man, the Dark had to admit that he was curious. Joshua was born in the wrong era, the Dark realized. Joshua belonged to the times of titans, angels, and demons. He should've existed in the Times Before.

And there waited Joshua, a smug smile gracing his lips. Black Swan lay on the floor between the two men as if it had been carelessly discarded. The Dark's breath caught. His quarry. His adversary. His master. His warden.

The chamber was six sided, each wall a mosaic of glass tiles depicting a mythical image: a green serpent rising from an emerald; a black swan wings outstretched, mouth wide in a hiss; an orange tiger preparing to pounce, jaws extended in a roar; a yellow wasp darting from the face of a sun; and a red falcon diving from a sky of fire.

The sixth mosaic was made mostly of black glass. He squinted, as if that could somehow clarify the image. As he stared at it, he recognized the backdrop as a dark forest, and there was a creature in that forest staring at him. It had eyes that glowed yellow. He thought he saw the outline of a body. Maybe it was a wolf or a cat. Those eyes belonged to a true predator.

The floor was a mosaic of a grotesque frog head. Set in the eye of the frog was a slot the size of a man's hand.

"How many did you kill to get here?" Joshua asked, snapping his attention away from the slots on the floor. "Ten? Twenty?"

"One of them was your brother. I ripped his spine through his chest."

Joshua's grin faltered but he replaced it quickly. "He was already dead. A broken man undeserving of the *Crooked Hand*. When we were kids, people used to think he was my father. Before he took his first wife, he looked like a grizzled veteran of a thousand wars. And before he reached his thirtieth year, he hobbled like a man three times his age. What kind of life is that?"

"I'm not here to offer platitudes."

"You've come to kill me?" Joshua stood with hands behind his back while the Dark circled.

"You imprisoned me," the Dark spat.

"I found you when you were no more than a thought, a cast off from another era. Barely a memory. I hid you."

"You used me."

"You can be great again, like the Times Before."

"Don't wait," the Other said. *"His words are like magic and he'll corrupt you to his will like he has everyone else."*

"His words cannot harm me," the Dark answered.

Joshua regarded him quizzically. "I don't plan on harming you. I plan on releasing you. All the power is in your hands. My years of planning all lead to tonight. Placing you inside of Nathaniel, keeping Jane close to me, setting the foundation for the Rominratu—and now it all rests with you."

"I have promised you control, but you must do this one thing. Otherwise, I'll cast you back into the dark and I'll never let you out."

The Dark took a step. Despite his contempt for the Other, he feared him—what if he *could* cast him back into the abyss? The Other's presence welled huge inside of him. He sensed the anger and determination, once the very emotions that he used to exploit now threatened to overwhelm him. If he didn't act now, the Other would attempt to wrest control away from him.

Not that it was a tough choice.

The Other conjured an image of Jane and with it the accompanying storm of anguish and helplessness. Those feelings burst in the Dark and he staggered. Jane's vacant eyes started at him, her throat torn open. Her lifeless lips mouthed words. She blamed him.

The Dark attacked. Joshua was quick but Creed's blood still flowed through the Dark's veins. Joshua tried to parry and dance away but the Dark saw through the ploy easily, caught an arm, and sent the man cart wheeling across the chamber. He landed awkwardly but regained his feet.

"What was Creed's part in your plans? Did you intend for me to drink his blood and gain his strength?" The Dark saw the doubt in Joshua's expression before it was replaced by a wry smile. "A wildcard? He was from the Times Before. I smelled it on him."

"He was a—"

The Dark didn't let him finish, attacking with punches, kicks, and elbows. Joshua tried to defend but he was overwhelmed by the Dark's ferocity. Several blows landed, bloodying Joshua's chin and opening a cut along his forehead that leaked blood.

The Dark pulled him into a hug, planning to crush him, able to watch closely as the life left him.

Joshua, however, pivoted then dropped. The Dark's shoulder, weakened from the earlier crossbow bolt, betrayed him and Joshua freed himself and wheeled backwards.

As he retreated, he gathered up Black Swan and brandished it before him. "What did Nathaniel promise you?" Joshua gasped.

"He promised me you."

"I can give you much more. I can give you everything you once had."

"You don't have the power for that."

Joshua engaged with a two-handed strike. Black Swan sang, its song like the hum of a thumb over fine crystal, the blade moving so fast that the Dark could barely register its arc. White light spilled from the blade and the Dark ducked under the attack, dropped to his hands, and wheeled a kick, sinking both feet into Joshua's midsection with a satisfying grunt. Joshua fell but recovered with the grace of an acrobat, slipping sideways and had regained his feet. He wiped blood from his eyes.

"You're going to have to better than that, Nate." Joshua came at him again. The Dark gathered two blades from his bandolier. Tried to parry but Black Swan sundered his dagger, the end falling with a clatter to the floor. Joshua followed up and though the Dark side stepped, the blade sliced into his hip. He stumbled but quickly locked away the pain.

"I don't want to kill you," Joshua said, failing to push his advantage. "I want to free you. To return to the Times Before. We can do that. Tonight."

The Dark threw a dagger. Joshua batted it to the side with a metallic ping. That was only a decoy. The Dark whirled and drove a dagger deep into Joshua's thigh, then brought a forearm up into chin and sending him sprawling backwards and knocking Black Swan from his grip.

His memories were filled with Jane, filled with visions of her lifeless body. The Dark didn't chase away those memories. Though they belonged to the Other, he'd use them. Channel the hatred.

The Dark lunged upon him, knees crashing into Joshua, emptying his lungs with a violent gasp, followed by the crunch of ribs snapping like kindling. The Dark's fist struck his jaw and cracked Joshua's head back into the stone. Dull thud. More fists.

Joshua's fingers reached into the Dark's mouth—a desperation move—and threatened to rip open the side of his face. The Dark swivelled, biting, molars crunching his forefinger. Perhaps these teeth had some use after all. Bone splintered. Joshua didn't react as blood sputtered into the Dark's mouth. When Joshua retracted his hand, several fingers were ruined. The Dark spit out the remainder.

"Listen..." Joshua gasped.

"No, don't listen."

The Dark broke Joshua's nose and shattered his cheeks. Maybe because he was so badly beaten, but Joshua appeared emotionless. The Dark wanted him to suffer and the more he remained impassive, the harder he struck.

He cradled his skull and using the last of Creed's power, he began to crush. Joshua's hands flailed at the Dark's face, but the fingers were ruined so they couldn't find the soft spots like his eyes and nose.

Orgasmic pleasure welled from the Other. Joshua's skull began to crack.

But Joshua was a man of limitless determination, and he arched his back, the sudden motion surprised the Dark and giving Joshua a short respite.

"I'll set you free," Joshua slurred through broken teeth. "You kill me...you're trapped forever."

The Dark's gaze flicked over to the knives. "*Yes. Use the knives. Cut him badly. Slice him into a thousand pieces while he watches.*" Where would he start? The fingers working up to the wrist? The face, careful to leave the eyes so he could watch his own dissection? The genitals? So many choices.

He caught movement out of the corner of his vision. The Dark turned but there was no one there. Only the image of the black swan. Had it moved? He was certain that before it had been in flight, mouth open. Now it was standing as if humanoid, chest puffed out in defiance.

More movement. The Dark whirled. The murals had shifted.

It was like he was staring through glass into another room. The green serpent uncoiled. The serpent's yellow eyes fixed on him, it's emerald-green body twisting upright like a cobra ready to strike. It stretched taller than a man, its body thick like an oak tree. The Dark realized that the serpent was looking at him. The snake slithered forward until it was no longer part of the mural but was a living entity in the room.

The Dark turned his attention to the wall with the black swan. The bird had risen onto its hind legs and walked upright, proud chest puffed out in an act of defiance. Its eyes were the deepest red and its bill a dark yellow. Behind, the dawn broke, rays of sun spilling across a broken field. The swan stepped from its mural to stand opposite the Dark.

The other icons pulled themselves from their murals as well and joined them in the Keystone, each becoming human-like, walking upright with distinct humanoid forms.

The orange tiger pulled itself from a jungle and let loose a guttural growl before crouching, tail swishing with an irritated flick. The Dark believed that the tiger was ready to pounce.

A man-sized wasp buzzed from the wall, its stinger dripping venom. A falcon screeched and majestically stepped into the Keystone. There was one totem missing. The sixth wall was bare—the wolf.

In all, the five totems joined them. A swan, a falcon, a serpent, a wasp, and a tiger. The sixth wall, the one with the wolf in the dark forest, remained oddly empty. Even though five mythical beings surrounded him and his mortal enemy lay broken on the floor, he stared at that sixth wall. Why was it empty? Where was the totem?

His gaze flicked to the black swan. The beast hissed and the Dark remembered. He remembered battling that swan through the Sour Lands for five months. They fought in the mud, in the mountains, and they fought in the air. The Dark remembered the stinging wounds along his hide. He remembered the wasp coming at him from the sky, its stinger plunging into him even as he tore its wings. The serpent constricting him as he clawed its face. The tiger throwing him from the mountains. He had battled the five totems for what seemed time without end. Eventually, they had cast him down.

The Dark tasted bile at the memory. They had cast him out of their sanctuary and sundered his body.

He looked back to the empty wall.

The Dark began to remember. He was linked to these totems, these creatures from the Times Before, when they ruled as deities. And perhaps they had been. But when their powers weakened and the Times Before had drawn to a close, they had cast him down.

As he looked upon the totems, he recalled histories with each of them. Allegiances, betrayals, kingdoms rising and falling.

"I can send you home," Joshua slurred. "Black Swan, the sword, is a key."

What had Creed said to the Other? *It is the key to limitless doors. Doors to infinite realms.*

"You are the Dark Wolf, the monster that hunts at night and prowls nightmares. You are from the Times Before, when man was still but a dream. Can you not remember what you once were? I have found the doorway to the era of your greatness, where you can be whole again. Where time stretches endlessly."

"How?" the Dark Wolf asked.

"Only you can do it. This Keystone is the doorway, but only you can turn the key." Joshua staggered to his feet and recovered Black Swan. He hobbled over to the Dark Wolf and handed it to him hilt first. "This is the key."

The Dark Wolf took the sword then stared down at the slots on the floor. *This is the key, but which door shall I choose?*

"Only you have the power to open the door."

"Then I can kill you."

"Only you can turn the key, but I was the one who prepared the door. Without me, all of this goes away."

"He's lying. He is not a sorcerer. Kill him."

But what if Joshua wasn't lying? What did it hurt to delay killing Joshua even for a few moments?

"Why did you do this?" the Dark Wolf asked.

Joshua spit a wad of phlegm and blood onto the floor. The man's face was swelling, a nearly unrecognizable mush. "Look at me. I bleed. Every day that goes by, I'm closer to death. No matter how strong or how skilled, Time is the fiercest of all my adversaries. This is my greatest battle. If you open the door..."

"Immortality?"

"Lives are so short. What does it matter what I do? What does it matter what any of us do to achieve our goals?" His words were forced, his breath hitching in his chest.

The Dark Wolf gazed at the totems and they acknowledged him in turn. A nod, a salute, a blink. He sensed from them a yearning. Without him they couldn't be complete. He remembered the absence of light when they cast him down.

"Kill Joshua. The rest can follow," the Other said.

The wall had become transparent. He saw their structure like a faint line, as if built with spider webs. Yet, the landscape wasn't Cresek-Tawn but an alien place. A war-ravaged city surrounded them, the buildings stretched so high it appeared they would topple under their own weight. They were gutted, burnt and scarred. How they could remain standing with such damage? Fires roared but it was so unbelievably cold that breath frosted.

A place of liquid fires. A place of nightmares. And he saw the demon from the ruined Palace of the Crucifixion. He stared at them with his blazing eyes, his face concealed by a hideous leather mask strapped to his skull.

The Beast on the Throne.

"We must hurry," Joshua urged. "The Beast on the Throne has found us. You have to turn the key."

"*That was not our agreement,*" the Other screamed. The Other was there, banging on the locks. He was stronger, much stronger than the Dark Wolf thought possible.

"I will be your servant," Joshua said. "I will do your bidding, but we cannot let the Beast on the Throne find us. You must act."

"Yes," the Dark Wolf agreed. He would return to the Times Before. He would turn the key and open the door to where he belonged, even if it meant taking the worm Joshua with him.

The Other would not relent so easily. He hammered on the door to regain control of their body. The Dark Wolf had to move quickly. He held the sword blade down, preparing to plunge it into the keyhole. Then he would return home to the Times Before.

"*No!*" the Other screamed and that door broke. Before the Dark Wolf could cast the sword into the hole, their body was paralyzed, teeth clenched so tightly that his jaw began to pop.

"*We cannot.*"

"We must."

"*No!*"

In the darkness, the mercurial shape of Dark Wolf lashed out at the Other. But the Other was powerful, and met him head on. The world shuddered as they battled. They twisted and turned.

Kill.

Mercy.

Survive.

The Dark Wolf attacked with fang and claw and Nathaniel retaliated with fists and fury. Neither would relent.

"Nathaniel," a voice whispered. At first, Nathaniel thought it was his imagination but it repeated his name. The voice didn't belong in the turmoil between him and the Dark Wolf.

"Nathaniel?" It was Jane's voice and the sound of it was sweet.

∽

My eyes opened and a shiver of excitement cooled my spine. Jane was with me. No wounds. Beautiful. My head lay on her naked chest, our bodies covered in the light sheen of our exertion. A cool breeze wafted through the open window. Outside, the night insects played their gentle songs.

"Jane." The name sounded so fragrant. She caressed my scalp.

"Rest easy, my love."

My words were choked. "I can't. I need to destroy him."

"Shhhhh. I'm here waiting for you. I will wait all eternity if I must. The battle is over. You have your freedom. Let them go. You can have me again, someday. Don't be his pawn. Don't let him use you like he's used everyone his whole life."

"I can't stand losing you. Not again."

"Don't let him destroy us."

"I failed you." My tears spilled onto her chest.

"No."

Her hands felt so good on my head. I was so weary. So tired.

"Quiet now, my love. Sleep."

I rested in her arms for hours. The beating of her heart was soothing, comforting. My heart desired for this to never end, but it inevitably would.

∽

When I opened my eyes, I lay at the feet of the humanoid wasp. It regarded me with its shiny, expressionless eyes and I couldn't tell whether it planned to stab me with its stinger or if I was beneath contempt.

I felt an emptiness in me as if someone had carved part of me away. I clutched at my chest but surprisingly found myself whole. Several feet away lay a body also rousing. I had never truly seen the Dark Wolf but I knew this to be the entity that had been inside of me all those years. I had cast it out.

I wondered if this sudden incompleteness was from the void left by the Dark Wolf, or from the hole that Jane had left.

The Dark Wolf staggered to its feet. Like the other totems, it was an amalgam of wolf and human. It looked at me, there was a moment of recognition, but then its stumbled to retrieve Black Swan.

Joshua was on his knees. A broken man but still with that lopsided grin. I felt the urge to strike him down. Destroy him before he won. And him winning meant that everyone else had lost. I wanted revenge so badly that sweat stung my eyes.

"Don't look so miserable, Nathaniel," Joshua said. "You're free now. We all are."

I wanted to scream that I wasn't free, that he'd thrown me into a box that I could never escape. But I couldn't speak.

The Dark Wolf plunged the blade into the keyhole in the floor.

Black Swan exploded in white light followed by a thunderous boom. Dust filtered from the ceiling and the air smelled metallic. The Dark Wolf held the hilt of the sword, body tense as if Black Swan was attempting to cast him aside. I shielded my eyes, the light stinging my skin like hail.

Then there was darkness and silence and I wondered if I had fallen into some bizarre dream state. This void stretched for what felt like hours yet I didn't feel the need to call out or explore.

Then gradually, I noticed the stars above me. I lay on my back on the hardpan. The vegetation was sparse and wind swirled the dust along the plains. With some difficulty, I raised my head. Joshua and the Dark Wolf were also rousing, Black Swan plunged into the earth between us.

I figured it to be just after twilight, the horizon holding an orange glow from the setting sun but dark enough so that the stars stood out in relief against the night. In the opposite direction was a city of such immensity that it seems to stretch the entire length of the world. The towers reached to the heavens, impossibly tall, the buildings blazing with unnatural light. I gasped at the sight.

The Dark Wolf pulled himself to his feet, sniffed the air, and howled. I knew that sound intimately but it still sent shivers down my spine. But it carried something a little different this time. Freedom. The Dark Wolf dropped to all fours and without glancing back, loped toward the city.

"The Times Before," Joshua said. "We made it."

"Why..." I stared at Black Swan.

"Death has been vanquished here. No sickness, no disease, no dying. You can come with me," Joshua said.

I regarded him. His face dripped blood from the numerous lacerations. Once, he had been pretty. I wasn't sure if he'd ever be pretty again. Yet despite all that, Joshua picked himself up with confidence and gazed at the city. Joshua left ruins in his wake and yet he was offering me an opportunity to go with him into this new world where life seemed never ending. One day, we both knew it would end—just as the Times Before did.

"You want me to go with you?"

Joshua tore his gaze from the city. "You think I did this to hurt you? I chose you to come with me. You are my only friend."

I couldn't reply. Joshua was as damaged inside as he was on the outside. I considered him a mortal enemy and he thought I would accompany him on this grand journey?

I proceeded to Black Swan and took the grip in my hand. The metal was almost too hot to touch but I closed my eyes and squeezed.

"There's no coming back if you do that," Joshua said. "We can live almost forever here."

I didn't have the energy to tell him that he'd taken away everything worth living for. I yanked on Black Swan and it remained fixed in the ground. I switched to a two-handed grip and heaved, worried that the sword was forever buried in the hardpan. Then it slide inch by inch from the ground. Finally it pulled free and there was a blinding light.

This time there was no void, only a vertigo-inducing vortex of light. I focused on the feel of Black Swan in my hand, using it in an attempt to keep me grounded otherwise I worried that my mind would shatter and I'd find myself lost in my own madness. Felt the texture of the metal work against my palm, the heat of the steel scalding my skin.

Then the world righted itself so quickly that I stumbled.

When I opened my eyes, I saw that I was back in the Keystone. The totems had taken their place back in the mosaics. I dropped Black Swan and it clattered to the floor, the sound echoing painfully through the chamber.

"Jane," I mumbled.

Then I collapsed, my anguish overpowering me. I was alone.

The city burned. The madness of the Rominratu was like a shooting star—a brilliant, short display. Now, Cresek-Tawn was trying to cope like a patient recovering from a debilitating disease. Buildings sagged on fire-weakened supports, clouds of sparks snapped into the air. Looters took the place of rioters. Small gangs raided homes and filled their arms with valuables.

I staggered through the city, gaze forward, ignoring the violence and chaos. My body was a map work of torment. Burns, festering wounds, sprains. None of it compared with the turmoil roiling inside of me. Cresek-Tawn had done it to me again.

My whole world had been disrupted. The Beast on the

Throne was real. Joshua had won, perhaps gone off to a fiery hell or perhaps having attained the ultimate goal of immortality.

For years, others had directed my fate. Tutors, scholars, flesh mongers, trainers, then Joshua. Once free from Joshua, I thought my fate was held in my hands alone. Now, the truth was no clearer. Had I ever been in control? I was a pawn, used to open Joshua's door to immortality.

As always, he had used everyone as instruments in his game of power. He had succeeded and I had failed. I didn't contemplate that for too long—bile surged at the thought.

And worst of all—Jane.

The lane down towards Phelps's estate was alive with fire. His imported trees were ablaze, their gnarled branches crackling and popping. The iron gates were open. Had I left them that way?

I forced myself into a run despite my wounds. Jane was in there.

I vaulted up the three steps of the front walk, both doors torn from the hinges. Glass crunched underfoot. Fire.

Looters gathered what they could, not noticing me. Some had been carrying torches but they had been discarded carelessly so that they could fill their arms with more loot. Fire licked along the walls. In moments, this whole place would roar into an inferno.

I grabbed the first looter. Twirled him around and slammed him into the wall, my elbow in his throat. Gold dishes fell from his grasp, eyes wide.

"You and your friends get out of here. Now."

He scurried from me and reached for a candlestick. Grabbed one then went for another. A kick in the pants sent him scrambling forwards.

"Now!" I screamed. My rage was returning. The other looters paused in their work. Worried glances my way. "Clear out now." Perhaps my appearance frightened them. Perhaps they already had all they could already carry. Either way, they quickly evacuated Phelps's house.

Thick gray smoke crawled along the ceilings. The room brightened as the flames increased. The fire stole the breath from my lungs. I wouldn't leave without her.

I hobbled up the stairs and rushed to her bedside. More smoke, stinging my eyes and lungs and my burns flared with the heat, and yet, I found relief when I saw Jane, exactly as I had left her with arms crossed on her chest, eyes closed peacefully. My gaze drifted to her throat and my breath caught. Such a terrible sight! She couldn't be taken outside like this.

A column of fire blasted through the bedroom. The downstairs had ignited. Only moments before we would be trapped inside. Would it be so bad to die with Jane? Except she had told me not to surrender to Joshua or this city.

I ripped a strip from the bed sheet beneath her, wrapped it around her throat like a white scarf and bundled her into my arms. Her body was stiff. I groaned, both from the emotional anguish pressing upon me, and from a wound in my shoulder. I had to lock the pain away so I could complete this last mission.

The house shuddered. Supports were collapsing. I took the stairs carefully. Impossible to breathe. My eyes teared with the smoke. I stepped over Phelps's body. Flames were everywhere. I rushed through the sitting room to the open doors. Down the steps. I gasped for a clean breath, barely able to see from the stinging smoke. I didn't stop until I reached the iron gates.

Off to the side, I laid Jane's body down carefully and sat beside her, watching Phelps's estate crumble piece by piece. For the last time in my life, I laid down next to her, exhausted, and slept.

The city was silent. The sun was bright and hot, the same as it had been for several lifetimes before me. Did anything out here ever really change? I lifted my head and gazed down the road. A few people wandered the streets, attempting to salvage what they could. A shift of my weight and I winced. My wounds, too numerous to count, would take months to heal. My shoulder throbbed and I inspected it. There was a hole directly through it and I seemed to recall a crossbow bolt exploding through my skin. I had to be a professional for this final job in Cresek-Tawn. Had to block out the pain.

I knew Jane needed a proper burial.

I ventured alone into the heart of the city, wandered into a stable and took a wagon. No one was there to stop me. I made several more stops for a shovel, food, water, blankets, traveling gear. No horses or asses remained; the few in the city must've been freed during the rioting. The wagon wasn't meant to be pulled by a single man but that was the only option.

I returned to the estate and carefully rested Jane in a bed of blankets on the wagon. Loading the rest of the gear, we began our trek from the city. The journey was difficult as the roads were strewn with debris and garbage from last night's chaos, and I had to pull it with one arm.

No patrols guarded the front gates. Who controls the city now? Such details didn't matter. Order would take days to be restored. Which meant the Rei or Megellin wouldn't even think of revenge for at least that long.

I considered taking her back to Havencastle, but that wouldn't have been proper. As much as I hated Cresek-Tawn, this was her home. I wasn't sure what we shared in Havencastle was even real, whether our time together was just an act to get at me, or whether we reignited our feelings for each other. I chose to believe the latter, though I'd never know for sure.

I buried her in the shadow of Cresek-Tawn.

I found a spot and dug throughout the afternoon in the hot sun, then lowered her carefully into the grave. As I filled in the hole, my eyes clouded with tears. I finished my task and paused.

"We finally made it, Jane." I wanted to collapse but if I did, I'd probably never rise again. I certainly didn't want to die here. For me to salvage any semblance of victory, I had to keep alive.

I couldn't leave a marker for her grave; it would only alert marauders and grave diggers. Once I left, she'd be alone forever. I stood there until the sun began to slide beneath the horizon.

Oddly, I felt so alone, not even the Dark to mock me from my personal darkness.

I finally forced myself to movement.

Time to go home.

My timing was perfect. Which was good. My crossbow was loaded with a deadly dose of poison-dart frog venom. I was in a foul mood and anyone who got in my way would find themselves the victim of a tiny frog from the tropics.

The Pariahs were still careless. Even after last time. And this wasn't a simple warehouse; this was their headquarters. They should've known better.

I didn't want a fancy entrance—I wasn't in the mood for my normal theatrics.

I threw the door open. As expected, there were curses and shouts. Five men, or rather, five humanoids, were in the chamber. Two were mutants, one was the black goblin, and the other two were Rapespawn. The black goblin named Bratic Snoot came at me first. I kicked him back, pinning him against the wall, one of my blades against his throat. My hand bow was levelled at the next attacker, a mutant with an oddly shaped face.

"Don't. No one has to die here."

They looked to their leader. Airlik Rendarrin, the whole reason I had gotten into this mess. He gave a nod and everyone retreated. Except for me. The blade remained at the black goblin's throat. He drooled on my hand. Disgusting. He was afraid. Now that was new. A frightened black goblin. These Pariahs had everything.

"I didn't expect to see you again," Airlik said.

"I have something of yours."

His eyebrows raised in surprise. "Something of mine?"

Replacing my hand bow on my belt, I used my free hand to pull the blade from its burlap sack on my back. Black Swan. Everyone in the room gasped as light spilled from the magical blade.

I thrust it into the ground, the sword swaying back and forth.

"My mission is complete. Now take the bounty off my head. Tell the Crusader to do the same."

No one paid attention to me. They all stared at Black Swan, even the fearful Black Goblin.

Airlik nodded absently. "Yes, yes."

"All debts are paid," I said. I wasn't going to tell them that the Beast on the Throne would come looking for it. I'd let them figure that out on their own.

I removed the dagger from Bratic's neck and I was out the door. They didn't even notice. They were staring at the sword, mouths agape in wonder.

∽

I drank alone. In the darkness.

How long had I been this way? I had lost count of the weeks.

I stared at the glass in my hand, the blinds drawn. My new safe house was in the basement of a morgue. There were only three small windows in the apartment, each set high on the walls. The quarters were gloomy but they best reflected my mood.

After a few days in Moregeth, I had migrated back to Havencastle. The Pariahs weren't going to hold our previous dispute against me, but Moregeth was a hard place. Cold and uncaring.

I sat in a low-set chair, my mind blank. Or trying not to think of anything.

It was hard to think about Jane, not because I missed her, but because I still wasn't sure whether she had hated me at the end, or if she had loved me. That was more painful to me than even her death. She, like the rest of us, had been Joshua's pawn. And I didn't want to play the endless games of what if.

A blind flipped up, sunlight spilling into the room. My eyes stung from the brightness. Someone was in the room with me. In my alcoholic haze, my hand reached for a crossbow but instead of grabbing it, I sent it toppling from the table.

"This isn't right, Nathaniel," the voice said.

"LaFage?"

"I heard you got back into town a few weeks ago."

"How did you get in?" My head hurt.

"You didn't lock the door. A careless mistake can get a man killed."

"Can it?" Another drink of brandy slid down my throat. *Why won't LaFage leave me alone?* This was when the Dark should've normally thrown in something about gutting the poor fellow but he was gone and I found my loneliness disconcerting.

He flipped up the other two blinds. More sunlight.

"You need to sober up," he said.

"Why do I need to do such a crazy thing?"

Now he opened the windows, the late autumn air chilling the room. Loathed to admit it, but the freshness felt good.

"Because I have a job for you."

"A job?"

"If you're not working, then you're not paying off your tab."

"I don't do that anymore."

"You've been here long enough, Nathaniel. I've given you weeks. Now it's time." LaFage grabbed the drink from my hand. Though he was smaller than me, he took it easily. Retrieving my crossbow from the floor, he handed it over.

"Alexis needs your help."

"Who's that?"

"She's the woman you duped into helping you get into the Syndicate, remember? You have to help her."

I remembered Alexis, though that felt like a lifetime ago. I liked her, if I remembered correctly. I didn't want anything bad to happen to her anyway.

Every time I tried to help, people died. People like Alexis, like Jane. No one wanted that anymore. Nothing positive came from my meddling.

LaFage must've seen the doubt on my face. "You help people, Nathaniel. It's what you do. That's why you went after Jane."

"And now she's dead."

"So you're going to let Alexis and her people die?"

My eyes closed and I wanted the world to disappear. When they opened, LaFage stood by me.

Kill. Kill. Kill. Except that wasn't the Dark Wolf. The Dark Wolf was gone. It was me, and that was even more chilling.

"She's in trouble?" I asked.

"The worst kind. O'Meara has shut everything down. She's the only one left standing, so what's left of the Syndicate is blaming her. You know what they'll do to her."

Yes, the Syndicate would be harsh. I didn't tell LaFage that Alexis didn't need my help, that shutting down the Syndicate had all been part of the bargain. But I had been fond of Alexis.

I sat for many long moments, LaFage staring at me.

Finally, with a heavy sigh, I dusted off my hat and put it on. Unsteadily, I crawled from the chair with LaFage's help. Time to go to work and save Alexis.

She was in trouble.

And I solved trouble.

www.ingramcontent.com/pod-product-compliance
Lightning Source LLC
Chambersburg PA
CBHW031110030726
47496CB00002BA/467